Sophie and
the Magic Flower

Gabriele Ewerts

Jacket Design: Christine DiGuiseppi

Available from Amazon.com and other book stores.

ISBN:1511842318

ISBN-13:9781511842310

To Bella and Pia-Sophie,
One who lent her hair, the other her name.

To Papa for giving me my first book,
And to Mutti for lighting the candles that day.

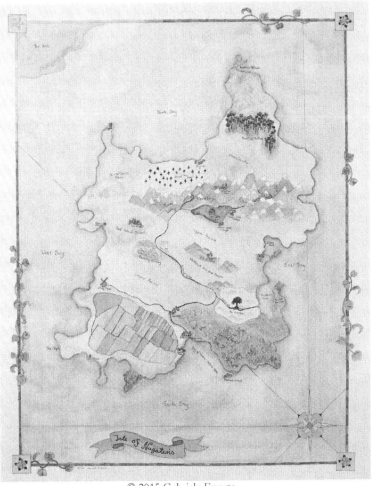

© 2015 Gabriele Ewerts

❧ *Chapter 1* ❧

Sophie perched on a branch of a gnarled ponderosa pine at the cemetery's edge. With her back pressing against the trunk, she hugged her right knee while swinging her left leg like a pendulum—tick-tock, back and forth. Her fingers picked at the tree bark, prying off bits. She flicked each one to a large stone near the roots, hitting it every time. The gum in her mouth had lost its flavor. Still, she kept turning it over and around with her tongue, from one cheek to the other and back again. A bubble grew from her lips. She let it swell, then popped it to start over. Her tongue reeled it in, and round it went again. Squish, squish. Playing with her gum didn't make her forget the tight knot in her chest, but she needed to do something.

Like a dwarf, the tree stood beside tall Douglas fir and blue spruce, and its crooked branch cradled her like a loving mother's arm. From her perch, she looked onto the roof of the nearby caretaker's shed. Beyond the shed, the majestic peak kept watch over the town and its small cemetery. Her eyes followed a straight line to Mom and Dad's grave and then to Tommy's.

A chilly gust clipped the last yellow leaves from the

few aspens that grew among the evergreens. The wind brought the smell of snow and tugged on Sophie's clothes as if wanting to pluck her off the tree, too. She hugged deeper into Mom's old leather jacket, watching Trudy stomp across the cemetery and plow over the hard, frozen path toward the tree.

"Kind, komm out of that tree!" Trudy called.

Sophie raised her gaze away from the small casket over the open grave. She blinked a few times into the gray clouds gliding over the pale November sun and let her gaze settle on the peak.

"Kind, komm now," said Trudy. "The funeral is starting. You will be all dirty and scratched up. You won't look nice." She threw up her hands. "And why those pink sneakers and the pink t-shirt? To Tommy's funeral?" She stopped a few feet away and looked up.

"Who cares?" Sophie threw Trudy a withering look, which grazed her foster mother's hat and face. Sophie pressed her lips together, biting down hard, the gum tucked away in her cheek.

"That is not true," said Trudy. "Everyone will care. Tommy would have cared."

"But he's gone, right?" The *he's* got stuck in her throat. Yeah, Tommy would have cared. For a little boy of five, he had been way too fussy about being clean. She shook her head, tightening her lips and her grip on the branch.

"We cannot change it anymore." Trudy sounded all choked up. "But we can say our last good-byes."

Sophie cast a furtive glance down, but only for a moment. Trudy's pleading look almost melted her heart—almost, like she cared.

Sophie pressed her lips into a thinner line, pulling her upper lip down, which made her sore red nose hurt even more. She wasn't a crybaby, but somehow her nose kept running, and she kept wiping it with the cuffs of Mom's jacket.

Trudy tugged a lacey white handkerchief from her suit pocket and dabbed her eyes, then blew her nose like a trumpet. The two thin black feathers on her hat quivered in the cold wind and gave a quick jerk when she swung around and stomped back to the grave where neighbors, teachers, and friends had arrived and gathered at the grave.

"Why do you not listen to your mother?" a deep, raspy voice asked.

Sophie startled, swayed, and dug her fingers into the rough bark but lost her grip and toppled from the tree. She fell back, sucked in air, and prepared to hit the ground hard. But something cushioned her fall, and she landed gently as if dropping onto a soft pillow. A strange smell laced the air. She sat and twisted to look behind her.

A six-feet-plus old man stooped in the shadow of the caretaker's shed. His light blue eyes twinkled strangely. His disheveled white hair and beard hung past his waist and framed his wrinkled face. He wore a hooded cloak over a long, gray tunic, and his right hand's long bony fingers shone white on the cloak's indigo sleeve. Something wasn't right. He clutched his left arm with its end wrapped in a white cloth with dark brown stains. She'd bet those stains weren't from spilled hot chocolate.

Sophie stared, then looked back to the grave. Trudy's name sat on the tip of her tongue. It would be easy to call for help. Nope, she could look out for herself.

"She isn't my real mother." She stood and brushed herself off.

"Ah, that explains it." He didn't say what he meant

but smiled, showing teeth with gaps between them.

"Who are you?" she asked and stepped back. Her eyes lingered first on the gappy smile, then dropped to the stained cloth, and returned to the grave. The scene turned watery and she blinked.

"Ah, the pain."

Sophie eyed the mangled arm.

"Sorry about your arm."

"Oh, I do not mean this." He winced when he lifted the arm a bit with his right hand.

Sophie looked away. If she stared too long at that stump, she would be sick, or worse, feel sorry for him. She wanted to do neither, but curiosity nudged her.

"What happened, I mean, to your arm?"

The man stepped from the shadow and stopped behind the tree so that the people at the grave couldn't see him. He shifted and adjusted his injured arm, wincing again while he watched the mourners.

Over by the grave, Trudy greeted Miss Wolcott, Tommy's kindergarten teacher. They hugged, held each other, weeping. Over the hill, the high school marching band stumbled into practice. The tuba's boom used to be funny, but now the boom rhymed with doom and gloom.

"I think she would like you to join her," said the old man, not answering her question.

"How'd you know what my foster mother wants?" Sophie glanced at him.

Leaning back, swaying a bit, the old man studied her out of eyes much like her own. Dad had always said they were like a beautiful summer's day, but with storm clouds in the distance. The old man's eyes flickered afraid and desperate like her own.

"She seems to care," he said and jabbed his chin Trudy's way.

"What the heck do you know?" Sophie raised her brows. "She just cares about rules." Sophie wiped her nose. "*And* she is a control freak."

The old man sighed. "Rules are good to have."

Sophie frowned.

"Of course, some rules are a bit strict." He gave her another gappy smile.

She hated it when adults pretended to understand. They were much more honest when they yelled.

Sounds drifted toward her. Mourners' voices mingled with the band's music. Adults talked in choked voices. Children cried their lungs out. The wind whooshed through it all and snatched the voices and music away. Here and there, a lonely snowflake zipped past.

"I feel for you, child. It hurts to lose," the old man said, "but perhaps I can help."

Sophie eyed the wrapped stump. "It's not the same."

They watched another family arrive. Dianne and her parents drove up and parked the car. Her friend searched the cemetery until she spotted Sophie by the pine. She made a step toward her, but Dianne's dad grabbed her arm and shook his head.

"Someone else seems to like you."

"Yeah. Right." A shaking sigh rushed past her lips. Yeah, she would like to be with Dianne. "Maybe I'll see what's going on over there."

"Well, then you should climb back into the tree." He smiled again, wider, more gaps showing. "The view would be more satisfying."

Sophie frowned and backed around the trunk, keeping it between her and the man. He stood taller than anyone she'd ever met. Pretending to be brave, she hid her fear in a frown, but she was ready in case he tried anything.

More people arrived and circled the grave. Was Tommy really in there? Earlier, she had stood beside the open casket in church, numb, gazing at his tiny still body. Trudy had pulled her away, saying Sophie was too young to see a dead person. Well, Tommy was her brother, wasn't he? Or had been anyway.

"Go on, join them."

Sophie shook her head. "He's gone now anyway," she whispered and sniffed. "What's the point?"

"The point is, child, that you have one last opportunity to say farewell."

Sophie said nothing and blinked a few times. What the heck did he mean? She never got a chance to say goodbye. And now? Now, it was too late.

"What I mean is this." He cleared his throat but the rasp stayed. "If you help me go home, there will be an opportunity for you to speak with your brother one last time."

Sophie's head jerked up.

The old man nodded. "Yes, there is a way to see your brother once more."

"How?" Sophie wrinkled her nose and squinted at him, searching his face for the truth.

The old man took a deep breath.

"There is a small catch," he said.

Oh, sure, there was always a catch. That's the adult's way of coming up with reasons as to why and what and never really keeping their word anyway. Her eyes strayed back to the casket, but for a second, hope rushed to her heart. And for a crazy moment, she thought she would to do whatever she must if it meant she could see

Tommy again, only once, and tell him she was sorry.

"The small catch is you must find an artifact that will help me to go home," the old man continued like she hung on his every word. "On the way there or back, if you pay attention, you might see your brother."

Sophie tuned him out. The guy was crazy. That's all.

The pastor from Trudy's church arrived. The service would be starting soon, like it had three years ago when Mom and Dad died. The big fist in her stomach twisted; the lump in her throat grew, choking her, making her cough.

The raspy voice continued, "You must go through the portal in the forest, past the gate over to the right, and run along the passage toward the light at the other end."

"Yeah, right," she said, but instead watched the people by the grave. She wanted to run and be close to the people she knew, but at the same time, the hurt in her heart kept her in place. Her feelings tumbled into an angry mish mash for not knowing what to do.

Out of habit, Sophie reached for her hair to twist it, but her hands came away empty. Why had she been so dumb? Now, she regretted having cut her hair to annoy Trudy. She dropped her hands and raised her shoulders so that only her fingertips peeked from the cuffs. Mom's jacket, still too big for her, had large pockets holding all the stuff she cared for: Dad's Swiss Army knife and his old wallet, Tommy's old teddy bear Mom had knitted for him, her cell phone and a charger, and a supply of gum that would last for several weeks. Mom had always said, "You can make things last if you don't indulge." She would remember that. In the old wallet, she had money stashed away, money she had stolen. She shouldn't steal, but she had to have some money if she wanted to run away with Tommy. Now Tommy was gone.

Hand in her pocket, she fingered the page from Trudy's parenting magazine. The advertisement said the adoption agency promised to bring parents and children together in a loving home. That's what she wanted. That's what she would get, right after the funeral. She would run to the adoption agency and ask for a new family.

"Child, are you listening?"

"'Course." The man sounded nuts.

He chuckled, then turned serious. "Listen, child," he urged. "I must return home to prevent something terrible from happening, but I cannot do so without your help."

Sophie peeked up to his face, down to her sneakers, then up again, and finally lingered on his arm and the stained sleeve.

"What happened?" She hugged herself, grabbing her upper arms, and pointed with one finger.

"I lost my hand defending my life." He shifted his arm and winced again.

"Someone cut it off?" Sophie backed up more, stumbled, and tripped over a root. Catching herself with her arms, she landed on her butt.

"Sophie, kind, komm over here!" Trudy beckoned her. "Um Himmels Willen, get up. You're getting dirty."

Sophie hugged her knees and ignored Trudy.

"What...?" Sophie twisted around. The man was gone. The same strange smell mingled with the cold air. Over by the grave, Trudy exchanged a few more words with the pastor.

"There is little time, child," the raspy voice said.

Sophie jumped. His voice came from somewhere close behind her, but she could see only the shed and the trees.

"Where are you? And what's that smell?"

"Sage," he said. "Child, listen. You must go through the portal in the forest. Look to your right between the trees."

Sophie looked past an old gate's rusty wings hanging more off than on its hinges and past the undergrowth between the Douglas firs. Way back within the trees, something weird shimmered and flickered like snowflakes twinkling in the sun.

"Once you are through the portal, you must run. Do not stop. You hear? You must keep running as fast as you can toward the light at the other end."

"What about my brother?"

Trudy stomped toward Sophie, her black shoes leaving scuff marks in the layer of snow that now dusted the ground.

"Sophie, komm here. Please!"

Sophie leaned forward. She was *not* going with her. *No way.*

"At the end of the passage, you will emerge into another forest," the old man said. "A path leads to the city of Gwern-cadarn-brac where you must go to Council Hall, and…"

"Sophie!" Trudy huffed like a steam engine without the steam across the cemetery. Sophie giggled.

"Child, are you listening?"

Was that man crazy?

"Sophie!" Trudy lumbered to a stop close to her.

"At Council Hall," the old man raised his voice, "you must…"

Trudy craned her neck. "Who is that talking?"

Sophie shrugged and glanced over her shoulder into the shadows. The sage smell tickled her nose. She sneezed.

"Sophie." Her foster mother jammed her fists onto her hips. "I'm talking to you."

Sophie's right hand curled around the smooth, round surface of a stone, the perfect size to fit her hand. Acting on their own, her fingers closed.

Trudy took another step forward. "Komm, now!"

No, I won't. Searing hot pain, fear and anger surged through Sophie. "I'm not going with you!" she yelled. "You're horrible! It's all your fault! I hate you!" She jumped to her feet. Her hand lashed out. The stone flew across the short distance separating them, and *thud!* hit Trudy in the forehead.

Sophie's jaw dropped. She stared.

Trudy did, too, for a second or two, then her eyes rolled up and her body folded like a big stuffed doll. Blood trickled between her eyes down her nose. Her head snapped back, and the hat with those ridiculous feathers rolled away like a loose tire.

What had she done? Sophie slapped a hand over her mouth. *Oh. My. Oh no!* What am I going to do? I didn't mean to.

A woman at the graveside screamed. Sophie started left, then right, and swung around. Where was the old man? Gone, probably. High tailing it so he wouldn't be caught here. Sophie dashed toward the old gate, arms pumping at her sides. People yelled, coming after her. With two long strides, she jumped past the rusty wings and ran into the woods. Earlier, the shimmer had been a little flicker, but now the setting sun peeked through the clouds, and she could barely make out any flickering between the trunks. Had she imagined it? She slowed down, unsure. Branches cracked behind her in the woods. Someone came after her. She had to get away.

Had the old man told the truth? Was there really a portal into another world? No time to wonder now.

With her arms extended in front of her, Sophie ran toward the shimmering light. As her hands touched it, a white light flashed, blinding her. She fell forward into a gray world. Fine sand filled the spaces between her fingers. The sage smell was mixed with the stink of singed hair and scorched flesh.

❧   ❧

Eigil gasped. For the entire conversation, he had hoped but not believed he could persuade the girl to help him. Her distrust had even masked the heavy pain shining in her eyes. Well, she had not wanted to help, but now she was on her way, and with good fortune, the precious few things he had managed to convey would prove beneficial to her at the right time.

"May the light brighten your path, child."

His shoulders slumped and his regret stung. A child. He had to rely on a child. Given the few choices he had, he should still have handled it differently. Perhaps the child would have a better chance than the men and women visiting the burial ground, although he worried about her pale face and red hair. Those features would not help her in Nugateris.

Eigil raised his head. The mourners hurried toward the injured woman on the ground. Blood spread over her face and she lay quite still. Pity surged through him, not so much for the woman but for the girl. Perhaps now she would have no one to return to and no reason to come back.

Two men bent over the woman, and after examining

her, one man jumped up and started after the girl.

No! The man could not enter the portal nor stop the girl. Eigil could not permit it. He winced as he let go of his left arm and hurried after the man. Extending his right hand toward the portal, he summoned his power. In a rush, the magic's warm tingle flared in his belly, surged up through his chest and shoulder, and down his right arm where it quivered in his fist. He breathed its strong sage scent enveloping him at the same time. His conscience would not let him harm the man, but stop him he must.

The man reached the gate's rusty wings and pushed through it, heading past the first trees. For a moment, the setting sun emerged from the clouds and cast the forest into a brilliant and blinding light.

In a straight line through the trees and above the man's head, Eigil released his power and let it hammer into the portal. The magic flashed purple and steeped the air with sage. With a white flare, the portal answered and threw the man back. He sat, shaking his head as if to clear it. Then the curtain of clouds closed once more. A gust snatched a few shimmering threads and took the sage scent, leaving the forest dark and silent.

Eigil retreated into the shadows. Well, he had stopped the man, but his success only brought the one result farthest from his mind—he had closed the portal. Now he could not return home, and without help, neither could the girl.

⋙ *Chapter 2* ⋘

Sophie stumbled and her legs buckled. She fell to her knees and swallowed the gum. For a second, she couldn't see anything through the shimmer. Then she made out Dianne's dad zigzagging through the trees.

A purple flash cut him off, leaving her to stare at a dark spot where the opening had been. The shimmer disappeared, and only a bit of the sage smell hung in the air.

"Trudy!" she yelled past a big lump in her throat. Of course, Trudy couldn't hear her. She had killed her with a stone. "Trudy, I didn't mean it. Help me! Trudy!" Her words fell flat and didn't even echo away.

Brrr. The chill made her shiver. She hugged herself and dropped to her knees. Her breath billowed in front of her face. Her phone! Maybe she should try to call Trudy. Her fingers curled around the cell phone in her jacket. She pulled it out, but the small display stared back at her like a black, dead eye.

"Nooo! This can't be." A sob bubbled up, but she swallowed and squared her shoulders. No, she wouldn't cry. She could handle it.

Gray and white fog swathes circled around her feet, thick and heavy, like a sluggish soup. Icy cold, colder than the cemetery, the air clung to her, and the fog snaked across the fine sand under her feet.

Sophie doubled the leather jacket in front of her, hugged herself tighter, and stood. What had the old man told her? Run to the distant light and don't stop, he'd said. Where was that light? She spun once on the spot in the gray and hazy gloom, searching. The old man had said she would see Tommy if she paid attention. Was this the place where dead people went?

"Tommy?" The name traveled nowhere and went dead as soon as it left her mouth as if smothered by a pillow.

Was she dead, too? She pinched her arm. "Ouch." Well, that felt normal enough.

She walked a few steps, stopped, did another turn, and groped the air around her. Maybe the opening was there somewhere and she just couldn't see it. Some of what the old man had told her seemed true. Despite pretending she'd heard little, she'd still caught quite a bit. Now she had to figure out the rest on her own. Once more, she faced forward.

"Tommy?" Again, the name fell dead into the grayness.

The fog swirled and agitated, slithering around her ankles. She stepped back, sideways, and took another step forward. Where was the light? A tingling up and down her spine urged her to run. She uncrossed her arms, zipped her jacket all the way to her cold chin, and tucked it down. Out of the breast pocket, she pulled a blue and pink pack and folded the gum into her mouth. Better.

Her feet kicked up the fog like fall leaves, the way she'd done on the trip to Vermont with Mom and Dad one fall. She clung to the thought. Together with the gum in her mouth, it made her feel braver. She broke into a jog, but there was no light anywhere, only more dreary grayness and that fog.

A shriek to the right sent her into a crouch. She jerked her head from side to side. Her chest tightened and felt heavy like someone was standing on it.

"Tommy?" She yelled and peered into the gloom. "Is that you?" Of course, it wasn't; he was dead, but the old man had said she would see him. Of course, he had played with her. How could she ever see Tommy again, or Mom and Dad? Shaking, she tightened her arms around her ribs. Would she die, too, right here and now?

Figures glided from the fog, some tall and thin, some squat and round, but all resembling people.

"Tommy?" This time she whispered.

They were coming to get her. She knew it. Her kneecaps wobbled when she straightened her shaking legs. Ghostly figures lifted their white arms and reached for her. Their mouths gaped wide like empty holes ready to swallow her. They glided and slithered closer. None even looked like Tommy, only like scary weird ghosts. The fog snaked into more ghosts, forming them bigger and more solid. What did they want from her? Up ahead in the near distance, a light flashed then shimmered like the one in the cemetery.

More ghosts approached with extended arms, fingers spread widely and curled like claws ready to snatch her. The old man's raspy voice spoke in her head, "Run and do not stop until you reach the light."

Sophie threw her body forward and broke through the white forms. High-pitched shrieks raced after her. She slammed her hands over her ears. Oh no, they wouldn't get her. Her legs carried her forward as fast as she could make them go. She gasped for air past the heart hammering in her throat.

Ahead, the light grew for a moment, but then it shrank again. All around her, pale white hands reached for her. Even their wispiness didn't make them less real. She twisted away and ran faster. Maybe they could catch her, maybe they couldn't. She wouldn't wait to find out.

The light ahead shrank more every second, closing. The shrieks rose into sirens. Sophie screamed right along, pressing her hands hard against her ears. She stumbled ahead. Almost there. The shimmer surrounded a small opening like a wobbly window, a ring big enough for her to dive through. Tall trees stood on the other side. Maybe she had run in a circle. Maybe she would be back home again. Like a diver, she stretched her arms out in front of her, reached through the shimmer, and pushed off with her feet. The light flashed and sparked as she dove through it. She hit the ground, sliding forward on her tummy, and skidded to a stop. A sage-and-apple smell stung her nose before her face grazed the dirt.

❧ ❧

Soft grass and a strong, rich earthy smell tickled Sophie's nose. "Ha-choo." She sneezed again. "Ha-choo."

A gentle breeze cooled her face. For a minute or two, she waited for her heart and breath to slow before she raised her head. With a scowl on her face, she pushed herself up and sat back on her heels. Some buttercups lay squashed by her knees. She lifted the limp yellow blossoms. "Sorry about that."

She had come out in the woods somewhere, a clearing

overgrown with grass and wildflowers. What did the old man tell her to do next?

Giant trees bordered the clearing, reaching skyward with massive trunks ten kids holding hands couldn't have circled. Birds chirped high above in the branches. Here and there, a chipmunk flitted across the ground, and two squirrels chased each other up a tree. After the strange gray passage, this all looked normal enough.

Sudden crackling and sizzling sounds made her twist around. Oh no, the portal closed. How would she get back home? With a few sparks and tiny flashes, the shimmering ring narrowed, got smaller and smaller, and disappeared. What now?

Sweat trickled down Sophie's back and from her armpits. Mom's jacket now felt way too heavy and hot in this warm weather. She unzipped it and shrugged it off.

Suddenly, the chirping stopped; the breeze and all sounds ebbed away.

Whoosh!

She spun around. Dozens of tennis-ball-size yellow-green fireballs streaked past the massive trunks like shooting stars, and in a blur, came at her across the clearing. Strong peppermint-smelling gusts swooped down from the treetops as if to knock the fireballs off course.

She dropped the jacket, and aiming for a spot between the trees, ran pushing against the gust. She zigzagged to avoid the fireballs, but they followed her and hit her all at once. Fire and light stung when it grabbed her, knitting a fine but strong net of fiery ropes, binding her like a fly caught in a spider's web. Sophie screamed. A nasty, burned sour apple smell overpowered the peppermint scent and stung the inside of her nose.

"Help!" She twisted and flayed her arms. The ropes pulled tighter, and the harder she struggled, the tighter they got.

"Help!" She screamed as loudly as she could. "Hel…." But the ropes squeezed the breath out of her and cut her off.

The gusts calmed to a strong wind, then to a light breeze, and ended in a soft sigh ebbing away through the forest, like the trees wanted to say, "Sorry, we tried."

Her vision blurred, and she felt queasy. Soon, she hung paralyzed in the net in the middle of the clearing, held up only by the yellow-green ropes. The net squeezed, quivered and hummed like electricity. Short spurts of breath pumped from her mouth; drool trickled from one corner. *Mom. Mom, help me. Dad. Trudy.* Only silent thoughts nobody heard anyway. Then she blacked out.

⌖ ⌖

"A girl?" Flynden scratched his head, making his motley cap dance as they watched the girl walk in the clearing. "Why would Master Eigil send a girl and not come himself?"

"Get down," Pelifeles hissed. "Now."

"Why?" Flynden got his answer right away.

Whoosh. Yellow-green magic flashed within the trees all around the clearing and shot out in tiny spheres trailing strands of light, heading straight for the girl. Whoosh. Gusts rushed into the clearing at the same time, bending bushes and grass almost flat.

Flynden threw himself on the ground and flattened his body behind the bush where he hid with Pelifeles. Even the cat crouched low.

"What's happening, Peli?" Flynden raised his head a tiny bit.

"Stay down."

The girl pushed against the wind. She screamed when the magic caught and ensnared her.

"Peli, can we help her?"

"Not yet. Stay down," the cat hissed once more. "That's Councilor Makimus' magic. He's set the trap for Master Eigil."

"But we must do something."

"I thought you didn't like girls."

"I don't, but …" Girls were a pain, but that didn't mean they should be hurt like this.

The girl screamed again. Flynden raised his head and peeked through the branches. She stopped struggling and hung as if dead in the magic net, her face pale in the yellow-green light. The gusts died down to a breeze, then ebbed away, and birds sang and twittered again.

"By the light, Peli, she is dead." Open-mouthed, he stared.

"Not if we're quick enough." The cat arched his back, shivered and shook from head to toe, then dashed beneath the branches and across the clearing toward the girl.

Flynden squeezed through the bush. His tunic snatched on some of the thorny branches, adding another tear to the ripped garment. He eyed the magic net hanging there, waiting, humming like a sleeping beast. Flynden's heart raced. He gasped.

"Peli, wait!" He hurried after the cat.

The girl's head lolled to one side. The net hummed louder now as if filled with a thousand bees. The heat singed his skin when he stepped closer. He flung up his arms, stepped back, and eyed the net from behind his elbow.

"Peli, is she alive?"

"Barely."

"What can we do?" This was all wrong. His stomach churned.

After sniffing the net for a bit without touching it, Pelifeles retreated and joined Flynden.

"Can you get her out?" Flynden asked.

Pelifeles licked his paw, maddening slow. "I think so." He gave another lick to the paw before he focused his yellow eyes on Flynden. "I can rip a hole into the net and widen it for a short while. I'm no match for Councilor Makimus' magic, but I can do a bit of damage." He lifted the corners of his muzzle into a weird grin. "If you help me."

"How?"

"Pull her out."

"I'm not sticking my hands in there."

The cat rolled his eyes. "You want to help the girl?"

Flynden nodded.

"Then do as I say. As soon as I cut the magic, pull. Ready?"

No, Flynden wasn't, but if they didn't do it, the girl would surely die. It looked like she had stopped breathing already. He gulped and swallowed.

Once more, Pelifeles faced the net and stood still. All at once, his fur turned bushy and glowed. The glow brightened to a white light and engulfed him. He padded forward; his nose jutted ahead toward the net. Angry yellow-green sparks attacked him, hitting his fur, trying to fight him off. Pelifeles pushed ahead. Little by little, first his nose then his head cut through the strands. His own light brightened and met another shower of angry sparks.

Then ever so small, a hole opened around the cat and grew. White light flashed and flared as he pushed in deeper. The hole widened with it, and soon, it grew big enough to pull the girl out. Flynden swallowed again and reached in.

❧   ❧

Sophie lurched. Her upper body lifted off the ground. A pair of small, dirty hands pressed her shoulders back into the grass. *Air! She needed air.* She gulped like a drowning person. The painful breath made her cough until she threw up.

A boy's face with a freckled nose and cheeks bent over her. His light brown eyes widened with fear, brimming with tears. A colorful and patched cap, shaped like a big beanbag, hung askew on his light brown curls. Beside him sat a black and white cat looking rather calm, the way cats do, with its yellow eyes round and wide. She reached out to touch its soft fur.

"Well, she's alive," the cat said.

"Huh?" Sophie flinched and snatched her hand back. *Had the cat said that?*

"Um, hello," the boy said and scratched his head, making his cap wobble. "How are you feeling?"

Sophie cleared her dry throat and tried to swallow.

"Bad," she croaked.

The boy fumbled with the leather string around his chest and uncorked a bladder attached to it. He tipped the opening to her lips, spilling water all over her face. Sophie spluttered. Her own trembling hands grabbed the bladder, and together, they managed to get some water into her mouth.

Sophie gave him a crooked smile.

"Thanks."

The yellow-green net, now torn apart, still hung in the clearing's center and only snippets wriggled in the air like a snake hacked into pieces.

"What's that?" Sophie pointed.

"A trap," the cat said. "A bit longer and you would've been no more."

Sophie stared at the net.

"You got me out of it?" Her eyes swiveled between boy and cat.

The boy nodded, then shook his head. "Um, Pelifeles did, but I helped a little."

"Thank you. Both of you." She tried to sit up but fell back into the grass. "Where am I? And who are you?"

The boy exchanged a glance with the cat. The cat blinked once, almost like a nod.

"I am Flynden." The boy sat back on his heels, straightened a little, and held out his hand. "But you can call me Flyn if you want," he added and made himself a bit taller.

"I'm Sophie. Sophie Gardener." She shook Flynden's hand.

"You're a gardener?"

"No, that's just my family name."

Flynden grinned. "That's my friend, Pelifeles." He pointed his thumb toward the cat. "He's my brother Kir's spirit mate."

"Hi, Pelifeles. What's a spirit mate?"

"Enough talking," Pelifeles growled. "If you can manage to stand, Sophie, we must leave now. The man who set the trap will be coming to check what he has caught."

"What man? Why would he do this to me?"

"It wasn't meant for you," Flynden said.

"For the old man?"

"You met Master Eigil?" Flynden's eyes bulged, and he forgot to close his mouth.

"Enough talk, I said." Clearly annoyed, Pelifeles flicked his tail. "We must leave."

"Come." Flynden grabbed Sophie's hands and pulled her up. "Peli is right. We have to leave now or there will be trouble for all of us."

Ragged strands from the net of light still twisted in the air, but only for a few seconds longer. A gust swept through the trees and into the clearing, chasing away the last ones. Then the net was gone.

Sophie stood. Dizzy, she swayed, leaning against the boy. Flynden pulled her arm across his shoulder, and she walked on shaking legs beside him.

"This way," Pelifeles said and headed toward a gap in the trees.

Sophie and Flynden trudged after him, one step at a time, like she'd been sick with the flu for days. Mom had always fussed and cared when she was sick. The thought of Mom gave her strength.

"By the light," Flynden said.

"What?" Sophie eyed the forest.

They stopped.

"Look." The boy pointed to the left where in the distance between the trees two lights appeared. "Over there."

"More of those lights?"

"No. Worse."

"What could be worse?" Sophie shivered and her stomach gave another turn.

"Makimus, maker of the light," Flynden said, and

tugged and pulled her along. Together, they took shelter in bushes between the trees. The effort of walking even the short distance left Sophie breathless.

"Wait," she gasped.

"Keep going," Pelifeles said from somewhere within the shadows. "This isn't far enough."

Shadows lengthened, and the darkness of the forest swallowed them. Somewhere in the distance, a bell tolled. Ding. Dong. Ding. The deep, slow ring sounded more like a gong than a bell. Ding. Dong. Ding.

Sophie craned her neck and kept walking. The lights bobbed toward the clearing, and soon, two men with long hair and beards stepped from the trees' shadows. They each carried a tennis-ball-size globe in the palm of one hand; one globe glowed yellow-green, the other orange.

"Come," Flynden whispered. "Hurry." He pulled on her arm, tightened his grip around her waist, and pulled her farther into the shadows. Holding on to a humongous tree, they peeked around the trunk.

The bigger of the two, a man maybe seven feet tall, held the yellow-green light, same as the net. Sophie gave Flynden a sideways glance. Pelifeles slunk into a bush and out of sight.

"Let's run," whispered Sophie.

Flynden whispered back, "Too late."

The men strode into the clearing; both were dressed in long tunics like the old man in the cemetery. Compared to the old man's clothes, their garments were clean, not ripped and bloody; the fine cloth was embroidered with stars, sun and moon. As they moved, their golden belts made of links shaped like suns tinkled.

Who are they? Sophie mouthed to Flynden, but the boy

shook his head and pressed a finger to his lips.

The taller man with white wavy hair extended his arm with the globe in front of him and swept it left and right. When he got to the spot where the net had hung, the yellow-green globe sparked and the light sizzled. He closed his fist, the light disappeared, and he circled the spot, searching the ground.

Sophie gasped.

The man bent down and picked up Mom's jacket from the flattened grass, straightened, and with raised eyebrows, he regarded it with a frown. The man handled the jacket, probing each pocket with one hand.

Sophie slapped her hand over her mouth to stifle another gasp. Wide-eyed, she stared at Flynden; he stared back. *So much for hiding.*

The other man, reed thin and a bit shorter, had lustrous brown hair laced with silver. He took his orange globe and ventured farther into the clearing to where the portal had been. No sparks jumped off his hand. Swinging his outstretched arm back and forth like a lantern, he searched a larger area. A deep scowl etched his face into a stony mask, making him look mean. He stopped and swiveled once on the spot, then closed his fist too, and the orange light vanished.

The forest stood as if breathless. No gusts or breezes stirred the air; no birds chirped; not a leaf rustled. Sophie held her breath, too.

The taller man squinted at his companion before they both swung toward the trees. Sophie and Flynden huddled close.

"Let's run." Flynden pulled her arm.

They swung away from the tree and rushed deep into the forest. All weariness forgotten, fear giving her strength, Sophie ran after Flynden. She didn't care how much noise she made, if she could only put as much distance as possible between herself and the big man with the yellow-green light. She stumbled and fell often. Each time, Flynden helped her to her feet. They kept running.

A thick trunk lay across their path. Pelifeles clawed his way over it. Sophie and Flynden scrambled after him. As her feet hit the ground on the other side, her right ankle bent. She cried out. Flynden stopped and pulled her up. No way she could keep running. With Flynden's arms around her, she hobbled along.

Soon, they reached a forest path, about a car's width, strewn with pine needles and brown leaves. They could walk faster here, but they could also be seen a long way off.

Every step hurt. Sophie limped beside Flynden, moaning, both casting anxious glances over their shoulders every few seconds. They hadn't gone far when the two men emerged from the forest onto the path behind them, but then the path curved left, and Sophie, Flynden and Pelifeles slipped around the corner.

Ahead, not far now, open gates three stories high and set into a high stone wall waited for them. Flynden pulled her toward them. The path ended at a wooden bridge leading them over a moat and through the gates.

Pelifeles dashed in front of them onto the bridge. In no time, he had disappeared along the cobblestones into an alley on the other side.

"Wait!" Flynden shouted, but the cat either couldn't hear him or didn't want to.

Sophie fell to her knees and groaned. With Flynden's help, she scrambled up again. They turned and watched the two men striding around the bend in the path. With renewed effort, Sophie hobbled over the bridge's last half, under the portcullis and into a town with cobblestone streets and stone houses. Two guards came running from a gatehouse and watched them pass. When they saw Sophie, they gasped and fell back.

It must have been the bright pink t-shirt and the pink sneakers. Sophie grinned despite the pain shooting up her leg from her ankle. But she was wrong because Flynden ripped off his cap and jammed it onto her head, pulling it low over her forehead and covering her red hair.

He veered left up a steep hill. People hurried past, carrying baskets with bread and vegetables or paper packages. Men, women, and children eyed them suspiciously, but no one stopped. A stitch in her side turned into a knife-sharp stabbing. She gasped, and her stomach heaved again.

"Let's hide somewhere," she said. "My ankle hurts too much."

"No, keep going." Flynden pulled her along, disregarding her complaints. "We'll be worse off if the councilors catch us."

The steep cobblestone street slanted upward even more. People stared at her pale face and her bright pink clothes. Nobody dressed like her. Most of the women and girls wore long, simple brown or gray dresses. Only some women donned colorful gowns trimmed with lace or bows. Long brown or black hair framed their golden brown faces. Men wore short tunics and leggings with short boots or buckled shoes. Dark beards covered their brown faces beneath a shock of black or brown hair. No wonder they stared; not one of them had fair skin, blond hair, or red hair like her.

Sophie and Flynden hurried up the hill. The street curved and rose with no end. Flynden climbed, never missing a step like the steep climb didn't bother him at all. Sophie struggled along, huffing and moaning the whole way.

Dusk settled on the city and shadows danced around them with each passing streetlight—small globes like those the two councilors held in their hands. Only these lights glowed white and sat like jewels on the tops of metal poles.

Cobblestone alleys cut between houses to the right, and a thick stone wall without doors or stairs ran along to the left.

Maybe if she picked one of the dark alleys, she could get away. It felt wrong to leave Flynden after he had saved her, but maybe he would catch on and follow her. She had to try no matter what.

Light from pit fires spilled onto the cobblestones from a side street. Men and women emptied stalls, carrying crates with produce into the houses for the night. A short way down the street, a huge round fire pit stood ablaze where flames licked at a pig roast. A man rotated the spit, singing. His happy song drifted over together with the yummy smell of roasting meat. Sophie's stomach growled.

No cars lined sidewalks; there weren't any sidewalks. Nothing looked modern or familiar. No one walked around with a cell phone or anything like that. Horses or cattle pulled these people's pushcarts and wagons. They seemed to be living in the dark ages.

They passed the street. Dogs barked through iron gates set in walled-in courtyards. A white cat with black paws sat on a low wall, eying them with interest, but it wasn't Pelifeles with his pinkish-white ears and half-black face.

Up ahead to the right loomed another dark alley. Sophie tensed. As they drew level with the alley, the lights of a busy street gleamed at the other end. *Time to run.*

Sophie threw off Flynden's arms, swiveled on her good foot, and rushed into the alley.

"No!" Flynden's voice echoed after her. "Wait!"

Was he crazy? No way would she stop now. Instead, she poured her energy into running as fast as she could make her hurting ankle go.

Yellow-green fire lashed around her legs. She stumbled and fell, hitting her head on the cobblestones. Flynden's cap slipped off her head. For a second, her sight blurred. She kicked at the yellow-green light strands that were gripping her leg and nipping her like a dog.

In no time, the councilors' faces appeared above her. The yellow-green light tickled her forehead where it had hit the stone, warmed her face for a second, and was gone.

Sophie blinked. Flynden squeezed between the two men, his eyes wide with fear and a look saying, why didn't you listen? People gathered around them and stared. The big man, who Flynden had called Councilor Makimus, lifted her off the ground.

He shouted, "Stand aside! The child must be taken to Council Hall." He tightened his arms around her. "Remain calm. You will be safe."

All around them voices rose, repeating, "By the light, a pale one." Women shrieked and screamed. The man's arms tightened around her body. Sour apple smell assaulted her nose and robbed her senses.

❧ *Chapter 3* ❧

"Promise you'll hide until I come back." Thistle pushed Bramble back into the shadow at the mouth of an unused sewage tunnel.

"I want to come with you, Thithle," Bramble said.

"You can't come."

Bramble furrowed her brow the way Da used to when he looked angry. Thistle bit his lip, stifling a smile.

"Why not?" she asked for about the tenth time.

Thistle sighed. Fine. One more time. "I told you, it's too dangerous. What if someone sees you?"

"People see *you*."

"Listen, Bramble, I need to do this alone. I promise I'll come back with food and sweets, but first, I have to earn some coin."

"But why can't I? I always came before." Bramble's pale blond curls danced around her shoulders.

Thistle sighed again. Why did she have to look at him with those big blue eyes? He had to stay firm. What he had planned might be dangerous if he failed. Better have her safely tucked away.

"Bramble, listen." Thistle grabbed his sister's face with gentle hands and squeezed her cheeks, making her mouth pucker. "I won't be long. Talk to Rosie until I come back. Maybe if I get enough coin, I'll get you a new Rosie."

"I don't want a new Rosie. I love Rosie."

"Fine." Thistle rolled his eyes. Anything to keep her happy. Ma's hand-made cloth doll in Bramble's arms looked at him with only one button eye. The ends of both arms were frayed from Bramble's constant sucking. Rosie's dress had disappeared long ago. He imagined giving Bramble a new doll, one he had seen in the doll maker's shop at Council Plaza. He could almost see her face light up with joy when he gave it to her. His plan had to work.

"Be a good girl and stay until I come back." He let go of her face. "Promise."

Bramble lowered her head and cried. He wiped her tears with his dirty hands and smeared her face, making dark streaks on her pink cheeks. If he could only find a place for them to wash. She needed a new dress and stockings; hers had holes in them. The stitching on her booties had broken, leaving big gaps between the soles and the upper leather. When the Turning Bell tolled at dusk, things would be different because he would have coin to buy new ones for her.

"I have to go now." He covered her hair with her scarf and tucked the stray curls under it. "Make sure the scarf doesn't come off." He stood. "Stay hidden the way I told you. Don't come out, even if someone calls you."

"What if the man with the big rings comes?" She leaned forward a bit and sniffed.

Something dropped in Thistle's stomach.

"Don't think about that man, and don't talk about him. We didn't see anything. Remember."

"But I did."

"No, you did not, Bramble. Please."

Bramble cried harder. "I want Ma."

Not that again. His throat tightened as if two hands squeezed it, like those hands with the big rings around Ma's throat. Thistle shook his head to rid himself of the picture.

Bramble cried louder. "I want Ma."

"I know. Me too." He knelt down beside her and clutched her in his arms, making the scarf come off so that her pale-blond curls tumbled from their hiding spot. By the time Thistle had swallowed the lump in his throat, Bramble stopped crying. He let go of her.

"What if Bron comes?" she asked.

"Don't talk to Bron and the others. Promise."

She nodded and smiled at him. "I don't like Bron."

"I don't either." He grinned back.

He adjusted his cap and hoped no strands of his light hair showed.

"Be good now."

She gave him a quick nod.

He strode away, looking over his shoulder, making sure she stayed put.

Bramble had settled back into the shadow, but her frayed booties remained in the light. He hesitated. No, he would never get away if he kept fussing. She would do fine. Bramble was smart, even for five, and most of the time, she listened to him.

He hurried from the alley by the city's outer wall into one of the busier streets. The men he sought played at the small market square two levels up. He had watched them often. Always the same four men played and always for a lot of coin. He had a chance to win a Game of

Stones. Da's voice still rang in his ears with the game's rules, but Da didn't teach him to play for coin. He had warned him not to. It ruins your character, he'd said. *Why?* Da never explained. But Thistle saw no other way. The few Leas he received from helping at shops or out on the farms were never enough to take care of Bramble. Everyone wanted his help, but no one wanted to pay a ten-year-old boy. He didn't want to steal like Bron and the others. Yet, he had taken the playing stones from Bron. No, he had borrowed them. He would give them back as soon as he'd won. The stones would be in their hiding spot before Bron would even miss them.

He ran up Cobblestone Main. A big, mangy dog on a chain tried to nip his ankles. Thistle swerved, jumping over crates and barrels, laughing at the barks following him.

Breathless, he reached the small market square halfway up to Council Hall. Bakers offered their bread, buns, and cakes stacked on tables. Thistle's stomach growled. He would buy buns and cakes in a little while with the coin he won.

Stalls lined most of the shops around the square. Some farmers offered fruit, like apples, pears, cherries, and peaches, while others sold different fresh vegetables, anything from sweet red potatoes to tomatoes. Big pens in the square's center held sheep and pigs. Cows lowed as farmers considered them for purchase. A farmer's wife had brought a milk cow and women stood in line for fresh milk.

"I offer you twelve Tres for that cow." Two farmers haggled over a light brown cow with a big round belly.

"Twelve Tres? Has the darkness gotten you? The cow is with calf. Twenty-five Tres or I'll keep her."

Thistle hurried past men and cows to the farthest

corner of the square where he knew he would find the four men playing the Game of Stones. Soon, he spotted them in their established corner at the foot of a fountain where a large flat stone lent its smooth surface to draw a big circle. One of the men straightened from his crouch, massaging his long legs.

"That's it for me," the tall man said and walked away.

"Hey, come back," one of the players, a fat dirty man, shouted.

"Na, need what I have left to feed my family," the man called over his shoulder and kept walking.

Thistle bustled up the steps toward the chalk circle.

"I want to play."

Onlookers and the remaining three players stared at him.

"You've got coin?" the fat man asked.

Thistle nodded, pulled his only two Leas from his pocket, and stuck his hand out. A booming laugh answered him. People watching joined in the laughter.

"Better hold on to those, lad. You won't have them much longer."

"I got stones, too," Thistle said, shoving the bronze coins with the leaf on them back into his pocket. He fumbled with a string around his neck, pulled a pouch from beneath his tunic, and shook the round gray stones—five small hazelnut-size stones and a bigger walnut-size one, onto his palm. "Five Bits and a Fire," he said.

The men looked at each other and grinned. Thistle could figure out what they were thinking, but the men were wrong. He would show them.

"Step up then, lad, step up. Starting a new game now."

For a moment, Thistle panicked. What if he lost the Leas? Bramble would go hungry until he earned more, and he didn't want to think about what would happen if he lost the stones. He would have to win the first game for sure.

"Go on," the fat man said. "Place your Bits."

Thistle knelt close to the outer circle without touching the line and placed his five Bits on the line of the smaller inner circle. The men placed theirs along the same line until each man had only the Fire left.

"Go on, lad." The fat man grinned. "You first."

Thistle swallowed and pulled the two Leas from his pocket, placing them beside his knees. The three men pulled out their coin, Tres, large ovals with an engraved tree.

If he won the first round, he would get three Tres besides his own two Leas. He weighed the Fire in his hand for a moment and eyed the Bits he wanted to hit. He curved his fingers into a fist and placed the Fire onto their crook, his thumb resting lightly behind it. His hand shook. Thistle leaned forward, took a deep breath and held it. He not only had to hit the Bits, preferably his own and some of the others, but also keep his Fire within the outer circle.

Flick. The Fire shot from his fist, and click, click, click, hit his own three and one of the fat man's Bits before it came to rest still within the larger circle. Thistle exhaled and sat on his heels. The crowd pushed closer and watched.

The fat man frowned. "Not bad, lad," he said and played next.

Flick. His sausage-like thumb flicked his Fire and overshot the smaller circle. The round stone stopped on the large circle's line, almost rolling out, not hitting a single Bit.

"Aaah." The crowd sighed.

The fat man's frown deepened.

The other two men took their turn, and faired no better than the fat man, each hitting only one Bit, their own. They handed over their Tres and Bits. Thistle tried to hide his excitement and relief. The men's frowns told him they weren't happy about losing their coin and Bits to him. They would play until all Bits were gone, taking turns flicking the Fires.

Thistle won almost every round until he had enough coin to last until Harvest time. Careful not to smile, he furrowed his brow instead.

The fat man won one round, and one of Thistle's Bits. Thistle's stomach clenched with fear. He had to leave with all five Bits and the Fire. Fortunately, he had enough coin and the Bits now to offer the man a trade for the one he had lost.

Absent-mindedly, the fat man rubbed the Bit he had won from Thistle between his thumb and forefinger. Thistle played his turn. Flick. Click, click. Thistle took out the last two stones and ended the game. He won.

Suddenly, the fat man jumped.

"What is this?"

He stuck his hand under Thistle's nose. The Bit sparkled on his palm.

Oh, no! It had been painted, and the fat man had rubbed off the paint. He should've known Bron would do something like that, painting forbidden stones to make them look like regular ones. Thistle cringed. He should've checked.

"You cheat." The fat man's face turned crimson. "You are playing with cove pebbles."

Thistle stared and shivered. How could he say he

hadn't known? If he did, he had to admit he stole the stones. No, borrowed them.

"What's the meaning of this?" The other two men came to their feet.

"Give it here!" Thistle shouted. He snatched the Bit from the fat man's hand and scooped up some of the money and his other stones. He backed away from the men and bumped into the round body of a woman. She grabbed him by the neck.

"Not so fast, you little cheat." She shook him so hard his cap slid off. Seeing his white-blond hair, she shrieked and dropped her hands.

The fat man lowered his red face to Thistle's level, fuming. His nostrils sprouted black hair, and his breath stunk of drink.

"So, not only are you a cheat but also a pale one."

"Not!" Thistle yelled.

People widened the circle, giving them more room; their laughter now sounded strained and nervous.

"Then what's with that hair of yours? Eh?" The fat man stood nose-to-nose with Thistle. "You will have to answer for this. Don't think you scare me into letting you go."

"But…," Thistle stammered. His knees knocked together hard. He could barely keep standing.

The fat man grabbed Thistle's tunic front.

"The councilors will judge what's to be done with you." He jerked and pushed Thistle before him. "Pick up the stones and coin and come," he ordered the other two men. "Don't pocket them."

"You mean…?" One of the men looked puzzled.

"I mean, the councilors will decide about the stones and coin. Don't fret, they'll give us the coin."

Thistle tore himself from the man's grip, making for a gap in the crowd, but another man caught his arm. "Going somewhere, lad?" He grinned, but not in a nice way. The crowd watched with glee but kept their distance.

The fat man grabbed the back of Thistle's tunic, pressed his large fist into Thistle's spine, and pushed him to Cobblestone Main. People backed away and stared; no one had a friendly look to spare. He wished he still had his cap to hide his light hair. Dread settled in his stomach, and his guilt stirred it. With hunched shoulders and hanging head, he climbed the hill with the men and the crowd.

Much too soon, they reached Council Plaza. The plaza bustled with its own market. Amidst the market stalls stood the Mother Flora's fountain, its water splashing merrily from the statue's hands.

When Thistle had taken Bramble here, they had watched the fountain, and the people, and the fine wear meant for only the wealthy. Those had been fun times, but now, the Mother Flora's stone face cast its stern gaze down on him. *Bramble.* A fist closed around his heart. What would become of her now? What would the councilors do to him?

The Council Hall's white façade with its tall, wide, stained glass windows sparkled in the sun. The fat man pushed him up the wide marble stone steps at the foot of the carved wooden doors. The other two men pulled the two wings wide enough to let them through. Thistle craned his neck back to the crowd, twisting and trying to pull free. As he did so, he had one last look of the plaza and the crowd. By the Mother Flora's fountain stood Bron, one fist raised and shaking it. His other fist tightened on Bramble's arm. She cried into the hem of her dress so that her ripped stockings showed. *How often had he told her this wasn't proper?* Bron shook Bramble. *What would he do to her?*

"Bramble!" Thistle screamed. His legs buckled, but the fat man yanked him up and shoved him through the doors. The heavy doors banged shut behind them, cutting off the plaza, Bron, and Bramble.

❧ *Chapter 4* ❧

The light faded quickly as the sun set over the city. The Turning Bell in the bell tower of Council Hall announced the Flora's turning at sundown. Instead of going back to Bramble with coin as he had promised her, he would now be punished for stealing and playing with magical cove stones. The law forbade playing with these stones in a regular game. Everyone had to have the same stones to keep the game fair, but he hadn't known they were cove stones when he stole them from Bron.

The fat man knocked on another set of double doors. They waited for quite some time until a young servant pulled one wing ajar, standing tall and peeking at them through a narrow opening.

"What brings you to Council Hall?" he asked.

"We bring our grievance against this boy." The fat man pulled Thistle in front of him so that the servant could see him. The young man widened the gap between the doors. His brown eyes flashed to Thistle, then away. Black hair framed his face like a helmet. His dark-green tunic showed the Council Hall's emblem over his heart, a golden-centered daisy with silver petals.

"Wait here," the servant said and strode away leaving

the doors open for the three men and Thistle to step into the large hall. There they huddled and watched the servant disappear through a narrow door at the hall's other end.

No, he wouldn't cry. He wouldn't show the fat man how scared he was. Still, tears stung his eyes and the hall in front of him swam, mingling with the frightening memory of Bron clutching Bramble with a nasty sneer on the thief's face.

Thistle had never stolen anything in his life, and his gut had protested when he took the playing stones. His gut had never told him wrong before. Why had he ignored it this time? He knew why. Because Bramble was dressed in rags and her stomach growled every day, and because he couldn't buy enough food for her. Now, he would be paying for ignoring his gut, and Bramble would still go hungry.

Thistle balled his fists. He would fight Bron for taking Bramble. His fists trembled, and he dug his nails into the palms. He knew the councilors would punish him, but he didn't know what that punishment would look like. That was the worst, not knowing. His heart sank lower, all the way down into his stomach and throbbed there. His head ached, making it hard to think. A heavy feeling pressed on his chest as if the fat man sat on it.

If only he hadn't stolen the stones. If only he hadn't left Bramble behind. If only he had taken her with him when she begged him to. If, if, if. He could wish all he wanted; it would change nothing now.

From the small door off to the side, the young servant reappeared.

"The councilors will be with you presently," he said and beckoned the three men and Thistle to follow him up the center toward a long table with seven high-back chairs. The fat man pushed Thistle ahead. Thistle wobbled along on shaking legs; his lower lip trembled. The men's heavy boots echoed on the stone floor as they walked along the raised benches standing in rows against the walls to both sides. The last rays of the setting sun peeked through the colorful stained glass windows, casting red, yellow, green, and blue patches onto stone and wood.

"Please wait here." With those words, the servant disappeared a second time.

The big man grunted something. The other two men shuffled their feet, twisting their necks and startling with every sound. From their looks, they had never been inside Council Hall and neither had Thistle.

Thistle snuck a peek at the ceiling. Open-mouthed, his eyes drank in the richness of the dark blue paint with silver stars, a silver moon sickle, and one golden sun at the ceiling's center. He imagined visiting only to enjoy the colors and looking at the Mother Flora's pictures in the high stained glass windows.

Footsteps sounded from behind a set of double doors to the left and tore Thistle back to the fat man's fist on his neck. The doors swung wide, and six High Council members strode into the hall. Thistle knew them all by name and had seen them before, not up close like this, but at ceremonies in the city and then only from far away. The councilors entered the hall with their long robes swishing on the stone floor, hands crossed in front of them and hidden by long sleeves. They took their seats one by one at the table. Some regarded him with gazes down their noses, but all stared at his white-blond hair a moment too long. The middle chair at the table remained empty.

Councilor Makimus, sitting closest to the left of the empty chair, cleared his throat.

"Well?" he addressed the fat man. "What has brought you before the High Council of Gwern-cadarn-brac?"

The fat man shuffled forward. He tightened his fist on Thistle's tunic, dragging him toward the table.

"Councilor." The fat man bowed. "We," he looked behind him and included his two companions with an arm's sweep, "have brought our grievance against this boy."

Makimus lowered his head and regarded Thistle from beneath heavy brows. He smiled, but somehow the smile looked all wrong and worse than a scowl. Thistle shivered. Sweat broke out all over his body and made his tunic and leggings stick to his skin.

"What has he done?"

"He won a lot of coin from us with this." The fat man placed the pouch with Bron's playing stones on the table.

"Hm." Makimus' eyes flicked to the pouch then back to the man's face. "Our laws permit for youngsters to play."

"Yes, of course, Councilor." The fat man bowed again. "But…"

"You said he won?"

"Yes, but…"

"Did he, indeed?" The smile widened and showed a row of white teeth.

The fat man wrung his hands. The tightness in Thistle's chest did not lighten even a little bit. Something was wrong. The councilor seemed to be toying with the fat man, or with him.

"Yes, but these are unlawful playing stones. I mean, in a regular Game of Stones, Councilor."

Makimus reached for the pouch. His sleeves pulled back and exposed hands with large rings on each finger.

Thistle gasped and froze. The man with the big rings. He remembered those strong and graceful hands. A large ring adorned each finger. He remembered the one on the right hand's middle finger, a flower with a blue stone center surrounded by silver petals. He had seen those hands only once, the night Da and Ma died, but he would never forget them.

Makimus emptied the stones into his left hand. Beside him, skinny-like-a-scarecrow Councilor Druce Lar leaned over to examine them as well. The other four councilors bent forward for a closer look.

"Well, I see. These are stones from Sunflower Cove, disguised with gray paint." Makimus looked up. "What have you got to say for yourself, boy?"

Thistle lowered his head, afraid to look at the councilor, hoping his fear wouldn't show. The silence within the hall weighed heavier the longer he waited to answer. He had to say something, but instead, he wanted to run as fast and as far as his legs could carry him. He knew he wouldn't get far. The fat man's fist on his back reminded him.

"I didn't know they were special," Thistle admitted, keeping his eyes downcast.

"How did you come by these stones?"

What should he say? Thistle swallowed hard, but the lump in his throat wouldn't go away.

"Well?" Makimus prompted him.

"I won them in a game." There was no way around the lies. As much as he disliked Bron, he didn't want to bring him into this, nor did he want to tell about Bramble. His gut feeling nudged him. Bramble must stay out of this. Whatever it took, he had to keep her a secret, even if the councilor found out what Thistle had seen.

When Makimus asked, "You won them with regular stones?" Thistle knew he was in trouble, but he nodded to the floor anyway.

"Where are your stones?"

"I gave them to another boy who hadn't any."

"I see."

The two words stung. "These stones seemed to be better," Thistle tried to explain. "But I didn't know why." He looked up. "I didn't know. Honest. By the light."

"Do not soil the light with your lies," Camshron said in his high voice, sending more shivers down Thistle's back and arms. Every time Thistle had seen Councilor Camshron, he had a scowl on his face and never seemed to smile; he only sneered the way he did now.

"I'm not lying." Thistle shook hard. His voice trembled. "It's the truth. Honest."

"Still, even if this is so, it is unlawful to use these stones in a regular game," Makimus said.

"But I didn't know…"

"We will keep these stones," Makimus addressed the fat man. "You may keep the coin."

"Thank you, Councilor." The fat man bowed lowest yet. "What about the boy? Will he be punished?"

"Leave him to us."

"My companions and I believe he is a pale one." The fat man seemed disappointed.

"The boy's hair and complexion are not his fault," Druce Lar cut him off with his deep voice. Tulio nodded, but the other councilors took in a sharp breath.

Thistle wanted to shrink into the stone floor. An uncomfortable silence filled the hall. He chanced a glance at the table. The councilors' eyes seemed to miss nothing as they looked down on him.

"We will determine what needs to be done, my good man," Makimus said at last, his smile wider than ever, dismissing the three men, but the fat man still hesitated.

Thistle's heart plummeted. He knew he could outsmart the three men, but not the High Council. They had great powers, or so he had heard. Tears he had tried to stop wet his cheeks. He would die. He knew he would.

Thistle cast a pleading look at Druce Lar and Tulio. They wouldn't harm him, would they?

Druce Lar's bearing had not changed. His warm gray eyes still regarded him with kindness. Tulio, the jolly councilor, frowned, his usual smile gone. Thistle looked along the table. Camshron's eyes narrowed to slits, while Darach pressed his mouth into a thin line. His one good eye now cast a steely glance at Thistle, but Thistle trembled when looking at the other one, the glass eye. Rumors said he could see better with the glass eye, right through people. Lombard's head shook a bit and he fussed with his cane. His watery eyes fixed on Thistle, making it hard to guess what he thought.

"You may go now," Makimus said and rose. "We will take care of the boy."

The fat man tightened his fist on Thistle, hesitated a moment longer, then pushed him away. The three men backed away, bowing all the way to the hall's middle, where they swung around and hurried through the double doors, running from the hall.

❧ *Chapter 5* ❧

As the door banged shut behind the three men, silence settled in the hall. The Turning Bell had rung when they arrived, and golden sunrays had streamed into the hall. Now, darkness slipped into the city and Council Hall, sucking all colors out of the stained glass windows.

"What is your name, son?" Makimus' wide smile flashed above Thistle.

"Thi, Thistle," he stammered. He hadn't meant to give his real name. It had popped out.

Lombard's hand shook as he pointed at Thistle. "Where are your parents, Thistle?" The old man leaned forward.

Thistle wanted to say dead, when his gut told him differently.

"They are doing business with a merchant."

"And left you exploring the city on your own?" The old councilor's voice filled with disapproval. "What are their names? They must be found at once."

Thistle kept his eyes on his dirty feet, wriggling his toes. He could not give his parents' names. If he did, Makimus would know him, if he did not already.

"They went to Harbor Town."

"Their names." Camshron slapped his hand onto the table.

Thistle flinched.

"Left alone for a few moments, and right away you got yourself into trouble." The lack of warmth and compassion in Darach's stern voice added to Thistle's growing fear. He kept his mouth closed. If he got away in one piece, he would never steal again. By the light, he promised. He would work hard. He would take Bramble out of Gwern and go to Urbinter, or Windy Fields, where nobody knew them. Tears stung his eyes anew.

"I assume, Darach," Councilor Druce Lar spoke, "that in your youth trouble was not a stranger to you?"

"I was a special child."

"Yes, of course, but that did not exempt you from right and wrong. On the contrary, as a special child, you would have had to set an example for the regular children, would you not?"

"What is your point, Druce Lar?"

"My point is, Thistle is still a child, a smart one at that, and has an aptitude for getting himself into trouble, as boys do."

Thistle looked up. Druce Lar's eyes twinkled once more. Gratitude washed over him. Da would have spoken like this.

"However, he has to be taught a lesson." Camshron's sour remark twisted the good feelings into fear again. "I suggest he should come with me. I will teach him right from wrong."

"None of that," Makimus spoke up. "For not being forthright with the Council, he will be locked away for five days with only bread and water. Time enough to consider his wrong ways."

Tulio, Darach, and Lombard nodded their consent. Camshron flared his nostrils but said nothing. Druce Lar frowned. His stern gaze rested on Makimus.

"I do not agree."

"That may be so, Druce Lar, but since I am acting High Councilor at present, I will make the decisions as to what punishment the boy will receive."

The two councilors locked gazes for a moment. Thistle hoped Druce Lar would win the silent sparring.

But then, Druce Lar nodded.

"Very well." He rose. "Then I will choose the room for him and make certain he will not receive the worst end of the bread."

"You are coddling a thief," Camshron said and pushed back his chair. "The punishment is…"

"The punishment is harsh." Druce Lar cut him off. "We do not know for certain if the boy is guilty. We have only the three men's testimony." He twisted in his seat and called, "Stace!"

The young servant stepped forward from his place behind the table and acknowledged Druce Lar with a nod.

"Take Thistle to the baths, wash him and give him clean clothes. Then bring him to the kitchen. I will meet you there."

Stace nodded and grabbed Thistle's arm.

With a stern but kind manner, Druce Lar addressed Thistle. "Stace will take care of you, son. Do not fear."

Thistle nodded at his feet.

"You must promise to do as you are told and not try to run away."

Thistle nodded again.

"If you give us your parents' names, we will find them and ask them to come for you."

Thistle stole a quick glance up. Druce Lar gave him a smile and the twinkle returned.

Thistle hated lying to the councilor, but he could not give his parents' names. He shook his head and remained silent.

"Very well. We revisit the subject later." Druce Lar nodded to Stace.

The servant pulled Thistle from the hall. As the double doors to the hallway banged shut behind him, Thistle let out a shaky breath.

⮞ ⮜

Stace dragged him down a long, wide hallway, but when Thistle followed obediently, Stace let his arm go. He took long strides causing Thistle to run after him.

"Come along then," the servant urged him, flicking his hand impatiently.

Thistle watched Stace walk ahead in his fine tunic that was gathered with a beaded belt around his waist. He wore fitted brown leggings, and sheepskin boots softened his steps. Thistle glanced down on his own shabby clothes and cringed.

Colorful and finely stitched tapestries of the Flora and their Garden adorned the walls between doors set deep into alcoves. Magic orbs glowed in silver brackets and brightened the hallway, but not enough to chase all of the shadows away. Soft rugs with lustrous pile and patterned with blue and gold swirls muffled the sound of their steps. Thistle's eyes tried to take in the splendor, craning his neck left and right, missing nothing.

Soon, the hallways narrowed. Here, no rugs covered the stone floors and no tapestries adorned the stone walls. Stace veered left and right, and right and left again, then across an intersecting hallway, then left and right again, until Thistle's head spun. He wouldn't have known how to find his way back even if he tried hard. They walked through a shadowy stone city until the next turn brought an arcade letting in air and moonlight. A flower garden spread between high walls. Thistle slowed and stared. Lighted orbs and the moon shone onto a golden statue of the Mother Flora in a fountain's center. Wide rows of sunflowers and daisies footed the fountain. Red, purple, and yellow tulips, yellow daffodils, and blue irises spread to both sides of a turquoise and blue mosaic path winding through the garden from one end to the other. Climbing pink, red, and yellow roses scaled the stone walls. Blooming lilac mingled with the flowers' heady scents.

Never had Thistle seen such a colorful and splendid garden. For a moment, his spirits lifted until Stace pulled on his arm and hurried him along to the arcade's end and into another windowless hallway.

"Come," he said. "First, the bath, then to the kitchen. We must not keep Councilor Druce Lar waiting."

They must have walked many leagues down long hallways when they entered through a doorway into a large chamber with three high lancet windows at the opposite end. Tiny orbs along the walls reflected in six white marble basins, three on each side against the walls. Every one of the basins had a shiny brass water pump at one end. Water steamed from one of them when Stace pumped it to fill the basin. Thistle ran his hands along the basin's smooth rim. Bramble would like this. He imagined her splashing around in the warm water, making the floor and shelves wet within her reach.

"Undress," Stace said, "and climb into the water." He took a square piece of fragrant soap and a washcloth from a narrow shelf above the basin and handed it to him.

Thistle breathed in the soap's lavender and lemon grass scent. Ma had liked both these scents and had trailed them throughout the house. The thought of Ma brought tears to his eyes. He sank into the water, hoping Stace hadn't seen them. The thought of Ma also brought back the memory of the man with the big rings, Councilor Makimus. In spite of the hot water, Thistle wiped the shivers away along his arms.

Stace walked to a set of shelves in a shallow alcove halfway down the chamber. Folded garments filled the shelves. Stace pulled a pair of leggings and a tunic from the middle shelf and held them up. He shook his head, refolded and replaced them. He picked another set from a lower shelf, shook them out and nodded as he walked back to Thistle.

"I think these will fit you well enough." He placed tunic and leggings on a wooden stool beside the basin. "Now do not dawdle and be quick about it. I will return shortly."

Thistle looked across the softly-lighted room to the high windows. The moon looked back at him.

As Stace's footsteps slipped away, Thistle began lathering his arms and legs with the soap until he smelled like lavender and lemon grass. It took some scrubbing to remove all the grime between his toes. When he thought he had done a good job, he leaned back into the warm water, closed his eyes, and drifted off.

The sound of heavy footsteps echoing in the hallway startled Thistle awake. That wasn't Stace. Someone else was coming. Thistle climbed from the basin, and without drying himself off first, he wriggled into the tunic and leggings. As he pulled his head through the neck opening, the steps stopped. Thistle looked up and his breath caught in his throat.

Councilor Makimus stood in the doorway. A wide smile split his face; his teeth gleamed and somehow gave him a snarling-beast look.

"Well, well, well, we are clean." The councilor stepped into the chamber.

Where was Stace? Why wasn't he coming back?

"Come." The councilor beckoned with one hand, rings flashing in the tiny orbs' soft light.

A lump grew thick in Thistle's throat. His heart fluttered like a caged bird within his chest.

"Councilor Druce Lar is waiting for me in the kitchen," he said as firmly as he could.

The smile disappeared. "Unfortunately, Councilor Druce Lar was called away on a rather important errand. You will be in my care instead. I trust that suits you?" Sharpness edged the councilor's voice.

Thistle wanted to shake his head but nodded instead.

"Where is Stace?" Thistle balled his fists and twisted them into his tunic's hem.

Makimus ignored the question and turned toward the door. "Come."

When Thistle opened his mouth to ask again for Stace, the councilor held up one hand. "Enough."

"Where are we going?" Thistle asked.

Makimus gave no answer but stepped into the hallway and beckoned Thistle to walk ahead. Thistle cowered and slunk past the big man.

The councilor took him a different way than the one he had come earlier with Stace and into an ever-darkening hallway leading down into a rough stone passage. The councilor hurried him around the corners, fingertips resting on Thistle's back, directing him wherever he wanted him to go.

"Here we are," he said, lowering his voice. The smile reappeared.

They had reached an ironclad door. Makimus gathered his yellow-green magic in one hand and pressed his hand against the lock. Sour apple smell filled the space around them and made Thistle sick. A moment later, the lock clicked and the door swung ajar. The yellow-green light shone down a few steps into a dark round opening looking like a beast's open jaws, but it was only a dry unused sewage tunnel like the one where he and Bramble had made their home.

Makimus pointed into the darkness. Thistle shook his head, but the councilor's hand brushed against his back and pushed him forward. Terror spurred Thistle into a dive beneath the big man's arm. He sprinted away, but after only a few steps, yellow-green ropes tightened around his ankles. Thistle stumbled as the ropes twisted up and around his torso and bound his arms to his sides. He struggled, but the harder he fought, the more the ropes tightened. The sour apple smell stung his nose until his head swam and his stomach heaved.

"Stace!"

The ropes cut off his scream and squeezed the breath from his lungs. He gasped. His body jerked once or twice then hung limp. Makimus walked toward him. Thistle's eyes grew heavy as the ringed hands picked him up off the floor.

૭ *Chapter 6* ૭

Sophie flinched and bolted upright. Who screamed?

A full moon peeked through a small open square high up in the dark wall; its light didn't quite reach the floor, but cold air drifted down from the opening and touched her face. Straw crackled under her as she rolled onto her stomach, her nose wrinkled with disgust. Phew, what a stink. Worse than a public toilet.

Something small scurried past her, then something else. What was that? Maybe mice? Mice weren't so bad. They were cute. She liked mice. She tried to stand but a sharp pain shot from her ankle to her hip. She lost her balance and collapsed against a rough stone wall.

"Ouch." Sophie bit her lip and blinked away the tears. She probed her swollen ankle and moaned. Maybe it was broken. She slumped back and hugged her knees, burying her nose between them to block out the rotting stink. Was she left to rot here, too?

If only she hadn't thrown the stone at Trudy. If only she hadn't run away. But what else should she have done? Not throw the stone and listen to Trudy. Duh. What if she'd killed Trudy? Then her picture would be hanging in the post office like all the most wanted. Well,

૭ 55 ૭

if the police saw her now, they'd be happy. No danger to anyone. She didn't mean to hurt Trudy. She really didn't. She had been so scared and lonely—and angry. Yes, Mom and Dad and Tommy were gone, but she wasn't alone. Trudy cared and had always been nice to her, annoying and fussy sometimes, but nice. If she could only undo what she'd done. Ifs didn't help. She had to find a way out of here and back home. Trudy would come looking for her, if she was alive, that's for sure. Another if. How would Trudy know? Would she post a picture on the missing persons wall in a store? Nobody would ever find her here in this dungeon.

Again, she blinked and wiped her face with her t-shirt's sleeves. No use feeling sorry for herself. She got herself into this; she would have to get herself out.

Sophie groaned as she stood and ground her teeth together. She hobbled along the wall, keeping one hand on the stone. Straw crunched under her sneakers.

A spider web crossed her face. She brushed it away. Hopefully, the spider was small and somewhere else. When she reached the cell's corner, her fingers searched along the next wall to another corner and another wall, and then her hands found a wooden door. A lock with a keyhole sat at waist height but with no handle or doorknob. Farther up, a barred window was set in the door's center a bit higher than her head. Sophie grabbed two bars and pulled herself up to look at what lay on the other side, but only darkness peered back at her. With a sigh, she lowered herself back to the floor and tried to rattle the bars, but they wouldn't give. She slapped the wood and kicked the door. Of course, it was locked.

"Ouch!" She should've used the good foot.

She slid down the door and sank into the straw. A

small flap no bigger than two hands wide opened in the door's bottom. It swung in and out but was way too small for her to squeeze through. She slapped the door again.

Outside the cell, something scurried past the door. A rat or something else? Sophie held her hand against the flap to prevent that something from coming in. Maybe the locked door was a good thing. She could always try to get away when someone came to check on her, if someone came.

Sophie crawled away from the door into the nearest corner. Four walls, a door, and a floor littered with dirty straw; mice and spiders as roommates; nothing else. Her whole world had shrunk to a cell smaller than her bedroom at home. *Home.* She curled into a tiny ball, hugging her knees to her chest. Complaining about her room to annoy Trudy had been her favorite past time. Now it sounded really stupid. What hell had she put Trudy through every day? And what for? For caring for her and Tommy? For giving her a really nice bedroom? For cooking her favorite food of roasted chicken, peas and mashed potatoes? For providing medical care for Tommy? Sophie frowned and furrowed her brow. Well, that was another thing, wasn't it? Trudy's care hadn't saved Tommy.

Something rustled outside the door again. She had to keep the flap shut. She crawled toward the door when something black and white and furry pushed through the flap. Sophie kicked out with her good leg.

"Stop kicking, Sophie, or I'll bite you."

"Pelifeles!" Sophie squeaked and sat.

"Ssh, quiet."

Sophie knelt. Her fingers touched soft fur and she

scooped Pelifeles into her arms. While she snuggled him close, he purred and his white fur glowed, making her feel calm and safe.

"Feeling better?"

"Much." She released the cat back into the straw. "How did you find me?"

"Cat's privilege." Then he said, "It's rather complicated."

Sophie rolled her eyes. "Where's Flynden? Is he okay?"

"I'm here, Sophie," Flynden's voice sounded through the flap. "We've come to get you out."

"Great." Sophie bent forward. "But how did you get away from those men?"

"The councilors had only eyes for you. I stood back and mingled with the crowd, then followed them."

"All the way here?"

"No, Peli found a way and I followed him."

"You're awesome." Sophie stroked the cat. Pelifeles had settled beside her and purred like a little motor. "What do we do now?"

"You do nothing," Pelifeles said. "Stand back. Flynden and I will take care of it." He slipped back through the flap and vanished.

"Where are you going?"

"Stand back, Sophie. Peli will release the lock."

A door slammed in the distance. For a second there was silence, then steps approached.

"Flynden?" Sophie whispered. Nothing. "Pelifeles?" Silence.

Sophie scooted to the far wall. Now that Flynden and Peli were here to get her out, she didn't want anyone to show up. She tensed. What should she do?

Through the barred square in the door, a greenish light jerked and flickered closer and glistened on the moist stone ceiling outside the small window. The steps stopped outside the door. A trace of sour apple made her stomach turn. Sophie hugged her knees closer and pinched her nose, breathing through her mouth.

A head appeared in the square, and for a moment, two eyes looked through the bars. Yellow-green light flared in the keyhole and released the lock.

The sour apple smell exploded into the cell. Sophie bit her teeth together and set her mouth into the grimmest, meanest line she could come up with, but when the door creaked open, fear paralyzed her anyway.

Makimus' garments rustled as he stooped into the cell.

"Ah, there you are," he said with a jovial smile like he'd come over for coffee. He held his hand with the yellow-green light high and took in the cell with her in the corner. "I apologize for the accommodations. Show your cooperation, and you can move to a more agreeable place."

Sophie gripped her legs hard so that he wouldn't see her shaking. His toothy smile reminded her of some neighbors Tommy and she'd stayed with for a short while after Mom and Dad died. They always used those kinds of smiles when they wanted her to do something she didn't want to do. Time and again, she knew they really weren't nice when they smiled like that. For Tommy's sake, she'd found courage, but now with Tommy gone, she would have to find some for herself.

She ground her teeth and pulled her mouth's corners down.

"Why the grim face?" The toothy smile grew wider. "I came to talk," he said.

Sophie pressed her back into the wall. The sour apple smell hung between them, a not-so-subtle reminder that talking wouldn't be all he would do if he chose to. Her chances were tiny if he used those yellow-green magic ropes again. With Makimus in it, the cell seemed to shrink even more. She had nowhere to run.

Never taking his eyes off her, Makimus took a step to the left, turned, then took one to the right. There wasn't much room for strolling back and forth. His long silvery robe with the fancy stitching rustled the straw.

"Now." He stopped, the robe's hem touching her sneakers. He brought his hands forward and clasped them in front. His cold eyes fixed on her. "Let us pretend we are here for a friendly visit, a chat to get to know each other."

Yeah, right. Friendly visit my butt.

Makimus waited a few seconds, his smile faltered.

"Come, child, why are you in Gwern-cadarn-brac?"

Sophie glowered at him. "We, I, I'm sightseeing while my parents are doing business."

"Gwern is certainly a place of beautiful sights. What is your name?"

"Um, S, Sam." She didn't want to give her real name, and maybe it would help if she pretended to be a boy. Maybe. Now, her short hair came in handy.

"And?"

"And nothing." Sophie brought up her chin.

The smile faltered again but returned right away as if he had to remind himself to stay friendly.

"And where did you say your family is from?"

"The North." It just popped into her head.

"Where exactly in the North?"

Oh no! What was she going to say?

"We live on a farm."

"Near Mountain View?"

"Yes."

His smile sparkled. "I see. The North. That explains the hair and the skin. Some people even think you are a pale one."

"A pale one?"

"I trust you know the pale ones' legend?"

Sophie held her breath, but stopped herself just in time from shaking her head, no. This was getting trickier every minute.

Makimus fingered his beard while he eyed her pink t-shirt and sneakers, and her black jeans.

"What crop does your family grow?"

"Potatoes." Why had she picked potatoes? Surely, they must have those here. "We have cows, sheep, and chickens, too."

"Interesting."

She knew she was in trouble as soon as he had said it.

"Very interesting indeed." His white teeth caught the greenish light and gave him a sick look. "Unfortunately, child, Mountain View lies in Nugateris' most arid area, high in the mountains, and no farmer would ever consider farming there, potatoes or other crops."

Sophie swallowed.

"Shall we begin again?" He leaned forward, his smile gone, his furry white brows knitted together. "Where have you come from? You do appear to be a pale one. I can almost believe it myself. Have you come through the portal or the Mists?"

What did he mean? Silence was the only weapon she had. She clenched her teeth to stop them from rattling.

"Where did you find this tool?" He pulled Dad's

Swiss Army knife from the folds of his robe. "This is not made in Mountain View." He held the knife under her nose with the hand that didn't have the yellow-green light.

Sophie tried to snatch it. "Give it back," she yelled. "That's mine." But as soon as her fingers touched his hand, greens sparks burned and zapped her. She flinched and shrank back. Pain shot up her arm into her shoulder.

"Now, now, Sam," Makimus said while he closed his fist and slipped the knife back into the folds. "Not to worry, I will keep this tool until we find out more about you." Honey-sweet, his smile spread across his face. His eyes brightened to a lighter gray like dirty ice before he leaned back and turned his other hand palm up, too. Yellow-green sparks danced between the fingers of both hands.

Sophie shook. I won't, I won't, no I won't tell him anything, not even about the old man in the cemetery. She closed her eyes, waiting for the ropes to hit, bind and strangle her, but nothing happened, only garment and straw rustled. She squinted.

The smile returned.

"Well, we will try another time. Shall we?" He stepped to the door and regarded her a moment longer, the smile gone. "Perhaps if you stay a while, you will change your mind. Isolation and hunger can break the most stubborn people."

He flicked a few yellow-green sparks off his hand like water drops. The sparks burned and stung like needles where they hit her face and hands. Sophie flung her arms up.

"Until I see you again." His humorless laugh echoed

off the stone walls. The door banged shut and the lock clicked into place once more. Sophie listened to his steps and laugh receding down the passage. She exhaled and slid onto the straw. A few minutes later, a door banged shut in the distance, then silence.

❧ ❧

It seemed an awful long time she'd been huddling on the floor before Pelifeles' whiskers tickled her cheek. Outside the cell, a pair of feet shuffled.

"Phew, that was close," Flynden whispered through the bars in the door. "We heard everything." The boy growled like a mountain lion. "That horrible man. The people of Nugateris look up to him. Everyone trusts him. If only they knew."

"No point in growling about it. We have to get Sophie out," Pelifeles said and rubbed his head against her, purring. "Flynden and I will open the door."

She tried to grab him, hold on to him for comfort, but he jumped through the flap into the dark.

"Stand back now, Sophie," Flynden said.

Sophie righted herself against the wall, still shaking, and waited. Of course, they would get her out this time. Pelifeles had gotten her out of the magical net, so a dungeon door couldn't be a problem. But as Pelifeles' white glow lit the keyhole, the door in the distance banged open and shut a second time.

"Please hurry," Sophie whispered and balled her fists. "Please get me out of here before Makimus comes back to get me."

"Be brave, Sophie." Pelifeles slunk into the cell. "It might not be Makimus."

Sophie grabbed the cat to stop him. His white glowing fur zapped her hands. She dropped him.

"No grabbing," he hissed and disappeared.

"Come back, Peli, I'm sorry. Flyn?"

Perhaps Pelifeles was right. The steps shuffling along the passage didn't sound like Makimus. She backed up into the far corner and sucked in her breath, waiting.

Soon, a soft white light flickered along the wall and stopped outside the door. Two dark, dull eyes gazed at her through the barred window. Then they disappeared and the small flap swung in. A hand pushed a bowl and a dented cup through and let them clatter onto the floor. The flap swung in and out, squeaking. Without a word, her visitor shuffled away. Not long after, the door slammed again in the distance and the dungeon fell silent.

Sophie puffed out her breath while her teeth rattled like she had a chill. Pelifeles hopped through the flap.

"You're supposed to eat this?" the cat hissed and shook. "I wouldn't. Perhaps the stupid mice will. Maybe."

A bread's end piece covered with mold lay in the bowl. Makimus had known she couldn't eat that and would starve to death. That's what he'd meant when he said, isolation and hunger can break the most stubborn people.

"Let's get out of here, quick, before someone else comes." Sophie wrung her hands. Her pleading sounded scared and stupid all at once.

"Peli, come out of there. We need to open the door." Flynden sounded impatient.

"Fine. Wait here," the cat said.

The flap squeaked, and he mumbled, "Always rushing."

"Peli," Flynden grumbled. "We have to hurry. Honest."

In seconds, the cat's white magic flared once more, the lock clicked, and the door sprang open.

"You can come out now, Sophie," Flynden said.

"I can't. My ankle is hurting. I can't stand on it."

They rushed to her side. Flynden pulled down the sock of her injured ankle.

"That looks bad," he said. "Pelifeles will heal it."

The cat sniffed the swollen green and blue ankle first, then wrapped his tail around it a time and a half before he made his fur glow again. The white light surrounded the ankle, and after two short zap-zaps, it faded away.

Sophie marveled at the now-normal-size ankle with no bruises. She scrambled up and tried it. "Wow. You fixed it. Thanks, Peli."

Pelifeles gave her a weird grin, and his whiskers twitched.

They hurried outside and Sophie started down the passage.

"What are you waiting for?"

"Not so fast. We need to lock the door again, so nobody will notice right away that you're gone."

"Great idea. Can you do it?"

Pelifeles ignored her stupid question. "Close the door and stand aside."

She shut the door. In the few moments it took her to back away, the cat pressed his paws against the door and relocked it with his magical light.

"Now, we can go." Pelifeles jumped into the dark passage. "What are you waiting for?" He mimicked Sophie.

Sophie giggled. "Where are we going?"

Flynden grinned and grabbed her arm. "We'll go see my brother Stace. He'll help us figure out what to do next."

∾ *Chapter 7* ⤚

Thistle held his aching head with both hands as he sat and squinted into the gloom. A dark red flower swayed as if standing in a breeze. The stem grew from the middle of a dark puddle and radiated a warm faint glow like dying ambers into the gloomy darkness. His fingers scratched the hard-packed dirt beside him and grabbed something stick-like. He picked it up but dropped it right away. Bones, hundreds of bones.

He remembered snippets of how he got here. The yellow-green ropes had almost strangled him, and everything had gone hazy and fuzzy. Makimus had carried him a long way, down and farther down. Thistle remembered the councilor's low menacing voice vibrating in his chest. He had tried to grapple with the councilor's angry words and the yellow-green magic on his skin. He would be teaching Thistle a lesson for flaunting his light hair and pale complexion, he had growled, but Thistle had been too weak to struggle or to understand.

Soon after, Makimus had lain him onto wooden planks. The planks lifted for a few moments before they descended, like a bucket lowered into a deep well. Dread more than fear rose up to meet him like water. When his mind cleared and he could think again, he still had no inkling of what Makimus meant.

Thistle raised himself onto his knees. Still dizzy, he fell back and eyed the glowing dark flower and the thin and thick bones, like those he had seen on his home farm when an animal had died or had been slaughtered for food.

Thistle scrambled to his feet, stumbled, and hit his head on a rock behind him. Dazed, he stood for a moment, trying to grasp what his discovery meant.

He reached out, searching. Rough stone and rock walled him in. A cave? He placed one hand on the rock and walked along the wall in shadows that wanted to swallow him. Like small travelers, his fingers explored every crevice of the wall, a rugged mountain range turned sideways with peaks and valleys, and with trickles of water for rivers. Blackness pressed down from above. He walked without end until he understood that Makimus had thrown him into a deep round pit the size of Council Hall.

Bones crunched and broke under his bare feet, jarring the silence. Thistle tried avoiding them, but there were too many. He slipped on something soft and squishy by a roundish object and bent forward. In the flower's glow, a skull's empty sockets stared back at him. His fingers came away smeared dark red and sticky.

Thistle shrieked and jumped toward the center where the dark flower swayed. He trembled, gulping for air, searching the dark. But no wild beast came for him. There was only the flower, the bones, and him. He sucked in a few shaky breaths and thought of Bramble's cute little face and her messy blond curls; it gave him the strength to push forward on his hands and knees. He would find a way out. He must. Without him, Bramble would be lost. He didn't dwell on how lost he was himself that moment. He thought of Bramble's blue eyes and gathered the courage it gave him like a cloak around him.

Avoiding the scattered bones, he approached the flower. Shreds of a black and white hide, long crushed bones, and some remaining innards lay scattered around the stem. Beautiful but somewhat repulsive, the flower stood almost twice his height. Thick fleshy, blackish-green leaves, the size of a man's hands, grew from the stem as thick as a man's thigh. A strange white glowing border rimmed the dark red petals. The open blossom, a blood-red daisy, swayed and turned lazily as if catching sunlight, but no sunlight pierced the darkness. Why was it glowing? Careful not to step onto the hide or into the blood puddle, he touched the fleshy leaf that felt like an animal's warm skin. The flower gave a shudder. He snatched his hand back and scurried away. Where could he run and hide? He twisted on the spot. Where was the way out?

He tried to skirt the bones, but gave up and instead listened with perverse pleasure to the crunching sounds they made when he stepped on them. He peeked into the darkness near the wall, searching for a door or tunnel. After doing two rounds in the pit, he had found nothing. No door. No tunnel. No way out.

Thistle looked up. He would climb out. The rocks stuck out enough to grab and stand on. If he tried hard enough, he might make it.

Thistle kicked some bones aside to make room at the foot of the wall. His fingers and eyes searched crevices and outcroppings for the best route. Taking a deep breath, he began to climb.

Thistle climbed until large rocks formed a ledge above his head and stuck too far out to climb around. Small cold droplets teased his face while his hands searched for hold. The stones turned slippery and he lost his grip. His toes slipped. He didn't even have time to cry out. His breath caught in his throat as he fell the distance he had climbed, landing with a crunch on top of the bones.

For a few moments, he lay still, dazed, and tired before he struggled to his feet and moved a few steps to the right. Again, he made it up to the ledge, but no farther, and hung in the air, his feet dangling in space, before his hands slipped off the rock. He fell and crashed into the bones again.

Over and over, he tried. Each time he fell, a crunch followed and assured him that soon his own bones would be breaking. While he caught his breath, he lay still, staring into the darkness above him. What if he never made it out? He shivered and curled up into a tiny ball. He cried his pain and fear into his curved arm. He hated to be weak and helpless. He hated crying, even if nobody saw him doing it. Bramble's picture filled his mind, bringing a little light into the darkness.

For a long time, he lay like this, not quite awake, but not quite sleeping either, when he noticed the flower moved more than the earlier gentle swaying. First, the blossom's glow flared like a torch, then it dimmed a bit. The whole flower trembled while the stem and leaves lengthened. Only the Flora did this, but they weren't dark red. Thistle scrambled to his feet, backing against the wall.

Fur erupted on the leaves and stem. The blossom grew solid and filled out and two sets of ears appeared. The petals' white border morphed into a white stripe starting between those ears and running all the way down its long muscular back to the tip of a lengthening tail. It ended in a bushy knot flicking and twitching like a whip.

Thistle panted. A beast. The bones. The blood. It would eat him, too. Scrambling, he clawed the pit's wall and the air above him for a way out. Breathless, he circled the pit, searching, peeking into every crevice. He sobbed, choking and coughing. He fell to his knees but jumped up again the next instant, his eyes on the beast that was still growing and forming.

Thistle stretched his arms over his head as if he could summon help. *Please, please, by the light, someone, anyone come and help me.*

The beast grew longer, bigger, and hairier. Four thick leaves lengthened into strong legs. Long claws formed at the end of large furry paws.

Now fully formed into a feline beast, it stretched its muzzle into a wide yawn, showing sharp teeth extending over its lower jaw. Eyes like glowing coal blinked. It hadn't seen Thistle yet. He gave the wall another try and climbed, hoping he would make it past the ledge this time. He cast a quick glance over his shoulder.

The creature crouched steps away. It roared when it saw him and watched him out of slits with red wild eyes. Its long tail twitched and swished, and its deep growl hummed all the way through Thistle's rib cage. When he came to the ledge, he dared not move his hands or breathe although the height made him feel a bit safer.

The creature hissed below. Thistle craned his neck and looked down.

"You will not make it out that way." The muzzle formed the words. "I have tried it time and again without success."

Thistle flinched, lost his grip and fell, screaming.

๑ *Chapter 8* ๑

From the dungeon cell, Sophie and Flynden stole through the dark passage. Pelifeles' fur glowed and lit the way, its light glistening on the moist stone walls. Each time Sophie bumped into the wet and slimy stone, she shuddered and hurried on. Soon, they reached another locked door, maybe the one that let in her unwelcome visitors.

"Here." Flynden pulled his motley cap from his shoulder bag. "Put the cap back on. You won't fool Councilor Makimus now, but it'll hide your hair and might deceive everyone else."

Sophie tugged the cap low over her ears and forehead.

"Ready." She grinned.

"Let's go then," Flynden whispered.

Pelifeles opened the lock with his magical light. They cracked the door and listened. Small white globes lit the passage. Pelifeles dimmed his fur until it stopped glowing.

"Come." Flynden waved to Sophie.

They slipped through the door, locked it again like the cell door, and tiptoed after Pelifeles who jumped along the passage, leading them away. He slunk around every corner with a purpose, never hesitating. Stark gray stone walls hemmed them in. A few lighted globes here and there gave them a hazy soft light to walk by. Luckily for them, they met no one because there was nowhere to hide.

The passage ended at a stairwell. They sneaked up the few stairs and peeked around the corner into a brightly lit windowless hallway. Flynden held a finger to his mouth. Sophie nodded. They slipped along the walls and followed Pelifeles.

Soon, the hallways' looks changed. Tapestries hung along the walls, and simple rugs covered flagstones. The tapestries showed battle scenes. Armies of fair people with light hair fought those with dark skin and black hair, like the people she had seen in the streets. Above the battles, monsters in the clouds bared their fangs. Sophie shivered. What did this mean? Had this happened in Nugateris at one time and people recorded it on these tapestries?

There were doors along this hallway set back in alcoves, offering hiding places should they run into anyone. Pelifeles slunk ahead, his tail disappearing around the next corner. Sophie concentrated so much on the tapestries that she startled when Pelifeles suddenly turned around and came back.

"Someone's coming," he hissed.

Flynden pulled Sophie into an alcove they had just passed. They pressed into the shadows and listened to the approaching footsteps. Only one person. Sophie held her breath and crossed her fingers.

Pelifeles raised his hackles, and his tail went bushy like a bottlebrush. But then he sat, smoothened his fur, and curled his tail around his paws. So, it couldn't be Makimus or Pelifeles wouldn't be so calm. Beside her, Flynden scrunched up his face and tensed. The footsteps came closer, and a very tall skinny old man with long hair and beard, dressed like a councilor, appeared and walked past the alcove, then stopped. "Hm." He backed up and peeked into the dark where they stood.

Flynden let out his breath with a big whoosh and stepped forward.

"Young Flynden," a deep voice said, startled. "It is you. What are you doing here?"

"Oh, hello, Councilor Druce Lar. I got lost looking for our cat. It's gotten away again. I need it at home to catch mice."

Wow, Flynden lied to the councilor, and he was good at it too, better than she was. Somehow, it made her sad.

"In the middle of the night?" Councilor Druce Lar asked, looking down his nose at Flynden. "Could it not wait until morning?"

"Um, the house is full of mice. They're keeping me awake."

"That many, eh?" The councilor shook his head. "Perhaps Apprentice Kir would be a better choice to take care of the mice. I will talk to him."

Flynden looked worried. Pelifeles slunk out from the shadows and around their legs, meowing.

"Well, there is your cat." Councilor Druce Lar bent down to scratch Pelifeles behind his ears but glanced past Flynden into the shadow where Sophie stood. "I see you brought a friend."

"Um, that's, yes, my friend helped me find the cat."

"You know the rules, young Flynden." The councilor sounded stern. "No visitors without prior permission, especially not this late."

"I wanted to ask Stace, but we couldn't find him anywhere."

"I see."

Councilor Druce Lar beckoned Sophie forward. His warm gray eyes widened when the light fell onto her pale freckled face. When he scanned her with raised eyebrows from motley cap to pink sneakers, she knew right away she wouldn't be fooling the man with Flynden's cap or any other disguise. She wanted to say something but her mouth had gone dry. Instead, she gave him a lopsided smile, which he didn't return, but his eyes still twinkled in a friendly way.

"Run along then, boys."

Flynden didn't wait to be told twice and pulled Sophie along, but they hadn't taken more than a few steps when the councilor said, "On second thought, I will escort you to Stace's chambers. Come. Your brother will find a discreet way out of Council Hall for both of you." He glared at them from under his bushy brows until they both nodded. With a groan, he then bent to pick up Pelifeles, cradled the cat in his arms, and led the way down the hall.

Sweat dripped down Sophie's face. She bent forward and wiped it with her t-shirt's hem. Were they in trouble now? Her heart beat fast. She looked toward Flynden, but Flynden shook his head and pressed a finger to his lips as they marched after the councilor.

After turning an occasional corner and crossing umpteen hallways, the councilor finally approached a door in a shadowy alcove and knocked.

On the door's other side, all was quiet. The councilor knocked again, harder this time. A rustle came from inside. Something fell and hit the floor with a thud. Finally, a sleepy voice asked through the door, "Who is there?"

"Councilor Druce Lar."

A young man, all sleepy looking with tousled hair, yanked open the door and blinked at them.

"Councilor Druce Lar? Has something happened?"

"No, no, Stace, everything is fine. I am very sorry to wake you. These two young men have gotten lost and need to find a way home. Discreetly," he added after a moment.

Stace eyed Flynden with a frown and furrowed brows. When he looked at Sophie, his eyes widened just like the councilor's had. Why was it such a bad thing to have red hair and a pale face?

"I trust I can leave them with you?"

"Of course, Councilor. I will make sure they go home."

"Very well. Perhaps keep them in your room until morning." He turned to go. "By the way, Stace. You have not seen the boy, Thistle, who was brought to Council Hall this evening?"

Stace shook his head. "No, I thought you had taken him from the bath chamber. When I returned, he was no longer there."

The councilor stared, shocked, his face white, but he took a deep breath and composed himself. "No. He is not with me." He handed Pelifeles to Flynden and waved them all into Stace's room. "I must hurry. You take care of these two. May the light brighten your path."

"And yours, Councilor," Stace called after the councilor but the old man already strode down the hall, his long robe flapping around his legs with every step.

They watched him disappear around the corner.

Pelifeles jumped from Flynden's arm and padded past them into the room, tail and nose in the air.

"We've got things to discuss."

"Right," Stace said and combed his fingers through his tousled hair. "Come in, then." He flipped his hand impatiently, beckoning them into the room, glanced once up and down the hallway, and closed the door.

Flynden turned to his brother. "Stace, this is Sophie. Can you get her out of Council Hall without anybody seeing her?" Then he pointed at Stace, "This is my brother Stace," he said to Sophie and plopped down on the rumpled bed.

Stace sighed and shook his head, hands on his hips. Right then, he had something very Trudyish about him. "What are you doing at Council Hall in the middle of the night, Flynden?" He furrowed his brows again.

"We rescued Sophie. Pelifeles and I did."

"From whom or what, for light's sake?"

Pelifeles wove between Stace's legs and purred. "Councilor Makimus caught her in his magic net in the forest and threw her in the dungeon. He means to hurt her. We saw."

"I do not believe it."

"You'd better," Pelifeles said.

"Councilor Druce Lar knows about this?" Stace's eyes widened.

"No," Flynden said, "but I'm sure he smelled trouble when he saw Sophie. We could see it on his face."

Sophie nodded.

Stace narrowed his eyes. "Do not lie to me. What have you done to be in trouble with Councilor Makimus?" he asked Sophie.

"It's true. I came through the portal instead of the old man Eigil and got caught in the trap."

"You have seen Master Eigil?" Stace asked, and for a

second, he looked like Flynden, but the sameness stopped there. Flynden's brown and curly hair tumbled around his freckled pale face almost as light as hers, while Stace's sleek black hair, cut like King Arthur in Dad's old comic books, framed his brown skin.

Sophie nodded. "Yep, and he sent me here to get something to help him come home."

"You didn't tell me that." Flynden hopped off the bed. "What do you have to get?"

"Don't know," Sophie said. "Some artifact he talked about."

"What?" Stace and Flynden asked together, disbelief on their faces.

"What's the matter?" Sophie ping-ponged her gaze between the brothers.

Pelifeles jumped onto the table. There, he licked his white paws a few times, then the black tail before he said, "I think I know why Master Eigil sent Sophie."

"Oh?" Stace crossed his arms, cocked his head, and grimaced. Sophie, Flynden and Stace huddled around the table as Pelifeles whispered, "She has to take the Flora blossom to Master Eigil."

Stace's mouth turned into a downward crescent. "That is not possible." He shook his head.

"Why not?" Sophie asked.

"Yes, why not?" Flynden asked, too.

"I mean, why ask a girl to do such a dangerous thing?"

"True," Pelifeles said. "But Master Eigil might've been desperate and asked Sophie to help him, and Councilor Makimus must have figured it out and locked her up."

Stace threw the cat a doubtful look. Pelifeles licked his paws again, first one then the other, as if not at all concerned.

"Well?" Flynden poked the cat with his index finger in the side. "How do you know all that?"

Pelifeles hissed. His paw was poised to lash out, but instead of scratching Flynden, he first rubbed his face against the boy's hand and then pulled back.

"Told you. No touching."

"What, no biting or scratching? What's wrong?" Flynden examined his hand in front of his face, his mouth open.

The cat ignored the questions, settled on the table and tucked his paws in. He blinked a few times.

"I know this because I heard Kir tell Calleo that Master Eigil took the Celarim to keep it safe somewhere, but Councilor Makimus interfered and tried to stop him."

"What's a Celarim?" Sophie asked.

"It's a magical book," Flynden said. "A long time ago, the Mother Flora gave the council a magical blossom. It's set into the cover of the Celarim."

"You think Master Eigil took it?"

"Yes," Pelifeles said. "I believe so. In order to lead the Council and Nugateris, Councilor Makimus must have the book. He doesn't want Master Eigil to come back but he wants the Celarim." He blinked. "I don't know exactly where Sophie comes in."

"Did Master Eigil mention any of this to you?" Stace asked Sophie.

She fiddled with her t-shirt's hem and stared at her feet. "Not exactly. I didn't hear, um, all of what he said," she said. It sounded true enough.

Stace threw up his hands. "You did not listen to Master Eigil when he talked to you?"

"Well, no. He was all weird like and injured."

The brothers gasped.

"Injured? How?"

Sophie shuffled her feet and swallowed. "It looked like he lost his left hand."

"By the light!" Flynden shouted.

"Not so loud," Pelifeles hissed. "Don't you see?"

"See what?" The line between Stace's eyes deepened.

"The councilors must have fought and Master Eigil lost his hand that way, maybe holding the blossom. And now, he needs it somehow to get back. That's why he sent Sophie."

"Hm, and where do you think the Flora blossom is now?"

"Where do the councilors normally keep the Celarim?" Pelifeles asked.

"In the small library off the Council Chamber. I have not been in the room for some time." Stace shook his head. "If I understand correctly what you are hinting at, then the answer is no, definitely not."

"Let him finish, Stace." Flynden leaned forward.

"Oh, I know." Stace folded his arms across his chest again. "You want me to take the blossom. If I do and I am caught, I will be lashed and cast from Council Hall."

"No, no, of course not. Nothing like that." Pelifeles sat up. "But, em, you could take a look to see if the Flora blossom is there next time you to clean the room. That's all."

"I will not be part of this."

"But Stace, you'd be helping Master Eigil," Flynden said.

"You do not know that."

"Yes, you would be helping Master Eigil," Pelifeles said. "I'm sure."

Stace rolled his eyes.

"We have to help Sophie too, Stace. Please." Flynden

stepped toward his brother, but Stace twisted around.

"I want my jacket back." Sophie said. "Makimus took it."

"That is Councilor Makimus, please."

"He's a creep."

Stace's mouth twitched.

"Can we get into Councilor Makimus' chamber?" Flynden seemed eager for action.

"You would be a fool for trying, little brother." Stace shook his head.

"With Peli's help, I can do it."

"You can get us all in trouble with Pelifeles' help." Stace grabbed Flynden by the arms. "Listen, Flyn. I do want to help Master Eigil, but we have to be very, very careful about it. You understand?"

Flynden nodded, sitting down.

"I believe there is more to this," Stace said. "Something strange and dangerous is happening."

"Like what?"

Stace shook his head. "I cannot tell you."

"Why not? Let's find out." Flynden held up his hands when his brother renewed his frown. "Fine, Peli will find out. Nobody suspects him."

"Kir might not like it," Stace said.

"Why does *he* have to like it?" Sophie asked.

"Our brother Kir is a Council apprentice, and because Pelifeles is his spirit mate and must listen to him."

"Is that why Pelifeles can talk and do magic?" Sophie asked.

Stace nodded and turned to Flynden. "Kir cannot go against the Council. The vows he has given will not permit it."

"I didn't mean, help help." Flynden groaned and threw up his hands. "I meant looking the other way or something."

"I'll talk to Kir," Pelifeles said. "I think there might be ways around that vow."

"At least we can go and have a look." Flynden raised his brows and put on his most appealing grin. "Looking won't hurt anything. We would know then if we're right about Master Eigil and the Flora blossom."

Stace's unfocused gaze hovered somewhere in the room's middle above Flynden's right shoulder, and it looked like he thought it over.

"Well?" Flynden asked.

Finally, Stace nodded and focused on Flynden, his face serious. "One thing I know for certain, Master Eigil must return soon." He scratched his chin. "But Sophie cannot stay here. We must hide her somewhere. My room will be fine until morning, but then before the dawn bell tolls, you will both need to leave Council Hall."

"No we won't. Isn't it obvious Master Eigil wants me to help?" Sophie asked. "So, shouldn't I be doing something?" She tried to read the brothers' faces. "Shouldn't we find the Flora blossom and *then* get out of here?"

"You do not know what you are suggesting. Nobody should be seeing you walking around Council Hall." Stace shook his head. "As you have found out only recently, it is almost impossible to avoid being seen."

"I'll wear the cap." Sophie waved it in front of them. "And maybe some other clothes?"

"Excellent thought," Flynden said but Stace didn't look excited at the idea. "Well?"

Stace looked over Sophie's pink t-shirt and pink sneakers and nodded.

"Fine." He went to a cupboard and pulled two garments and a pair of cloth shoes from it. "Perhaps

get

these are a bit large for you, but try them anyway." He pointed to the curtain at the room's back.

Sophie took the clothes, hurried behind the curtain and entered a kind of bathroom tucked away in a small alcove. Back in one corner, a smooth stone pipe with a wide rim stuck up straight from the floor, and it took no time at all to figure out it served as a toilet. A stone sink was attached to the far wall beneath a few shelves. It had a small brass water pump. Sophie washed her hands and face, and felt a little better. She pulled off her sneakers and jeans and tried the soft gray leggings while she listened.

"So, what do we do?" Flynden asked.

"I will take you to the kitchen and say you are helping me with my chores." Stace said. "Everyone will like that, thinking I finally persuaded you to work."

"I'm not sure it's a good idea." Flynden squinted and folded his arms. "They might come to expect it all the time."

"So?"

Flynden sighed. "And Sophie?"

"Fortunately, Councilor Makimus gave me the task he did not want to bother with himself. He asked me to choose five new servants, sons from among prominent families. Now there will be six. Everyone is still unfamiliar with the boys. But…"

"But what?"

"He chose four men as personal servants—men, not boys—who would be serving him."

"You sure? I thought the councilors don't have personal servants."

"Exactly."

The leggings bunched up around her ankles but fit

okay in the waist and hips. She pulled the dark green tunic over her head and stuck her arms into the silver-embroidered sleeves. It fit fine in the shoulders and the length was okay, but the sleeves fell far over her hands. The cloth shoes fit like they were made for her. She rolled her t-shirt and jeans around her sneakers, stuffed the bundle behind the stone pipe, and stepped from the alcove.

"Well, how do I look?" she asked.

"Like a Council Hall servant," said Stace. "Unfortunately, the garments are far too big. Let me fold them in and tuck them into place. It will have to do for now."

He pulled a small wooden box from a drawer and went to work, folding the leggings in once and stitching them in four places. He had to fold the sleeves under twice before he could stitch them. The sewing job wouldn't pass Trudy's scrutiny, but it was okay.

"There." Stace grinned. "Now you are almost ready." He looked at her hair and face.

"Almost?"

"You cannot wear the cap, pretending you are a servant. We have to do something with your hair."

"Like what?" Sophie asked. "It's already short."

"I can disguise it." Pelifeles slunk around her ankles. "If you bend down and let me touch your hair, I can turn it brown and make it look like Stace's haircut."

Sophie squinted at the cat. "You sure?"

"Trust me."

"I don't know." Sophie ran her fingers through her hair. She'd appreciated having her ankle fixed and being saved from Makimus, but having magic done to her again didn't feel right. The yellow-green magic's sting still stuck in her mind.

"He can do it." Flynden nodded. "He saved you from the trap. Remember? Changing hair takes nothing at all."

"I think we could take polish and darken her hair," Stace said. "That ought to be enough." He rummaged behind the curtain for a minute and came up with a tin container filled with brown polish and a large wooden comb.

"Yuk." Sophie shook her head. "I like Pelifeles' idea better."

Pelifeles asked her to bend her head close to him and then touched his nose to her hair. She flinched as a bright light flashed once or twice. Fear bubbled up when she thought about the yellow-green ropes that had bound and stung her before. She wanted to cry out, but Pelifeles' magic didn't hurt and took only a few seconds.

"How do I look?" Sophie asked.

Flynden stood in front of her and grinned. "Perfect. You look like one of us now. Pelifeles even made your eyes brown."

"What?" Sophie blinked a few times. "Do you have a mirror, Stace?"

Stace pulled a small hand-held mirror from a drawer and handed it to her. Straight brown hair cut like Stace's framed her tanned skin, and brown eyes stared back at her. Even her freckles were gone. "Can you make me look like myself again when it's time to go home?"

"Certainly," Pelifeles purred. "Any magic touch will turn you back the way you were. So, don't let Councilor Makimus catch you."

She gave him a sideways glance and a frown and looked in the mirror again.

The room's window turned gray with the first morning light.

"Come, let us leave." Stace cracked the door a hand's width, peeked through the crack, then nodded and beckoned them outside. They slipped after him into the corridor. Stace closed the door, and with quick steps, they hurried down the hallway.

❧ ❦

The hallways stretched before them. Soft dark blue rugs with silver stars and swirls woven into the pile muffled their steps, and they moved ahead like ghosts. Why did she have to disguise herself anyway? They met no one.

Pelifeles slunk ahead, left around a corner, then right again, but slowed each time they crossed another hallway. Soon, Sophie lost all sense of direction. She would never find her way out of this place if she had to do this by herself. Flynden walked a step behind her and Stace. When she asked why, Stace told her a Council Hall servant, man or boy, had a privileged status and other children were subordinate at Council Hall and had to walk last.

Sophie peeked over her shoulder, grinned, and met Flynden's dark look. He didn't seem to like being subordinate. She walked beside Stace, her chin a bit higher. Then she blushed. Well, she wasn't a Council Hall servant either and should have been walking with Flynden. He and Pelifeles had saved her, twice, and laughing about his social status was a lousy way of paying him for his friendship.

Polished wood floors replaced the flagstones, and old faded tapestries hung between new colorful ones along the walls. When Sophie reached out, the fabric's smooth and shiny stitches rippled beneath her fingers.

Flynden poked her in the back and shook his head. Sophie withdrew her hand. Like the earlier ones, these tapestries told similar stories, but here, the newer ones featured roses, daffodils, irises, blue bells, and other flowers surrounding a daisy as large as a sunflower. Other tapestries showed a slender woman with long, golden blond hair draped in a white flowing dress. White flower petals framed her face. She stood beneath a giant tree, face lifted, one hand on the trunk as though talking to it. Off to the side, tall bearded men stood, wearing long robes and looked like Councilors Makimus and Druce Lar, and Master Eigil. The older faded pictures showed more battle scenes between monsters and armies of men and women. These men and women had blond and red hair and pale faces like her.

What did it all mean? She opened her mouth to ask Stace, but right then, a rhythmic clonk-clonk on the wood accompanied voices in the hallway ahead. Stace held a finger to his mouth. She closed hers and walked beside him. Her heart fluttered and sank from her throat down into her belly. Would her disguise work? What should she say if someone asked questions like Makimus had asked? Why hadn't she listened to Master Eigil? Maybe he could've told her a lot about this place.

Two old men rounded a corner dressed in long tunics with beards and hair to their waists. That's all she needed, more of those councilors. The frail-looking councilor used a cane making all the clonking noise; the other councilor had one good eye and one weird, ugly black glass one. Sophie cringed but couldn't stop staring until Stace poked her arm to make her look away.

Stace halted, held out his arm for Sophie to do the

same, and backed them against the wall. Flynden did the same, and the three stood like soldiers as the councilors drew level with them.

"I say he is going too far this time," croaked the man with the cane.

"Not now." The man's good eye swiveled to the spot where they stood. "Stace." He gave a curt nod. His eye flicked to Flynden and Sophie.

"Councilor Darach. Councilor Lombard." Stace inclined his head.

"Are those the new boys?" Lombard croaked and stepped closer to eye Sophie and Flynden. "They need washing."

Before the old man could linger and ask more questions, Darach quickened his step and pulled Lombard with him, making his companion hobble alongside. They disappeared around another corner, and only the cane's clonk-clonk echoed for a while longer.

Stace exhaled with a shaky sigh. His pale lips in a chalky white face threw Sophie and Flynden a lopsided grin like saying it wasn't so bad. He swung around and walked ahead.

Sophie fell in line with wobbly legs. Surely everyone up and down the hall could hear her heart pounding. If she got out of this in one piece, she would never ever think of running away again.

Pelifeles appeared from an alcove, his tail twitched in a nervous kind of way.

Sophie glanced sideways at Stace but he faced ahead without acknowledging her. When she peeked at Flynden, he looked pale beneath his freckles; fear and worry scrunched up his face. Soon, the smell of freshly-baked bread made Sophie's stomach rumble. Stace beckoned her and Flynden closer. Pelifeles sat at their feet.

"I will talk for us. If you are asked something, Sophie, let me answer for you," Stace whispered.

Sophie leaned in.

"Remember, you are a new servant, and it is fine not to know answers or the things expected of you."

She nodded.

Stace paused, tucked down his sleeves, squared his shoulders, and raised his chin. "Flynden, for once, stay out of trouble."

Flynden rolled his eyes and grimaced.

Stace gave him a stern look. Sophie's mouth twitched into a grin, but then she received the same stern look herself and pressed her lips together.

She and Flynden made serious faces. If this worked, they would be the luckiest people in the world.

"Let us proceed." Stace waited for Sophie and Flynden to get back in line and marched down the hall.

Soon, the mix of laughing, talking, and murmuring separated into men's basses and boys' high, sometimes squeaky voices. The next turn brought them to the dining hall's open door. Long benches flanked rows of equally long wooden tables pointing toward a large fireplace the length of the entire back wall. Seven different-size cauldrons hung over individual fires and gave off yummy vegetable and meat stew smells. A boy about Sophie's age stirred one cauldron, his face shiny with sweat. Repeatedly, he wiped his face on his sleeve. Each time he rested the large spoon, a tall round man with an enormous belly threw him an amused look, which made the boy stir faster. The big man's long chestnut and gray hair hung down his back. He had tied his long beard with a ribbon, keeping it out of a cauldron while cutting carrots into it.

"Wait here," Stace said out of the corner of his mouth. "I will find the new boys and we will leave immediately."

Stace marched straight toward the big man. Pelifeles jumped ahead and slunk around the man's ankles, purring.

"Pelifeles," the man chuckled. "You know where to find good food, my furry friend." He took a small bowl, picked out a few meat pieces from the stew and placed it on the floor. With a groan, he straightened.

"Ah, good morning, Stace," the big man said. "You must try my stew. The new greens I have been cultivating add an exquisite flavor." The man filled a wooden bowl to the rim and held it out to Stace.

"Thank you, Councilor Tulio." Stace took the bowl. "It looks and smells delicious, but I must find the new servant youngsters and show them their work."

"On an empty stomach? You could use a bit more meat on your bones, young man. What I've seen of the new boys, they are a bit on the thin side too." His mouth stretched into a wide smile amongst his beard's bushy hairs. "How are they going to do their work without breakfast?"

Sophie's stomach rumbled. Mmm, the stew did smell good. Flynden must have thought so too because he stepped away from the door and headed straight to the big man. "Ah, young Flynden." Councilor Tulio chuckled. "I have been wondering. Where have you been?"

"Exploring." Flynden thrust out his chest and stood taller.

"The ancient forest again, I suppose?"

"Of course."

Councilor Tulio wagged his finger at him. "Not

getting into trouble again, are you?"

"Me? Trouble?" Flynden shook his head.

They both laughed when he said that, and Councilor Tulio showed no disapproval. He seemed to enjoy Flynden's cheekiness. Sophie liked the man. He looked kind and jolly like Santa Clause.

Stace picked his way to the hall's rear to a small table where five boys sat huddled together, looking a bit lost. He asked them to get up and follow him.

Flynden and Tulio continued their banter a few more minutes. Flynden told stories of small cute animals he had seen in the forest while he shoveled stew into his mouth from a bowl Tulio had handed him. When he had emptied the bowl, he held it out and the councilor filled it again.

"That's my boy," the councilor said, but Flynden took the bowl and joined her again, handing it to her with a spoon.

Sophie shoveled meat, carrots, potatoes and some other greens she'd never seen, and wouldn't have eaten on any other day, into her mouth. Even if it had tasted like cardboard, her stomach growled and rumbled. She would've eaten anything right now.

Flynden went back for yet another bowl. Did he always eat so much? Maybe not or he wouldn't be so skinny. Maybe he didn't get enough to eat at home.

The dining hall hummed and buzzed with talking and the clattering of plates and utensils. No one paid attention to her in the shadows. Small boys and teenagers sat together with older men. All wore Council Hall servants' uniforms. Their black and dark-brown hair was cut like Stace's and hers. Some of the older men's hair showed the gray of old age, but none had blond or red hair. Sophie fondled her hair, grateful all over again to Pelifeles for disguising her.

Suddenly, benches scraped on stone. Every man and boy in the room stood and bowed his head. Makimus and three young but equally tall men entered the dining hall through another door at the hall's side. Flynden elbowed Sophie in the side and pushed her farther into the shadows. She rubbed her ribs and gave him a dirty look.

"Ouch," she whispered. "Why did you do that?"

"Get back."

"Yeah, I wasn't going to run out there and say hello." Miffed, she kept rubbing her ribs, but then she stopped being mad. He was just looking out for her.

Makimus raised one hand in greeting. Men and boys sat back down. Eating and talking resumed.

"Those three with Councilor Makimus are the Council's apprentices." Flynden stood straight like Stace, shoulders back, chin raised. "My brother Kir's the tallest one with the black hair. The one with the brown wavy hair is Calleo. The puny one is Vaughn."

Vaughn stood a lot shorter than the others. He was skinny and had a nervous and restless look about him. As he fidgeted with his robe's sleeves, tiny reddish-brown sparks jumped off his fingertips.

Makimus placed a hand on Vaughn's shoulder, extending the other one, inviting him to sit. Vaughn flinched but tried a smile. He scooted onto the bench and placed his hands flat onto the table, which stopped the sparks.

Nervous Nellie. Sophie wrinkled her nose.

The councilor took a seat beside Vaughn, Kir, and Calleo. They began talking to each other, their voices drowned out by the overall din. Calleo used sign language, his fingers flicked his words and he nodded once in a while.

Stace guided the five boys, already dressed in servants' uniforms, to the door.

"You have to try my stew, Makimus," Tulio hollered. "It tastes exquisitely."

"I am certain it does," Makimus said without smiling. "If you have added meat this time, I will try your stew."

"Of course, I have added meat. Listen to him." The big man jammed his fists into his non-existing waist. "What would a stew be without meat, I ask you?"

"Rabbit food, Tulio," Makimus said. "Let us have some then."

Tulio grinned and ladled generous portions into four bowls, handing them to a boy who carried them to the councilor and the apprentices.

Kir and Calleo sat with their backs to her, but Makimus and Vaughn faced her. Sophie stared. As if he sensed her, Makimus looked up and toward her. She stiffened. Could he see her? Would he recognize her? She pressed deeper into the shadows. Her breath came in short spurts. For a second, his eyes lingered before he lowered them to his stew.

She wanted to run, but her legs wouldn't move. Fear rooted her to the spot. She squeezed her eyes shut. When a hand grabbed her shoulder, she gasped and almost cried out, but Stace only wanted her to get in line with the other new boys.

❧ *Chapter 9* ❧

Sophie put one foot in front of the other, trying to keep pace with the boys, when instead she wanted to run. Keep calm. You can do it. The little food she'd eaten churned in her stomach as she and the boys walked in twos behind Stace. Three of the boys were maybe her age, around eleven or twelve, the other two maybe nine or ten. The boys whispered non-stop. Sophie kept quiet. Every other step, she looked over her shoulder past Flynden and Pelifeles and farther down the hallway. She relaxed a little bit when neither Makimus nor his yellow-green magic came after her to bind and strangle her again, but she kept peeking over her shoulder, stopping every time, so that the boy behind her bumped into her. Again, she was glad Pelifeles had changed her hair, and her eyes, too. They would've given her away now as the boy's black angry eyes looked into hers.

"Sorry," she said and faced forward.

Stace marched them down hallways with polished wood floors, his arms swinging in rhythm with his steps. Sky-blue rugs covered the wood and muffled their steps until they reached a two-winged floor-to-ceiling wooden door. The door's right wing was carved with a sun, the left with a moon sickle, and instead of stars, both sun and moon were nestled among daisies. Stace lined up the group in a half circle around him so that they faced him and the closed doors. He clasped his hands behind his back and looked at each boy.

"Now," he said as he bounced a little on the balls of his feet. "Behind these doors," he began and jabbed his chin sideways. He didn't turn but kept looking at them like a teacher. Sophie grinned, which earned her an extra stern look from Stace. It didn't help that Flynden stood right behind her, poking her. She whirled around. Flynden rolled his eyes and made a face. Sophie giggled.

"Pay attention," Stace snapped.

They both faced him and the doors, and tried to keep their faces straight.

"Well, now," Stace began again. "This is the entrance to the Council Chamber where the Council of Gwern-cadarn-brac meets," he said. "In the Council Chamber, important decisions are made and judgments are pronounced." Stace gazed into each boy's eyes. "Your first day at Council Hall will begin with cleaning it."

They all groaned and started talking at once. It seemed no one, including Sophie, had expected to be cleaning the first day. Maybe they had expected something more glamorous. Well, they were servants, weren't they? She would have a chance to snoop around during the cleaning without anyone suspecting her of wrongdoing. Flynden and Pelifeles would help.

"Silence!" Stace clapped his hands.

Sophie fidgeted and picked at her tunic's seams. The shoes Stace had given her didn't fit well after all and rubbed her heels. There would be blisters soon. She shuffled her feet back and forth, earning her another stern glance from Stace.

"You need all of us to clean one chamber?" One boy whined. He looked a bit haughty with his upturned nose.

Stace raised his brows. "Yes, all of you. Is that a problem?"

The boy shook his head, even though he looked like it was a problem for him.

"Fine." Stace grabbed the two carved handles. "See for yourself then." He pulled and the double doors swung wide.

"Ah." A joint sigh greeted the magnificent hall beyond the doors.

"Wow," Sophie said and her mouth fell open.

A bit like in a church, colorful light fell on the chamber floor as the morning sun streamed through the high stained glass windows repeating the sun, moon, and daisy pattern. They certainly liked those flowers here.

"Follow me, boys." Stace headed for a small door off to one side and opened it to a broom closet. Umpteen wooden buckets stacked beside brooms leaned against the wall. Rags, small wooden soap containers, and metal cans with oil filled a large shelf on the third wall. Instead of smelling musty as those cleaning things sometimes do, fresh and clean lemon scent filled the room. Trudy would have liked it. Beside the shelf in the corner stood an old-fashioned water pump, but this one was polished brass and didn't look old at all. Sunrays reached the pump and made it sparkle even more. Stace showed them how to pump the handle and fill the buckets with water. He instructed three boys to scrub the floor, and the other two to oil and polish the long wooden benches down the chamber all the way to a door at the other end.

Stace pointed to Sophie.

"You will be oiling and polishing the Council table and chairs." He demonstrated how to apply some oil to a rag, rubbing and circling the rag on the table's fine dark wood. "Take your time and do it properly," he said when Sophie attacked the table with rag and oil. "Slow and steady does it." He gave her a curt nod. "Flynden," he called. "You will assist with this task." He handed his brother a rag and an oil can, and took the other boys away to the benches. Then he walked up and down the chamber, supervising his crew with encouraging words.

Sophie slowed her hand, making small even circles with the rag. She liked the oil's pleasant lemony smell, and after a while, she even enjoyed the work. Trudy would've been proud of her.

A hush fell over the chamber, except for the scrubbing and shuffling the boys made. With loud scraping noises, Flynden and Sophie pulled the seven chairs back from the table to reach the tabletop on that side. They met in the center near a door that stood closed directly behind the table. Soft light flickered from the gap beneath the door.

When they finished polishing the table, they continued oiling the chairs. Sophie had pulled one closer to the door, which made it convenient to eye the door without anybody noticing. Pelifeles had snuck up on them and sat beneath the very same chair, ears pricked, blinking his yellow eyes once in a while.

Flynden leaned toward the door. Way too obvious. She waved her rag into his face, grabbed his sleeve, and pulled him toward the table, pretending to polish the top.

With their backs toward the door, Sophie asked, "Is that the room?" She wiggled the rag toward the closed door.

Flynden nodded. "I think so."

Pelifeles slunk around their ankles.

"What do you say, Peli?" Flynden squatted and petted the cat.

"I say we go in."

"Now?" Sophie asked and sneaked a peek at Stace and the boys.

"Sure, let's have a look."

A loud knock on the heavy doors at the chamber's other end slowed them. Hands stopped scrubbing and polishing. Stace hurried to the door and someone on the other side exchanged a few heated words with him.

"Wait here," Stace said aloud, swung around and strode toward them, clapping his hands twice. "Please leave through the doors we came in." His face had turned red, and he looked angry. Looking like a mother goose, his arms swept them from the Council Chamber. "Take your buckets and rags. We will continue later."

A relieved sigh went through the group. The boys seemed more than happy to take a break.

"Join them," Stace said to Flynden and Sophie.

"But why?" Flynden asked. "Who's at the door?"

"Never mind," Stace said and swiveled Flynden around by his shoulders. "Close the door behind you."

Flynden and Sophie grabbed their rags and oil cans and hurried toward the door. Down the chamber, a young, dirty, and disheveled man shuffled in and stood waiting, looking nervous. His fist tightened around a little girl's arm. She was maybe four or five and dressed in a frayed dirty dress that may have been light blue at one time. A dirty scarf was wrapped around her head and hid her hair. She cried and trembled and tried to pull away from the man. What was that guy doing with her?

Flynden stopped. "Why is Bron here?"

"You know them?"

"The man, yes." Flynden frowned. "That's Bron. Where he goes, there is trouble."

"What's he doing with the little girl?"

"Don't know, but I'm sure it isn't good." Flynden pulled Sophie with him from the chamber. "Come on, we can't stay in here. The Councilors will be coming," he whispered when they had joined the other boys.

Sophie didn't need to be told twice. They hurried out, but at the last minute when the door started closing behind them, Flynden stuck his foot in the door. "But we can watch," he added with a grin.

❧ ❧

Sophie and Flynden watched through the gap between the doors as Bron strolled down the chamber's center, pulling the very reluctant girl with him.

"Lemme go." The little girl tried to pull her arm from Bron's grip. He looked mean. She clearly didn't want to be here. Bron squeezed her wrist and dragged her with him. She cried out, planted her feet and tried to pull away from him while her other fist pummeled him.

"Are we going to see Thithle?" She squinted up to Bron and tugged.

"Quiet." He didn't even look at her and yanked her forward.

She cried, "No."

"Be quiet, I said."

"No, I won't." She pulled hard on her arm and made Bron stagger. "Lemme go."

The slap on her face cracked like a whip. She stumbled back and would have fallen had he not yanked her straight again. A red handprint spread across her cheek.

Sophie cringed and pressed her lips together. One foster father had slapped her like that and she would never forget it. Her nostrils flared. Heat rose to her face. Breathing hard, she jerked her fists up, nails biting into her palms. She held her elbows away from her sides and widened her stance. When Flynden grabbed her arm, she realized she had stepped forward, ready to have a go at Bron.

"You're mean and bad," the girl screamed.

"Stop crying or I'll leave you with the councilors. They'll teach you."

Bron jerked her forward and stopped close to the Council table. The girl wrinkled her nose and sniffed.

"I want Thithle."

"I want Thithle," Bron mocked and laughed. "Your big brother won't be coming to help you, little girl. I will give you to the meanest councilor and he'll turn you into a mouse so the cats can eat you."

"No, please don't. No." She cried and tugged her arm again, but he held her tightly. She wiped her runny nose on the hem of her dress, smearing it all over her face. "No, please. I'll be good. I promise."

The creep. Sophie balled her fists tighter. How could he abuse the little girl like that? Stace would be back soon and put a stop to it. He had left through another set of doors halfway down the chamber. One side of the doors stood ajar a bit. If Stace didn't show up soon, she would go in and get the girl away from Bron. Someone had to stop him. How she would love to punch that guy.

Bron laughed, but not a happy laugh. His long oily ponytail twisted down his back. His dirty tunic and pants hung on his skinny body. He looked like he wasn't getting enough to eat either. If he hadn't been so mean, she would've maybe felt sorry for him.

The middle doors swung open and Makimus and Camshron strode into the Council Chamber. The girl trembled, tugged and twisted her arm, but Bron's fist tightened.

The councilors walked around the table and stood tall, scowling down on the dirty man and the little girl. Camshron looked even meaner than Bron.

"Please, come forward." Both councilors sat, and Makimus beckoned to Bron.

"I need to speak only to Councilor Makimus." Bron pulled the girl with him. She leaned back, refusing to walk, trying to slow him down. He wouldn't slap her in front of the councilors, would he? She dragged her feet and punched him with her little fist, but Bron squeezed her wrist. She started to cry and ended up walking like he wanted her to.

All too soon, Bron and the girl stood in front of the long table, facing the stern and unsmiling councilors.

"What brings you to Council Hall?" Makimus drawled. He sounded annoyed and bored, like let's get this over with.

"A grievance against this girl's brother, Councilor Makimus."

"Then why did you not bring the brother?"

Bron looked down.

"He was already brought to Council Hall, not too long ago."

"I want Thithle," said the girl. "I want my brother."

Makimus chuckled, but his frown appeared again.

"If this Thistle has been brought already, what would we want with his sister?"

Bron swallowed. "Because he took something from

me. I'd like to have it back." He tugged on the girl's arm. "I've brought the girl in exchange."

"We have no use for a girl. Go." Camshron's face darkened even more.

"See?" the girl said to Bron, a triumphant look on her face, and she tried again to tug her arm free.

"Wait." Makimus leaned forward. "Take your scarf off, child." He pointed at her with one hand. Each long graceful finger, and even his thumb, wore a ring sparkling in the sunlight.

The girl hiccupped, froze, and stared at his hand with the rings on it. She trembled harder and a little puddle formed on the floor at her feet.

"What is the matter, child?" Makimus smiled at her but his smile disappeared and his face became thoughtful, seeing how she had peed herself.

The girl cowered and whimpered.

"Quiet, Bramble. Nobody's hurting you." Bron shook her, but he trembled, too.

"Bramble?" Councilor Makimus stood and he seemed to grow into a giant. The girl whimpered and pressed her free fist again her mouth.

"So, what about our bargain?" Bron pressed, watching Councilor Makimus come around the table. Camshron stood, too, watching.

"In a moment," Makimus said and walked around to the table's other side, reaching for the girl. She screamed and fell to her knees. For a moment, Bron still grabbed her arm, but then he let go and she collapsed on the floor.

When the little girl screamed inside the chamber, Sophie shivered and rubbed her arms.

Makimus yelled, "Stace!"

"You were supposed to have gone with the other boys," Stace whispered as he rushed past Sophie and Flynden. Through the gap, they watched Makimus bending down to the girl in front of the table. Tiny yellow-green sparks danced from his fingers, moving up and down her small body. Bron stood off to one side, staring terrified at the girl on the floor. He shook hard, itching, shifting his feet, looking like ants crawled all over him.

"I bet he regrets coming here," Sophie whispered into Flynden's ear.

Flynden nodded.

"Take the girl, wash her, and put her to bed." Makimus grunted as he lifted the girl and straightened. He handed her to Stace. "She is exhausted and starved." His voice became stern. "When she wakes, feed her, and do not let her out of your sight."

Stace nodded but wrinkled his nose as he received the girl into his arms. He rushed toward the doors. Flynden pulled them open a bit to let Stace pass. Too preoccupied with the girl to tell them off, Stace left the door open a crack. He grumbled to himself while he hurried down the hall, holding the girl away from him. Her dirty wet legs dangled over one arm, her head bobbed up and down over the other, and her white blond curls danced with each of his strides.

Poor little girl. Makimus scared everyone to death. Sophie peeked over Flynden's head, while he bent forward pressing his face to the gap between the doors. Makimus walked back to his chair.

"Step forward, Bron." His voice rang cold and

commanding through the cavernous chamber. "What is the meaning of this? Bringing this neglected child to us. What have you done to her?"

"I have done nothing to her, Councilor. Thistle, her brother, lacks the skill to look after her and gambles away all his coin. Lets her go hungry. That's why she's so thin."

Bron wrung his hands, his shoulders hunched. He tensed and his eyes widened with fear. His face went pale like he would puke any second.

"Where are the children's parents?"

"How would I know?"

"You seem to know these children," Camshron said in his high voice. "But you do not know where their parents are?"

"No, Councilor. I mean, yes, Councilor." Bron bowed, trembling now. "I don't know where the brother and sister came from. They live in the streets."

Makimus gazed at his folded hands in front of him on the table, tipping two fingers together. When he looked up, he asked, "What has the boy Thistle stolen from you?"

"Playing stones."

"Which you have stolen from someone else."

"That's not true."

Makimus pulled a pouch from the folds of his tunic and emptied marble-size stones into his cupped hand.

"Then why are these pebbles from Sunflower Cove disguised with gray paint?" He extended the stones on his palm toward Bron.

Bron said nothing and looked at his feet.

"Answer." Makimus' voice boomed.

Bron's Adam's apple danced in his throat with every swallow, but he said nothing.

"Answer," Makimus repeated.

"If I can have them back," Bron said, "I'll return them to the rightful owner."

"You can have nothing. You will be fortunate if I let you go unpunished."

Bron flinched and took a step back. For a moment, he looked as if he would run.

"Tell me what you know." Yellow-green sparks jumped off Makimus' fingertips. Bron shrank within himself and looked like he wanted to make himself as small as he could, perhaps even disappear into the cracks of the stone floor.

No such luck, buddy. Sophie had to grin. She didn't know Bron, but she didn't like him already. How could he use the little girl to get some playing stones back? In a hurry, she changed her mind though, when the yellow-green fire gathered in Makimus' hand and snaked across the table, reaching for the thief. Bron stumbled backward. Like a snake, the yellow-green magic slithered off the wood, down to the floor, and across the small space separating it from the thief. It licked at Bron's boots and wound around his legs. Bron kicked at the magic snakes, but it made no difference. Then his mouth gaped wide with a soundless scream.

With a thud, the doors closed in front of Sophie and Flynden, cutting off their view, and almost their noses. Sophie jumped. They swung around, facing Councilor Druce Lar. Behind him, Councilor Tulio had lost his merry smile and fixed them with a stern glance. Then came Councilors Darach and Lombard, who didn't look too pleased either about seeing them there.

"Off you go, boys. This is no place for you to be," Druce Lar said.

"Yes, Councilor," Flynden said and pulled Sophie with

him. Sophie walked sideways down the hallway and watched so that she would miss nothing.

Druce Lar pulled the doors apart again, and in a line, the councilors strode into the Council Chamber.

"What is the meaning of this, Makimus?" Druce Lar's voice boomed before the doors closed behind him.

"Let's find Stace," Flynden said.

Sophie nodded, feeling sick.

They broke into a run.

❧ *Chapter 10* ❦

"It's us, Stace." Flynden knocked, his nose pressed to the wood as he spoke to the door. "Let us in."

The door cracked a sliver.

"What are you doing here?" Stace whispered through the crack.

Flynden and Sophie pushed past him and squeezed into the room. Pelifeles slunk in after them. Where had the cat been the whole time?

"We saw Councilor Makimus use his magic on Bron," Flynden said.

Stace's eyebrows scooted up, his eyes widened for a second, but then he furrowed his forehead. "He did not."

"He did." Sophie nodded with emphasis. "We saw it. But then all the other councilors came and stopped him." She panted and took deep breaths. "Councilor Druce Lar sent us away, and we couldn't find out any more."

"You were not supposed to witness what the councilors are doing in the Council Chamber. It is not allowed."

"Where is the girl?" Flynden looked around the chamber. "You didn't leave her for Councilor Makimus, did you?"

"Shush. Of course not." Stace shook his head and walked toward the curtain. "You can come out now, Bramble." Stace pulled the curtain aside. Bramble, now scrubbed clean, her rosy cheeks gleaming, stepped from the alcove behind the curtain. Her curls still hung wet on her shoulders from the bath. She wore a tunic like a dress, the sleeves rolled up while the hem reached past her knees. Fear stared from her big blue eyes.

"Since you are here, I will take all of you out of Council Hall. Now. No arguments."

"What about the Flora blossom?" Sophie asked.

"Never mind the blossom," Stace said.

"Never mind?" Sophie threw up her hands. "Isn't it the whole reason why your Master Eigil wanted me to come here?"

"No arguments, I said." Stace stood in front of the children, hands on his hips. "It is far too dangerous if you remain. I will take you as far as the road to Urbinter. Flynden, you know the path that cuts through the forest?"

Flynden nodded.

"Go to the Garden and speak with the Mother Flora. She will know what to do." To Bramble he said, "You will go with them, Bramble, because it is safer than staying here."

"Where is Thithle?" Bramble asked. "He must come, too."

"I do not know where your brother is, Bramble, but I promise I will keep looking for him." Stace petted her on the head and gave her a small smile.

"I will not leave without the Flora blossom. I just can't." Sophie frowned and crossed her arms. "We have to get it first," she said. "We just got to."

"I won't leave, too." Bramble crossed her arms like Sophie and mimicked her scowl.

Stace bit his lip, but the corners of his mouth twitched anyway. "You are only guessing because you do not know if that is the very thing you must take."

"But Master Eigil…"

"Not now," Stace cut her off.

Sophie still stood with crossed arms and a scowl on her face. She wouldn't back down.

"I need to get the Flora blossom." Sophie squeaked and swallowed. "I'm scared of Makimus, but maybe we can stop him and his plans, whatever they are, if we get the blossom and bring Master Eigil back."

"Listen," Stace said. "Sit." He pointed to the bed and grabbed a chair for himself.

He pulled Bramble onto his lap. Sophie and Flynden sat on the bed while Pelifeles jumped onto the table and licked an empty bowl. Stace placed the bowl on the floor. The cat followed and continued licking, not missing a beat.

"Now listen." Stace whispered and leaned forward. "As long as the councilors are meeting in the Council Chamber, we cannot do anything and have to wait. If you stay here, you may not receive another chance to get away. Now is the right time." He held up one hand to stop Sophie from interrupting. "I know how important it is to take the blossom with you and bring Master Eigil back, perhaps more than you do, but if Councilor Makimus catches you again, he will not let you go a second time. You have seen and felt for yourself what he will do. If you cannot go back to get Master Eigil, then we are all lost. Do you understand?"

"Then how can we get the blossom?" Sophie asked.

"We can't do anything if we're miles away."

"I do not know." Stace raised his hands, palms up. "You could ask the Mother Flora, she will know."

"I got it," Flynden cried. "We let Peli spy on the councilors and let us know when they're leaving the Council Chamber. Then we'll get the Flora blossom and leave."

"That sounds too easy, little brother. Believe me, it is not."

"I didn't say it is or would be, but it might work. We could even ask Peli to steal it."

Pelifeles twisted to look straight at Flynden, shook himself and went back to licking the bowl.

Stace rubbed his chin with two fingers and made a face. Bramble giggled.

"You cannot stay here," he said. "Councilor Makimus will be looking for Sophie and Bramble, and there is a good chance he will be coming first to me."

"We could go to Kir's or Calleo's chamber," Flynden said.

"We cannot."

"Why not? I'm sure they would help."

"I told you before, the apprentices are bound by their vows. They will have to notify the councilors."

"Yes, one of them but not Makimus. They could go to Druce Lar, right?" Sophie asked.

"True." Stace started pacing the room. "But…"

"Do you think Druce Lar would give us away?" Sophie said. "The way he yelled at Makimus when the councilor tortured Bron sounded like he wasn't happy with Makimus either."

"It still does not mean Councilor Druce Lar would help us."

"I think he would," Flynden said. "We could ask him."

"I believe it is unwise." Stace stood. "Your first idea sounded better. Let us send Pelifeles first."

Pelifeles licked his paws slowly, first the right one, then the left. At last, he padded over to the door, tail flicking. Stace cracked the door a bit, listened, and opened it a bit more. The cat jumped out and vanished. Stace shut the door. Now, they only had to wait, but for how long?

❧   ❦

Pelifeles didn't come back right away. Stace paced the room from window to door, moving a book from the table to a shelf, folding and refolding leggings and tunics on another, and every so often, he opened the door to check the hallway before continuing to pace. Once in a while, Flynden or Sophie jumped up with, "I think I heard something," and Stace lunged for the door.

Sophie gazed out of the window. When Flynden and Pelifeles had rescued her from the dungeon and they'd come to Stace's room, she'd thought they were underground somewhere, but Council Hall sat on a high cliff, overlooking a rugged bay. Waves crashed against the rock, spraying foam and water halfway up the cliff. Fog swirled farther out on the ocean low to the water. Farther down the coast to the right, big sailing ships with two or three masts moored in a harbor. She remembered Flynden lying about his father and her parents doing business in Harbor Town. He must've meant the place with the ships.

Flynden teased Bramble and played with her until she giggled and squealed.

"Stop it. You are making too much noise." Stace sounded tense and irritable.

When they got hungry, Stace pulled some food items from a cupboard and served fresh soft bread, cheese like mild cheddar that Sophie liked, and water. They ate in silence, but before they could finish, a soft scratch on the door interrupted them. Bramble heard it first.

"Pelifeles is back." She pointed to the door.

Stace rushed to let the cat in. Pelifeles padded back and forth, and slunk between their ankles, wrapping his long black tail around legs with every turn, tickling them.

"So, what did you find out?" Flynden asked.

"They're looking for you, Stace," Pelifeles said. "You have to go or the councilors will become suspicious. Makimus is wondering what is taking you so long with the girl."

Bramble's eyes popped when Pelifeles started talking.

"The kitty talks?" she asked and reached for him. Pelifeles let her pet him and purred.

Stace shook his head. "I have been neglecting my duties."

"No, you haven't," Flynden said. "You've been helping us. That's more important." To the cat he said, "Why didn't you come back earlier, Peli?"

Pelifeles sat at Bramble's feet, with his big yellow eyes blinking. He rounded his back and pushed into the girl's hand, purring like a motor.

"Come on, Peli, what did you find out?" Sophie asked, but Pelifeles just licked his paws. "Come on, we haven't got all day."

He gave her a look like don't push me or I won't say anything. Sophie rolled her eyes.

Pelifeles moved away from Bramble and said,

"Makimus let Bron leave."

"Good." Stace nodded. "You children should leave, too."

"But…" Flynden jumped up.

"No, Flynden, it is too dangerous. Perhaps Councilor Makimus let Bron leave, but that does not mean he would let Sophie go, or Bramble. I am not sure what he wants with Bramble or what he has done to her brother, but it cannot be good. I am willing to risk being sent from Council Hall to see you safely away, but we must leave now."

"They wouldn't send you away," Flynden said.

"Oh yes, they would, especially if Councilor Makimus finds out I have been helping you."

"Makimus announced he and Camshron would be visiting the Mother Flora," Pelifeles said.

"What?" Stace scratched his head. "When?"

"First thing in the morning," the cat said.

"Did he say why?"

"He wanted to discuss things with her."

"By the light!" Stace sat down at the table. "What to do?"

"Why don't we get the Flora blossom while he's gone?" Sophie asked.

Stace shook his head. "There are still the other councilors to think of. You cannot walk into the chamber and take it like that." He snapped his fingers before her face.

"Why not? Maybe they'll help if we tell them what we know. They saw what he did to Bron."

"I doubt they will help." Stace stood and started pacing again. "You are coming with me. Now. All of you. Up, up." He waved with his hands. "We are going right now."

"Can't we try? Please, Stace," Sophie pleaded.

"I haven't told you all of it yet," Pelifeles said and licked his paws.

"What else did you hear?" Stace asked and ignored Sophie's plea. He sighed and sat down again. "Finish then and make it quick, Pelifeles." He put his elbows on the table and his head in his hands.

"The councilors argued with raised voices," Pelifeles said. "I've never heard them do that before." His yellow eyes blinked once or twice. "The other councilors are unhappy with Makimus because he claims the Mother Flora is too powerful and the Council should have more authority when it comes to choosing the mothers who bear the special boys."

"Why's that?" Sophie asked. "I don't get it. What does that have to do with us?"

"Never mind that now," Pelifeles said. "It means, Councilor Makimus is after power and it could mean he wants to harm the Mother Flora." The cat paused.

Stace, Flynden and Bramble gasped.

"I think Councilor Makimus wants the Celarim so that he can carry out his plans, but Master Eigil spoiled everything for him when he fled with the book right out of Nugateris."

"Master Eigil didn't have a book when he talked to me," Sophie mumbled.

"He could've been hiding it somewhere," Flynden said.

"I have changed my mind." Stace suddenly said and pushed his chair back to get up. "We must take the Flora blossom and warn the Mother Flora." He gave them a grave look. "First, you will hide here until morning. I must attend to the councilors, or they will become more suspicious. In the morning, as soon as Councilors

Makimus and Camshron have left Council Hall, I will take you to the Council Chamber, but on one condition." He stopped to take a deep breath. "I need your cooperation. Everyone's, even yours Flynden. Understood?"

They all nodded.

"Right then." Stace went to the door. "Not a word, a sound, or anything."

Again, they nodded.

Now they had to spend another night in this awful place, but it would be okay for a little while longer if she wanted to help and make it home. Well, Makimus made it awful; otherwise, this place and the people were quite nice.

Stace looked out into the hallway.

"Stay here," he said. "And remember, no noise."

"Why do I have to stay?" Flynden argued. "Nobody's looking for me. I can help."

"You can help by staying out of trouble." Stace grinned. "I will lock you in. It will be safer for you." With those words, he slipped out and shut the door. A key turned in the lock. Then Stace had gone.

❧ *Chapter 11* ❦

Flynden jumped to the door and tried the knob.

"I don't believe it! He really locked us in." He swung around. "Peli, can you open it?"

"Of course, I can," Pelifeles said, "but I won't."

"You're as bad as Stace."

"Or as caring."

"I agree with Flynden. Shouldn't we do something instead of just waiting?" Sophie asked. "If Makimus comes looking, a locked door won't stop him."

Pelifeles jumped onto the table. His yellow eyes blinked up at Sophie.

"A valid point," he said. "I suggest as soon as we hear something outside, we'll hide behind the curtain."

"You mean that's doing something?" Flynden crossed his arms and plopped onto Stace's bed, his face scrunched into a frown. "A fabric curtain won't stop Makimus either."

"I can do a trick to the curtain," Pelifeles said. "Or this chamber. Or us."

"Then he knows for sure because he can sense other magic," Flynden said.

"We can hide under the bed," Bramble squeaked.

"Thithle and I always do that at home."

Flynden flopped onto his stomach and hung upside down over the bed's edge.

"There isn't enough room for all of us."

"Then what do we do?" Sophie asked. They were caged, locked in, stuck, and if Makimus came, there would be no place to run or hide.

"I don't know," Flynden grumbled, rolled onto his back and crossed his arms behind his head.

Well, what could they do? Sophie looked around the room. The table strewn with crumbs, four cups and a pitcher, and a plate with cheese would give them away. Flynden had messed up the bed. If Makimus came and looked into the room, even if they hid under the bed, he would know right away that Stace had visitors.

"I know what we do," she said. "We clean and tidy this room."

"You're mad." Flynden said. "What for?"

"It'll look like only Stace was here. Duh."

"I'm not doing any cleaning."

"Then at least get off the bed, lazy butt, so I can straighten it." Sophie pushed Flynden aside and fluffed the pillow.

"Yes, stop arguing and help, Flynden." Bramble stood in front of Flynden. Her scowl made him laugh.

"Okay, little girl," Flynden said and scooted off the bed. "You win." He ruffled her hair and smiled.

Together, they tidied the room. Flynden made the bed and even did a good job straightening the blanket and pillow. Sophie handed Bramble the plate with cheese. The girl carried them behind the curtain and came back with a cloth. Sophie wiped the crumbs off the table with it, straightened the chair and pushed it in its place, then stood back. She found a broom in the small alcove and swept the whole room, chasing Flynden, Bramble, and Pelifeles with it. Bramble squealed.

"Ssh, not so loud." Sophie stopped sweeping. "All this work will be for nothing if someone hears us." She put the broom away and they all sat on the rug in front of Stace's bed.

"So what should we do now?" Sophie crossed her legs and held onto her knees. Bramble scooted up beside her and mimicked the pose. Pelifeles snuggled up on the little girl's lap.

"How come you can talk?" Bramble asked.

'It's a secret," the cat said.

"Why?"

"If I tell you, it won't be a secret." Pelifeles tickled her chin with the tips of his ears. Bramble giggled.

"Let's make a plan." Flynden hugged his knees. "How will we get into the room in the Council Chamber, take the Flora blossom, and find the fastest way out?"

"Sounds way too easy." Sophie shook her head and put one arm around Bramble. "We walk in and walk out, right?"

"No. I mean, we have to make a plan because with a plan we might have a chance of getting out."

"Okay, don't start," Sophie said.

"Yes, don't start." Bramble said, scowling again at Flynden.

Sophie chortled. The girl was too cute with her little button nose, a pout more like a scowl, and her lisp. Tommy had been cute, too, in a different way though. He'd had Daddy's straight nose and he didn't have a lisp, but he could say funny things, too, like mimicking one of their foster fathers in a mock deep voice. She blinked a few times. Flynden would be calling her a crybaby if he saw. She rubbed her eyes pretending they itched.

"We should get some Z's," she said when she thought her voice would sound steady.

"Get what?" Flynden cocked his head.

"Sleep." Sophie curled up on the carpet and closed her eyes. Bramble snuggled against her. "We can't do anything else. We can talk all we want, but until Stace lets us out and tells us what's going on, we can't make any plans. So, sleeping will be the best thing, and we'll be rested." Now she sounded like Trudy. Sophie frowned and shifted her shoulders and legs until she found a comfortable spot. The bed was tempting, but it had to look unused. She squinted at Flynden. "Well?"

"Sleeping sounds better than working." Flynden grinned and rolled into a ball, facing Sophie and Bramble, and was asleep in seconds.

Soon, Bramble's and Flynden's breathing became slow and even. Pelifeles snuggled up beside Sophie's head and purred her to sleep.

❧ ❧

It seemed like she had slept for only a few minutes when something cold tickled her nose. Sophie bolted upright in the dark and didn't remember where she was.

"Someone's coming," Pelifeles hissed.

Then she remembered Stace's room. Bramble stirred beside her but didn't make a sound. Flynden moved in the shadow across from her. He lifted Bramble into his arms. Together, they rushed behind the curtain. A greenish light flickered through the key hole. Steps stopped on the door's other side. The sour apple smell crept into the room and stung her nose.

Oh no! Makimus would get them now. She held her breath. Please go away. Please.

They huddled as far back into the alcove as they could, pressing their backs into the shelving on the wall.

The lock clicked and the door creaked open. The sour apple smell assaulted the room, the alcove, and Sophie's nose and lungs. Flynden's warm shoulder pressed against hers, somewhat reassuring, but Bramble trembled in his arms. Sophie reached over, put a hand over the girl's mouth, and placed a soft kiss on her hair.

First, Pelifeles sat like a furry statue outlined in green by the curtain, then he jumped. No, Pelifeles. No, don't go out there. The curtain moved. Beyond the curtain, he hissed and spat. Cloth tore and ripped. Makimus' feet shuffled. Panting, he kicked. Pelifeles cried out. There was a dull thud and silence again.

"I have to talk to Stace about cats at Council Hall," Makimus mumbled. "We have better ways to take care of mice." He sounded disgusted and moved across the room, his clothes rustling, swishing over the floor. The door creaked and closed.

They waited a minute or two. Was Pelifeles okay? Or was he…? She couldn't even think the word. She wouldn't. He had to be okay. He saved them.

Sophie's kneecaps wobbled. Beside her, Flynden lowered Bramble and stepped to the curtain where he crouched. Sophie and Bramble huddled closer. In the dark, they crawled into the room and searched for the cat's body. Pelifeles lay near the door. Makimus hadn't made it far into the room.

"Is he okay?" Sophie whispered.

"I don't know," Flynden whispered back.

Bramble sniffled. "The bad man."

"Stop making so much noise. Makimus will hear you and come back." Pelifeles hissed.

Phew. Sophie let out a long breath. She'd held it the whole time.

"I don't think we should stay here," Flynden said and moved over to the door. The door creaked and light cut into the room.

"Flyn, no," Sophie said. "He might still be out there."

Flynden stood; half his face and body showed in the light's beam falling across the floor all the way to the curtain.

"Come, let's run."

From somewhere down the hallway, steps approached in a hurry. Sophie and Bramble scrambled up. Flynden rushed with them behind the curtain again. Pelifeles disappeared under the bed. The much lighter steps slowed near the door. Someone sucked in his breath. The door creaked, and light flooded the room.

"Flyn?" Stace whispered. He sounded scared. "Sophie?"

Flynden pushed the curtain aside.

"By the light," Stace said. His face was whitish-gray and looked older than before. "What happened? The door stood ajar. I thought…" He didn't finish the thought.

"Makimus came," Sophie said. "Pelifeles saved us and almost got himself killed."

"By the light." Stace ran one hand through his neatly combed hair until the bangs stuck up straight. "Makimus hurried past me in the hallway and said something about cats and mice, and I knew he must have been here. How else would he know about Pelifeles?" Stace gulped.

"Then he told me he was leaving for the Garden immediately, looking at me sideways when he said it."

Stace went to the door and pressed his ear against the wood.

"Not to worry," Pelifeles said. "He's not out there now."

Stace nodded. He sat on the bed and beckoned them closer. They gathered around him.

"We go as soon as Councilors Makimus and Camshron leave to visit the Mother Flora. There will be no better time, maybe no other chance. I believe Councilor Makimus suspects something because he came looking for you here."

"What about the other councilors?" Sophie asked. "Where are they?"

Stace rubbed his upper arms and shivered. "Councilors Darach and Lombard retired to their chambers after breakfast. Councilor Tulio announced he would be working in his herb garden, and Councilor Druce Lar had me fetch Kir and Calleo. He said he required their assistance."

"What for?" Flynden asked.

"I do not know, little brother, but I believe you were right, we have nothing to fear from them."

"How do you know?" Sophie asked and threw up her hands. "They're council members and you said they took some kind of vow."

"Kir wouldn't," Flynden growled. "He wouldn't tell on us, and neither would Calleo." His face took on a thoughtful look. "I'm not sure about Vaughn. He's an odd one."

"He is fine, Flynden," Stace said. "You do not know him well at all."

"If you say so."

"If it makes you feel better, he left Council Hall and went walking."

"Sure, going to see his mama, isn't he?" Flynden mocked. "Everyone knows where he goes when he thinks nobody is watching."

Stace shook his head. "You should not talk bad about Vaughn. Kir and Calleo trust him, and so do the councilors."

"Well, perhaps they do not know where…"

"Enough, Flynden," Stace cut him off. "Vaughn is fine. You are not the only one who finds out what is going on. The councilors and the apprentices know a thing or two, and so do I."

Flynden crossed his arms over his chest and scowled.

What was that all about? They should be worrying about getting the Flora blossom. Fast. No more dawdling, Mom would say.

Flynden opened his mouth to say something else, but Sophie was quicker.

"So, once we have the blossom, how do we get out?" she asked. "We didn't come up with anything while you were gone, at least nothing helpful."

"I believe there is a way," Stace said. "We need Pelifeles' help. Where is the cat now?"

Pelifeles slunk from under the bed and blinked his big yellow eyes. Stace scratched the cat's ear and smiled.

"Good. Now listen."

They huddled closer, settling around him on the rug. Bramble took her thumb from her mouth and stared at Stace. Sophie hugged her close. Flynden scratched his head.

"It will be tricky, even with the councilors gone. This is what we must do," Stace said, and they listened quietly to his plan.

❧ ❧

The window in the room changed from black to gray to lighter gray. It would soon be morning. Stace peeked through the crack of the open door.

"Stay close now, and no talking."

He swung the door wide, and one by one, they tiptoed out and hurried after him down the hallways. Flynden watched their backs while Pelifeles slunk ahead. Sophie held Bramble's hand and pulled her along. Bramble kept up on her short legs and said nothing. Tommy would've moaned and groaned the whole way.

Sophie's stomach clenched into a hard knot. If only this would work. If they were lucky, she'd be home soon, and Master Eigil, too. Then she could tell Trudy how sorry she was. Sophie crossed her fingers. First, she had to get that dumb Flora blossom.

A short while later, back where the soft thick carpets lined the Council Hall's floors, they rushed past the floor-to-ceiling windows and tapestries on the walls. They met a few other servants, but Stace strode ahead, nodding to them, and sent them away with quick instructions for some task or other. No one questioned him. No one stopped them.

From somewhere down a hallway, delicious smells of fresh bread reached Sophie's nose. They had to be close to the kitchen. Her stomach forgot to clench for a moment and growled instead. She ignored it. Right there and then, she could've eaten ten bowls of Councilor Tulio's yummy stew.

After the next turn, they faced the Council Chamber's heavy double doors. Without stopping or hesitating, Stace pulled one wing open, wide enough for them to slip inside. They hurried across the short distance to the table and behind it to the narrow door.

"Is it locked?" Sophie whispered and reached for the doorknob.

"Wait," Stace said. "Do not touch the door."

Pelifeles sauntered up blinking his yellow eyes at them. He gave his front paws a quick lick before he walked back and forth in front of the door, once, twice, then again.

"No wards," he said.

Stace frowned.

"What is it, Stace?" Sophie asked.

Stace didn't answer, scratched his chin, looking thoughtful, and shrugged. "Quick now." He grabbed the doorknob, turned it and pushed the door in.

Sophie held her breath. No alarm. What had she expected? A siren? She breathed out.

For a second, they stood there then rushed into the small room and stood waiting, searching only with their eyes. Dead silence surrounded them. Heavy velvety curtains covered one side of the room, probably a window, because from a crack where the fabric's edges met, the morning sun cut into the room and gave them enough light to look around the otherwise gloomy space. A nasty smell hung in the air with the dust motes.

They jumped when Bramble sneezed. She snuffled into her sleeve, wiping the snot all over her face. Stace held one finger to his mouth to tell her to be quiet. She nodded, but now wiped her nose with her tunic's hem. Stace pulled a cloth hanky from his pocket and helped her, whispering in her ear.

They waited two minutes, but when nothing happened and nobody came to get them, they breathed with relief.

Sophie pinched her nose to cut the nasty smell. Where did it come from?

Bookshelves lined the walls, cramped with red, black, and dark green leather-covered books. Some spines had a subtle new look while others were cracked and faded with age. Most were as large as coffee table books, but here and there, a small paperback-size volume was wedged between them. There must have been more than a hundred books. In the middle of the room, tall wrought iron holders with tennis-ball-size globes adorned each corner of a square pedestal, one step up. Seven narrow cylindrical columns with flat wooden surfaces on top stood a little bit taller than Bramble—three in the front, three in the back, and one in the center of the pedestal. On six of them, large books lay open. Their pages were marked with shiny red ribbons, as if someone had just stopped reading a minute ago. On the column in the center lay a gray cloth sack the size of a big down-filled mitten with something inside. Brown stains covered the cloth. Was the Flora blossom in it? Why was it such a big lump? Wouldn't it be smaller more like a brooch?

Sophie looked at Stace and pointed to the sack. When he nodded, Sophie rushed forward, but he grabbed her shoulders.

"What?" She hissed, almost like Pelifeles. "Do you want to get out of here or not?"

"Of course," he whispered back, "but let Pelifeles check first. There might be wards around it. Although, there seem to be none anywhere. It is rather peculiar."

Sighing and rolling her eyes, Sophie stepped back from the pedestal. This time, Pelifeles moved quickly and jumped up. Stace, Flynden, and Bramble stood near the door. Bramble wrinkled her nose and pinched it closed with her thumb and finger. With one hand on the doorknob, Stace cracked the door and peeked out. When he turned back to them, he nodded and waved Pelifeles to hurry up.

The cat circled the middle column with the cloth sack, turning first left then right, and finally sat, blinking up at them. He shook himself, sending off a bunch of cat hair to mingle with the dust motes in the shaft of light from the window. Bramble sneezed again. They looked toward the door and held their breaths. Nothing moved. No sound. Nobody came.

"Did the shake mean there are no wards?" Sophie asked.

Pelifeles licked his paw again. "No wards," he said. "But there's something odd about it."

"Like what?"

The cat blinked a few more times. "Like something evil. You shouldn't touch it."

"How can the Flora blossom be evil?" Flynden asked and came up to stand beside Sophie. "Nothing from the Flora could be bad."

"True, but there is something else in the bag," Pelifeles said and blocked Sophie from the column.

Sophie took a deep breath. "There's only one way to find out." She grabbed the sack's corners, tipped it over, and shook it a bit. A withered hand, almost like a skeleton but still with gray mottled skin over the bones, slid from the bag and tumbled onto the wooden rest. Sophie gagged and dropped the bag. The hacked-off hand's grayish-green fingers curled into a fist. Bones and straggly tendons hung from the wrist with dried blood, dark brown like the stains on the old man's sleeve. The hand stunk somewhat awful like sulfur springs, milk left out on the counter, and rotten meat all mixed together. On their own, the fingers unfurled slowly. On the hand's palm lay a beautiful jewel shaped like a flower. Its delicate golden petals curved away from seven stones making up its composite center. The stones sparkled where the sunlight touched them.

"Wow," Sophie said. "It's beautiful, even if it stinks."

Flynden's mouth hung open as he stared. "Master Eigil's hand," he whispered.

Sophie grimaced and pinched her nose. "What do you think?" she asked in a nasally voice.

"Master Eigil needs this," Stace said. "You saw him with his left hand cut off. He would have lost it while holding the Flora blossom."

"You shouldn't touch it," Pelifeles said again. "The hand is evil."

"How can a hand be evil?" Sophie asked and inched back toward the pedestal.

"Because it's still alive, that's how."

"Then how do we take the Flora blossom from it?" She looked at the others like they all had an answer ready, but nobody said a word.

Bang! One of the big doors in the Council Chamber slammed. Someone was coming.

Stace pulled the door shut, his eyes wide with panic. Pelifeles raised his hackles and made his tail look like a bottlebrush.

"What now?" Sophie whispered and searched the room. They could get out through the window.

Stace must have thought the same because he rushed to the nearest one and ripped the curtain away. It wasn't a window at all, but a double door leading into an ornamental garden. Stace fumbled with a latch. They would get out but how would she take the blossom from the hand?

Loud voices approached the door.

"Who is in the library chamber?" Makimus shouted.

Why was he here? He was supposed to be gone.

Sophie had no time to guess or wonder about it. She had to do something, and do it fast. She bent to pick up the sack.

Stace unlatched the patio door and pushed it open. His Adam's apple bobbed up and down below his white face. Bramble whimpered and trembled. Stace grabbed her and clamped one hand over her mouth to keep her quiet. Flynden stood frozen on the spot, looking from the hand with the blossom to the Council Chamber's small door to Sophie.

Steps and voices grew louder, closer now. Sophie pulled the sack over her right hand like a glove. As soon as she touched the hand, three fingers curled over the Flora blossom, but its thumb and index finger clamped over Sophie's wrist through the cloth. She gagged and tried to pry the hand from hers, but it wouldn't let go. The cold fingers squeezed her wrist like a vise. Pelifeles hissed. Flynden tried to help her, but when he reached for the hand, his fingers flashed with a white light. He jumped back.

"What's that?" Sophie whispered, twisted and shook her arm, but the hand squeezed her wrist. "Please, get it off. Quick." She wanted to cry out. It hurt so much.

Flynden stared amazed at his own hands and made no move.

Pelifeles hissed. "We have to get out. Now. Run."

The voices had almost reached the door. As if coming

out of a trance, Flynden shook and shivered, then grabbed Sophie's free arm, wrenching her toward the garden door. They had no time for pulling the curtain or closing the door. Already, Stace raced with Bramble in his arms toward an archway at the garden's end, not sticking to the colorful stone walkway but crashing through the flowerbeds. Sophie and Flynden trampled after him, crushing forget-me-nots, roses, daisies, and tulips.

They dashed toward the archway when Makimus shouted behind them. Sophie glanced over her shoulder. He stood in the open patio door, his hand alight with wicked yellow-green light, aiming at her.

Flynden pulled her around the corner and out of sight, and they raced into a shadowy hallway.

❧ ❧

Sophie shivered and gagged as they ran through Council Hall after Stace.

"Stop, Flyn," she gasped. "Can't run anymore. Gotta throw up." The words had barely tumbled from her mouth when the vomit followed. She bent over and threw up in a corner underneath a colorful tapestry. Maybe Stace hadn't noticed any of this and raced ahead, his steps fading away. When she shook her arm again to get the gray hand off her wrist, the thumb and finger squeezed tighter. "Ouch." Sophie sank to her knees. Her hand turned blue. "Please get it off, Flyn. Peli, please."

"Keep going," Pelifeles hissed, not jumping ahead this time. "There is no time right now."

"Come," Flynden urged. "We have to keep up with Stace." He grabbed her from behind under the armpits and pulled her up. She stumbled along, bile rising in her throat again. Was the pain or the hand making her sick? Pelifeles had said something was evil about the hand. She was sure of it because only something weird and evil could still be alive and make her sick like this. She wanted to get it off now but didn't dare shake her arm again or it would squeeze even more, or maybe do something worse.

They rounded another corner and almost crashed into Stace and Bramble.

"What is taking you so long?" Stace asked, panting, as he skidded to a stop.

"Sophie is really sick, Stace," Flynden said. "It's the gray hand."

Stace glanced at the Sophie's face then at her hand with the gray hand attached to it, and grimaced. "No time now. I am sorry, Sophie. Hurry." He turned on the spot and raced ahead again.

Sophie tried to keep up, but now she started to feel dizzy on top of nauseated. Without Flynden guiding and pulling her along, she would've been lost. When they raced around another corner, Stace waited by a closed door. He unlatched it, and they stumbled out into a courtyard with stone walls on all sides.

Servants washed cloths and sheets in stone basins, slapping the wet fabric against the stone. They looked up and watched them run to a wooden gate in the wall. Stace yanked it open and pushed Sophie and Flynden out into a narrow cobblestone alley. As soon as he slammed the gate shut after them, shouts rose on the other side. Makimus' voice rang loud and clear.

"This way," Stace called and raced down the alley.

Flynden could've easily run ahead with his brother,

but he stayed with her, hanging onto her good arm. Pelifeles stayed at their heels. On wobbly legs, Sophie stumbled ahead as fast as she could with no idea where they where going. What did it matter? As long as Makimus didn't catch them.

"Stop, Flyn. I can't run anymore."

"Come, only a little farther."

He wouldn't let go or stop. Why didn't he listen? She wouldn't make it. He should save himself.

The alley curved to the left. Sophie peeked over her shoulder. Four men (or eight?) dressed all in black like karate fighters emerged from the gate into the alley and sprinted toward them. They looked like normal men, but they were fast.

Stace cut around the next corner into an even narrower alley with Bramble clutched in his arms. The girl was looking over his shoulder, her curls dancing around her frightened face. Stace dashed around another corner and was gone.

Flynden slowed for a second looking from side to side. Pelifeles hissed a warning. The men rushed toward them.

"In here," Flynden breathed and pushed her through a door to the right, and shut it behind them. They pressed against the closed door to catch their breath. The men ran past the door, their steps fading away.

"Where are we?" Sophie panted. Her whisper echoed into a dark stone tunnel.

"Ssh." Flynden hissed almost like Pelifeles. "This is a tunnel to the sewers. I've hidden here before," Flynden whispered. "Come." They tiptoed into the chilly, damp tunnel where the air smelled dank and foul, but not as bad as the gray hand. Water dripped somewhere.

After a few minutes, the tunnel sloped down like a

chute. Sophie gasped. Flynden let go of her arm. They slipped on the wet stone, fell onto their butts, and started to slide. Rough stones bruised her arms, legs and back. The hand on her wrist slammed into the stone and tightened its grip on her more. Sophie cried out and tried to find a hold somewhere to stop the slide, but she kept sliding and bumping into the stones. It hurt but not like the vise grip around her wrist. She bit her lip until she tasted blood. The slide was short, and soon they slid to a stop at a narrow ledge. Below ran a small stream stinking worse than dirty toilets and even worse than the gray hand squeezing her wrist. Sophie gagged, and her stomach heaved. Flynden jumped aside just in time for her to throw up again. Exhausted, she sat back on her heels.

A faint glow came down the tunnel as Pelifeles slid toward them. His white fur glowed and lit the wet stones all around.

"You could've chosen somewhere less wet," Pelifeles hissed and flicked his paws. "This is disgusting."

"One good reason why Makimus won't be looking for us here," Flynden said and frowned. He sounded disgusted, too. "Pelifeles, can you take the hand off Sophie's arm?"

"I might."

"Please, Peli. It hurts so much," Sophie begged. "It's squeezing my hand right off."

"Let me see." Pelifeles sniffed the hand when Sophie shoved it under his nose. "Hm, I think it could work," he mumbled. "As soon as the hand lets go, pull your arm away."

"Okay."

"Ready?"

Sophie nodded.

"Flyn, when the hand lets go, pull the sack over it," Pelifeles said.

"No. Didn't you see the light sparking off of my hands before?"

"Never mind your hands now. Do what I say."

Flynden frowned and looked at his hands but scooted closer on his knees.

Sophie cried out when the gray hand tightened even more. It would break all the bones in her wrist.

For a moment, the cat sniffed the hand, then bit into the thumb's fleshy part. Sparks exploded like fireworks off the hand and bounced everywhere. Sophie squeezed her eyes shut but when the hand let her wrist go, she snatched it away, clutching it close. The gray hand opened, dropped the Flora blossom, and tried to grab the cat around the neck. Pelifeles let go and jumped backward but wasn't quick enough. The fingers tightened around one of his front paws.

Pelifeles hissed and spat. More sparks jumped off him and the gray hand, too. Flynden pulled the sack on like a glove, grabbed the hand and tried to pry it off Pelifeles' paw. With a tiny explosion, the hand let go but threw Pelifeles a few feet. Right away, the hand grabbed Flynden's instead like shaking hands with him. Flynden's brows furrowed and he didn't look like himself anymore with his face all scrunched up and distorted into a frightening grimace. With his other hand, he grabbed the gray one by the wrist. A blinding white light flared from his hands. The hand wriggled like a caught fish. Then the white light sparked, flashed, sizzled, and finally winked out.

Flynden's eyes widened, and his mouth hung open. As soon as he dropped the gray hand, it crumpled, leaving a tiny pile of ashes.

"Wow." Sophie stared. "How did you do that?"

Flynden moved his head from side to side and said nothing, staring at his hands and the ashes on the stone.

"Flyn, are you okay?"

First, she thought he would throw up because he looked like he was gagging, but then he sobbed.

"Flyn, what's the matter. What happened?" Sophie leaned over, placing one hand on his back. He shrugged her off.

"I, I killed Master Eigil's hand," he sobbed.

"It wasn't Master Eigil's hand anymore, Flyn." Pelifeles padded over. His fur was singed a bit but he looked okay otherwise. "It was something evil, made so by Makimus to guard the Flora blossom."

"What's happening to me, Peli?" Flynden cried and kept holding up his hands like they hurt or didn't belong to him.

"I don't know, Flyn," Pelifeles said and his yellow eyes blinked in the dark. He pushed his head into Flynden's side. "Looks like you might not be who we think you are."

Shouts echoed behind them in the tunnel. The men had caught up with them.

"Come on, we have to leave," the cat said and jumped away.

Sophie scrambled up and pulled on Flynden's arm. "Come on, Flyn." She started after Pelifeles with his softly glowing fur when she remembered the Flora blossom. "The blossom, where is it?" Sophie whispered.

Pelifeles came back and searched in the dark. "Over here," he said.

The blossom sparkled, and she jumped to pick it up.

"You shouldn't touch the Flora blossom with your

bare hand, Sophie," Pelifeles said.

"Why not?"

"Not sure. We don't know what its powerful magic will do to you."

"Okay. Then where's the sack?" She searched the ground and found the sack near the hand's ashes. Like before, she slid her hand into the sack and picked the blossom off the floor. Even through the cloth, warmth spread into her hand and arm. She didn't have time to wonder if this was good or bad because more shouts sounded in the darkness behind them.

"Let's go, Flyn." Sophie pushed him.

Flynden shook his head as if coming out of a trance and dropped his hands. Together, they rushed into the tunnel, Pelifeles leading the way.

❧ ❧

They ran along a narrow ledge down the stinking tunnel. Sophie pinched her nose and tried to breathe through her mouth, but the stink was so bad she could taste it, too. Yuk. When would they get to the end of this? Fresh air wouldn't come soon enough.

Daylight's narrow beams speared from airshafts onto the ledge as they ran past them—almost like riding in a car past streetlights. Pelifeles was no longer glowing because the lights' round patches showed enough of the ledge.

The running feet behind them echoed louder and closer. It sounded like an army coming after them. Then the tunnel curved and light shone up ahead. Sophie ran faster, her arms pumping at her sides. She squeezed her fist tight around the sack with the Flora blossom.

Pelifeles cleared the tunnel ahead of her and disappeared around the corner. Then Flyn and she were out, too. Squinting into the sunlight, they veered left. Sophie sucked in the fresh air.

"This way," Flynden panted and took the lead. Pelifeles was gone.

Sophie and Flynden rushed together into the forest, away from the sewage canal that curved to the right. Thorns and branches snatched at them as they crashed past trees into bushes. Flynden zigzagged between trees, and Sophie followed. The four men dressed in black sprinted from the tunnel behind them and would soon catch up. Flynden and she would have to hide somewhere. They couldn't outrun those men.

Sophie and Flynden burst from the trees onto a wide path. Flynden swung left, heading down that path. Sophie stayed close. Here, it was easier to run but the men would catch up quickly.

The path wound through the woods, blocking the view ahead and behind. Where was Flynden going? Her breath whooshed in her ears competing with her pounding heart.

The men crashed through the bushes, way too close. Sophie and Flynden doubled their efforts and ran harder around the next bend. Up ahead, Makimus stood in the path's middle, arms raised, his wicked yellow-green light glowing in his hands. He threw it at them and hit Flynden in the chest. With a scream, Flynden stumbled and collapsed onto the ground.

Sophie wanted to help but had to hide the blossom, fast. Makimus would have her any second, too. She flung herself into the bushes to the right. The thicket wasn't as dense here. She dashed between the trees, the men closing in behind her. Her eyes darted left and right. Up ahead, a tree stood twisted and bent. As soon as her gaze fell on the hole in the trunk a bit higher than her head, she made up her mind. She sprinted up to the tree, raised her hand, and like a basketball player, slam-dunked the sack with the blossom without missing a step. Then she circled back. Makimus would have her soon anyway but not the Flora blossom. Would she stay strong and not tell him where it was when the yellow-green ropes tightened around her?

She scrambled from the bushes onto the path close to where Flynden lay still and fell to her knees beside him. *Phew.* He was still breathing.

Makimus was striding toward them. Would he kill her now? Her throat tightened and she struggled for air. Camshron was coming up behind Makimus with a sneer on his face. No help would come from him.

Makimus raised one hand and sent a string of yellow-green light her way. She ducked, but not fast enough, and it hit her in the chest. She tingled all over from her scalp to her toes. The magic stripped away Pelifeles' disguise and she looked like herself again. She kicked and screamed when it wound around her torso until it cut her off and squeezed the air from her lungs.

Camshron cackled like an old woman.

"What did you do with the hand and the Flora blossom?" Makimus demanded, low and dangerous. His voice was somewhere above her, his feet and his robe's hem swam before her eyes.

"Lost it," Sophie breathed. She wouldn't tell him anything.

"The truth."

"Back in the sewer," she choked. Any second now,

she would pass out or die. "It fell into..." The yellow-green ropes squeezed tighter and she collapsed on top of Flynden. *Mommy, help me*, she pleaded with the beloved face in her mind. Then everything went black.

❧ *Chapter 12* ❧

Sophie came to with a fuzzy mind buzzing like a beehive. At least she was alive. How long had she been out? Where was Flynden? She tried to kick, but her arms and legs wouldn't move. Only her eyelids did. Makimus had done something to her. Somewhere up ahead, a tiny voice whimpered. Bramble? What happened to Stace?

She hung over someone's shoulder like a potato sack. One of the men who chased them? The man made no sound, his fingers dug into her legs as he marched through the darkness. How could he see anything? Sophie tried to scream but her voice wasn't working either. Soon, her captor stopped and placed her on the floor. A torch hissed and flickered, blinding her. The heat from the flame was so close it seared her skin. A rotting smell rose from nearby. The sewer again?

Makimus towered over her. "I shall return," he said and stepped back. "Perhaps when you have had time to think, you will tell me the truth about where you came from and where you have hidden the Flora blossom. Until then…" He turned away.

Camshron cackled his high-pitch laugh somewhere in the darkness behind Makimus.

Another man placed Bramble beside her. The girl rolled into a ball and grabbed Sophie's arm, still whimpering and crying. *Ssh, it's okay*, Sophie wanted to say, but no words made it out of her mouth, only drool.

Four ropes tightened on all four sides of her. The floor that was really some kind of wooden platform now rose off the ground. In the torch light, two men operated a crank and a pulley connected to a beam, lifting the platform with the thick ropes. The men swung the beam around and pushed the platform forward. She had to get Bramble and herself off this thing. Still, she couldn't move. The platform swung back and forth and wobbled. Another man stepped up, and together the men released the crank. Makimus and Camshron stood watching; they rose while she and Bramble sank.

In the next moment, when Sophie could move her arms and legs again, she rolled onto her hands and knees.

"What are you doing?" Sophie screamed.

The platform sank below the councilors and the men's feet, leaving only the rocks' black sharp edges and darkness. Sophie pried Bramble's fingers off her arm and edged to one side, digging her fingernails into the wood when the platform slammed into the rocks. Far below her, something glowed red. A fire? Far above, the torch light flickered like a faint star. Down and down the platform went. With every foot it sank, it turned darker, but soon, the glow far below them tinted everything red like a setting sun. Sophie scooted back to the center and hugged Bramble close. The little girl trembled and whimpered, grabbing fistfuls of Sophie's tunic. The platform swung back and forth, bumped into the rock, and quivered. Sophie gasped when it dropped a foot, but then it steadied and kept sinking fast.

"Ssh, Bramble." Sophie made soothing sounds, but Bramble didn't seem to be listening. "I have to look where we're going. Okay?" Again, she had to pry the girl's hands off her before she could roll onto her stomach and peek over the edge. A big red and black flower moved as if standing in the wind, or like swaying in an under-water current. Some kind of rubble and debris littered the ground, but she couldn't make out what it was.

With a thud, the platform hit the bottom. No, she wouldn't get off. The platform was the one thing that would get Bramble and her back out.

No sooner had she thought it, the platform tipped, and Bramble rolled off. Sophie reached for the girl while grabbing the wood, holding on as best as she could, but her fingers closed on air and Bramble rolled into the dirt. The platform bounced up and down. Sophie dug her fingers into the wood. Splinters pierced her skin, and pain shot through her hand up her arm. Finally, her hand lost its grip, and she slid off the platform, landing beside Bramble.

"You creeps!" she yelled.

They both sat and watched the platform jerk and move up much faster than it had come down. In no time, it disappeared into the darkness. The torch now flickered far above, but not for long because soon the platform blocked it. For a second, the light appeared again but then winked out, and then there was nothing but black above.

Bramble wailed. Sophie put her arms around the girl and pulled her close, patting her head. Fear and panic settled in. How would they ever get out? She took a few calming breaths but shook so hard that her teeth rattled and butterflies fluttered in her stomach.

Bones littered the ground, lots of them. They looked way too big for people's bones, but some were smaller and could be from people. Would Makimus let her die here, too? He'd said he would be back. But how long would Bramble and she have to be down here? The stench rose off the ground, those bones, and the black and red flower. Sophie shuddered and hugged the girl closer, hoping to give and get comfort.

Despite being stinky, the flower radiated warmth. Just in case, Sophie grabbed Bramble and pulled her as far away as she could into a niche with fewer bones. Sophie kicked the space clean and sat Bramble on the ground. Her gut feeling told her it would be safer to stay away from the flower. Kicking more bones aside, she sat beside Bramble and cradled the girl's head in her lap.

"It'll be okay, Bramble." She pushed the hair off Bramble's face while whispering her name.

"I want to go home. I want Thithle," Bramble cried.

"Ssh, I know. We'll find a way out," Sophie said. How would she keep that promise? She didn't even know where they were other than the obvious dark pit.

They sat and watched the dark red flower swaying. Bramble cried for a while longer but then fell asleep in her arms. Sophie grew tired, too, and her eyelids closed. She tipped to the side, righted herself, but in the end, she fell asleep anyway.

❧ ❦

"Wake up, Sophie."

Bramble's voice reached her from far away. Two small fists punched her arm.

"Wake up, quick."

Sophie surfaced, taking a moment to remember where she lay. She sat and rubbed her eyes. "What?"

"There, there. Look." Bramble's fingers dug deeper. "Red eyes. A beast. It will eat us."

Within the darkness, two red eyes blinked, and blinked again.

"Ssh, it's okay, Bramble. I'm here." Sophie pulled the girl closer. What could she do other than hide her fear so Bramble wouldn't be more scared?

A bushy white stripe lit up and glowed on top of a feline's head, starting between the brows, travelling over its head, down the back, along the long tail, and ending in a bushy tuft. The stripe lit the stone walls and the bones. Larger than a lion or cougar, the cat creature crouched unmoving, blinking lazily, and its raspy breath broke the stillness following Bramble's words.

Sophie grabbed Bramble and pulled her farther back into the niche, never taking her eyes off the creature.

"Bramble," Sophie whispered into the girl's ear. "Did you see where it came from? Where it came in?"

Bramble trembled and nodded.

Great, that would be their way out if they could get to the door without being pounced on.

"Where is the door?"

Bramble shook her head. "No door," Bramble whispered back. "It was a flower first and now it's a beast."

A funny queasy feeling churned in Sophie's stomach. The flower is the beast; the beast is the flower. More no-good magic and no way out after all. Hopefully, it had eaten before they came and wasn't hungry anymore. Now all those bones made sense.

"Bramble," she whispered closer to the girl's ear again,

"you think you can climb with me up the wall?"

"You won't get a foot off the ground before I have you." The creature hissed and raised itself onto its plate-size paws.

Sophie and Bramble pressed into the niche, pulling their knees up to hide behind.

"There is no way out," the creature growled. "I tried. Many times. More often than I care to remember."

"Who…who are you?" Sophie asked as calmly as she could, but her teeth rattled in her mouth, making her stutter.

"Never mind who I am. Who are you?" It lowered its muzzle. Foul breath stank up the air in the niche even more. The whiskers twitched.

Maybe if she talked to it and kept it distracted, sooner or later someone would come and rescue them. Flynden and Pelifeles had found her before. Stace would help. The other councilors wouldn't stand for this. Someone would be coming. She had to believe it. This remote ever-so-small hope gave Sophie some courage.

"I am Sophie." She raised her voice and placed her hand on her chest. "This is Bramble." She grabbed Bramble's shoulders but looked at the creature.

"I am neither dumb nor deaf, girl. No point in yelling," the creature growled.

Sophie would have backed up more if the rock wasn't already poking into her back. It looked funny the way the creature moved its muzzle, and its nose twitched from side to side.

"Sorry. I didn't mean…"

"I know what you meant. Never mind." The creature rose and stretched its long legs and large paws forward. It stuck up its behind while whipping its tail in the air once, then twice, before settling back and tucking the front paws under the way Pelifeles did.

Bramble sat open-mouthed, watching it.

"Who brought you here? No, no, don't tell me, let me guess." The creature thrust its nose forward, closer. "Councilor Makimus."

Sophie nodded. "You know him?"

"Know him? You jest." The creature roared. Long, dirty canine teeth protruded from the upper and lower jaw. More jagged teeth lined the dark red gums. "What have two little girls like you done to displease the high and mighty Councilor Makimus?"

"We stole the Flora blossom," Bramble said before Sophie could stop her, nodding to give her words more importance. Ever since the creature had spoken, Bramble seemed no longer afraid of it, merely curious.

"What are you talking about, child?"

"She means that we stole something and Makimus caught us." No point in telling the creature the whole story.

"Hm, stealing is wrong. Did your mothers not teach you that?"

"Yes, but we had to this time." Sophie wanted to justify her behavior for some reason without giving the real reason away.

"Yes, we had to," Bramble said. "The man with the big rings hurt Ma and Da."

"He hurt many people, little girl." Then the creature hunkered down even closer. "Where are your ma and da now?"

"They have gone to sleep," Bramble sniffled. "Forever."

The cat creature moved even closer, nose raised

toward them. The big slits in its nose flared, taking in their scents.

"Something smells familiar about you, little girl." The nose moved closer. "The light hair. The blue eyes."

Bramble reached out with her hand, but the creature pulled back.

"Do you have a brother, little girl?"

"Yes, Thithle." Bramble nodded. "But I don't know where he is."

"I know where he is," the creature whispered. Its glowing white stripe lit the way as it jumped away from them, flinging bones everywhere. "Come."

Sophie held onto Bramble and watched the creature slink through the pit.

"Come," it said again.

Bramble struggled free, got up and walked toward the creature. Sophie tried to snatch her back, but the girl shook her head. "It says it knows where Thithle is. I want to look."

"No, it's too dangerous." It might eat us, she added in her mind.

As if Bramble had heard her thoughts, she said, "It won't eat us. It wants to show us where Thithle is."

Sophie hesitated. Well, the creature could've eaten them already.

"Okay, let's see."

Hands clasped, they followed the creature over and around the bones to the pit's other side. Sophie tried to slow Bramble down, but the girl pulled her hard, unfazed.

The stripe on the creature's back glowed like an eerie white snake wriggling through the dark pit and lit the bones and rocks for seconds before it moved on. The creature crouched low in front of a wide cut in the rock. It sniffed something on the ground, raised its head, and regarded them through red slits.

"Come."

They inched closer. Bramble gasped, let go of Sophie's hand, and rushed forward. The creature slunk aside.

"Thithle!" Bramble fell to her knees beside a kid curled up way too close to the creature's paws.

Sophie eyed the creature and sidled around it. The kid had white-blond hair like Bramble's; dirt and sweat caked it to his head. Thank goodness, there wasn't any blood. If Bramble hadn't said his name, Sophie wouldn't have been able to tell it was a boy. His clothes were ripped and dirty like the rest of him, but his chest rose and fell. Thank goodness, he was still alive.

"Thithle," Bramble whispered and placed her small hands under her brother's head, trying to lift it. "Thithle, it's me, Bramble, and Sophie. Look." She pointed to Sophie, but no matter what she said or did, the boy didn't move. Bramble started crying, calling his name over and over. She looked over to Sophie. "Is he gone to sleep forever?" she asked.

"No, Bramble, he's still breathing, but maybe he's hurt."

Her eyes flicked to the creature who watched them.

"I will not eat you," the creature said and backed up, placing its head onto the big paws.

Sophie knelt beside Bramble. She felt the boy's chest, neck, head, and limbs. She had no idea what to look for. What if he had broken bones? Would she be able to tell? He didn't seem to be hurt, but he'd gone off somewhere deep inside of himself and didn't respond to Bramble or seem to notice anything around him.

"Thistle?" Sophie gently shook him. "Thistle, can you hear us?"

"Thithle, can you hear?" Bramble mimicked.

The boy whimpered and curled into a tighter ball, then lay still again.

"What happened to him?" Sophie rounded on the creature. "What did you do?"

The creature lifted its head.

"I have done nothing. He fell from the wall as he tried to climb up and has been lying there like this ever since." It blew out through its nose, and the stinky breath sprayed dust all over. "He is not injured, only afraid."

"How do you know?"

After letting out another breath, the creature said, "I can smell his fear."

"Thithle, you don't have to be afraid anymore," Bramble shook her brother's shoulder. "We'll help you."

The creature snorted.

"Don't be afraid," Bramble said again.

Thistle whimpered and covered his head with his arms.

"It won't eat us." Bramble shook her head. "The kitty's nice."

Sophie almost snorted too but decided to say nothing. Whatever Bramble did to get her brother out of his funk was fine with her, and maybe Bramble was right about the creature.

After a bit more coaxing, Thistle raised one elbow and peeked from under it, first at Bramble, then at Sophie, and at last at the creature who stared back at him.

"How come you're here, Bramble? What happened?" he asked in a tiny voice.

"Bron. He took me to the councilors and said they would turn me into a mouse. He wanted his stones, but the councilors wouldn't give them back. When I saw the man with the big rings, I was scared. Then I don't remember until I woke up and Stace took care of me."

"Who's that girl?" He pointed at Sophie.

"That's Sophie. She and Stace and Flynden stole the Flora blossom, and I helped. Makimus caught all of us."

Thistle sat up and hugged Bramble close. "He knows who we are."

"What do you mean, knows who you are?" Sophie sat cross-legged before them.

"He knows we saw him?" Bramble opened her eyes wide. What the creature hadn't accomplished with its terrifying looks, the thought of Makimus did. Bramble trembled and leaned into her brother.

"Yes, Makimus took one look at us. How could he not notice our hair and skin?"

"Explain yourself, children, you are holding me in suspense." The creature raised its head higher. "What did you see Makimus do that he wants to hurt you? Is it because you are pale ones?"

Thistle sat straighter, still holding on to Bramble. "We are not pale ones," he said.

"Yes, you are, boy. Now explain why Makimus wants to hurt you."

Sophie had been called a pale one, too. Were pale ones just people with blond or red hair and light skin like hers or did it mean something bad?

Thistle glowered at the creature, as though forgetting for a second that he was afraid. Then he said, "A few moons ago, Bramble and I were playing in the storage cellar beneath our kitchen. Ma forbade us to play there and would shoo us out when she found us. But that day she didn't see us. We crept up the stairs to the cover and watched her through the cracks. Then the man with the big rings came…" Thistle wiped his nose and eyes on his sleeve. "We saw only his hands. They grabbed Ma's neck and squeezed. Yellow-green light filled the kitchen, and sour apple smell seeped all the way into the cellar." Thistle sniffed and pulled the snot back into his nose.

"Go on," said the creature.

"Ma fell to the floor, the hands withdrew, and the man left."

Bramble nodded. "I wanted to help Ma, but Thithle held me tight and covered my mouth so I was quiet."

"We waited, but the man with the big rings didn't come back." Thistle took a deep breath. "Then we climbed from the cellar and ran to Ma. I knew when the eyes of our farm animals went all glassy and staring, they were dead. Ma's eyes were like that and I knew. Bramble shook her, thinking she was sleeping. She didn't understand."

"I understand," Bramble cried. "I do. Ma is gone away. Sleeping forever." Then she started crying in earnest.

The creature stuck its nose toward Bramble and purred, a loud rumble deep in its chest.

Thistle pulled his sister closer and clutched her against him. "Ssh."

"And your da?" the creature asked.

"Da lay in the barn, crumpled in the straw. He had glassy eyes, too."

"Didn't you know who the man with the big rings was?" Sophie asked.

Thistle shook his head. "Not until the men brought me to Council Hall."

The creature sprang away and roared, kicking more

dirt and bones around. Sophie and the siblings cowered, but it did no harm. It started pacing and circling the pit, sniffing them each time it passed. After the third time around, it stopped close to them and crouched.

"Makimus betrayed the High Council, his gift, and the vows he made. He has abused and killed people. He must be stopped—and punished. If I could get my paws on him, I would rip him apart."

"Yes, rip him apart," Bramble growled and clenched her fists, banging them together, then pulling them apart like ripping something in half.

"We will have our chance, little Bramble," the creature purred and gazed at the girl. "If someone comes to rescue you, you must promise to take me with you."

"I promise," Bramble said.

"Not so fast, Bramble, we don't know if we can keep the promise," Thistle said.

"I want to promise. We rip him apart."

Bramble did her fist thing again and hissed. Sophie cringed listening to Bramble talk like that, but she wouldn't mind punching and hitting Makimus a few times herself.

"Where have you come from?" The creature rounded on Sophie with an unsettling stare. "You do not talk, smell, or look like one of us."

"Em. I…" Sophie stuttered. Should she tell the creature? Why not? What could it hurt? So, she talked about Tommy's funeral, but left out the part where she hit Trudy with the stone. And how she met the old man Eigil, then ran through the gray passage, and everything up to the point until Makimus caught them.

Bramble nodded when her name came up like she wanted to make sure the creature believed the story.

"So, you see," Sophie finished, "we think I have to take the blossom home with me because Master Eigil needs it. He must know about Makimus and the bad things he's done. Now we're stuck down here and can't go anywhere."

The creature said nothing for a long time until Sophie wondered if it had even listened because it had its eyes closed. After a while, the eyelids parted, and the creature squinted out of red slits.

"Master Eigil is a good man, a brave man. He knew. He knows everything."

"Everything what?" Sophie asked.

"Everything," the creature said before it got up and moved back to the pile of bones and skin in the pit's center. There, it stood on all four paws for a little while, mumbling to itself. A few minutes later, it pushed off with its front paws and balanced on its hind legs that merged into a stem. Roots spread from it and slithered over the bones into the ground. Its front legs and paws shortened into branches and leaves and more grew from the stem. In the end, the creature bent its head back and gave a final growl before the head morphed into the crimson blossom making the pit glow red.

❧ *Chapter 13* ❧

"We have to go back and find them." Flynden balled his fists.

"We can not go back, Flynden, I told you a hundred times." Stace threw up his arms and groaned. "I am sorry."

"I don't care. We have to go back. No matter what." Flynden's back hurt, but he wasn't going to give up. The lashes still stung. Well, Stace had received an extra ten lashes and lost his position at Council Hall, which would have to hurt even more, but he wasn't complaining. He even excused the punishment. In his opinion, they had done wrong.

After their lashings, guards had dropped them outside the city gates with nothing but their shredded clothes on their stinging backs.

Now, they rested in a small clearing not far off the road to Urbinter arguing about what to do next. Pain stoked Flynden's anger, determination, and the want to hurt Makimus back. Makimus had ordered the men in black to take Sophie and Bramble away. Where to? He didn't know. Maybe back to the dungeon. He wanted to go back to Gwern to find out, but Stace wouldn't let him and didn't want to listen. Maybe he should go back alone. With Pelifeles, they could free the girls. Maybe Stace was right, they could never go back to Council Hall in broad daylight. Anger balled like a tight fist in his stomach. They had to find a way to free Sophie and Bramble. Flynden kicked the fallen tree Stace sat on and stubbed his toes.

"Ouch!" He hopped around on one foot. Now his foot hurt, too.

"Calm down, Flynden." Stace's face reddened, his brows furrowed, and very unlike him, he narrowed his eyes into mean slits. "We must think about this first. Makimus figured out our plan. I think he set a trap for us and we walked right into it."

"How so?" Flynden crossed his arms and frowned at his brother.

"I do not know." Stace dropped his arms and hung his head. "Somehow he must have found out. He may have discovered that Sophie had gone missing from her cell."

Stace eased himself forward, took a few deep breaths, and placed his hands onto his knees while he scrunched up his face in pain.

"We need another plan," he said. "A better one than we had. We have to find out where Makimus has taken Sophie and Bramble."

"Then let's go back and find out." Flynden jammed his fists into his waist. "I bet Pelifeles knows where they are or knows how to find them. Maybe we can ask Kir and Calleo, or even Councilor Druce Lar. They'll help." Breathless, Flynden slumped down beside his brother.

"Perhaps." Stace groaned, bending forward, stretching his back. "But we cannot go back to Council Hall. Councilor Makimus made it clear. We will be punished again, perhaps worse. Where is the cat when we need him?"

"I don't know, but we can't leave Sophie and Bramble."

"I did not say that. I fear for them, too," Stace said.

"Then what do we do?" Flynden banged his fist into the fallen tree and received a few splinters. Soon every bone and patch of skin would be bruised.

"We need help from someone who has the power to make a difference." Stace winced as he lifted his arm and scratched the top of his head, then laid a hand on Flynden's arm. "We will visit the Mother Flora and ask her." He stood. "Master Eigil trusts her and often confided in her. He told me so himself. I think we can trust her as well." Then he grimaced. "She might even have a remedy for our backs."

Flynden agreed, but a heavy lump settled in his stomach. They were wasting time and he felt like a coward for not going back right away to look for Sophie and Bramble. Tears came unbidden and he wiped them away. As powerful as the Mother Flora was, could she stop Councilor Makimus? Would she offer help when she found out they had stolen the Flora blossom from the Council Chamber? They would find out soon enough.

With his mouth set in a grim line and a hanging head, he followed his brother down the narrow path deeper into the ancient forest.

❧ ❧

In the pit, a squeaking noise woke Sophie. She blinked into the gloom.

The creature-turned-flower cast its red glow from the pit's center. It had not changed back. *Phew*. Better that way. Though it hadn't eaten them and had even been quite friendly, it had scared her, and maybe it would eat them later.

Bramble had slid to the ground beside her brother and lay curled up with her head on his crooked arm, sleeping. Poor kids. They had been through so much. How could she ever complain again about anything after all they'd been through?

Bramble's white-blond hair curled around her face, one lock hugging her ear. Gently, Sophie touched it and the soft lock curled around her finger.

Sophie searched the darkness above her for whatever was making the squeaking and rattling sounds. Way up, a light blinked on and off, blocked ever so often by the swinging platform rattling toward them.

"Bramble. Thistle," she whispered, excited. "Wake up. Someone's coming."

Bramble whined a bit, but sat and rubbed her eyes. Thistle woke instantly, peering into the dark above them.

"Someone's coming to take us out?" he asked, disbelief and hope mixed in his voice, and he pulled Bramble onto his lap

"Hopefully," Sophie said.

"The man with the big rings?" Bramble asked and pressed against Thistle.

"Maybe. I hope not." Maybe Makimus came to check if she'd changed her mind. Sophie shook her head. No fat chance she would tell him anything.

"I'm not going if he comes. I stay with the kitty," Bramble cried.

Sophie didn't like the idea, but if she had to choose, it

would be the creature and the pit for her, too.

"Come on, we'll go hide," Sophie said and lifted Bramble out of Thistle's arms.

They scrambled into a dark niche. Something furry scurried away. Sophie shivered and hugged Bramble. The girl squirmed and started talking, but Sophie shushed her.

"Be quiet, Bramble. Just in case. Okay?"

Bramble nodded against Sophie's chest and calmed down. Beside them, Thistle hugged himself, rocking back and forth, trembling.

The platform squeaked into view tinged with red from the flower's glow and landed with a thud on the ground. A slim tall figure wrapped in a cloak stepped off. It couldn't be Makimus because he was bigger than this person. Sophie stayed hidden with the siblings and watched. The figure walked around the flower, bending close, then stepping away and looking at the bones. The person stopped and straightened, pushing off the hood. Apprentice Calleo looked exhausted and worried. He balled his fist, twisted it around, and opened it to a deep yellow light forming into a ball on his palm. He flung the ball into the air and it zoomed straight to where the light hung at the pit's rim. A licorice scent filled the pit. Sophie's mouth watered. A licorice stick would be nice now. She would like that, or better yet, licorice-flavored gum.

Calleo watched the light disappear above his head before he whirled on the spot, his face sad and serious.

"Calleo, we're here," Sophie called and crawled from the niche.

"Calleo, we here," Bramble echoed right behind her. Thistle trailed after them.

Calleo's face brightened with a big smile and relief,

and suddenly, the gloomy pit didn't look so gloomy anymore. He ran toward them and scooped Bramble into his arms, hugging her close. Bramble giggled as he placed a big kiss on top of her head and sat her on the platform. He urged Sophie and Thistle with frantic hand movements to join them before releasing another licorice-smelling ball of yellow light into the air. He tugged twice on the platform's rope.

"I want to say bye to the kitty," Bramble said and before they could stop her, she hopped off the platform.

Calleo shook his head and tried to grab her, but Bramble was quick and ran toward the flower.

"No!" Thistle yelled.

"Bramble," Sophie called. "Come back!"

"No!" Bramble yelled. "We promised."

Sophie shook her head. "Not now. The kitty has to stay."

Bramble didn't listen and touched one of the fleshy leaves. "Come, kitty, we have to go." Her voice rang loud and clear like a bell.

At the sound of Bramble's voice and the touch of her hand, the flower shook and shivered, and began to turn.

"No, Bramble, come!" Thistle screamed. "Don't touch." He tried to pull her away, but Bramble struggled with him.

Sophie jumped off the platform and rushed to help him. The flower morphed fast, its leaves and stem elongated into limbs while the head shaped from the blossom.

For a moment, Calleo stared. Horror showed on his face before he grabbed Bramble around her waist and pulled her away. Sophie stood watching, mesmerized by the flower's changing. The plant grew until it stood taller than Calleo. In seconds, the creature crouched before them. First, no one moved. Then Calleo pushed Sophie toward the platform and grabbed the siblings together, dashing after her.

The creature roared and reared. Calleo gathered his magic in both hands and flung it into the beast. The creature shrieked. Singed fur mingled with the pit's stink and the licorice smell. *Yuck.*

The creature came at them, furious but not hurt. Calleo gathered Sophie and the siblings behind him on the platform and jerked the rope a few times. Slowly, too slowly, the platform rose. The creature jumped, incensed and screaming.

Calleo's next volley hit it in the face, throwing it back. Stumbling and twisting, it rolled into the dirt and right back onto its paws.

The platform rose, quicker now. The creature jumped high, trying to reach them. Bramble wrestled herself away from Thistle, latched onto Calleo's leg, dug her fingers into the leggings, and tore at his leg.

"No, don't hurt the kitty. It only wants to come with us."

Calleo flinched. The second he didn't pay attention, the creature jumped once more and sent the platform careening into the rocks. Sophie dug her fingers into the trembling wood. On hands and knees, she tried to stay put. Calleo stumbled, but grabbed Bramble and kept one hand on the rope. Thistle hung onto a rope on the platform corner.

The creature fell back, rolled over onto its feet, and attacked again. Its front paws pulled the platform down the few feet it had gained. With one paw, it reached onto the platform and clawed the wood. Sophie jerked away, but the claws caught her and ripped across her back and legs. Her screams bounced around the pit and echoed off the rock.

Calleo let go of the rope and sent two magic volleys into the creature's face. With a high-pitched scream, it fell back, kicking the platform with a whack into the rocks. With a lot of luck, they managed to stay on. Swinging back and forth, it rose at last without stopping. Sophie hung on with her legs dangling over the side. Calleo grabbed her tunic and pulled her up. Pain exploded up and down her back where the claws had injured her. Red-hot sparks flashed before her eyes. She lay flat on her stomach and caught a final glimpse of the pit's bottom.

The creature curled up and pawed its face. Woozy, Sophie dropped her head onto the wood.

❧　❧

The platform jostled and jerked. Pain ripped through her, keeping her from passing out. It took forever to reach the rim, but once there, the platform shook and quivered one final time and settled on the ground. Murmurs greeted her. She tried to move and open her eyes, but she couldn't even move her eyelids. The pain gripped her tighter. She wanted to cry out, but she only moaned because her mouth wouldn't work either. Someone lifted her. More pain sliced through her back and legs.

"A narrow escape," a familiar deep voice boomed close to her ear. "Where did the creature come from?"

The flower. It's the flower, she wanted to say but couldn't move or talk or explain anything. For a few seconds there was silence. Did Calleo sign his answer?

"How did it come to be in this pit?" the deep voice asked.

More silence.

"Perhaps," the deep voice said. "Let me look after the children first."

Gentle bony fingers examined her back and her legs. More screams came with the pain. Then a cool gentle feeling spread through her and took the pain away, soothing her. A fresh lemony scent tickled her nose.

"Sophie?" The deep voice called her. "Child, can you hear me?"

Yes, yes. Those words rang only in her head. Her lips didn't move no matter how hard she tried. Her eyes obeyed this time and opened like two little butterflies. Druce Lar's lined face with his warm gray eyes looked down on her. Then there were four eyes and two faces swimming in and out of focus, making her dizzy. Something wet ran down her cheeks.

"You will be fine, child," Druce Lar said, and his gentle fingers brushed along her forehead. His voice lifted away, no longer close. "Calleo, take Nelwyna and the children to the ancient forest and hide. Hasten. Go now."

Strong arms lifted and cradled her. So gentle. Daddy? Was that Dad picking her up? Mommy? Where was Mom? Had they come to take her home? Tommy, too?

Her body rocked in the cradle of two strong arms carrying her away.

She dreamed of home, walking through the empty house. Mommy? Daddy? Tommy? Where was everyone? She ran into the backyard, slipped and fell, and hit her head. When she got up, she sat on the floor in her friend Dianne's room, playing by herself with Barbies. This would be her chance. Dianne had told her about her mom's piggy bank in the big bedroom. Sophie sneaked from the room, across the hall and the soft carpet with the orange and turquoise southwestern pattern, straight into Dianne's mom's bedroom where the big walk-in closet stood open. On the top shelf above the clothes, the piggy bank hid beneath spare pillows. Dianne had called it a piggy bank but it was only an old shoebox stuffed with money. She grabbed one bundle of twenty-dollar bills and shoved them into her jeans pockets. Now, she could run away with Tommy.

Steps came up the stairs. Someone called her, telling her Trudy was taking Tommy to the hospital. Sophie ran and ran and ran, but she couldn't make it. The ambulance reached the far end of her street. "Tommy!" Sophie screamed. Trudy leaned out of the window, waving and calling. "We don't need you. I'll take care of Tommy." No! No! Tommy! Wait for me! Without stopping or even slowing down, the ambulance disappeared around the corner, taking Tommy away—forever.

The arms still held her tightly, cradling her. While she drifted, time seemed to pass slowly like wading through honey. A fresh peppermint smell laced the air and made her breathing easier. A breeze stirred her hair and cooled her hot face. Close by, a horse nickered. Its rich smell reached her. A horse? She liked this dream better. Did Dad get her a horse? Did he want to surprise her?

Gentle arms lifted her onto the back of the horse. Hands placed hers onto the horse's neck. She grabbed the coarse mane. Someone lifted a kid onto the horse behind her. Was Tommy coming, too? Then someone else sat behind Tommy. Mom?

"I apologize, Nelwyna, but we need to ask this of you. Go with Calleo to the ancient forest. Try to find Flynden and Stace." Druce Lar's voice again. *Who was Nelwyna?*

"How am I supposed to know where those boys are?"

A raspy voice asked and sounded like an older woman who smoked too much and drank a lot of whiskey.

"I assume they are between here and Urbinter or the Garden, somewhere within the ancient forest."

"Fine. Now I am a beast of burden, am I?"

"Nelwyna, we need your help. If someone can find them, it would be you."

"Fine, I said. But I do not have to like it, do I?"

Someone slapped the horse on the neck. It shook its head as if to shake it off, like it was annoyed.

"Hold on." Druce Lar stepped away. "You will be safe with Nelwyna and Calleo. Listen to them."

Would this woman Nelwyna help them? Sophie couldn't ask. Her voice still didn't work. Did the woman own the horse? As the horse walked and swayed, small hands grabbed her tunic from behind, digging into her sides. Hold on, Tommy.

Sophie managed to croak but those words stayed in her head. She slumped forward, and the horse's even rhythm rocked her to sleep.

❧ *Chapter 14* ❦

Sophie drifted from darkness to light and back. She sank deeply only to be tossed up again like the ocean playing with a piece of driftwood. The horse rocked her from side to side; with every move, the pain stabbed and sliced her. Voices reached her from far away, some familiar, some new. Why did they whisper?

Pine tree and leafy smells mingled with a peppermint scent and tickled her nose. Breathing made her ribs hurt, but at the same time, the cool fresh air soothed her. A gentle breeze caressed her face, and after a while, she drifted off again despite the pain.

Hours, days, maybe months later, she had no idea, someone lifted her off the horse and laid her on the ground. When she opened her eyes, five white faces, a cat, and a horse stared down at her. Night had come and Pelifeles' fur glowed, giving them all a ghostly look.

"Hi." The word scratched her throat as it slipped passed her lips.

Calleo's scrunched up face relaxed into a smile. Pelifeles' whiskers tickled her cheek. Flynden grinned and let out a shaky laugh. The horse's breath grazed her forehead and nickered softly. Stace squatted beside her, holding a cup. He exhaled sharply, but his face looked lined, old and exhausted.

Bramble and Thistle knelt beside Flynden, their blue eyes wide and brimming with tears. Bramble's lower lip trembled. Strange, the three looked like they were related. The same eye shape, the straight noses, and the delicate features, except Flynden's hair was sandy colored not white-blond. They said they were from different families, but Flynden looked nothing like his brothers Kir and Stace and much more like Thistle and Bramble. When Thistle's and Flynden's faces lost their scared look, they even grinned the same way.

"About time," Pelifeles growled. "Thought you'd never wake up."

Bramble reached out and cupped her face. "Sophie, you feel better?"

"A bit."

Calleo took the cup from Stace and tipped it to her mouth. The cold water soothed her dry throat. She gulped it down. Some water dripped out of the corners of her mouth onto a clean tunic someone had dressed her in. When she had enough, Sophie pushed his hands away. Calleo nodded and his smile grew wider. Wouldn't it be nice if he could talk?

"Bramble and Calleo told us what happened." Flynden sat cross-legged by her head. Some curls hung over his forehead. "You're lucky."

"I'd say." Sophie craned her neck to look at him. "I didn't really think the creature would attack us. It was almost friendly before."

Calleo signed something.

"What's he saying?" Sophie asked.

"Calleo thinks it was his fault," Flynden said. "His

magic threatened the creature."

"It had magic, too." Sophie looked at Calleo. "How do you think it came to be down there?"

Calleo's face darkened, and he made one short quick sign.

"Makimus," said Flynden. "Who else could be behind a creature in a pit and throwing people in there for it to eat?"

"We must stop him," Sophie said and sat up. The forest and the faces swam and spun around her. Her stomach turned over and she lay back before she had to throw up.

Stace and Calleo nodded.

"How?" Flynden asked, but someone different answered his question.

"Master Eigil can stop him, but he must be here to do so." The horse spoke with the same raspy voice she'd thought belonged to an old woman. It shook its head, ruffling the long ebony mane. Its forelock fell over a tear-shaped white blaze, the only light mark on the whole body. The graceful tail swished like a soft black veil, and the fetlocks curled above shiny black-blue hooves like someone had taken a curling iron to the hair.

"You can talk?" Sophie's mouth fell open.

"I am Nelwyna, Master Eigil's spirit mate."

"Like Pelifeles?" Sophie asked.

Nelwyna's nostrils flared as she breathed out. "Well, accidents happen."

Hackles raised, Pelifeles hissed and swiped at Nelwyna's soft nose, but she jerked her head up.

"Stop!" Flynden grabbed Pelifeles, but dropped him right away as if stung. A few sparks jumped between the cat's fur and Flynden's fingers.

Pelifeles hissed. "I won't let the nag insult me."

"Do not call me a nag, fur ball."

Calleo clapped his hands like thunder, silencing them. He shook his head, his face stern. He signed something. The horse snorted and the cat crouched low to the ground, hackles lowered.

"What did he say?" Sophie asked.

"He told them to stop," said Stace.

"It sounded more like shut it."

Stace nodded. "There is no time for bickering now. A truce would be welcome."

Sophie grinned, looking at the two animals. Funny, but she liked it. A horse and a cat talking and arguing. Lots of spirit in those mates.

"So, what do we do now?" she asked.

Calleo signed something again and Stace translated.

"First, you have to recover. Then we will visit the Mother Flora and ask her."

"Whoever this Mother Flora is," Sophie said. "Can she put up a good fight against Makimus?"

"The Mother Flora does not fight," Nelwyna said. "It is her whole reason for being."

"What is?"

"The Mother Flora and her children exist for the sole reason to keep peace and to heal the land and the people."

"Then how can she help us?"

"Well, child, if we knew we would not have to go and see her, would we?"

Sophie wanted to roll her eyes, but she decided against it. Nelwyna seemed a bit touchy.

"Can we go *now*?" Sophie asked. "We can't wait until I'm better. Who knows how long that'll take?"

Calleo flicked his fingers.

"What's he saying?"

"Calleo will give you healing herbs to speed up your recovery," Stace said. "In a few hours you will be fine to travel."

Calleo gave her a reassuring smile and nodded.

"Why can't Pelifeles help me?" She asked. "He's fixed my ankle before. Surely he can do this quicker than some herbs."

Calleo pointed at her and shook his head.

"Calleo says because the creature has magic and left some in your wounds when it scratched you, Pelifeles' magic might cause more harm than good. Both magics might interact in a bad way."

"Calleo's herbs won't?"

Calleo shook his head again and signed.

Stace said, "The herbs are a strong plant remedy and do not have magic."

"Sounds good to me." She grinned, relieved. Better not mess with more magic.

Calleo sprinkled some of those herbs from a pouch into a cup of water and made her drink it. Cool and soothing, the drink traveled into her stomach and spread from there through her whole body, taking away the pain and making her sleepy again. It felt like magic anyway.

Sophie woke in the night to Flynden's calling. What's happening? She struggled out of her sleepy mind and opened her eyes. The pain in her back and legs had dwindled into a dull ache. Her whole body felt stronger.

Pelifeles' light flared and showed Kir striding across the clearing with a pack slung over his shoulder. Everyone exhaled with relief. When Kir reached them, he swung the pack around and plopped it on the ground.

As soon as it had settled with a clatter, they surrounded him and bombarded him with questions. Calleo's fingers flicked a mile a minute. Flynden and Thistle shouted all at once until Kir held up his hands.

"One at a time, please." His serious features changed into a boyish grin.

"What's happening at Council Hall?" Flynden asked.

"Has…has Makimus found out we escaped?" Thistle shook while Bramble clung to him.

"I think he has," Kir said. "Councilor Makimus was in the worst mood I have ever seen him in. He stomped through Council Hall, yelling at the servants. He was short with the other councilors and me. He couldn't ask obvious questions about you, which would mean admitting his secrets. Sometime after the midday meal, he announced he would be spending time in his chambers until the turning bell tolls at dusk, but Master Druce Lar believes he is making plans to come after you."

Kir's voice sounded deep and calm; and he moved with elegance like a noble prince. He must have sensed Sophie staring because he walked over to her and squatted beside her. "Master Druce Lar has sent me to warn you. You must leave now. We will carry you."

"No, I will carry her," Nelwyna piped up. "We must hurry. Master Eigil must return. The sooner we can accomplish this, the better for us all."

Sophie grinned. *Way to go.*

Kir and Calleo lifted Sophie onto the horse.

❧ ❧

They walked single file into the woods. Giant trees like sequoias and redwoods hemmed in a narrow path.

Nelwyna scraped past some that stood too close. A strong peppermint smell lingered all around.

They trekked through the dark woods. Here and there, the moon peeked through the trees' canopy, sending only a feeble light down to them. Pelifeles' fur glowed ahead of Nelwyna, leading the way. Calleo walked behind Nelwyna. His deep-yellow magic flickered in the darkness. Behind him, Stace carried Bramble. Thistle and Flynden tiptoed ahead of Kir who brought up the rear, his hand cupping his purplish-blue magic that smelled like lilacs.

After some time, they reached a small clearing where snatches of fog hovered over the grass like a cottony-cloud blanket.

"We will rest here for a short while," Kir told them.

They sighed with relief. Together, Kir and Calleo lifted Sophie off Nelwyna's back, placed her onto a blanket in the grass, and covered her with another one. She threw it off. *Phew.* Way too hot. After drinking Calleo's herbs, her strength had returned, but when she tried to stand, she swayed. Calleo and Flynden jumped to help her lie back down.

Cross-legged, Flynden plopped down beside her and grinned.

"Looks like you're feeling better."

"How can you tell?" Sophie grinned back.

"You're not looking half dead anymore." He rocked side to side, back and forth, making himself more comfortable.

Calleo placed his hand on her forehead and nodded. His fingers flicked something to her.

"He says you'll make it," Flynden said.

"Thanks to him," Sophie said and grimaced. "Thanks,

Calleo. I'm sorry I've been such a pain in the neck."

Calleo clutched his neck, bent his head sideways and grimaced like he had a pain. They laughed. He patted her shoulder, nodded, and walked over to Kir who sat cross-legged in the grass with Pelifeles on his lap. Thistle and Bramble huddled close to Stace. Nelwyna grazed a few feet away.

"Who is Trudy?" Flynden asked.

"How do you know about Trudy?" Sophie pushed up on one elbow. "I never told you about her."

"You were talking in your sleep." Flynden grinned. "Don't get upset." He held up both hands when she frowned at him.

"Okay. Fine. Trudy's my foster mother," she said.

"Why do you call her Trudy not mother?"

Her eyes stung and she swallowed away the lump in her throat.

"You fine?" Flynden leaned forward.

Sophie nodded but didn't look him in the eye. "Because she isn't. My mom and dad were killed in a car accident."

"What's a car?"

"Never mind." She'd forgotten they didn't have cars here, and she didn't feel like explaining everything.

"You talk like you don't like your Trudy. Is she mean?"

No, Trudy was strict, but not mean, and mostly kind and generous. Sophie shook her head.

"No, she's really nice, and, um, I'm the one who's been really mean to her. I threw a stone at her." *Maybe I killed her.* She didn't want to say this out loud. It would make it more real than she wanted it to be.

Flynden wrinkled his brow, making him look a lot like

Stace or Kir. "Why were you mean to someone who's nice to you?"

She blushed. "Um, I was mad at her because she stayed with Tommy when he died, but I wasn't there."

Flynden shook his head. "Then why did you get angry at her? You should've thanked her."

Sophie nodded, her face getting hotter. For a moment, they said nothing and listened to the murmurs of the others. A soft breeze stirred the leaves high above them. Somewhere in the branches, an owl hooted.

"How 'bout you? Where's your mom?" Sophie changed the subject.

"Never met my ma," Flynden mumbled.

"How come?"

"Da told me she died when I was born."

"Oh." Open-mouthed, Sophie stared at him. "I'm so sorry, Flyn."

Flynden looked down and away. She reached out, but then pulled her hand back. Maybe he would slap her hand away or would get mad if she felt too sorry for him. She waited.

"Kir and Stace are my half brothers," he said. "Da took a new wife after their ma turned Flora giving birth to Kir."

"How does that work?"

"She lives in the Garden. You can ask her or the Mother Flora later. They can explain it much better than I ever could."

Kir opened his pack and handed out apples and nuts. He even had some dried meat strips for Pelifeles. He looked more like a warrior than a thoughtful, caring guy. When she said so, Flynden laughed.

"Most people are wrong about Kir. He's full of

surprises. He's even been taking lessons from Councilor Tulio. Soon, my brother will be a master cook."

When Kir handed her an apple and some hazelnuts, he smiled at her. Had he heard everything she'd said? Her face grew warm again.

"How are you feeling, Sophie?" Stace asked.

"Much better. Thanks."

"Good," Kir nodded to her. "We have to keep moving. Makimus' men will be following us, perhaps Makimus himself." He rearranged some things his pack. "The sooner we reach the Garden the better. You can hide there."

Nelwyna had wandered off a few steps. She suddenly raised her head and tensed, standing still like one of those statues in a park, ears pointing forward into the dark forest. Pelifeles stood almost as still, ears pricked, hackles up, growling.

"What...?" Before Sophie could finish her question, a roar rumbled through the woods. The next moment, something jumped into the clearing—the creature from the pit—the white stripe on its back glowing like a white snake in the dark.

How did it get out?

Everybody screamed and scrambled up, dashing toward the trees.

Kir shot volleys of his purple-blue magic into the beast. It back-pawed him, sending him backward into the darkness. Bramble screeched and tried to get to the creature.

"No!" she screamed. "Don't hurt the kitty. No!" Thistle held onto her and pulled her away with him toward the trees. The creature came on. Calleo hammered his own deep-yellow magic into it, but the creature threw him aside like Kir. Screams filled the forest. A strong wind howled all around them, kicking up dirt and leaves, twirling it into funnels. Pelifeles launched himself at the creature at the same time Nelwyna charged, but the two spirit mates accomplished as little as the two apprentices did. The creature threw them back and knocked Stace out of the way at the same time.

"No!" Bramble screamed again.

The white stripe along the creature's back glowed brighter and pulsed like electricity, sending all but Flynden tumbling away. Sophie fell back, the air knocked out of her. They lay paralyzed, unable to get up and interfere when the creature rounded on Flynden. He fell on his back, struggling to get up, trying to get away. He scrambled on hands and feet backward, looking like a crab scuttling across the clearing.

The creature loomed over Flynden, pinning him down with one big black paw, but instead of biting or scratching him, it started purring like a loud motor, then sniffed his face, and nuzzled him. The white stripe on its back glowed even brighter. A hush fell over the forest, not a leaf stirred.

First, Flynden tensed and went rigid. His eyes bulged. In the next second, he grabbed the paw. With a crack and a boom, a blinding white flash burst from his hands. He flung the creature away. It flew through the air, landed on its back halfway across the clearing, and rolled onto its paws. It stared at Flynden with red glowing eyes and a look of great surprise. A moment later, it swung around and disappeared into the dark forest.

❧ *Chapter 15* ❦

A gentle breeze stirred the air and the forest sounds returned. Another owl hooted. A mouse scurried through the grass and disappeared into a tiny hole, perhaps glad to be alive and make it home to the burrow. A deer ventured to the clearing's edge, its tail flicking, ears alert, its eyes soft but watchful.

Sophie scrambled to her feet. Kir and Calleo rushed up from where they had fallen. Stace brushed himself off. Thistle emerged from the trees, pulling a crying Bramble with him, keeping his arms around her.

"Ssh, Bramble, it's fine," Thistle tried to comfort her, but the girl didn't even look up.

Flynden's face had lost all color, his lips had turned white. They trembled. His eyes widened with terror. He sat up and looked to the spot between the trees where the creature had disappeared. He mumbled something, shaking all over.

"What, by the light, was that?" Nelwyna asked and snorted like the whole thing had left a bad smell in her nose.

"Are you okay, Flyn?" Sophie asked, kneeling down beside him.

Flynden didn't answer. He hugged himself and kept staring into space, mumbling. Pelifeles snuggled onto his lap but Flynden didn't touch him.

Stace grabbed Flynden's shoulder. "What is it, Flynden?" He scrunched up his face, worried and scared.

Sophie leaned forward, trying to catch Flynden's words.

"It knew me," Flynden whispered. "It knows who I am."

"What do you mean, Flyn?" Sophie took his hands. They rested cold and clammy between her warm ones. "You've never been into the pit, right?"

"I felt as if I knew it, too. Like someone familiar from a long time ago." He shook himself out of his trance and looked around. "And then… and then…." He couldn't seem to finish the sentence. He blinked a few times. "I was scared. I couldn't move."

"We all couldn't," Sophie said.

"And then… then something gathered in my chest and coiled. It was almost like before but much, much stronger. Something angry, furious burst out of me and flung the creature away."

"You have magic, Flyn," Pelifeles said. "And you didn't even know." He pushed his head against the boy's hand. "I sensed something special about you, but different, much different." Pelifeles sat on his haunches and blinked his big yellow eyes at Flynden. "Your magic has no scent and it's blinding white. Powerful and strange."

They stared at Flynden while Pelifeles' words still hung in the air.

"But how? Why?" Flynden asked. "I'm not a special child." He looked off into the trees again.

Calleo and Kir exchanged meaningful glances. Calleo's

hands flicked a few signs. Kir nodded.

"We should leave. Now," Kir said and picked up his pack. "Stace, go to the Garden and talk to Mother. She will arrange a meeting with the Mother Flora for you." He slung the pack over his shoulder. "I will return to Council Hall and report what has happened to Master Druce Lar."

"You cannot go alone, Kir." Stace stopped his brother with one hand. "Not with the creature roaming the forest."

"You are right."

Calleo flicked his hands until both Stace and Kir nodded.

"What are you guys talking about?" Sophie stood.

"Kir and Calleo will return to Council Hall. Together, they will be safer," Stace said and gave her a quick smile. "We still have Nelwyna and Pelifeles to help us."

"Well, the creature is powerful. Pelifeles and Nelwyna weren't able to do much," Sophie said.

"Perhaps Flynden will save us again next time."

Bramble jumped up and balled her fists.

"We mustn't hurt it. The kitty is nice. It doesn't want to hurt us."

"What do you mean, Bramble?" Stace squatted in front of her. "How do you know what it wants?"

"It told me." Bramble looked at the ground and fidgeted with her tunic's hem. "It wants Flynden, but she doesn't mean to hurt him, either."

"She?" Kir said. "How do you know this creature is female?"

"Her name is Eleta, and she told me," the girl said, nodding to make sure they believed her.

"What else did she tell you?" Flynden jumped up and

grabbed Bramble's arms. "What do you know?"

"She, um, she told me no more." Bramble sniffed and tears rolled down her dirty cheeks, leaving little wet trails. "She is so sad." The girl hiccupped. "She wants to kill the man with the big rings."

"Makimus." Now, Sophie too looked off into the trees. "He's the one behind this, isn't he?" She gazed at the others. "It's him we've got to worry about. Maybe this Eleta, this creature, can finish him off."

The three men sucked in their breaths, but Thistle, Bramble, and Flynden nodded.

"You are talking about a member of the High Council." Stace frowned.

"So?" Sophie jammed her fists into her hips. "It doesn't seem to stop him or make any difference to him. He's abusing his power, right?"

"But…" Stace looked from Kir to Calleo, but the two apprentices both shook their heads.

"Well, he's the one who caused Master Eigil to flee. He's the one who abused that Bron guy. He threw Thistle, Bramble and me into the pit, hoping the creature would finish us off. Who knows what else he's up to?"

When no one said anything, Sophie snatched the blanket off the ground. "We need to get going. Maybe this Mother Flora has some idea what to do."

Stace had stared at his feet, but now, he lifted his head and nodded, his face determined. "Be careful," he said to Kir and Calleo. "I will leave word with Mother about where you can find us."

Calleo handed Sophie a pouch with some crumpled up leaves and a small metal tin. He flicked his fingers a few times.

"He says, the tea will make you feel good and will

take the pain away," Stace explained. "The ointment in the metal tin is for the wounds. Someone must apply it to your back."

"Thank you, Calleo." Sophie stepped forward to hug him but changed her mind, dropped her arms, and stepped back again. Heat rose from her neck into her face. Gee, now she blushed again. To hide her embarrassment, she asked, "Can we use it on Flynden's and Stace's back, too?"

Calleo nodded, then hugged Bramble and Thistle, petted Nelwyna on the neck, then with a quick nod good-bye all around, he headed for the trees. Kir placed one hand on Stace's shoulder and ruffled Flynden's hair, waved to everyone else, and took off after Calleo. In a few short moments, they had jogged to the clearing's edge and disappeared into the dark.

❧ ❧

"Let's go," Pelifeles said and slunk off where another path led into the trees.

Stace helped Sophie onto Nelwyna, and at the last moment, lifted Flynden up, too.

"I hope you do not mind, Nelwyna." He made a slight bow to the horse.

"What if I do?" She snorted. "Would you take him off again?"

"He has been through quite an ordeal. And…"

"Never mind. Let us proceed," she said rather haughtily and jumped ahead. Her front hooves lifted off the ground, and she kicked off with her powerful hind legs. Sophie grabbed her mane. Flynden held tight around Sophie's waist. Together, they slid forward.

"Easy!" Sophie yelled.

"I am making sure you two are paying attention," the horse said and slowed to a walk.

"Mean," Flynden mumbled.

"I heard that," Nelwyna snorted. "If you are not careful with your words, you will walk." She kicked her hind legs back and Flynden fell forward, pushing Sophie up her neck.

"Enough," Sophie said. "We need to keep going and stick together. So, stop bickering, okay?"

"Well said, dear." Nelwyna shook her head, tousling her mane and slapping Sophie in the face with the long strands. Sophie pressed her mouth together. If she said anything now, the horse might do some other stupid thing.

On quiet hooves, Nelwyna strode after Pelifeles. Stace, Thistle, and Bramble hurried after them, but Bramble slowed them down, and they fell farther and farther behind. Soon, Sophie couldn't see them any more way back down the path because they had vanished into the dark.

"Nelwyna, we have to wait for the others." Sophie leaned forward and patted the horse on the neck. She twisted to see around Flynden, who also gazed over his shoulder. "They shouldn't be walking by themselves. If the creature comes back…" She let the sentence hang unfinished in the air.

The moon's yellow light darkened the already deep-purple shadows even more.

"Well, the little girl said the creature did not mean harm to us. So why worry?" asked Nelwyna, but she stopped.

"We don't know for sure, do we? Even so, what about being a bit considerate?"

Nelwyna snorted and shook her head.

"Very well, we will wait."

It took quite a while before their friends caught up. Stace carried Bramble and Thistle jogged closely behind him.

"Nel…Nelwyna," Stace panted. "Can Bramble ride with you as well?"

"Who do you think I am?" huffed the horse. "I am Master Eigil's spirit mate, not a beast of burden."

"Please." Stace leaned forward and lowered Bramble to the ground. He clutched his side. "Please?"

"Oh, very well then." She held still while Stace lifted Bramble onto her withers in front of Sophie.

Sophie put her arms around the girl and kissed her hair. Bramble leaned into her and lifted her dirty, tear-streaked face up, giving Sophie a small smile. In the moonlight, the girl looked tired and afraid.

"It'll be fine, Bramble," Sophie whispered, hugging her close. The girl said nothing and faced forward.

Nelwyna walked a few minutes. Soon, Thistle kept tripping over his own feet. After considerable begging from everyone, Nelwyna agreed to let him ride behind Flynden on her rump. She then took short measured steps for Stace to keep up. They walked in silence and only the dull rhythmic thuds of Nelwyna's hooves mingled with the night sounds. A breeze stirred the leaves overhead, making a whooshing sound, carrying the peppermint smell all around, soothing and calming. Sophie leaned back while Flynden leaned forward, and they swayed back and forth with the horse's strides. A large bird swooped past on great wings and settled ahead on a small tree. Some animal farther off in the darkness screeched. Then silence again.

Nelwyna and Stace walked for the remainder of the night, resting a few minutes here and there. Pelifeles never showed his face once. When the morning's first gray shimmered through the trees ahead like a tunnel's end, Nelwyna stopped. The path ended at the forest's edge where the cat sat looking out over grassy plains and rolling hills.

"What took you so long?" Pelifeles said without turning when they reached him. "One would think with long legs like yours, you would've been a bit quicker."

To her credit, Nelwyna lowered herself only enough to give him a dismissing snort but didn't take the bait. Perhaps she was as tired as the rest of them since she had to carry four children all night. Stace moved to the front, stood beside the cat, and gazed over the grassy field toward a low stone wall, winding left and right, along the bottom of the nearest hill.

"Where are we?" Sophie sat up straight and glanced over Nelwyna's head. A gentle breeze stirred her hair and brought the smell of the ocean and memories of an Oregon beach vacation with Mom and Dad. Sophie's stomach clenched and she swallowed hard to get rid of the lump in her throat. Not too far in the distance, waves rolled against the shore.

Stace pointed ahead and to the left. "Over there is a small gate in the Garden's wall."

"Let's go then," Sophie said.

"We are not permitted." Stace shook his head. "No men or boys are allowed to enter the Garden, and only sometimes, the councilors and their apprentices are permitted." He lifted Thistle off the horse.

"Why's that?" Sophie asked.

"The Flora set those rules and we must obey."

"But this is an emergency." Sophie threw up her hands and twisted around to Flynden.

"Sophie's right," Flynden said. He slid off Nelwyna's rump and walked up to Stace. "We have to find the Mother Flora quickly. I'm sure she won't mind."

"I am *not* so sure, Flynden." Stace crossed his arms over his chest.

"Well, if we don't hurry," Pelifeles piped up, "the Flora will have turned and we won't be talking to anyone until the dusk bell tolls."

To the east, the indigo sky with its pinprick of stars turned paler by the minute and moved up to make room to a widening pale blue and gray band. The sun would be following soon.

"What do you mean by *the Flora will have turned*?"

"Like the kitty," Bramble said, "they turn into flowers when the new day begins."

Sophie opened her mouth, then closed it again.

"So, you mean, em, the Garden? They're creatures, too? Em, I mean." What did she mean? She took a deep breath and shook her head. "Let's hurry. We can't stick around here."

"Flynden, Thistle, and I cannot go," Stace said. "We will wait here within the trees. Bramble and you can enter with Nelwyna and Pelifeles. If you hasten, you could make it to the Garden proper before the turning begins. Pelifeles knows where my mother Amabel lives."

"Come on," Pelifeles hissed and parted the tall grass, only the tip of his black tail showed where he walked toward the stone wall.

"See you later," Sophie called over her shoulder. "We'll be back soon."

Nelwyna broke into a trot, then broke into a slow

canter, but slowed and stopped by a wrought iron gate.

"Can't you just jump the wall, Nelwyna?" Sophie asked.

"No, I cannot," Nelwyna said and shook her head vigorously. The movement traveled along the smooth body. Bramble and Sophie scrambled to hold on, grabbing and clawing the mane, and almost sliding off her back.

"Oh dear, children." Nelwyna raised her neck and they righted themselves. "Really now. Can you not hold on properly?"

"Yes, we can," said Sophie, fuming, "but you're not making it easy."

Nelwyna ignored her and walked to the gate until her shoulder butted against the metal.

"One of you has to dismount and open the gate," she said. "I will not crash it." She raised her nose in a huff and waited.

"Fine." Sophie tucked her right leg behind Bramble, over the horse's back and slid down.

The gate looked old and rusty but its latch worked. Sophie pushed the gate in and climbed onto the low stone wall, ready to mount again, when Nelwyna walked past her and kept going.

"Close it again."

"What?"

"Close the gate," Nelwyna said. "Manners dear, manners."

"You should be talking." Sophie frowned but closed the gate.

Instead of waiting though, Nelwyna trotted away from the wall, forcing Sophie to jog after her. *If I catch that horse, I'll kick her.*

❧ ❧

Flynden watched the girls and the spirit mates cross the distance to the wall and the gate. He shook his head, watching Nelwyna goad Sophie into opening the gate but not letting her ride again. Soon, they disappeared over the first hill toward the Garden proper. Sophie yelled after the horse to wait for her.

Not too long ago, he would have laughed, but now nothing seemed funny. Now, his life seemed scary and uncomfortable. Ever since he'd destroyed Master Eigil's hand, and after the creature had pinned him to the ground and magic had burst out of him, he didn't feel like himself anymore. In the Council Chamber, it had been a small curious feeling, nothing scary, and he had shrugged it off. Now, this magic had violated him. He had always liked himself. Nothing special. A regular boy. Yes, he had wanted to work as a servant at Council Hall like Stace, but that would've been special enough for him.

Flynden hugged himself. Tears stung his eyes. What was happening to him? He looked at Stace, who pulled him into a one-arm hug and squeezed his shoulder, saying nothing. He and Stace hugged little, but now he liked having his brother's arm around his shoulders.

Thistle stood close by, watching and looking scared. Flynden smiled, but Thistle only frowned back.

"I'll wait by the wall," he said and marched off. When he reached the wall, he sat down and kicked the stone with his heels.

Stace dropped his arm from Flynden's shoulder and they rushed after Thistle.

"Wait, Thistle," Stace called. He hurried forward, but before he got to the wall, Thistle swung his legs up, around, and over to the other side. As soon as the feet hit the ground, vines snaked from the soil and latched onto him, winding like ropes around his ankles and legs.

"Come away from there, Thistle," Stace yelled. "You are not allowed in the Garden."

"I'm only sitting on the wall," Thistle said and tried to struggle free of the vines.

"Your legs are in the Garden." Half laughing, half frowning, Flynden helped Stace pull Thistle's legs free, but as soon as they grabbed him, the vines latched onto them too, binding and squeezing them until they couldn't move.

The more Flynden pulled, the tighter the vines bound him. They slithered like snakes around his chest and neck, starting to cut off his breath. Flynden struggled fiercely. Thistle and Stace didn't fair better. Anger rose in his chest and with it, the magic inside stirred and coiled like before. Unbidden, it burst from him.

Thistle gave a stifled scream. Stace gasped.

Did he hurt them? Not likely, but they looked at him questioningly and somewhat accusingly.

The vines let go of them as quickly as they had appeared and slithered back over the wall and into the ground.

"That hurt," Thistle said and rubbed his arms. "Whatever you did, Flynden, that hurt too."

"I didn't mean to." Flynden stepped back. "I got angry. Not quite like before in the clearing when the creature came, but angry all the same, and then I felt the magic again. It lashed out at the vines."

Even Stace rubbed his arms. "You will have to learn to control it, Flynden. You might hurt someone. Your magic stings! I feel like I have been sitting in an ant hill."

"Sorry, Stace, I didn't mean to," Flynden said. "I only wanted the vines to let go of us." No, he hadn't wanted that, or had he? He only remembered being angry, but when he thought harder, yes, that's what he had wanted because those vines were holding and strangling them. Maybe he could talk to his magic and tell it what to do? No, that was silly.

He nodded. "I'll try." Everything happened too fast. How would he have time to think before this happened again? The magic didn't rise with his thoughts but seemed to wake with his feelings.

Thistle stepped away from him but only leaned against the wall this time. He cast a scared look to the other side, then at Flynden. When he saw Flynden watching him, he turned away.

"We should not be out in the open like this," Stace said and rotated on the spot as if expecting someone or something to jump out at them.

"I'm not leaving." Thistle's frown deepened. "You can go back to the trees, but I'm waiting here until Bramble comes back."

"Fine." Stace sat and leaned against the wall. "We will stay."

Golden rays of the rising sun shot over the hills, coloring the gray morning yellow and orange. They watched the sun's sliver cut into the horizon.

A bit later, Thistle came away from the wall and lay down in the tall grass. Flynden went to lie down close to him, wanting to reassure the other boy it would be fine, but when he looked over, Thistle's eyes were closed and his chest gently rose and fell. Stace stayed by the wall, not letting down his guard or relaxing his vigilance.

"Go to sleep, Flynden," he said. "I will be watching."

Flynden rolled onto his side, resting his head on the crook of his arm. In his chest, a strange tense feeling kept him uncomfortable. He couldn't explain the feeling. It nudged him as if it wanted to tell him something. After a while, the morning sun's warm rays made him sleepy. He wanted to tell Stace he shouldn't be watching alone, but then he closed his eyes instead.

❧ *Chapter 16* ☙

Sophie ran after Nelwyna but didn't have a chance keeping up. Pain stabbed her back and legs as her feet pounded the ground.

Nelwyna trotted ahead with her long graceful legs. She let her catch up a few times, but each time Sophie almost grabbed the tail, the horse kicked out and sped up again. Horrible tease. Sophie kept jogging, and because she kept her eyes on the horse and not on the ground, she missed a rabbit hole, stumbled and went down. Now her knees hurt, too. She brushed herself off, glowered at Nelwyna's disappearing butt, and limped after the horse.

Bramble stayed on the horse, and even though she bounced left and right, she always righted herself in time and bravely dug her fists into the mane.

Sophie must have run close to two miles over rolling hills in record time when she saw the branches and leaves of a huge tree rise above the crest of the next hill. As she stumbled up the rise, the tree seemed to grow even more. At the top of the hill, she stood and stared.

Down in a valley around the giant tree, weeping willows stood side by side with Quaking Aspen and pink, red, and white-leafed blooming trees Sophie had never seen before. The huge tree stood like a skyscraper in a small town's center, reaching high into the sky.

Nelwyna slowed and let her catch up. Sophie bent over and held a stitch in her side; sweat was running down her back and was sticking the tunic to her skin. *Kick that horse.*

"Pretty," Bramble said and pointed down the hill.

At first glance, the grove seemed like a simple copse of trees, except for the tall one in their midst of course. But when Sophie squinted, she made out small houses built on, around, or in almost all of the trees, including the giant one. The large and small houses seemed woven like baskets or lobster traps. Fenced-in gardens with dark and rich soil, but with nothing in them, surrounded each tree.

Nelwyna trotted down the hill, once again leaving Sophie behind. Tinkling laughter and women's voices drifted toward her. A sudden flurry of activity made the place look like an anthill. Women and girls hurried up and down the paths that crisscrossed and intersected the tree town.

"Come," Nelwyna said, "it is not far now."

Some women and girls spotted them, pointing. Nelwyna whinnied a hello and strode down a wide lane between trees and houses. Soon, she veered right onto a smaller path, turned left, then right again, until they were deep inside the town, and the trees blocked the hills behind them.

Sophie lagged behind and stared back at the women and girls who eyed her curiously. Most were no taller than Bramble. Their pale skin and white-blond or light brown hair shimmered silvery green, like they ate too much spinach or something. Tiny little white petals framed their faces along the hairline, down their cheeks and chins. They stood slender and willowy, like fairies from a fairytale. Women and girls watched them pass but no one stopped or spoke to them.

Nelwyna finally slowed enough to let Sophie catch up.

"How do you know where you're going?" Sophie whispered, skipping along, close to Nelwyna's head.

"Pelifeles pointed the way," the horse whispered back. "I will let you do the talking." She gave a snort.

"What do I say?"

"Well, girl, tell it like it is." The horse shook its head to mask her words. "First of all, tell Amabel we need to see the Mother Flora immediately."

Sophie nodded.

"We are almost there." Then Nelwyna went quiet as they drew up to a garden in front of a tree house.

A woman, in her forties maybe, hurried down a walkway woven to the tree trunk. It spiraled to the ground from the house up in the branches. The walkway swayed and sagged under her feet. The woman looked up, hesitated for a moment, but kept moving until she reached the ground. She came over to them, her face furrowed. In a worried kind of way, her eyes flicked sideways to the tilled soil in the garden.

"What brings you to the Garden, girls?" She looked from Sophie to Bramble. "Oh, is that Master Eigil's horse?" She petted Nelwyna's neck.

She wore her hair loose and long down her back. Some silvery gray-green strands showed at the temples of the otherwise black hair. Unlike the short and slender Flora, she stood tall and stout, and her eyes, cheekbones, and chin made her clearly Kir and Stace's mom.

"Amabel? Are you Amabel?" Sophie gushed, rushing forward.

"Yes, yes. What brings you?" Amabel asked.

The woman's clipped tone took Sophie off guard. "Um, I'm Sophie and that's Bramble." She pointed to the girl. "We need to talk to the Mother Flora. Master Eigil has sent me." She stretched the truth a bit, but this was an emergency, wasn't it?

Bramble nodded in her cute way, eyes big, like saying, yes, that's right.

"The Flora are about to turn." Amabel's eyes flicked again to the soil patch, then to the spot where the sun flashed the first rays over the horizon. "Come. We have only a few moments."

When they had only taken a few steps, the most beautiful woman ever followed Pelifeles down the path.

Sophie's mouth fell open. More graceful than a ballet dancer or a statue of the holy Mary, the woman approached, almost gliding toward them, hands and arms extended in greeting with a swan-like grace. Her soft, flowing white gown draped around her slender figure taller than the other Flora but shorter than Amabel. Her golden-blond hair hung wavy to her ankles and shimmered with a bit of green, too. Bright white flower petals, larger and whiter than the others', ringed her face.

So, this had to be the Mother Flora. What did she expect? An old nun?

"Welcome to my Garden, children," the Mother Flora said, still steps away. Her voice sounded lyrical, a soft soprano, like a pleasing song to the ear. "Pelifeles has beckoned me to come. What need do you have of me?" She reached them and patted Nelwyna's neck. "What a pleasure to see you, Nelwyna."

The horse nickered softly but said nothing. The woman cocked her head and regarded Sophie. Long blond eyelashes with a hint of green surrounded her silvery eyes.

"We need your help." Sophie sighed and her eyes glazed over, awed by the woman. A moment later, she shook herself out of her reverie. "Master Eigil has sent me. He needs help to get home. He asked me to get the Flora blossom and I did, but then I had to hide it because Makimus came after us and caught us, and now this creature is after us and Makimus too and we don't know where to go from here." She gulped some air after her words bubbled out so fast. "Can you help us?"

The Mother Flora smiled and placed her fingertips on Sophie's arm. Warmth spread from the spot where the fingers rested and made Sophie feel calm again. Without squinting, the woman gazed into the rising sun. A moment later, her glance lingered on Bramble. She reached up to the girl's foot and smiled. Bramble's eyes got even bigger and rounder, looking at the beautiful woman beside the horse.

"It is time for turning," the Mother Flora said. "I need more than a few moments to listen to your story and decide what help I can give." To Amabel she said, "Go on, child, and prepare for your turning."

Amabel bowed ever so little. "Thank you, Mother Flora. May the light brighten your path." With another quick bow, she hurried back to her home.

"And yours, child." The Mother Flora beckoned to Sophie and Nelwyna. "Come. Follow me."

Sophie glanced over her shoulder at Amabel who dug her toes into the black soil. Would she do the same thing the creature did in the pit? There was no time to stop and watch because the Mother Flora already hurried down the path, and with a swish of her gown disappeared around a fence corner.

"Come on," Sophie urged Nelwyna forward, flipping her hand.

The horse followed but mumbled something like, "No respect. Not a dog."

❧   ❧

With a straight back and hands clasped before her, the Mother Flora led them through her Garden town, halting here and there to exchange a few words with one of the women or the girls. Her long hair swung like a pendulum with her steps. In all of the gardens, women and girls dug their toes like Amabel into the freshly-tilled dark soil. Some women looked tired, settling and burrowing their feet while sitting on the ground. Some women struggled with toddlers or babies who didn't want to keep still. One toddler ran away, squealing with delight. Still others planted seeds beside them where they settled in the tilled soil. All this would have been like a strange bedtime ritual, except for the morning sunshine and no one was going to bed. Some older girls waved to Sophie when she walked past their garden. Gee, she'd never met anyone so friendly.

"Come, Sophie, hasten now." Nelwyna slowed and urged Sophie under her breath.

"Will they all turn?" Sophie stopped and swiveled on the spot.

"Yes, but come," the horse whispered and picked up the pace again, "there is no time now."

Sophie jogged after Nelwyna. Bramble twisted on Nelwyna's back, taking in the flowers, the trees and the gardens, smiling all around her. She waved to the girls her own age, who waved back, friendly and eager, staring at her the same way she stared at them.

Soon, the giant tree seemed to rise straight from the ground, closer now. A short while later, Nelwyna trotted from the narrow path out into a large, perfectly cut grass square set between flowerbeds, flowering trees and bushes. A colorful mosaic stone path like the ones in the Council Hall gardens divided the grass and flowerbeds. In the square's center grew the massive tree, taller and thicker than any redwood tree. Sophie bent her head back and stared up into the branches. Woven from reeds, stairs with rope railings wound from the roots to branches higher up where they ended on narrow porches of small tree houses. Even higher than that, birds chirped and darted in and out of the leaves. A small cottage nestled between the thick roots, cradling it like giant arms and fingers.

Nelwyna's hoofs stopped at the edge of the fine stone path leading up to the cottage door where the Mother Flora waited for them. Pelifeles sat at her feet and blinked his yellow eyes at his friends, his tail swishing over the stone.

"Come this way," the Mother Flora said, beckoning them around the side to the back of the cottage. A tall and thin older woman, not a Flora by the looks of her, greeted the Mother Flora with a bow at an open gate in a low stone wall.

"It is late, Mother Flora," she said. "You must hurry."

She had wrapped her gray and blond hair into a loose bun at the nape of her neck. When she looked up and noticed Bramble on the horse, her eyes widened in shock. She stopped and stammered, "Is that? It cannot be."

"Yes it is, Gritta, but you must come and assist me." The Mother Flora guided her to a small garden in the center of a courtyard.

Sophie trailed with Nelwyna and Bramble after them.

"My apologies for being so late, Gritta, but it could not be helped," the Mother Flora said. "The girls are my guests and have come with a message from Master Eigil. Please make them comfortable while they wait."

Gritta listened to the Mother Flora but eyed Bramble the whole time. After a moment, she shook her head as if to clear it.

Why did the woman stare at Bramble like that? Did she know her?

"Of course, Mother Flora, I will take care of the children," Gritta said in a peculiarly distracted way and helped the Mother Flora step into a small stone tub with a wide rim. While the Flora sat on the rim, Gritta kneeled before her, washing the Flora's feet, then drying them like a newborn baby with a clean white towel.

The whole time the Mother Flora kept her eyes closed. The white petals around her face began to grow, the green shimmer of her skin deepened, and a soft sigh escaped her lips.

Gritta glanced up and placed the towel on the rim. One arm under the knees, the other supporting the Mother Flora's back, she swept the tiny woman up and carried her to the prepared soil in the small garden. With a deep sigh, the Mother Flora dug her feet, toes first, side by side into the soil, a look of pleasure and relief washing over her face.

"We will speak soon, children," she said. "Gritta will take care of you. Some milk for the cat. Hay for the horse." The whisper of her last words faded away.

Sunrays flashed through the trees, hitting the tiny garden where the Mother Flora stood. Like the creature in the pit, her legs formed one stem. With a soft rustle, her arms stretched out and divided into leafy branches. The white gown dropped and lay like a white soft ring around the stem. Her head tilted up toward the sky and the golden rays, while her face faded into the head of a large daisy flower with snow-white petals. In a few moments, the Mother Flora had morphed into a huge daisy, sunflower size, but unlike the creature, the Mother Flora stood beautifully and serenely, not dark and scary.

"Wow!" Sophie stared open-mouthed. "Wow," she said again because she couldn't think of anything else to say.

Nelwyna shook her head. Bramble sat, her eyes big, her mouth open. A silence settled over the courtyard and the tiny garden. All through the Garden town, the same rustling repeated over and over, like a breeze sweeping through it, but not a leaf stirred in the trees.

❧ *Chapter 17* ❦

The sun rose white and cold over the burial ground but had no warmth to loosen his stiff joints. Eigil huddled within his cloak on dirt-filled bags stacked in one corner of the small shed, a small square structure he could cross with two long steps. He had found shelter within since the girl had disappeared into the portal. Seven bitterly cold nights and miserably hungry days, and still, the girl had not returned. The few seeds he brought had sustained and nourished him for half the time without giving him the satisfaction of a hearty meal. Now he had used up all of the seeds and his strength began to ebb away, leaving only a hollow feeling in his stomach. Perhaps being so far away from Nugateris weakened his body further, but he could not be sure. Yet, a smidgen of hope remained that the child would return and nudged him into sliding his legs off his makeshift bed.

His feet dropped onto the wooden floor strewn with dirt, broken earthenware, and rusty nails. A man of his position should not make his home in a shed such as this, but it mattered not. Here, he was not High Councilor of the Council of Gwern-cadarn-brac, but a beggar and fugitive, a man on the run. The burial ground's caretaker, an older haggard-looking man, used the shed for tools and storage. The man had come every other day, each time bringing a brown bag with bread, meat slices, and fruit, and leaving it on the wooden surface where he sometimes worked with tools. When Eigil had peeked into the bag the first time while the man busied himself outside by the graves, the food's smell had made him dizzy with hunger and he had considered stealing some. Yes, it was low and demeaning for a man like him to steal another man's food, but he must survive, he must return to Nugateris.

Eigil stood, cradling his left arm that would not heal, and shuffled over to the door and cracked it a sliver. The grounds lay empty and still in the morning chill, frosted over like his favorite sugarcoated sweet bread. He hesitated because leaving the shelter would expose him to the chill and anyone visiting the graves, but the walking would be good. He would stretch his legs and keep the blood circulating. The hinges creaked when he opened the door wide. He stepped forward and stopped, halting in the doorway, unmoving.

Close to the shed, on the only bench within the burial ground, the girl's guardian sat hunched at one end, her shoulders trembling. The feathers on her hat twitched and trembled with the movement, while the hat sat lopsided on her head, showing the bandage wrapped over her forehead. Sadness lined her profile.

To lose one child and then the other so soon after. Not knowing where the child had gone or if she would ever come home. With heavy heart, Eigil wished for the guardian's sake too the girl would soon return.

The woman sighed and pulled a small, square white cloth from her coat pocket. She dabbed her eyes with it before balling the cloth into her fist, pressing it to her nose.

Eigil watched her for a moment, surprised she had not heard him open the door. Would she hear it if he now closed it? Would she suspect something if he left it open? He held his breath and bit down hard when he let go of his injured arm. He stretched out his right arm, gathered the magic and cupped it in his hand. She would smell the sage. A soft, cold breeze fingered his hair and cloak and scattered the already-weak scent and his doubts. Good. The magic draped him in a thin cloak of invisibility and dampened most of the noise he made, but not all. He left the door open.

"Who's there?" the woman called and straitened, twisting to look over her shoulder. "Sophie?" Her gaze lingered on the open door, but she did not rise.

Eigil remained close to the shed. His hand shook with the effort of keeping the magical cloak around him until his fingers began to curl inward on their own. If his fingers closed, she would see him. Should he permit it? For an instant, Eigil wanted to reach out. Loneliness and fear ached in his belly worse than the stump of his arm. He stepped away from the door, inching toward the bench and the woman who huddled there.

"Who's there?" she asked a second time, but now more resigned as if her hope had dissipated.

Eigil halted, hesitating. What should he do?

The woman waited a moment longer, listening, twisting around on the bench, searching the burial ground for the noise maker before she bent her head once more.

His magic weakened. She had heard him despite his effort to cloak himself. He lifted one foot, stepping toward the bench. He reached out with his hand cupping the magic. No, he should say something first, otherwise she would startle if he touched her shoulder while she could not even see him. Slowly, he closed his fist and took a breath to speak. What could he say to her?

Eigil stood behind the bench within reach when a growling and sputtering noise announced the caretaker's carriage. Eigil knew the sound by now. The old man drove one of those horseless carriages, which emitted ill-smelling vapors and moved with a strange kind of magic. Almost all visitors to the burial ground had come in ones like it.

With effort, wasting much of his ebbing strength, he cloaked himself once more.

The caretaker's carriage sped toward the shed and the bench, its wheels kicking up dirt and skidding to a halt.

"There, there," the caretaker yelled as he jumped from the carriage and pointed where Eigil had been visible behind the bench a moment earlier. "A weirdo, standing behind you. Right there." His chest heaved. His outstretched hand trembled with excitement.

The woman twisted around, looking through Eigil.

"What are you talking about?" She gave him a stern and questioning look, pressing her lips into a thin line. "There's nobody there."

The caretaker stamped his foot. "No, course not. Not now. He was sneaking up behind you. Right there." Again, he jabbed his finger toward Eigil behind the bench. "Come away from there."

"I think you're imagining things, my good man. I don't see anyone." The man stomped around the bench, but his watery eyes searched in vain.

Eigil backed up too fast, stepping on his cloak's hem,

tripping. The caretaker made so much noise he did not seem to hear Eigil's stumbling and losing his balance, nor did he see him fall. *By the light!* Now, he would have to lie here on the cold ground until the man and the woman had gone. If he got up, his body would leave signs on the frozen ground, giving him away.

"He was here. I tell you." The caretaker kept pointing. "Look, the door of the shed is open. Damn, he was in there." He came around the bench, heaving and sputtering. "Wouldn't surprise me if that guy had something to do with your kid disappearing."

Eigil lay still. The moist chill penetrated his garments and made him shake with cold. He bit down hard to keep his teeth from rattling. As soon as they left, he should take the Celarim and find another place to hide now that the caretaker had seen him. No, this was not going well at all. What should he do? For the hundredth time, Eigil wished he had taken different actions, but how could he have foreseen that the magic would carry him out of Nugateris? He had wanted to go north to Mountain View where some of his distant and loyal relatives would have taken him in. But Makimus with his twisted ways had intervened and caused the plan to fail. If Eigil would not return and the councilor's actions were left unchecked, Makimus would bring an end to the Flora and everyone dear.

Eigil's hand shook with anger, cold, and mounting weakness. Already his body's outline shimmered, giving him a few short moments before becoming visible once more. Eigil waited until the caretaker had turned his back to him and sat. If he could make it behind the shed, and from there to the trees, he would be safe for now. With great effort, he maneuvered his legs under him and managed to raise himself onto his knees. Fear gave him strength. The stump of his left arm throbbed painfully with his racing pulse. It caused him much difficulty to keep his breath shallow and quiet. Yet, he wanted to scream his pain and frustration.

The caretaker sat down on the other end of the bench, still talking to the woman.

Eigil raised one shaking knee. It took him three tries before his leg obeyed and pushed him up onto his feet. Behind him, the frosted ground showed his body's imprint, but a bit of help came with a brief gust of wind rushing through the trees. Eigil waved his hand at the same time and stirred leaves and frost, destroying the telltale shape on the ground.

Eigil backed up and had almost reached the shed corner, when *crack* his foot broke a brittle branch in half.

The caretaker whipped around. "There!" He shouted. "There. You see him? Told you."

Eigil froze where he stood, doubling his effort to remain cloaked. The woman jumped up. She stood, not saying a word, and stared past the caretaker's outstretched arm and his pointing finger.

Had she seen him as well? As long as she could not validate the caretaker's claim, perhaps she would continue saying the man imagined things.

Eigil could not count on this. He waved his arm as he backed up farther, erasing his footprints as he went. When he had turned the shed's corner, he put his last strength into remaining upright and invisible and shuffled as fast as his wobbly legs would carry him into the shelter of the trees.

❧ *Chapter 18* ❧

Flynden woke with a start and sat. The grass swayed in the breeze rolling off the ocean. He looked through the tall stalks toward the forest. Something had woken him, but he couldn't say what. Beside him, Thistle still slept. Stace, who had decided to stay awake and keep watch, had nodded off anyway, sitting with his back against the stone wall, snoring.

The skin at the nape of Flynden's neck prickled. The strange magic tickled inside his belly. He craned his neck to get a better look at the forest and the rolling hills around them, but everything appeared calm and quiet. Too calm. Too quiet. No bird calls. No squirrel chatter.

The sun had traveled almost the whole sky and now hung low in the west, casting a warm glow over the grass, making the tops look like golden wheat. Why had Pelifeles gone with Sophie? He didn't have to go. He could've stayed with him and warned him. Now, he had to find out by himself, maybe too late. They all seemed to think he could wield his magic and solve their problems, but he didn't know how. He didn't know what it would do, or what *he* would do. This boy he had become no longer felt like him, and he was scared and lost without the cat, especially now. He pushed the thoughts aside. He had to believe he would be a match for whatever happened.

A woman in the service of the Flora had brought food and water to them earlier in the day, but she'd brought little news of Sophie and Bramble, and none of Pelifeles and Nelwyna. The Mother Flora had invited Sophie and Bramble to be her guests and had asked them to wait until the turning at dusk to speak with her at length, the woman had said. She had left them with a full belly and more questions.

Flynden reached over and placed a hand on Thistle's shoulder. The boy opened his eyes but didn't cry out in surprise or act stupid like some kids do when you want them to be quiet. Flynden started to like Thistle. He held one finger to his lips. Thistle nodded and sat as well.

"What?" he whispered.

Flynden shook his head and beckoned Thistle to follow him. Together, they crawled to where Stace was still fast asleep and snoring. His mouth hung open, and drool dripped from one corner down his chin. Flynden and Thistle grinned at each other before Flynden shook Stace's arm. Stace woke with a big snort.

"What? What is happening? Who is coming?"

"Ssh, Stace, it's only Thistle and me." Flynden crouched before his brother. "You were supposed to keep watch," he said. "Something woke me."

"What?" Stace rubbed his eyes. He sat up straighter and craned his neck a bit, scanning the grass and the forest. With his sleeve, he wiped the drool off his face.

"Not sure. My neck prickled something fierce," Flynden said. "The magic in my belly is coiling again."

Thistle sat down beside Stace, a bit closer than

normal. Stace gave him a sideways glance.

"You think the creature is coming back?"

Flynden twisted his torso, still on his knees, and faced the trees. The dark purple shadows between them hid whatever lay there.

"Don't know." Flynden shrugged, but his innards squirmed. If the creature came back, he was sure the magic inside him would fight again. Last time, it had left him helpless, stunned, and scared. He didn't like it then, and he wouldn't like it now.

"What if Councilor Makimus comes?" Thistle asked with fear in his voice as if he were more afraid of the man than the beast.

The three exchanged uncertain glances. No one said a word. Flynden wasn't sure himself what he liked less, Makimus or the creature. He would rather not see either one again.

The breeze died away and the hills fell silent. Flynden tensed, crouching lower. Stace and Thistle huddled on hands and knees. When Stace made a move to stand, Flynden waved him back down, shaking his head and mouthing the word *no*. Stace sank back onto his heels and put one arm around Thistle's shoulders.

Flynden raised his head once more. There, close to the nearest trees, the tall grass parted.

❧ ❧

The setting sun's golden light teased her face through a window. Sophie blinked and wrinkled her nose. She couldn't remember falling asleep. One moment Bramble and she had sat at the table in Gritta's small cabin, drinking tea, and the next moment, she lay on this bed.

All the running and the pain must have knocked her out.

The bed stood along one wall, the small window above it. Bramble lay beside her, sucking her thumb in her sleep. Gritta had left the cabin.

Sophie sat and swung her legs to the floor.

"Ouch."

Big holes in her leggings exposed her knees. Scraped skin and dried blood peeked through the fabric. She limped across the room to the cabin door where she stood for a moment and let the evening breeze fan her hot face and ruffle her hair. Flower and grass scent filled the air. Sophie sneezed into the crook of her arm and looked over her shoulder. Bramble whimpered but kept sleeping.

The sun sank behind the trees, blinking at her here and there from between the trunks while the wind brushed through the crowns. Sophie walked to the stone basin where Gritta had washed the Mother Flora's feet. Water splashed from the small fountain into the basin. She cupped her hands to catch it, drinking some. After she had splashed water on her face, she sat on the stone rim.

The large daisy that was the Mother Flora, beautiful and perfect, stood as before, the large blossom turned toward the sun. Sophie watched the sun setting. Would the Mother Flora turn back into a woman soon? Sophie itched to ask her questions and hoped the woman had answers.

Where were Pelifeles and Nelwyna?

"Pelifeles?" Sophie called. "Nelwyna?" She was surprised, but relieved, when the horse whinnied not far away. Soon, Nelwyna's sleek black body clip-clopped toward her. The tear-shaped white blaze on her forehead bobbed up and down like a lantern as she walked down the path and stopped by the gate.

"You have finally decided to wake?" Nelwyna snorted. "Sleeping all day. Tz, tz." She shook her head, sending her mane flying.

"I was tired from all the running," Sophie said, feeling angry. "Bramble is still sleeping."

"You are right. Perhaps you both needed the sleep."

"Where is Pelifeles?"

"How do I know what that feline is doing?" Nelwyna snorted.

"Come on, Nelwyna, stop bickering. We've got better things to do. Can we look for Pelifeles?"

The horse stuck her nose over the gate, cocked her head, and regarded Sophie with one black eye. For a second, she looked as if she would argue again.

"Fine. Let us look." Not waiting for Sophie, she trotted away.

Sophie shook her head and jumped up. "Nelwyna! Wait!" Pain ripped through her back and legs. Her knees buckled and she sank to the ground. "Ouch."

"What is it?" The horse stopped and called back. "By the light, what happened?"

"I need your help. Come back. Please," Sophie added in her nicest voice. Stop being such an idiot, she wanted to say, but the last thing she needed right now was Nelwyna walking off and making her run after her again.

Well, trying to be nice wasn't working. Sophie stared at Nelwyna trotting away.

"No! Please, come back!"

Nelwyna stopped, swiveled on her hind legs like a circus pony, and galloped back. With a powerful kick, her hind legs pushed off, and she landed in a dust cloud and tufts of grass beside Sophie.

"Gee, I thought you were going to leave me here." A lump in her throat made her cough. Sophie blinked a few times.

"Where does it hurt, girl?"

"It's my back and thighs," Sophie cried. "I think the wounds ripped open again, and my knees hurt a lot."

"Hold still," Nelwyna said and pushed her soft nose against Sophie's back.

What was the horse going to do? With a groan, Sophie twisted around.

"Hold still, I said."

"Calleo said he thought Pelifeles' magic would do something weird when I asked why Pelifeles wasn't healing my back."

"Well, I am not Pelifeles, am I?"

"No, you're not."

First, Sophie's back warmed and tingled, then the warmth moved down her legs, through her knees all the way down to her feet, taking the pain with it.

Sophie touched her legs. The wounds were covered with scabs, and the pain was gone. She scrambled up. "Thanks, Nelwyna."

"Never mind," the horse said gruffly. "Can you climb onto my back? I cannot help you with that."

"Sure, come over here." Sophie used the low wall around the courtyard as a step and swung her right leg over Nelwyna's back.

"Hold on," Nelwyna said.

Sophie had enough time to grab the mane before the mare jumped toward the wall and sailed over it. On the other side, she slowed to a walk and stopped.

"Well, where would you like to start looking?"

"How about we check on Flynden and the others first? Maybe Pelifeles is there." Sophie scooted forward on the horse's back, clamping her legs against her sides. "Have you checked on them?"

"Why would I? It is not my turn to watch them, is it?"

Sophie rolled her eyes. "Okay, let's go now and check," she said and dug her heels into Nelwyna's side.

The horse snorted and didn't move. "You do not have to kick me, girl. I know when to walk."

"Sorry." Sophie waited. "Well?" she said after a while. "Are we going or what?"

"I was thinking."

"About what?" Sophie sat back and sighed. What a blessing, horses normally didn't think and talk. It made things a lot easier.

"About Bramble." Nelwyna shifted her weight, making Sophie lean to one side. "Should we take her with us?" She stretched her head backward and eyed Sophie with one eye.

"Um." Sophie looked back to the cabin. "Nope. We'll let her sleep for now. Let's go." Sophie petted Nelwyna's neck.

"Very well." Nelwyna snorted and without warning, she lunged into a canter, almost toppling Sophie off her back. The horse trotted along the paths between houses, gardens, and trees, cutting corners here and there through yards without fences, but being careful not to step on any flowers, Flora or not. After a short while, Nelwyna stopped again, making Sophie slide onto her neck.

"I was thinking, Sophie," Nelwyna said. "The Flora will be turning soon and the Mother Flora might be wondering where you have gone. Should we not wait for her instead of running off?"

"We could be back before the Mother Flora changes again."

"Hm." Nelwyna straightened her neck. "The sun will be gone in a few short moments." She took a few steps.

"Can you not do something magical to get to the boys faster?" Sophie leaned forward and teased. "Aren't you a spirit mate like Pelifeles?"

"Do not compare me with that feline, please. To answer your question, yes, I can do certain things, but I am not Master Eigil." The horse stopped. "Let me think." She cocked her head. "Hm."

Sophie sat back but kept a tight grip on the silky mane. Maybe Nelwyna would lunge ahead again once she stopped her thinking.

"Well?" Sophie prodded Nelwyna's withers with a finger. "Any luck?"

"Not yet. I have many thoughts to sift through."

The sun sank lower, fast. Nelwyna was right. Maybe they should go back and wait for the Mother Flora.

Two small birds chased each other from tree to tree in the evening breeze. A fat black squirrel with tufted ears sat on a fence post, grooming itself. Another squirrel, this one a bit slimmer, joined it on the fence. In the garden behind it, where only that morning one of the Flora had sewn a few seeds, tiny flowers peeked through the soil. Wow, those Flora grew fast.

Sophie breathed the warm air with its soft flower scents. Then she sneezed again. Her mouth went dry. Some more water would be great.

"Come on, Nelwyna, it's getting late." Sophie wiggled her legs a bit but didn't dare kick the horse in the ribs.

"Has no one ever taught you to be patient, girl?"

"Well, yeah. I've been told that patience is a virtue."

"Rightly so. Now, practice what you have learned."

Sophie sighed and rolled her eyes. Nelwyna showed lots of Trudyish qualities. Instead of being irritated though, Sophie warmed to the horse's funny ways, the way she had warmed to Trudy's. But now she was stuck here and couldn't get back. If she ever saw Trudy again, she swore she'd be nicer to her.

"I have found an answer," Nelwyna announced and lifted her head. She bent her head around, her black eye sparkled with golden sunlight.

Sophie raised her eyebrows and leaned forward.

"We will turn back and consult the Mother Flora."

Sophie dropped her shoulders and sat back.

"After all your thinking, you've come up with that?" She shook her head. "Why did we leave in the first place?"

"You were the one who wanted to leave."

No, it wouldn't be good wasting time with arguing. Sophie grabbed the mane tighter and squeezed her knees against the horse's sides. "Never mind. Let's go back."

"Fine."

Nelwyna walked in a circle around the small garden and trotted back through town. Sophie bounced on her back and tried to stay up, looking stupid. Maybe running wasn't so bad after all. Shadows stretched and lengthened. Here and there, a rustling became louder than the breeze. Maybe they would reach the Mother Flora the moment she turned. Ooh, that would be cool. Fascinating as the Mother Flora's turning into a flower had been, it would be neat to see it the other way around, too.

A short while later they arrived back at the Mother Flora's house. Sophie slid forward, hugging the neck just in time when the horse stopped.

"You're really having a good time doing this, don't you?"

"I have no inkling of what you are talking about, girl." Nelwyna gave a little snort and shook her head and neck, shaking Sophie's arms off.

Sophie scooted back, swung her right leg over the withers, and jumped down.

"Good horse," she said and patted the sleek neck, then danced out of reach because Nelwyna gave a loud angry snort. Grinning, Sophie opened the garden gate, stepped through it, and let it bang shut behind her. She threw a glance over her shoulder. Nelwyna looked like she had her brows furrowed, if a horse could do such a thing.

A hush fell over the Garden town; all sound was gone for a moment like someone had flipped a switch. Right after the silence, the rustling swelled like crinkling tissue paper. The rustling and crinkling drowned out the wind and the birds in the trees.

Sophie sat down on the stone bench as the large daisy in the small garden began turning.

The lush green stems and leaves paled, changing in seconds. The stem split in half close to the ground, thickened, and shaped into slender legs. Two thinner stems higher up formed into two graceful arms with the biggest leaves at the ends stretching and curling into fingers and a thumb for each hand. The main stem twisted and thickened until a slender body emerged with a graceful neck holding the giant blossom, which now lowered to face them. The Flora's face appeared within the center, her eyes closed with a wrinkle between her brows. *Did the turning hurt?* Behind the petals framing her face, the long golden hair fell almost to her ankles as if she had taken out hairpins.

Gritta hurried from her cabin with a white gown over one arm, Bramble on her heels.

"Ah." The Mother Flora sighed and raised her shoulders, rolling them back and forth. She placed her hands on her hips and bent back to stretch her torso. First one leg, then the other, she stepped from the dark soil like a ballet dancer. "The turning seems to be harder the older I become." Her smile smoothed the wrinkled forehead. "I see you have waited for me, child."

Gritta helped the Mother Flora into the gown.

"I wanted to check on Flynden, but then Nelwyna and I thought it would be better to wait for you." Sophie leaned forward and looked into the woman's face.

"I will send someone to see how the young men are faring," the Mother Flora said.

"With all respect, Mother Flora," Gritta said. "I sent a woman this morning to bring the boys bread, fruit, and water. She returned, saying they were well."

"Yes, but, I'm worried," Sophie said and wrung her hands. "I want to make sure they're okay. Something could've happened during the day."

Gritta frowned at her. Sophie stared back without blinking.

"Rose! Lily!" The Mother Flora called. The breeze carried her soft melodic voice into a neighboring garden. Two petite and delicate women—even shorter than the Mother Flora—hurried over, still stretching the kinks from their arms, legs, and backs. One had crimson rose petals framing her dark-brown face with a green sheen to it. The other woman's features were white with a spring-green tint. The lily-white petals around her face glowed rosy in the sun's last warm rays.

Both women stepped to the gate and said, "What is

your need, Mother Flora?"

"I would like you to go to the gate by the forest and see if the three young men waiting there have need of anything."

"As you wish." Rose and Lily inclined their heads and right away hurried down the stone path.

"Not to worry, child. Your friends will be fine. Come." The Mother Flora took Sophie's arm and guided her to the cottage's back door. The sun plunged below the horizon, leaving a red-orange band on the bottom and dark blue sky above where stars sparkled like rhinestones on velvet. The moon rose round and yellow in the east.

"Now, child, let us find out what must be done to help you and Master Eigil." She pulled Sophie through the cottage's doorway.

Sophie ducked into a room like a kitchen with no stove or fireplace. Woven reed chairs stood around a long table in the center. Colorful wool rugs and runners lay on top of woven reed mats covering a hard earth floor. A hallway led off the kitchen farther into the house. A big cupboard with many drawers and doors took up one wall, and in the corner next to it stood a sink with a small shiny water pump.

The Mother Flora invited her to sit at the table and took a chair across from her. Gritta walked in with Bramble, and while the little girl scooted onto the chair beside Sophie, Gritta took four seashells from the cupboard: a shallow one like a plate and three small ones like mugs without handles. She plunked the mugs in front of them and with unsteady hands, poured water from a pottery carafe, so that some water slopped over the rim. The plate, she filled with small fruit pastries.

Sophie's mouth watered. She licked her lips.

Nelwyna stuck her head through the open door and leaned forward until the whole cottage creaked under her weight.

"So tell me, child, how did you come to be here? How did you meet Master Eigil? What did he ask you to do?" Then she laughed a tinkling laugh and stretched her hands toward Sophie across the table. "I apologize. I should ask one question at a time. Please forgive me. I am rather anxious to learn what has befallen my friend Eigil. I would like to know how I can help."

"Okay. No problem." Sophie shifted, uncomfortable under the woman's silvery gaze. The chair creaked when she leaned back. She rocked forward and took a deep breath. "It all started when my little brother died." Already, she had to swallow hard a few times and picked on a loose reed on the tabletop to hide her sadness.

The Flora reached over and gave her a reassuring pat on the hand.

Sophie pulled her hand back and looked away, but her gaze fell on Nelwyna who watched her, too. Sophie blinked. No, she wouldn't cry. She sniffed, grabbed the end of her tunic sleeves with each hand and wiped her eyes. Bramble snuggled against her arm. The Mother Flora waited quietly. Sophie sniffed a few more times, but then she had it back together.

"Anyway, I sat in a tree in the cemetery, watching the people by the grave when this old man suddenly stood beside the tree and started talking to me." Shamefaced, Sophie kept her eyes down and played more with the loose reed, remembering how little she'd paid attention to Master Eigil. In a few short sentences, she explained what had happened before she got to Nugateris and after, but she didn't mention the part about throwing the stone and finished with, "After our rescue from the pit, I woke in the forest clearing where the creature attacked us." She lifted both her shoulders and arms in a helpless gesture. "How would it have gotten out? Flyn fought it off and after it was gone, Kir and Calleo went back to warn the councilors and we came here. That's it, more or less." Then she added, "Flyn discovered he's got magic."

"Flynden? Fabrice's youngest?" The Mother Flora rose, alarmed. "He shows magic?"

"Yes. It's how he fought the creature."

The woman lowered herself back into the chair. "By the light," she murmured and stared at the shell she turned round and round with her small slender hands. She said nothing for a long time but got up from the table. When Gritta, who had leaned against the cupboard the whole time, wanted to refill her cup, the Mother Flora waved her away and refilled everyone's cups herself. Deep in thought, she moved around the kitchen but kept her thoughts to herself until she sat again.

"I am sorry, child, you had to go through this because of Master Eigil, but I assure you, he would not have asked for help if he needed it not. He must return to stop this madness."

"You think he can?" Sophie asked.

"I believe so." The Mother Flora nodded into her cup. When she looked up again, her silvery eyes were moist and shimmered even more. "We must help him. You must do as he says. I am certain the Flora blossom is what he needs. Take it back with you and help him come home."

"Sure, but how? Makimus is after us, and the creature, too."

The Mother Flora rose and paced along the table. "I am worried about the creature." She stopped. "You said she was like a Flora, turning?"

"Yes." Sophie nodded. "Why?"

The Mother Flora continued pacing and sighed. "Because for several years now, I have been aware of a presence like the Flora, but strangely so. I could never quite touch it with my thoughts. It would not let me come close." She shook her head.

Sophie wrinkled her brow. What did the Mother Flora mean?

"The presence was not hostile, but hesitant and shy. It could have been this creature. It puzzled me, but I believe it means no harm." She stopped and said to Sophie. "Perhaps it needs protection from Makimus."

"That's true," Bramble said. "The kitty's nice. It wants to help and to be safe."

"How do you know, child?" The Mother Flora sat and leaned toward the girl.

"The kitty told me." Bramble nodded hard. Her curls danced around her face. "The kitty is scared like us."

"Hm." The Mother Flora rested her chin on one hand. "Perhaps a possibility," she whispered to herself.

Sophie threw up her hands.

"Why did Makimus chase Master Eigil away and kept the creature in the pit? I don't understand why he's doing this."

"He craves revenge, child. He wants to take power from Master Eigil and the Flora. We are standing in his way." The Mother Flora lowered her voice even more, so that even Nelwyna leaned in closer against the doorframe. The cottage creaked and moaned.

"He is trying to …" She couldn't seem to finish.

"Do what?" Sophie took the Mother Flora's hands and held them, squeezing gently. "What's he trying to do?"

"Harm the Flora and me. Eliminate us all."

Sophie slapped a hand over her mouth and stared.

"Oh no," she mumbled behind her hand. "Why?"

The Mother Flora shook her head.

Sophie dropped her hand.

"That's so, so... That's horrible. But why?"

"For some time now, I've known that he hates the Flora," the Mother Flora said. "He does not want to be dependent on us and the seeds we gift to the High Council. Nor does he want the Choosing to continue because it took his mother from him and made him who he is."

"What's the Choosing?"

The Mother Flora sat and folded her hands on the table, staring ahead without seeing like gazing inside herself.

Say something. Sophie wanted to shake her when the silence dragged on. Why didn't she say something?

When the Mother Flora's eyes focused, she blinked and said, "When the council apprentices complete their apprenticeship and become councilors, the High Council of Gwern-cadarn-brac requests a Choosing where a woman with child is chosen to receive one of my regular seeds." The Mother Flora brushed a lock from her face and folded her hands again. "It is entirely voluntary and not all women come, but most do."

Sophie sat with her mouth open and remembered to close it when the Mother Flora stopped talking for a second. The woman's mouth twitched with a smile.

"When the children are born, they stay with their mothers for only the first year of their lives before the mothers surrender their sons to the High Council. The seed also changes the women. They become Flora, and I invite them to live in the Garden."

"Like Amabel, Kir's mom?" Sophie asked.

"Yes, like Amabel." The Mother Flora nodded. "Not all women come. They do not have to live here. Some prefer to live close to their families."

"Do they get to visit each other at least?"

"Of course, the mothers go to see their sons or the boys come to the Garden."

"But they cannot be together anymore all the time?"

The Mother Flora shook her head.

"No, they cannot. It is sad, but it has to be like that to preserve the peace and keep everyone safe."

How sad for the boys and their mothers. It sounded awful. And why would it keep everyone safe?

As if the Mother Flora had read her thoughts, she said, "It is not all bad. The councilors love the boys like sons. And like a father, each councilor teaches the apprentice all he needs to know to live life well and to control the magic."

"Like Kir and Calleo."

"Yes."

"So, that's what happened to Makimus too and now he hates you for it?" Somehow, Sophie could see the point of it. She would hate it, too.

"I believe so."

"What's got Master Eigil to do with all of this?" This didn't add up, at least not in her mind.

"Master Eigil overheard Makimus telling Camshron that he plans to take my three special seeds to grow the legendary seed tree." She paused. "I will not surrender them." Resolve and firmness made her words strong.

"Where do you keep those seeds?" Sophie asked. "Maybe you could hide them, so he'll never find them."

The Mother Flora flipped both hands over on the table, palms up, exposing tiny little slits in the middle of both palms. She lifted the left hand.

"In this hand, I carry the regular seeds like all Flora." She closed her eyes and furrowed her brows. The slit like a stoma on a leaf opened in her hand and a pea-size seed, perfectly round and spring green, popped out and rolled onto her palm.

"Wow." Sophie stared.

The Mother Flora lifted her right hand.

"This hand holds the three special seeds."

Sophie watched and waited, but the Mother Flora didn't pop out another seed.

"When my time comes, I will release one of these three seeds for my successor, who will carry her own three special seeds."

"What happens to the other two?"

"Let us call them spare ones," she said and curled her fingers into a fist. "Taking those three seeds from me by force would have dire consequences."

Sophie wondered what it meant, but the Mother Flora continued.

"Should Makimus succeed and take those seeds, all Flora will die with my passing and Nugateris will revert to what it was before the Flora arrived, dark and cold. Demons and pale ones will return."

"Why is everyone so scared of these pale ones? Aren't they just fair-skinned people with blond or red hair, like me?" She touched her hair and pointed at her freckled nose.

"There is no reason to be afraid. It is only a prejudice.

Having acclimated to the sun and warmth that is now common on Nugateris, most people are dark-skinned, but all people are descendents of the pale ones. Most seem to have forgotten that."

"We've got issues like that, too. I mean, people being treated differently just because they look different."

The Mother Flora nodded. "I can see how this is so where people remain ignorant of the truth.

"But there is one thing that is quite puzzling," the Mother Flora said. "You see, Councilor Makimus hates pale ones, although his parents were fair-skinned and blond like Bramble and Thistle, and you. He does not wish anyone to know and has tried all of his life to hide the fact that he is also a pale one." The Mother Flora sighed and leaned back. "A devoted son, he came to visit his mother often in his younger years. I do not know what happened to his father."

"Do you think…?" Sophie was afraid to ask.

"I am not sure what to think, child. I do not wish to think the worst." The Mother Flora held up her hands. "All I know is that Makimus wants the seed tree. He will be the most powerful man in Nugateris, master of all. Terrible things would happen. I believe Master Eigil took the Celarim to prevent harm. One foolish councilor thought it wise to write the legend of the seed tree into the book." She shook her head, her eyes sad. "Master Eigil must have lost the Flora blossom when he fled with the book."

"Pelifeles thinks Makimus cut Master Eigil's hand off when he tried to get away because Master Eigil had only a stump and no left hand when I saw him," Sophie said.

The Mother Flora gasped; her fingers reached up to her trembling lips.

"We can't let Makimus win. We must stop him." Sophie slapped the table and made them jump.

At the door, Nelwyna shied and whinnied, and almost broke the doorframe.

"Well said, Sophie, well said."

❧ *Chapter 19* ❧

Near the forest at the gate, Flynden crouched low, no taller than the wall. Beside him, Stace sat with his back pressed against the stone. Thistle pressed against him, shaking. Flynden held his breath; only once in a while he remembered to let it out in short, quiet bursts. The grass tips quivered and parted with something or someone moving through it, a bit to the left, then to the right, as if searching. Was the creature looking for them? Or Makimus? No, the councilor would not crouch low. He would stand much taller than the grass.

The sun dipped deeper and lighted the wall, the hills, and Thistle's white-blond hair fiery orange.

Flynden's neck prickled. He clenched and unclenched his fists. How would he know what to do? The magic in his belly stirred and churned, making him feel sick. Would it show him how to protect Stace and Thistle? He didn't know. He swallowed a few times. One thing at a time. He took a few deep, calming breaths. It helped for a moment, but then the fear was back.

The grass swayed with the wind, and once in a while, big lumps of it split apart, closer now. The waves rolling onto the beach sounded somehow louder. In the distance, a seagull cried and another one answered. Then silence again.

There, straight ahead the grass moved again. Flynden flexed his feet and ankles with all ten fingers on the ground before him. He could smell the rotten breath and the filthy fur. Close. Too close. He tightened his leg muscles and lifted his back end. He glanced sideways to his brother. Stace opened his mouth to say something, but Flynden shook his head, jabbed his chin toward the grass, raised one finger to his mouth, and with his hand palm up, pumping it in the air, he motioned Stace to get up. Stace rolled in one smooth motion onto his feet, squatting low and pulling Thistle up with him. The boy huddled on his knees shaking hard. Stace urged him to get up but Thistle looked too scared to move.

For a short moment, the grass parted enough for Flynden to glimpse red eyes in a sleek black face and tufts of white-blond fur on the head.

Then the creature jumped.

কু   কু

Night had settled while Sophie and the Mother Flora talked. Crickets chirped. Lightning bugs and moths flitted in and out of the window, attracted by the small white globes that the Mother Flora lighted with a touch of her hand.

"So, what do we do?" Sophie asked.

"First, you must bring the Flora blossom to me. Do you remember where you have hidden it?"

"Yes, in a hole in a tree outside the city. With Flynden's and Pelifeles' help I'll get it back for sure."

"Good. For reasons I cannot explain, you are able

to pass through the mists, but Master Eigil cannot without it."

This made Sophie proud. The Mother Flora and Master Eigil counted on her. She wouldn't let them down.

"The Flora blossom is powerful. The Flora gifted it to the High Council and they set it into the Celarim's cover."

Hurried footsteps interrupted her. Nelwyna withdrew her head and stepped aside. Rose and Lily slipped in through the door, exchanging quick glances. "Mother Flora," Rose gasped for breath. Lily trembled beside her. They panted like they'd been running.

The Mother Flora rushed to them. "What is it, children?"

"There," the women pointed outside the window. "There…at the gate…by the forest."

They all rushed outside.

Bright flashes lit the sky, some greenish ones, others a brilliant white.

"Oh no!" Sophie yelled. "Flynden! Stace! We have to help them."

"Thithle!" Bramble screamed.

"Nelwyna, would you permit us to ride on your back?" The Mother Flora bowed to the horse. "We would be much obliged if you would."

"Of course." Nelwyna stepped to the stone wall, even bending one front leg to lower herself and make it easier for the Mother Flora to climb up.

Sure, if the Mother Flora asked there was no problem with riding. Sophie grimaced.

With a young woman's agility, the Mother Flora stepped onto the wall and swung her right leg over the back. Sophie clambered up behind her.

"I want to come with you." Bramble raised her harms to be picked up.

"No, Bramble, you stay with Gritta. We'll be back soon," Sophie called over her shoulder.

Nelwyna jumped the garden wall, not bothering with the gate. Gritta rushed to grab Bramble because the little girl started to run after them.

The mare cantered through the town, but once out in the open, she stretched her long legs and galloped at full speed up the nearest hill. Sophie clamped her legs against the horse's belly. The Mother Flora's long hair whipped her face and arms and the wind brought tears to her eyes and pushed them into her tousled hair.

Moon and stars lit the way for Nelwyna as she raced through the night. Ahead in the dark, white light flashed and cracked like lighting bolts anchored to the ground. It mingled with yellow-green light above a fire roaring through the grass. Gray and black smoke billowed in the air. The stench of burned grass, burned fingernails, and sour apple mixed all together made Sophie gag.

Off to the side, something black and white streaked past the horse toward the fire.

"Peli!" Sophie yelled, but the cat didn't seem to hear and didn't slow down. Nelwyna must have seen the cat too because she picked up speed like someone had hit her on the rump. Her hooves thundered on the ground.

With a loud boom, a bright yellow-green flash overpowered the other lights and snuffed out the fire, leaving a scary darkness and silence. Smoke blocked out the twinkling stars overhead. Now mostly burned sour apple stank up the air.

Nelwyna slowed to a trot, to a walk, stopped, and nickered.

"What happened?" Sophie whispered.

The Mother Flora didn't answer and sat like a statue.

"Somebody say something," Sophie said.

When the horse and the Flora remained silent, Sophie yelled, "Flynden!"

"I think we are too late, child." The Mother Flora twisted around.

"No, we can't be. We have to help them."

Ignoring the possible consequences, Sophie kicked Nelwyna hard with both heels. "Go, Nelwyna. Go!"

With a powerful kick, the horse jumped with all four legs in the air and lunged forward, racing ahead. She skidded to a stop by the wall and sent her riders sliding up her neck.

Sophie didn't take the time to settle back, but flung herself off the horse and hit the ground running, racing along the wall.

"Flynden! Stace!" she yelled. "Thistle!"

The tall grass, now burned to stubbles poked Sophie's arms and hands as she groped in the dark, feeling her way along the wall on hands and knees until a bright light blinded her. She squinted at Pelifeles who appeared before her.

"My fault. All my fault," the cat murmured. His ears drooped, and he sat on the wall with hanging head.

"Where are they, Pelifeles?" Sophie screamed.

"Over there. Maybe dead. Maybe he killed them."

"Makimus?"

"No. Flynden. All my fault."

"No, no!" Sophie shook her head and hammered the ground with her fists. "No!"

The Mother Flora slid off Nelwyna's back, came up beside Sophie, and hugged her. "Where are the boys,

Pelifeles? Show me," she said and let go of Sophie, following the cat into the darkness.

Sophie scrambled up and after them. No, it couldn't be. Please don't let them be dead. Please don't let Flynden be the one. Please. She wasn't sure with whom she was pleading with but she kept doing it anyway.

Pelifeles began circling. Within the lighted circle lay Stace, Thistle, and the creature, all twisted and broken looking. Someone ran off into the dark toward the forest. Was it Flynden?

"Flyn!" Sophie screamed. "Flyn, come back!"

"He ran away." Pelifeles sounded pathetic.

Anger boiled up and made her feel sick.

"Then go after him! Go! What's the matter with you?"

Pelifeles crouched and said. "It's too late now. I should've been here to save them. This would've never happened if I'd stayed with Flyn."

Her anger vanished. Poor Peli. How bad must he feel? She reached out to pet him, pulled her hand back for a second, then caressed his white ear. He said nothing and didn't even seem to notice her touch.

"Could you maybe still do something for Stace and Thistle with your magic? Remember, you saved me from Makimus' net."

"Yes, but you weren't dead."

The Mother Flora knelt beside Stace and placed her hands on his chest. Her shoulders slumped. She hung her head.

Sophie knelt beside her. *Not Stace. Good, kind Stace.*

The Mother Flora stood, gave the creature a wide berth, and knelt beside Thistle. There she did the same thing with her hands, but then looked up.

"He is alive," she called.

Sophie glanced once more at Stace and placed the palm of her hand against his cheek.

"Sorry. I'm so sorry, Stace," she said. Her chest tightened and hurt so much, but she swallowed her tears, jumped up and hurried over to where the Mother Flora cared for Thistle.

"He has difficulty breathing," the woman said.

Sophie knelt on the boy's other side and crouched over him.

"Thistle? It's me, Sophie."

"He got us. He came." Thistle took a deep breath and grimaced like it hurt a lot, though Sophie couldn't see any injuries.

"Who did?"

Thistle moved his head from side to side. "Makimus came at us right after, after…"

"After what? What did he do?"

Thistle didn't answer. The Mother Flora gently prodded and probed along his torso, up his neck to the crown of his head.

"He is hurt, child. Let the questions wait."

They couldn't wait; they needed to know what happened.

"Thistle, where is Flynden?" Sophie asked.

Thistle's eyelids fluttered open again. "Don't know. And Bramble?"

"She's back in the Garden. One of the women there is looking after her."

Thistle closed his eyes. Then he whispered, "Flynden tried to protect us. The creature came. Then Makimus. The magic hurt." His chest quivered. "So much." Thistle swallowed hard, fell silent, and lay still, tears dripping into his hair.

An owl hooted in the forest. The wind picked up and carried the smoke away, but the smell of burned grass and sour apple lingered.

"Pelifeles! Nelwyna!" Sophie scrambled up. "Let's find Flyn." She took a few steps toward the forest. "Come on."

Nelwyna vaulted over the low wall with one easy jump and landed with a dull thud beside them. Pelifeles made his white fur glow again and cast a circle of light on the charred ground.

"Where were you anyway?" Sophie asked.

Pelifeles didn't answer and slunk away into the darkness. Sophie hurried after him.

"Come on, Peli, this is important."

"As if I don't know." Nose to the ground like a dog, he sniffed here and there, changed direction, and headed for the forest.

Nelwyna followed them, zigzagging a few steps behind, nose in the air. Their paths joined into one at the forest's edge.

Sophie peered past the first trunks into the purple shadows. The last thing she wanted was to go back into the forest, but if Flynden was in there, she would go. Somewhere deep in the forest, the owl hooted again. When the bird's call faded away, the forest fell quiet, more so than before it seemed. It was like someone had closed the door of a sound-proof room.

Pelifeles padded into the darkness. Light shot up the trunks where he passed. Sophie rested one hand on top of Nelwyna's neck and grabbed a fistful of her mane. Making little sound, they followed Pelifeles, keeping close to him as they walked deeper into the forest. Nelwyna's hooves thudded in the eerie silence. The forest stood still, like waiting for something to happen.

Earlier when they had come through the forest, a calming peppermint scent had been easy to breathe. Now, a pungent acidic smell irritated Sophie's nose and throat. She shivered and tried to hold her breath but gasped for air when she couldn't hold it any longer.

Sophie stepped on a twig that cracked like a gun shot, and she jumped. Nelwyna nickered and shook her head. They both stopped and listened. Pelifeles got farther ahead. His light glowed up the trunks now far away, then winked out and plunged them into total darkness.

"Peli!" Sophie called. "Where are you?"

No answer.

"Peli? Flyn?"

"That cat," Nelwyna said. "By the light, why does he have to be so difficult?"

Sophie laid her hand against the horse's neck and stroked the sleek coat.

"He isn't being difficult. He's upset because he believes it's his fault and he failed Flyn."

Nelwyna snorted. "Dumb little feline."

Coming from her, it sounded almost endearing.

"What now?" Sophie asked.

"We keep going."

"Without light?" Sophie reached for the withers.

"I am a spirit mate after all, am I not? I can do as well as the feline who has left us in the dark."

Sophie sighed. "Fine. Let's go." She didn't feel like arguing. They had to find Flynden. It was all that mattered.

She stumbled through the woods at Nelwyna's side. Where had Pelifeles' light shone last? Seconds stretched into minutes. Sophie shivered and tightened her fist on the mane. Nelwyna kept hoofing forward, her breathing louder in the stillness.

With a slap and a crack, a blinding light flared in front of them. Sophie fell backward and slammed into a tree.

"Ouch."

Nelwyna reared, whinnying. Pelifeles barred the way, hackles raised, and jumped sideways with a rounded back. His tail had gone bottle-brush.

"Stop," he hissed.

Sophie gulped for air. For a second, she forgot to breathe.

"Why did you have to scare us like that?" Sophie rubbed her arm where she had scraped it against a tree bark.

"You would've walked right into Flyn. That's why." Still hissing, Pelifeles dimmed the light though and smoothened his fur. All at once, he looked dejected again.

There, right on a pile of leaves, Flynden lay curled into a tight ball, not moving. Sophie crouched and placed her hand on his shoulder.

"Flyn?" She rubbed his arm. "Flyn, are you okay?"

He said nothing.

Nelwyna touched her nose to his face with a low rumbling nicker. She nudged him a few times, but still Flynden didn't move.

Fear gripped Sophie. Was he alive? To make sure, she placed her index finger on the side of his neck the way she'd sometimes done with Tommy. A pulse throbbed in Flynden's neck. Several sparks jumped from his skin to her finger and zapped her. She snatched her hand away and bent close to his ear.

"Flyn, are you hurt?"

"Don't know," came a muffled sob. "Hurt Stace and Thistle."

"No, I'm sure you just wanted to save them."

Flynden raised his head and gave her a sideways glance. "How do you know?" His head fell back onto the dark leaves. "You weren't even there."

Sophie frowned. "No, I wasn't. I'm sorry."

Flynden tried to sit up. Sophie helped him because he seemed too weak to do it by himself. She sat down beside him, wrapping both arms around him the way she had done with Tommy when he struggled with his asthma attacks. Flynden sniffed a few times, his nose running like he had a bad cold.

"The Mother Flora stayed with Thistle and Stace while we came looking for you," she said and hugged him close.

"Are they…?" Flynden swallowed. "How are they?"

Sophie looked at Pelifeles who closed his eyes and hung his head. Nelwyna did the same. So it was up to Sophie to tell him, but she couldn't get a word out. A big lump in her throat made it hard to breathe and impossible to talk. She didn't have to say anything, though. One look at her face and Flynden started bawling, twisting his head into Sophie's shoulder.

"It's all my fault," he sobbed.

"No, it isn't." Sophie shook her head and wiped away Flynden's tears with the sleeves stretched over her fist. "You didn't ask the creature to come after us. Did you? Or for Makimus to show up and attack you, too. If it's anyone's fault, it's his." She bit her lip, anger and loathing boiled up inside. If she only had magic like her friends, she would give Makimus some of it. "Master Eigil will deal with him."

"Well," Nelwyna cleared her throat. "He would have to be here before he could do anything, would he not?"

"True, but isn't there something we can do in the mean time?"

"For example?" Pelifeles asked. "Tie Makimus to a chair and hit him with a stick?"

Sophie grinned and shrugged. "Don't know. Something."

Nelwyna snorted. "The Mother Flora must have something in mind. She will tell us what needs to be done."

"Come on, Flyn, let's go back. You can't stay here."

Flynden rolled to his knees and stood. With Nelwyna's consent, he scrambled onto her back, using a toppled tree as a step. After some begging, she allowed Sophie to sit behind Flynden, just to hold him up, of course.

Pelifeles lighted the way but hadn't gone far when he stopped suddenly in the middle of the path and Nelwyna almost stepped on him. She snorted.

"What I really want to know," he said, blinking his yellow eyes, "is how you came to have magic, Flyn."

Chapter 20

They trekked back to the wall without speaking. Closer to the charred area, Nelwyna slowed and finally stopped where the Mother Flora still knelt beside Thistle. The Mother Flora must have called Rose, Lily, and other Flora who circled her and the boy. Off to one side, four Flora wrapped Stace's body into a white cloth. A knot in Sophie's stomach hardened into a hard, heavy weight that sank lower with every minute.

For a moment, Flynden sat motionless on the horse, staring, before he twisted out of Sophie's hug, swung his right leg over Nelwyna's wither, and slid off the horse.

"Flyn!" Sophie yelled and scrambled after him.

Flynden's legs buckled. Doubled over, he pushed through the circle of Flora and crawled to the spot where Stace lay wrapped like a mummy. Flynden scooped up the lifeless body and clutched it like a useless deflated lifesaver, rocking back and forth, his face buried in the crook of Stace's neck.

Poor Flyn. Poor Stace.

Feeling helpless, Sophie stood watching Flynden's shoulders tremble. The knot in her stomach grew bigger, and her body numbed. Something ugly grew from the knot and blossomed into envy. Where did it come from? She knew. It was because *she* never got to hold Tommy. *She* never held her parents either. They had died and gone without her being there, holding them, crying over them. She had never had the chance to say good-bye.

Her legs folded under her right behind Flynden. She reached for him, then changed her mind. Maybe it was better to leave him alone. She wouldn't want anybody to bug her; she would want privacy. She pulled her arm back.

Pelifeles had none of those problems. He slunk beneath Flynden's arm and pressed against his ribs. With his magic, he wrapped up the three of them like a small island of light on the blackened ground.

Sophie hung her head and hugged herself. Her eyes stung fiercely, and her raw throat hurt when she swallowed. Any minute now, she would be throwing up. Hot tears burned her eyes but she blinked them away. No point in falling apart. She'd be strong for her friends now. Her body trembled like it wanted to shake away the pain and sorrow. She rocked back and forth like Flynden, holding herself. A throbbing and whooshing filled her ears and blocked out other sounds around her. Nelwyna's warm, velvety nose pressed into the back of her neck for a moment before it lifted away again, but the warm breath still tickled her skin.

Many minutes later, Sophie rubbed her face with her sleeves but kept her burning, itchy eyes on the trio. Flynden had stopped rocking and sat holding his dead brother. The Flora began singing, a strange buzzing or a low hum filled the air with no real melody. More Flora came, creating an even wider, stronger circle around them all.

Also within the circle lay the creature. Its sleek black

body with the white-blond stripe down the middle slowly changed. The Mother Flora handed Rose a cloth to wipe Thistle's forehead, pushed herself up, and cautiously approached the creature.

Giving Flynden another glance, Sophie got up too and joined her. While they watched, the creature morphed into a woman. Powerful limbs changed into pale arms and legs and a slender white body. The feline features receded leaving a beautiful woman's face. Her long white-blond hair draped around her naked body. Bloody slashes crisscrossed her limbs; a big bleeding gash ran from her left shoulder across her chest to her hip.

The Mother Flora knelt beside the woman, one hand clamped over her mouth, her eyes wide and terrified. Her other hand hovered and moved in the air above the body like she wanted to touch it but couldn't decide where.

"By the light," she mumbled behind her hand. "By the light."

Sophie leaned forward and reached for the Mother Flora's arm. "What's wrong?"

The Mother Flora shook her head, back and forth, like a person gone mad. She let her hand drop and looked up, eyes brimming with tears and resting on Flynden and Stace a few feet away.

"Flynden," the woman on the ground whispered. "Flynden, please."

Loud and clear, the Mother Flora called, "Flynden, come. Quickly."

Something in her voice made Flynden turn his head. His eyes popped as he gazed at the woman on the ground. In slow motion, he lowered Stace's body to the ground and tried to get up. The Flora wanted to help him, but he pushed them away, shaking his head. With much effort, he heaved himself onto his feet and staggered forward like a drunken person but stopped after a few steps.

"Flynden." The woman's hoarse whisper still carried a bit of the creature's growl but also a gentle note. "Please come." She reached for him but dropped her arm, grabbing the charred ground instead.

"Who are you?" Flynden asked, took a few more steps, and knelt beside her, still out of reach. "How do you know me?"

The woman closed her eyes. The Mother Flora beckoned Lily to bring some white cloth. From a large pouch, Rose took leaves and placed them along the wounds. Afterward, they covered the woman's body, tucking the fabric around her.

Flynden approached until he reached the outstretched hand and knelt beside it but still not touching. "Who are you?" he asked again. "What happened to you?"

The woman's eyes fluttered open. She had turned completely human and with sad blue eyes looked up into Flynden's face.

"I am Eleta," she began, coughed, and stopped.

The Mother Flora took a small bowl with water from Lily's hand, and lifting Eleta's head, she held the bowl to the injured woman's lips. The water ran down her chin as the bowl tipped, but some must have gone down fine though because she stopped coughing.

"You must not exert yourself, Eleta," the Mother Flora said. "Rest."

Eleta moved her head from side to side. "My life is flitting away, Mother Flora. I must tell Flynden everything. He must know."

The Mother Flora closed her eyes, nodded, and like a

mother, moved some hair off Eleta's forehead. Flynden's eyes flicked back and forth between them, leaning forward, yet a big frown scrunched up his face.

"Ten years ago," Eleta began again as her eyes met Flynden's, "I was with child." She swallowed and her whole neck convulsed with the effort. "The High Council invited women with child to visit Gwern-cadarn-brac for the Choosing. It was an unusual request because a Choosing had taken place not long before. Rumors circled a chosen woman from the last ceremony had given birth to a sickly boy who would not live long enough to become councilor. Another boy was needed to take his place."

The Mother Flora covered her face and nodded into her hands. The woman's eyes flicked to her and back to Flynden.

"I did not want to go," Eleta said with a finality and strength. "I wanted to have my child, and I wanted it to grow up like a regular boy or girl." Again, her eyes flicked to the Mother Flora. "I wanted to remain a woman and bring up the child myself at home on our farm. The thought of giving him away and becoming Flora terrified me."

Eleta coughed again. After a few more sips of water, she was able to continue.

"My husband and my father bullied me into making the journey to the city. They talked about honor and riches bestowed on our family should I be chosen. My mother supported me. We both argued we were not wanting for anything because of my coveted weaving skills and the beautiful cloths I was producing. We also had the farm." She closed her eyes again. Her chest rose and fell with shallow breaths.

Did Eleta see the farm in her mind and her life the

way it had been ten years ago?

The wind brushed over the stubbles of burned grass, rustled through the trees, and stirred Sophie's hair and the Flora's long flowing gowns.

Eleta opened her eyes.

"I complied with my father and my husband as any good daughter and wife ought to. Yet, I was scared, a fear I could not push aside. I should have been proud, but I was not. A small hope wrestled with the fear. There was, after all, a chance I would not be chosen, I told myself, since the odds were in my favor. Only one woman would have to give her child and her life that night." Her breath rattled in her throat. "The ceremony began. The moon climbed the night sky and with it rose my fear." Eleta trembled and took another shaky breath. "Dancing and festivities filled the city. Yet, I stood with fear in my heart, not so much for myself but for my unborn child."

The Mother Flora cried into her hands now. Eleta lay quietly for a while.

Why was the Mother Flora so upset? Though Sophie knew already the story's bad ending, listening to how it happened sounded terrifying. Sweat and shivers tingled down her spine.

"As the moon approached the zenith, its beam came closer and closer to where I stood. I cried and prayed to the light, but when the gong rang loud and clear through the park, the moon beam had chosen me." Eleta moved her head from side to side. "I shook my head, not wanting it to be true, wishing it away. The Mother Flora guided me from the midst of the other women to gift me her sacred seed. Before I could make myself stop, I begged her, pleaded with her, and told her I did not want this." Tears trickled from the corner of Eleta's eyes and made big wet blotches on the white cloth. "No one was more surprised than I when the Mother Flora gave me the choice, telling me I did not have to accept this. The light would choose another woman by the next full moon. She squeezed my hands ready to make the announcement."

The Mother Flora took Eleta's hand now and held it, kissing it, pressing it against her chest.

"She had not taken more than a few steps when Makimus rose from his place amongst the other councilors and strode to intercept her. 'We will not have this, Mother Flora, the woman was chosen, she will obey,' he bellowed. The Mother Flora argued with him, but he would not yield to her wishes. The Mother Flora demanded to wait for High Councilor Eigil's return from a journey and make a final decision then, but Makimus would not hear of it. He was in charge. He would decide. Then he had me taken away under the pretence of wanting to persuade me." Sobs now rattled Eleta; her whole body shook as they racked through her. "He did nothing like this. Instead, he had me bound and confined to a dark room. Every day he came and fed me seeds, and every day he tortured me with magic. I could not see myself, but I felt myself changing. At first, I did not know what this did to me, but I knew it could not be good. My terror mounted. What would this do to my child?"

Sophie could no longer just sit and do nothing. She knelt beside Flynden and hugged him. This story was going somewhere much worse now.

Flynden shook as hard as Eleta, but he no longer cried. Now, he looked angry enough to punch somebody. He balled his hands into tight fists against his chest. Pelifeles hissed and a low growl rumbled in his throat. Nelwyna stood with hanging head but snorted so low it sounded like growling, too. The Flora stood and listened. After a few long heavy moments, Eleta continued.

"Then one day, a few hours before the birth of my child, High Councilor Eigil returned from his journey. He found me and promised to help.

"So, Councilor Eigil helped me give birth and let me spend a few moments with you. I named you Flynden. I begged him to take you first and keep you safe. He carried you away, and I never saw you again until the moment in the forest." Now a bitter smile stretched across her face. "It did not take him long to return. With him, he brought a dead baby boy, a few hours old like you. I still remember the dark hair and the light brown skin. Master Eigil never told me whom he took the dead child from. He wrapped the tiny lifeless body into the soiled cloth from the birthing and pressed the bundle into my arms. I still remember the sad smile on his face when he said, 'Only for a short while, Eleta, to fool Makimus.' I did not ask him where he had taken you, so that I would not be able to give away our secret."

Sophie let go of Flynden when he scooted closer to Eleta and cradled his mother's head in his lap.

"I trusted he would take me there as well, but he did not return quickly enough because Makimus came before him and was furious about the child's death. Fortunately, he never investigated and thought it was my child, but he punished me by taking me to the pit and leaving me there, feeding me dead animals and using me to terrify other unwilling victims."

Sophie gagged, but bit her lip hard and watched Flynden throw himself onto Eleta, holding on to her.

"Mother, oh, mother. Forgive me for what I've done."

She reached for his hair tenderly as if afraid to hurt him.

"None of this is your fault, Flynden. Perhaps it is all my doing. I wanted a normal life for you. I wanted to be happy, and I wanted happiness for you, but I only made my whole family unhappy."

"Why didn't they help you?" Sophie asked. "Did they never come looking for you?"

"No, they did not," Eleta said. "When guards carried me away, I pleaded and begged my father and my husband to help me, but the two only brandished their fists and disowned me, saying they no longer knew me."

"I could have done more," the Mother Flora whispered. "Perhaps I could have stopped Makimus, but I did not because I believed he would not harm you. When I later asked, he told me he had sent you home with your family. I believed him." The Mother Flora dried her eyes. "When your mother came to me, Eleta, and told me you never came home, we searched and asked, but no one knew where you had gone. We suspected wrongdoing, but we never found you. A short time later, I sensed a strange presence. I tried to communicate with you but never received an answer."

"I heard and sensed you too, Mother Flora, but I was angry, and I despaired."

"Child, I could have helped." She took Eleta's hand.

"Bitterness prevented me from answering you."

Flynden bent over his mother, sobbing. "I, I killed you, m…mother."

"Ssh, son, it is well. It was not you who wounded me." She clutched his hand, and he held hers with both of his like a precious gift. "You tried to protect and save us all with your magic. Yes, I will die, but because of you, I will not live out my life as a monster. I believe only you and your magic could have done this because you are my child, my beloved son." She squeezed his hands and moaned while spasms twisted her body. Her back arched off the ground. Flynden pressed her back down onto the white cloth.

"What is happening, Mother Flora?" Panicking, he looked at the Mother Flora, his eyes wide and scared.

"Listen, son," Eleta said, before the Mother Flora could answer. "There is more." Her gaze lingered not on Flynden but on the white cloth wrapping Stace's body. "Stace must have been a good brother to you, but he is not your real brother. Thistle is your half-brother and the little girl Bramble is your half-sister. My husband Braen took my unwilling sister Moirae as second wife and she gave birth to the two children. Thistle and Bramble told me in the pit some of what they knew. I stitched together the rest. What became of my parents, your grandparents, I do not know, but I do know Makimus killed both Braen and Moirae." Eleta went silent, her breathing even shallower now. "He released me from the pit with the promise I would kill Sophie, Thistle, and Bramble. I agreed and lied to him so he would release me."

Flynden looked confused when his eyes settled on Thistle's still body.

Of course, it explained a lot. That's why Thistle, Bramble, and Flynden looked so much alike.

"Your father died of grief when you did not return home after a while," the Mother Flora said and patted Eleta's other hand. "He could not bear what he had done and what he let happen to you. Your mother,

Gritta, being the stronger of the two, came to live with the Flora. She will be overjoyed to see you again."

Eleta looked over to the Mother Flora, and her voice steadied a little. "It will be too late. You cannot save me." To Flynden she said, "Son, I always imagined, no, longed to see you, to know what you would look like. Wondered how you grew up, fearing but hoping the magic would spare you. Now that I have met you, and see what a fine boy you have become, I am proud of you. Even though you do possess the magic, I hope it does not become the curse I feared it would be."

Her voice had gone so quiet. They leaned in closer for her last words.

"Mother?" Flynden bent forward trying to hold her, but Eleta's body didn't move anymore, and her eyes stared past Flynden into the night sky where the stars did the twinkling for them.

❧   ❧

In a long silent line, more Flora arrived from the Garden. They brought branches and reeds that they cut and wove into a long stretcher for Stace and Eleta. Without grumbling or complaining, holding her head high, Nelwyna pulled the stretcher toward the Garden's center. The Mother Flora saved Thistle's life, but he was weak and could not walk by himself, so she called Gritta to carry him.

When Gritta came and saw Eleta, the old woman sank beside the stretcher and gently touched the dead woman's face, which looked so much like hers, and Thistle's, and Bramble's, but most of all like Flynden's. There she knelt for the longest time, not crying, but staring at her daughter's peaceful face. The breeze teased some white-blond hair across Eleta's face. With a sigh, Gritta brushed it gently away, replaced the white cloth and rose with a groan. Nelwyna pulled ahead.

Bramble had come with Gritta. The whole time Gritta knelt by Eleta's body, Bramble had stood beside Thistle, holding his hand. Now, she grabbed a fistful of the old woman's skirt while Gritta picked up Thistle and cradled him in her arms.

The Mother Flora walked beside Nelwyna leading the procession back to the Garden town and her home. Like a guard of honor, the Flora surrounded them.

Vines slithered like snakes from the ground and tried to snatch Flynden's heels when he stepped through the gate into the Garden, but the Mother Flora brushed against one and they all slithered back into the ground.

Flynden never took his eyes off the stretcher with his dead mom and Stace. Although Stace hadn't been his real brother, he must have loved him very much. A mixture of wonder and grief settled on Flynden's face every time he gazed at Eleta like he couldn't make up his mind if he should be happy about meeting his mother, or sad for losing her so soon again.

Sophie walked beside him. She said nothing to him but took his hand. He squeezed hers. Anger boiled inside her and made her nauseated. How could one man destroy these lives? A whole family? She must stop Makimus, and part of her wanted to hurt him back. What good was this magic? At first, she had wanted some herself, thinking of neat things to do with it. Who wouldn't? Now, it seemed a lot like money. Some people used it wisely, others abused it. Well, maybe it wasn't the magic. Money didn't make people bad. Some people were bad and used the money in a bad way. Like the way it happened with the magic here, and not everyone had magic either, only a few.

Sophie shook her head. Some things were always the same no matter where you went, but she could help these people. How often had she felt helpless and powerless, but here and now, she could make a difference. If she went home and helped Master Eigil to come back to Nugateris, he could stop Makimus. If she tried to take on Makimus by herself, she wouldn't have a chance. She would be dead in two seconds flat, but Master Eigil with the other councilors and the Mother Flora had a real chance, and she would help them.

When they reached the Garden proper, Flora women and girls stood along the walkways and fences. They all sang their humming song. Peace sneaked into Sophie's heart and pushed the pain and sorrow living there to the edges where she could barely feel them anymore.

At the Mother Flora's cottage, Nelwyna let the Flora unhitch the stretcher. They carried the bodies into the courtyard, placing them on the ground near the fountain. There, they wrapped Eleta's body in white cloth as well, making her look like a mummy, too. Flynden knelt beside his mother until the Flora finished. Pelifeles pressed against him and blinked his yellow eyes once in a while. The big tree stretched its branches over Flynden and his mom and brother like a guardian angel, the peppermint scent strong in the air.

Gritta carried Thistle into the Mother Flora's cottage. He hung in her arms and seemed to be sleeping. Bramble kept one fist on Gritta's dress and skipped along.

"What's going to happen with Stace and Eleta?"

Sophie faced the Mother Flora's back as she followed the woman inside.

The Mother Flora stopped and turned, gazing back to Flynden, who huddled beside the bodies of his mom and brother.

"I have sent word to Kir, and to Fabrice, Stace's father. They will bury Stace in a small cemetery not far from the Garden, so that Amabel can be there, too. As for Eleta," the Mother Flora sighed, "she will be laid to rest in the Flora cemetery here in the Garden, honoring her that way."

She hurried after Gritta and left Sophie in the kitchen.

"Wait here for me, child. I will see after Thistle and be right back," she called over her shoulder.

Frustrated and sad, Sophie flung herself onto a chair at the table and dropped her chin into her hands, staring at the open door. *Wait, wait, wait.* She wanted to do something, not wait.

"I'm going after him!" Flynden yelled as he stomped in, his face all red and scrunched up, still crying. "He'll pay for this."

Sophie sat up and nodded. "How?"

"Somehow. I've got magic." Flynden threw himself into a chair beside Sophie, his hands balled into tight fists pummeling the table. White sparks danced off his knuckles and bounced off the tabletop.

"Hey," Sophie touched his arm. Zap. "Ouch." She pulled away. "You should wait for Master Eigil. He'll be a match for Makimus." This angry boy who'd come in wasn't like Flynden anymore.

"We can't wait for him." His fist slammed the tabletop and like a firecracker, his magic exploded all around the kitchen.

"Stop it, Flyn, you'll set the Mother Flora's home on fire."

"I don't care."

Sophie rolled her eyes. "Yes, you do."

Flynden frowned but buried his fists in his lap. "Who knows what Makimus will do if we don't stop him now." One angry tear plopped onto his fists. His mouth worked like a choirboy singing.

"Ssh." Sophie placed her hand on his back. "I'm sorry about your mom and Stace."

Flynden deflated like a cushion with no stuffing left; his shoulders slumped, and he hung his head, hugging himself. He rocked back and forth like his stomach hurt.

"Flyn?" Sophie kept her hand on his back and tried to look him in the face. "Master Eigil is all we've got. Makimus is too much for us. Even with your magic, you can't beat him. He's got much more practice and you'll just get hurt—or worse."

"I'm already hurt. Mother and Stace are dead. Now, it's his turn." Flynden's temper flared again for a moment before he shrank back down.

"Sure, he must pay," Sophie said. "But we need to make a plan first." Sophie withdrew her arm and faced the table and the open door again. The courtyard lay quiet now. The Flora's hum ebbed away, but no laughing or talking replaced it, like the Flora had left. "We'll do it together, Flyn."

He sat up straight again and nodded but didn't look convinced at all.

Gritta and the Mother Flora bustled into the kitchen. Gritta made tea while the Mother Flora sat at the table with them.

"How's Thistle?" Sophie asked. "Will he be all right?"

"Yes, his life is saved, but he still ill. It will be some time before he recovers and heals."

Flynden blushed and hung his head. The Mother Flora put her arms around his shoulders and hugged him.

"Flynden, you did not do this to Thistle. Your magic is white, pure white, and does no harm. Nor did you harm Stace or your mother. Because of you, your mother became human once more, and Thistle is still alive. With guidance and practice you can learn to control this magic."

"It won't help Stace and Mother now."

"No, it does not, but to know you did no harm is worth a lot, is it not?"

Flynden seemed to think about it for a moment. When he said nothing and shook his head, the Mother Flora continued.

"You cannot change what has happened, Flynden, but you can help from here on. Help Sophie bring back the Flora blossom so that she can help Master Eigil return to Nugateris. On the way, Pelifeles can teach you to control your magic. With it, you can protect Sophie and make certain she stays safe. If you learn to use it properly, no one, not even Makimus, will stand against the magic you have. You can thank him for this." She chuckled.

Flynden and Sophie exchanged surprised glances.

"Let us have some tea," the Mother Flora said. She drank the tea Gritta poured and hummed to herself. It wasn't exactly a happy tune, but it sounded peaceful and calming.

"Now," she said and shifted on her chair, arranging the folds of her gown. "We need a plan to trick Makimus into helping us."

"Why would we need *his* help?" Sophie asked.

Flynden gaped at the Mother Flora.

The Mother Flora smiled. "I think it is like this."

Sophie and Flynden bent forward missing nothing the Mother Flora had to say.

"When Makimus tried to stop Master Eigil, the magics collided and ripped open the portal into which Master Eigil fled. And now it is closed."

Bramble tiptoed into the kitchen and held one finger to her mouth.

"Ssh. Thithle is sleeping. You have to be quiet."

The Mother Flora chuckled. "He will not hear us, Bramble. I gave him something to sleep and heal." She reached for Bramble and smiled.

"Will Thithle be fine?"

"Yes, child, he will be." With her arms around the girl, the Mother Flora kept talking.

"So, you see, Makimus must be in the clearing and use his magic at the same time we use ours, I believe, or the portal will not open for you, Sophie."

"I don't like the idea—at all." Sophie shivered. *This was crazy.*

"We will be there to protect you. I promise," the Mother Flora said. "Flynden will do his part."

Sophie wanted to trust and believe, but standing in harm's way wasn't quite what she had in mind when she said she wanted to help. Flynden looked like he liked the idea even less. He needed to trust and believe in himself now more than ever. Before he knew he had magic, he had lots of self-confidence, and he would've done what the Mother Flora asked. Now, he had magic and he just looked confused and helpless.

"Now, finish your meal," the Mother Flora said. "Tomorrow, you will go and bring the Flora blossom to me for safekeeping until our plan is ready."

Sophie and Flynden ate bread and fruits for dinner while the Mother Flora checked again on Thistle. With a full belly, Sophie grew sleepy. Gritta showed them to a room with two narrow beds and a window facing east. As soon as Sophie hit the pillow, she drifted off to sleep.

The next thing she knew, the Mother Flora shook her awake.

"It is almost time for the turning. I did not want you to leave without saying good-bye."

"Huh?" Sophie sat and rubbed her eyes. The gray morning sky peeked into the window and turned the square from black to gray to lighter gray. The Mother Flora's outline appeared beside her cot like emerging from the darkness. Flynden jumped out of bed and crossed the room.

"Gritta prepared breakfast for you," the Mother Flora said and took Sophie's and Flynden's hands and held them. "Be careful, children, and return soon. Nelwyna and Pelifeles will go with you. And Flynden," she gazed into Flynden's eyes, "I am counting on you to protect Sophie. When you return, we will say our final good-byes to Stace and Eleta."

Flynden nodded and swallowed hard, but he didn't look like he knew how he would keep that promise.

"May the light brighten your path, children."

Too sleepy to say anything, Sophie nodded.

When the first golden rays shot over the windowsill, the Mother Flora rose and stopped by the door to glance over her shoulder before she hurried from the room. Sophie swung her legs to the floor. Outside, a rustle like tissue paper crinkling swept through the Garden town. Then all went quiet.

Sophie and Flynden rushed through the kitchen into the courtyard, but the Mother Flora had already turned back into a flower. Gritta stood there with Bramble in her arms. Pelifeles and Nelwyna were nowhere in sight.

While Sophie quickly washed her face at the fountain, Flynden knelt beside the two mummified bodies. For a few moments, she gave him privacy and didn't approach.

"You should eat, then leave," Gritta said. "The sooner you'll be back."

"I'm not hungry," Flynden said.

"You'll have to eat, Flyn." Sophie pulled his arm and tried to get him to go back inside with her. "You'll need your strength."

Reluctantly, he followed her into the cottage kitchen. Two baskets with bread and colorful fruit stood on the table beside two canvas bags. Sophie grabbed an apple and a loaf shaped more like a long thin bun, and stuffed the rest of the food into the two canvas bags. Flynden plopped into a chair, not helping, his eyes out of focus. She thrust an apple into his hand.

When she had wolfed down her own apple and loaf, she slipped the bag's strap over her head and held out the other one to Flynden.

"Let's go, Flyn."

Gritta joined them in the kitchen and released Bramble to the floor. The little girl ran up to Sophie and wrapped her arms around Sophie's legs.

"I want to come with you," she said, holding on.

"No, you can't, Bramble. You've got to help your grandma look after Thistle. Okay?"

The girl's lower lip extended past her upper one.

"Don't you want to stay with your brother?"

Bramble nodded.

"Then stay with your grandma and make sure Thistle gets well again. Okay?"

Bramble nodded again. The pout disappeared and a wide smile spread across her face as she took Gritta's hand, already pulling her away. "Come, Grandma, let's go and see Thithle."

Gritta smiled and followed Bramble down the hallway. "Good-bye, children. Come back soon," she called over her shoulder.

"Bye." Sophie headed to the door.

Flynden slung his bag over his shoulder. The whole time, he said nothing. Outside in the courtyard, he dawdled near the fountain.

"Come on, Flyn," Sophie urged.

He nodded but with no real enthusiasm. She pulled him away through the gate and out into the lane while he craned his neck to have a parting look at the two white forms.

Sophie and Flynden walked through the silent Garden town along the houses and gardens with the beautiful flowers. The sun had risen and a fresh breeze from the ocean rustled through the trees. A few women working for the Flora noticed them and waved. Soon, they reached the outskirts of the Garden town and faced the grassy hills.

"You know where we're going, right?" Sophie asked. "Because I'd never find the tree again by myself."

Flynden looked up and shrugged. "Course."

Sophie wrinkled her forehead and jammed her fists into her hips.

"Listen, the Mother Flora said you would help me. Now lead the way." She hated herself for being so short with him, but it might get him out of his funk and stop his moping.

Flynden shrugged again.

"Come on." Sophie pushed him.

Flynden trudged along, looking over his shoulder every so often.

She tried to pry him out of his moping with questions, but he only responded with yes or no or grunted something she couldn't understand.

"Hey, where do you think Peli and Nelwyna are?"

"Don't know."

Sophie sighed. At least Flynden kept walking. Maybe he would perk up later, but she worried. How was she supposed to find the tree with the Flora blossom if he didn't help? The tree grew somewhere near Gwern, but finding it without Flynden would take forever. The Mother Flora had said Nelwyna and Pelifeles would help too, and Flynden knew the way, but Flynden wasn't helping, and the spirit mates weren't there. So what was she going to do?

They trekked along over hill after hill until they crested the final rise and looked down to the low wall surrounding the Garden and the metal gate. On the charred, blackened area, new grass grew. How could that be? A bit to the right of the gate, Nelwyna stood beside Pelifeles, shaking her head. Pelifeles raised his hackles. Were they arguing again?

"Look, Flyn, there they are." Sophie pointed.

Flynden raised his head and his face brightened. A bit of a sparkle came back into his eyes, and he ran with her down the hill.

Out of breath, they reached the spirit mates.

"It's about time you two showed up," Pelifeles said, hopped off the wall, and slunk around Flynden's ankles. Flynden picked him up and hugged him close. The cat let it happen without his usual protesting hiss and magic sparks. Nelwyna nickered a soft greeting but said nothing.

"Can we ride on your back again, Nelwyna? It would make it so much faster, please?" Sophie asked in the most polite voice she could manage.

Nelwyna rolled her eyes. "By the light, I am becoming a regular nag."

"Please," Flynden and Sophie said together.

"Oh well, I do see the need to hasten. Step up then." She moved closer to the wall.

Sophie scrambled from the wall onto her back first. Then Flynden jumped up behind her.

"Easy, young man, I am not the youngest." The horse shook her head and sent her mane flying. "Off we go."

Pelifeles already padded away.

"Do you know where you're going?" Sophie called after him.

"Of course, I do." Pelifeles flicked his tale. The green blades of grass parted like water as he pounced through them.

Nelwyna stepped back a few paces. Sophie grabbed the mane and clamped her legs against the ribs. Flynden's arms tightened around her waist. With one big jump, the horse cleared the wall.

"Wait a minute!" Sophie shouted. She still couldn't believe the changed ground. Where the charred grass and the blackened earth had been, new shoots peeked through the rich, brown soil.

"What happened here?" Sophie twisted around to Flynden, but he shrugged, shaking his head.

Nelwyna said, "The Flora healed the ground and took away the damage the magic left."

"Wow. Just like that?"

"Yes, indeed. Enough talk." The horse trotted after Pelifeles, who cut a narrow aisle through the grass and his black-tipped tail wiggled from side to side.

Soon, they walked in the cool forest light, breathing the soothing and calming peppermint smell. Nelwyna slowed to a gentle walk and Sophie let her mind drift. Some butterflies in her stomach stirred already when she imagined what she still had to do before she could go home. After all this, she would never ever even think of running away from home again. Honest to goodness, she wouldn't. Trudy making dinner and tucking her in at night were good things she didn't appreciate. How stupid she'd been. Sophie shook her head.

"What's the matter?" Flynden asked.

"Nothing."

"Then why are you shaking your head? Are you worried we won't find the tree again?"

"Nope. Just thinking about home." She twisted and gave him a lopsided grin.

He tightened his arms and squeezed her waist a bit.

"You'll get home."

Sophie faced forward and sighed.

"It'll be fine," Flynden said and held her still a bit tighter.

✃ *Chapter 21* ✄

Only in the dead of night could Eigil now leave the forest and the pine tree's shelter with its low-hanging branches. Although grateful for the tree's shelter keeping away the falling white cold, he would have preferred to spend the nights in the shed. The caretaker had turned vigilant and before long, would discover him if Eigil had remained there. The old man came sporadically any time of day or night, as if his sole purpose in life had become the task of catching him, while Eigil's whole existence had become a matter of preventing the old man from doing so.

With each day, this task became harder. Cold assaulted Eigil from the outside, hunger from the inside, and he had not a single seed remaining to protect and feed himself. He clung with an iron determination to his life, a last strength he would need to call on his magic should it prove necessary to hide or perhaps defend himself. Of course, if he could take the Celarim from the shed and hold on to it, it would warm him, and he would not freeze to death.

There were moments when he considered letting the caretaker catch him and take him somewhere warm, and even provide food. At this point, he would not ask for much. He teetered close to the edge. If help would not come soon, from anywhere …

Eigil pushed the thought aside. He must act, not ponder his demise. Wishful thinking would not bring the things he craved. He must stay alive and return to Nugateris. He must save Marguerite, the Mother Flora, or she would be lost and her children with her. He must not let this happen and must right his wrong.

His joints protested when he uncurled where he lay beneath the white covered branches. His bones screamed when he crawled to the trunk and pulled himself to his knees. His body shook with the effort; his hand trembled as he latched onto the lowest branch. Then he pulled, bringing one knee up. Nauseated from hunger and exhaustion, he waited a moment, steadied himself, grabbed another branch, and stood.

The night turned bitter cold. Eigil eyed the shed through the branches. Leagues away, it seemed, but he would make it. Well past midnight, the caretaker had come. Perhaps he would not return again until morning. By then, Eigil could have walked to the shed and back with the Celarim without the man being wiser. Try he must because he lacked other options.

Again, he did not dare leave the burial ground. If the girl returned, he had to be here. If she found her way back…

He pushed that thought aside as well. Hoping the girl would return with the Flora blossom kept him going. If he stopped hoping, he would be finished.

One shaking step in front of the other, he pushed the branches aside and squeezed past them. He staggered from tree to tree, waiting beside each for a moment to catch his breath, until reaching a point with no trees where only graves lay between the forest and the shed. Here, he waited a bit longer until his breathing calmed, watching for the caretaker. The burial ground lay still, and those who rested there would not tell on him.

The white cold kept falling, and he could see no farther than the arch over the ground's entrance. It would cover his footprints, and the ones it did not, he would erase with a branch or stick. It would be less than perfect, but it would help. Again, he wished for the full strength of his magic and shook his head. When one had relied for most of his life on magical powers, it came as a bitter realization that most people without these gifts had to use their smarts to figure things out. If he made it out of this predicament in one piece, he would spend some time learning how to do things without using magic. It would be good practice. He would suggest it to the High Council.

Eigil stopped his musings. He was not back home, not yet, not even close. Staying alert and vigilant, like the caretaker, was his foremost responsibility. He steeled himself, gathered his strength and staggered out into the open.

So far to go. Eigil tottered to the nearest headstone, which stood along the oval path around the burial ground, a large statue of a beautiful woman draped in a flowing gown, one leg exposed. She stood on a pedestal and spread her protective wings over the burial site. He grabbed her leg around the calf, caught his breath for a moment or two, then thanked her and apologized for the misuse of her presence. He staggered off to the next stone, a large lopsided square that had sunk to one side into the soil. He searched for the next one to support him. Once again, he thanked the stone and its owner long gone, feeling silly, but he did not want to seem unappreciative or disrespectful to the departed.

He stooped to rest by another low stone. His breath came raspy and hoarse from his dry throat, hurting down into his lungs. He grabbed a handful of the white cold, letting it melt into water, tipping hand to mouth. Cold and soothing, the water trickled over his tongue and down his throat. Everything had a good side.

At last, Eigil reached the path and followed it left. The small amount of his remaining strength and energy ebbed away. Had he been healthy and strong, it would have taken a few moments to cross the short distance to the shed. Instead, it had taken all night, and now, the sky bled from its darkest indigo shade into a soft gray. Regardless, he must keep moving. If he remained here, anyone would see him instantly.

Eigil dragged himself hunched over the final distance to the shed, staggered and tottered to close the gap. Pain shot up his injured arm when he slammed against the wood siding. Panting, his eyes closed, his teeth clenched, he stood for long moments until he could gather a small amount of his magic to break the detachable lock securing the hasp and staple on the door.

Over the hill and down the road, a horseless carriage roared close. He held his breath, but sound and lights moved past, and the early morning went still again. Eigil exhaled.

He leaned against the wooden side, so that his good arm could reach. Gathering his remaining strength and power, he grabbed the metal lock and guided the magic into the keyhole. The familiar scent of sage wafted around him, weak and faint. A click released the lock's moveable shackle. Eigil removed the lock, pulled the door wide enough to slip inside as quickly as his aching bones permitted, then closed it behind him and shut out some of the cold. With a few shaking steps, he made it to the dirt-filled sacks and reclined on them.

Eigil needed only a few moments' rest to catch his breath. He must not fall asleep. He counted to twenty, concentrating on each number, and with effort, he pushed himself up. The Celarim was still stuck between the sacks and the wall. He sighed and closed his eyes. In his present state, carrying it would slow him, yet, there could be no quarreling about it; he must take it and leave. Groaning with pain, he pulled the heavy book with his good arm onto the sacks and hugged the tome with both arms to him like a beloved child. The Celarim responded, reaching out, embracing him with warmth and magic, and something like longing, as if the book too had been cold and lonely, waiting for his embrace. A bit of strength returned to his aching body, seeping into every fiber of his being and even relieving some pain in the stump of his left arm. He should have come sooner.

Eigil straightened, dropped his feet to the floor, and faced the door. With a heavy sigh, he braced himself and put weight on his legs. As he took the first step forward, the door swung open, quivering on its hinges as it slammed against the outer wall. Within the doorframe stood the old caretaker, brandishing a long three-pronged fork.

☙ *Chapter 22* ❧

"Shouldn't you be practicing your magic?" Sophie bit into the bread, then into an apple.

At Flynden's request, they had stopped in the same clearing where Eleta as the creature had caught up with them the first time. Flynden went to the spot where she had pinned him down. He sat there, refusing to say anything or eat or talk. Sophie sat cross-legged a few steps away, wanting to give him privacy but also wanting to stay close.

"Remember, the Mother Flora said Pelifeles could help you with it."

Flynden didn't answer, didn't even move.

She wanted to help him. But how? She didn't want to be pushy, but how else could she get him to help her? Though he still moped, he took his mom's death and all the stuff he'd found out about himself much better than she would've. When Mom and Dad died, she threw one tantrum after another, threw things, broke things, and made life hell for Tommy and everyone else around her. Flynden did nothing but stay quiet, brooding.

Nelwyna and Pelifeles patrolled the clearing. Pelifeles padded beside Nelwyna through the grass, nose in the air, sniffing. Nelwyna walked a slower pace to let him keep up. They looked at peace with each other, or maybe they'd found some kind of truce, for now anyway.

"Are you going to say something, Flyn?"

He made no move. He sat still, cross-legged, shoulders hunched, head hanging. He didn't cry, but maybe he did it inside, for himself.

"Peli! Nelwyna! Come over here," Sophie called. "We need your help."

Horse and cat came trotting over to Flynden. Nelwyna nudged him with her nose.

"Where's my spunky friend gone?" Pelifeles said and pushed his head into Flynden's leg. Tiny bright sparks jumped off his fur and zapped Flynden.

"Ouch," Flynden jerked his leg away. "Stop that."

"Get your behind off the ground." The cat pawed Flynden's thigh and zapped him again.

"Stop!" Flynden balled his fists and scooted sideways. "It hurts."

"Then do something about it." Again and again, Pelifeles butted the boy with his head or pawed him. Each time sparks jumped off his fur. Zap. Zap.

"Ouch. Stop!"

Nelwyna flipped Pelifeles with her nose onto his back. "There are other ways, fur ball."

"Stop nagging. He needs to learn how to use his magic and protect himself and Sophie."

Gee, now they quarreled again. "Can you guys stop fighting for a while?" Sophie stood and walked over to them. "You're supposed to help Flyn, not make it worse."

"Who's making it worse?" Nelwyna shook her mane. "Certainly not I."

Sophie rolled her eyes.

"Peli, can you instruct Flyn instead of zapping him?"

"I could, but is he listening?"

Sophie knelt across from Flynden, facing him. She raised her hand and poked his arm with one finger.

"Flyn?" She whispered. "I know you're sad and angry, but we need your help. You must learn how to protect yourself and us with your magic. Okay?"

At first, Flynden made no move at all, then he nodded. "I'll try." He sighed. "But I don't know if it works."

"It's all we're asking." Sophie pulled him up. "Come on, Pelifeles, tell him what to do."

The cat blinked at her then at Flynden. "It seems to work well when he's angry."

"It's true," Flynden said. "Back at the Mother Flora's home, anger and magic seemed to boil together in my belly and sparked through my whole body. Then it came out at my fingers."

"Isn't there a way where you can do this without getting angry all the time? It seems kinda uncontrollable then. You don't want that. Right?"

"I'm sure I'll be angry when we run into Makimus again."

"You want to keep your wits about you, especially then." Sophie turned to Pelifeles and Nelwyna. "What should he do?"

The spirit mates stayed quiet for some time.

"Well?" Sophie threw up her hands. They should hurry not hang out here in the woods.

"I suggest," Nelwyna said, "you look deep inside of yourself, Flynden, and search for the magic."

"Yep, close your eyes and concentrate." Pelifeles piped in.

Flynden closed his eyes. His brow wrinkled and then his whole face scrunched up. Nothing happened.

"Nothing." Flynden shrugged and opened his eyes. "I just can't do it on command."

"Try again." Pelifeles pushed him with his nose, sending off tiny sparks.

Flynden closed his eyes.

"Concentrate hard and look for the magic with your mind," the cat said.

Sophie walked to Nelwyna's side, and they both backed up, giving Flynden and Pelifeles room to practice. Flynden squatted, placing one hand in the grass like a football player ready to make a move. When nothing seemed to happen after a few seconds, Pelifeles pushed him again and again until Flynden's magic flared, draping him in a veil of bright light, pulsing. Flynden fell backward and flung Pelifeles away. The cat landed on his back, flipped around onto his paws, flicked his tail a few times, and started grooming himself right away.

"There you go," Pelifeles chuckled. "That's what you're looking for."

Flynden jumped to his feet, the magic faded and winked out.

"I'm sorry, Peli, I didn't want to do that."

"No, you didn't, but I did." A lick to his paw, a rub on his belly, the cat chuckled. "You have to learn how to do this on your own."

"I don't want to hurt you."

"It takes a lot more than that to hurt this feline, my friend." He pulled his black tail through his mouth, combed the tip with his tongue once or twice, then concentrated on his hind leg. A few more licks, then he rolled onto his paws, vibrating a few more dirt specks from his fur.

"Now, let's try again."

Before Flynden could stop him, Pelifeles had jammed his head against his shin. Zap, the magic stung him again.

"That hurts, you know. A lot."

"Then do something about it. Come on, you can do it."

Zap. Zap.

Flynden concentrated, straining like going to the bathroom. Pelifeles sat back, watched him, and blinked.

"Are you going to lay an egg or something?"

"Be quiet. I'm concentrating." Flynden squatted, crouching lower with every try.

"I see. Looks like egg laying to me."

Flynden rolled to one side and started laughing. Colorful sparks burst from his skin. Sophie giggled and snorted behind her hand. Nelwyna whinnied, nodding her head vigorously. Pelifeles clucked like a chicken and then laughed even harder.

"Fine, now we know your magic likes laughter, too. Try again." The cat padded up to him but didn't zap him this time.

Flynden sat up, still snorting and chortling. Snot ran from his nose.

"Follow my lead," Pelifeles said. "Close your eyes and with your mind find the spot where you first sensed the magic." Pelifeles closed his eyes and went still.

Flynden wiped his sleeve under his nose and shut his eyes, too. For a moment, he looked like he strained again, but then he relaxed.

"Find anything?" Pelifeles asked.

"Quiet."

The wind brushed through the trees and brought a whiff of calming peppermint scent into the clearing. A black bird trilled in a tree. Pelifeles purred.

Without warning, Flynden's magic exploded out of him and threw him on his back. When he jumped up, the light winked out.

"What happened?" Sophie asked.

"I heard the forest sounds far away. With my mind, I searched inside my body almost as if putting my hand into a deep pocket. When I reached my belly button, or somewhere around there, something stirred, like a gentle tickle, a soft light. It was more a feeling than seeing it." Flynden exhaled a shaky breath. "I tickled it back with my mind."

"You did it, Flyn." Pelifeles hopped up and down. "Try it again. Come on. You got it."

"It's scary and I feel stupid." Flynden threw himself on the ground beside a large root protruding from the ground.

"Never mind. Keep trying. If we run into Makimus, you'll have to feel confident, not stupid," Pelifeles encouraged him. "Try again," he hissed.

Flynden sat back down, crossed his legs, and closed his eyes, but kept peeking at Sophie. As soon as their eyes met, they started laughing all over again.

Pelifeles sat on his haunches, considered first his right, then his left paw, gave it an impatient lick and glowered at his friend. "Keep trying," he said.

"Nothing's happening." Flynden snorted.

Nelwyna nickered.

Pelifeles hissed. "Of course not. You're too busy laughing."

Sophie still giggled and took Flynden's side.

"You did okay, Flyn. I'm sure you can do it when you have to."

Flynden frowned. "Maybe."

"We should get going." Sophie got up. "We haven't got all day, guys."

"Let's go, then," Flynden said and ran laughing across the clearing, disappearing down the path leading into the trees.

"Wait!" She called after him, but Flynden ignored her.

Sophie scrambled after Flynden, but Nelwyna jumped ahead of her, knocking her sideways into the first tree. Sophie grabbed the bark, missed, and scratched her arm and shoulder before she fell to her knees.

"Hey, wait for me," she called and brushed herself off, but Flynden and the spirit mates had already disappeared into the woods.

Sophie turned on the spot. She was alone. The forest seemed suddenly so quiet, eerie like, and dark and gloomy underneath the trees. Goosebumps rushed up her arms and the back of her neck prickled. She sucked in the peppermint scent to calm herself.

"Wait for me!" she yelled, running after them.

The trees stood close together, crowding her and wouldn't show her more than a few feet of the path ahead. Her friends had gone, just left her here. As the knot of fear in her stomach grew, she zigzagged between the trees. She jumped over fallen logs, and dashed around the next big trunk, smack, right into Nelwyna's flank.

"Are you crazy?" Sophie bent over, resting her hands on her knees.

Nelwyna snorted, "You are making too much noise, girl." She sounded amused again. You could never tell with that horse. "You were the one who said we should hurry."

"Yes, but don't leave me back there all by myself. What if Makimus had shown up?"

"He isn't anywhere near here." Pelifeles blinked his yellow eyes. "We would've known."

"Yeah, but I wouldn't."

Flynden ducked beneath Nelwyna's belly. "Sorry, Sophie, but it was so funny."

"Not for me." She crossed her arms over her chest and stuck her nose in the air. "It scared me."

"Sorry," Flynden mumbled. "We didn't mean to frighten you." He looked sorry but she wanted to give him a hard time for a little longer. Just because. She turned away, looking off into the forest.

"When you're done moping, Sophie," Pelifeles said, "we do need to hurry."

Right. This was all pretty stupid. She nodded. "Okay. Where to?"

"It's not far now," Flynden said. "We're almost at the spot where the sewer comes out."

"How do you know?" Sophie looked around. "I can't see anything but trees."

"We know," Pelifeles said. "Because we've been visiting this forest a few times before you came."

Sophie grimaced and rolled her eyes. Flynden grinned.

"Then where is the path where Makimus caught us?"

"Up ahead." Pelifeles flicked his tail and took the lead. Sophie followed Flynden, and Nelwyna brought up the rear.

"You think Makimus is waiting for us?" Sophie whispered.

"You'd never know. Quiet now," he hissed.

Sophie grabbed Flynden's tunic in the back, holding on, and tiptoed after him. The boy looked over his shoulder, his face serious and scared. All the fun was gone. They trudged ahead. Sophie jumped at every noise, even though the forest sounded normal with the wind whooshing through the trees, birds singing, and squirrels chatting up a storm.

Maybe it would be fine. They would find the tree, get the Flora blossom, and be back at the Garden. But somehow, the knot in her stomach swelled a bit more and told her it wouldn't be so easy. Just nerves, like Dad used to say when she got scared and grew a knot in her stomach. If Mom and Dad were here, they would figure out something. They would look out for her. They would tell Makimus where to go.

Flynden stopped and ripped her out of her wishful thinking. Nelwyna's breath tickled her neck. Not far ahead, Pelifeles stood sideways. His fur stuck out, his tail a bottle brush. She could see the wide path right where he waited. Voices came from somewhere down the path, men talking. So, Makimus did leave someone there to watch. Would he be waiting himself? No, those men had higher voices than Makimus, and if they were regular men, Pelifeles, and maybe Nelwyna, too, could handle them.

The men passed, their voices faded, and Pelifeles' fur went smooth again. He padded back to them.

"Two men," he hissed. "They're patrolling the path."

"Are we close to where Makimus got us?" Sophie asked, squatted, and duck-walked forward.

"Yes, but we have to get to the other side of the path."

"You sure?"

Pelifeles blinked and gave her a look. "You're asking me?"

Sophie and Flynden crouched low. What about Nelwyna? Would those men see the tall horse? She twisted around to tell Nelwyna to hide, but the horse was gone.

"Nelwyna?" Sophie whispered.

"Ssh," Flynden pressed a finger to his lips.

Sophie searched the trees. A few steps down the path, the air shimmered like heat rising off pavement. "Nelwyna?"

With a soft nicker, Nelwyna's nose appeared for a second out of nowhere and disappeared just as quickly.

"Will you be quiet?" Pelifeles came padding toward her. "The men are coming back," he hissed. "When they turn around heading the other way, we'll rush across the path." His yellow eyes blinked at Sophie then at Flynden.

They both nodded.

"Wait for my signal."

They nodded again.

Sophie tensed. Flynden's face turned into a white mask with lots of freckles, but even those paled. She grabbed his hand and squeezed it; he squeezed hers back and swallowed hard, while watching Pelifeles crouch low underneath a bush by the wide path.

The men came walking back, talking and paying little attention to anything around them.

"Then, click, click, my stones hit the other ones, and I won," the one with a bushy black beard said.

"How much coin did you win?" his burly companion asked.

"Ah, wouldn't you like to know?" The first man chuckled.

They seemed to be talking about some kind of game as they strolled by. After a minute or so, the voices faded more and more in the other direction.

"Now," Pelifeles hissed and at the same time jumped from the bush across the path and disappeared on the other side into the bushes.

Sophie and Flynden started and rushed after him at

the same time. Nelwyna's hooves clonk-clonked right behind them. When they reached the middle of the path, Sophie tripped on a root, stumbled, and fell.

"Gee," she said, way too loud. She froze, so did Flynden.

Pelifeles jumped back out of the bushes. "Get up, girl. Come on, hurry."

At the same moment, the men came around the corner. Had they heard them? Nelwyna stepped right over Sophie and Flynden and stopped, placing her hooves close to Sophie's head and Flynden's arms, making the air above them shimmer like heat.

Sophie held her breath. *What now?*

Pelifeles rushed at the men and changed in mid-jump, now looking like a fox.

"Hey, look." The burly man pointed at the fox.

The men laughed as Pelifeles jumped in the air before he slipped through their legs and took off away from Nelwyna, Sophie, and Flynden. The men watched him go.

Sophie and Flynden didn't need any urging. As soon as the men turned their backs, they scrambled to their feet and dove for the trees. They crawled for some time and lay still until the men's laughter faded.

"Phew, that was close." Flynden panted beside her. "They almost got us."

"Where's Nelwyna?" Sophie whispered.

This time, neither head nor tail of the horse, nor a shimmer showed anywhere.

"Come." Flynden pulled her arm. "They'll keep those men busy giving us time to find the blossom."

Sophie sat and swiveled, walking her feet in a circle around herself, eying trees and bushes. Makimus had scared her so much when he came after her. How would she remember now one single tree?

"Anything?" Flynden asked, keeping his voice low.

She shook her head. Maybe another spot was better. She crouched and crawled along the trees, stopping ever so often to take a closer look. Nothing. How far had she run? She had thought the gnarled tree would've been easy to find again. She passed tree after tree. No luck. Where was it?

Flynden kept right on her heels. Maybe she should've described the tree better and then he could be looking, too. She took a breath to explain when he grabbed her tunic and pointed. Ahead, where the trees parted a bit, the gnarled tree with the big hole stared right at them.

Sophie nodded. "That's it," she whispered.

Flynden looked left and right over his shoulder. "Go get it. I'll watch out."

Sophie scrambled to her feet and made a dash for the tree. It had been quite easy to slam dunk the Flora blossom into the hole, but how would she get it out? The opening gaped above her head. With both hands, she grabbed it and pulled herself up. The black hole was just that, a black hole, and she couldn't see anything. How deep could it be? She needed to stick her arm in there to find out, but she wasn't strong enough to hold on with only one arm. She let go and stumbled back.

"You've got to help me up, Flyn. Come on," she whispered and pulled him toward the tree. "I can't reach."

Flynden seemed to think for a second, then knelt down and placed his hands on the ground making himself into a step. Sophie grabbed the bark, left and right and stepped on his back. Her shoulder didn't quite level with the hole, but she could stick her arm in now.

Other than spider webs and rotted wood that fell apart at her touch, she found nothing. Sophie stepped down.

"The tree is hollow," Sophie said. "I bet if I dig a hole at the bottom, I'll get the Flora blossom out through there."

They knelt and clawed the earth between two roots snaking away from the trunk.

"You look like two dogs digging for a bone," Nelwyna said behind them.

They jumped and banged their heads together.

"Why do you have to sneak up on us like that?" Sophie asked. "You could've warned us."

"I wasn't sneaking."

"Never mind." Sophie turned back around and continued digging. "This is the tree. It's hollow and I think we can dig the blossom out."

"Let me see." Nelwyna stuck her nose close to the hole they had already dug. "Hm."

"What?"

"Are you sure it is in there?"

"'Course, it is."

"Here, let me help you." Nelwyna swung around and kicked the trunk with her rear hooves. Whack!

"It's way too loud, Nelwyna."

"Um, well, perhaps."

Whack. She stomped her front hoof this time.

"Those men will hear us," Flynden said.

"I believe Pelifeles is giving them a bit of fun at the moment. I doubt they will notice us."

After the third whack with the hoof, the brittle wood broke away and the trunk spilled dirt, pinecones, acorns, and wood pieces. Sophie stuck her hand in and groped for the sack with the blossom, finding more pinecones and acorns, probably a busy squirrel's winter supply, until she fingered cloth and pulled it out.

"You did it, Nelly," Sophie said in a loud whisper, dancing on the spot. "You did it."

Nelwyna snorted and swung her big head around, coming nose to nose with Sophie. Sophie gasped and froze.

"Do not ever shorten my name in that fashion, girl. I rather dislike it."

"Sorry." Sophie backed away. "I didn't mean any disrespect."

Nelwyna ignored her. "Let us leave. Now," she said into the air.

Sophie looked away because she didn't want Nelwyna to see the grin she sneaked Flynden. Spider webs covered the dirty cloth sack with the blossom, but otherwise it looked fine. Like before, the weird warmth pulsed on her palm, alive, like it knew she'd found it. When Sophie slipped the sack into her pocket, the warmth seeped through the cloth into her leg.

"What's the matter?" Flynden asked.

"It's just so… It feels weird." Sophie shrugged.

"Let us hasten back to the Mother Flora," Nelwyna said. "It would be unwise for you to handle the Flora blossom with your bare hands."

"I still have to take it home and give it to Master Eigil, right?"

"Of course." The horse shook her head. "Nevertheless, it would be best if you did not handle it."

"Will it hurt me if I touch it?"

Nelwyna stared right through her as if she saw something in her mind or far away. After a few seconds, she shook her head, sending her mane flying, saying nothing, and started walking away.

Sophie and the Magic Flower

That looked like a no. Sophie wanted to shrug the weird scary feeling off but couldn't. She had the blossom now and could go home. Right then, home had never sounded so good. Maybe soon, she would be going back. Already, she could see her room and Trudy making the bed. She could smell the freshly ironed clothes and her favorite food of roasted chicken and home fries. Did those thoughts show on her face? They must have because Flynden stepped closer and placed a hand on her arm.

"You'll be home soon," he said. Tiny sparks danced off his fingers, making the Flora blossom flare in her pocket, like an answer to his touch.

Sophie slapped Flynden's hand away.

"Ouch." She grabbed her leg. "That's hot."

"What happened?" he asked and jumped back.

"As soon as your fingers touched my arm, the blossom burned me."

Flynden frowned. He held up both hands in front of him, studying them.

"Maybe it recognizes you or your magic," Sophie said. "Do you think that's a good sign?"

"I don't know."

"What is taking you so long?" Nelwyna had stopped and bent her head around, eyeing them with one dark eye.

"Okay, okay," Sophie said. "We're right behind you." She mouthed *come on* to Flynden and they hurried after the horse.

Nelwyna led the way back to the wide path. As they were crossing it, Pelifeles came dashing around the corner still looking like a fox with the two men running after him. They swung thick clubs at Pelifeles. All of it happened too fast for Nelwyna to disguise Sophie and

Flynden. Everyone froze, staring.

"There they are!" The man with the beard shouted. "And that's no ordinary fox, I'd say." He took another swing at Pelifeles, missing by a few inches.

Pelifeles jumped into the nearest bush and disappeared.

"Get on," Nelwyna said out of the side of her mouth. "Hurry." She bent one front leg and lowered herself.

Gee, Nelwyna offered to carry them? Sophie threw herself onto the horse, swung one leg over the back, grabbing the mane and hanging like a flour sack over the neck.

The men sprinted toward them.

"Stop!" The burly man shouted and threw his stick like a spear.

Flynden jumped onto Nelwyna's back and wrapped his arms around Sophie's waist. His magic flared and wrapped around them like a protective cloak.

"Ouch," Sophie cried.

"I need to hold on, Sophie, or I'll fall off."

"You're also doing something else."

The Flora blossom seared her leg. Flynden's magic burned her stomach where he held her and made her skin crawl and tingle in a painful way. Sophie bit her teeth together.

Nelwyna whinnied, straightened her leg and at the same time kicked her powerful hind legs, jumping across the path. There, she slipped into the bushes, picking the narrow path they had come on. Like a dressage pony, she pranced between the trees.

The men crashed through the woods behind them, closing in, yelling for them to stop by order of High Councilor Makimus.

Nelwyna trotted along the winding path, but the crowding trees made it hard for her to run. The men quickly closed in behind her. Whack! The burly man struck Nelwyna's rump with the stick. She screamed and kicked back, sending the man flying. Sophie and Flynden slid forward onto her neck. With a loud crack, the man struck a tree a few feet away and crumpled against the trunk. The bearded man stopped and brandished his fist at them before he went after his companion.

Flynden twisted around and stuck his tongue out at him.

"Please let go of me, Flyn," Sophie breathed. "The magic is burning me."

Flynden scooted back and placed his hands behind him on Nelwyna's rump.

"They will tell Makimus," Nelwyna snorted. "Perhaps I should kick the other one as well."

"No, let's get going. What if Makimus comes?" Sophie said through rattling teeth and shivered. "Or maybe we should go right away to the clearing where the portal is."

"The portal is gone. Closed," Flynden said. "The Mother Flora thinks it will take all of us, and Makimus, to open it again."

"We could try anyway, right?"

Flynden shook his head.

"Nelwyna, what do you think?" Sophie stroked the horse's neck. "Shouldn't we at least try?"

"I would not know how to begin. The Mother Flora knows. I say we go to the Garden."

Sophie grimaced. They weren't helping at all. Now she had the thing she needed and wanted to go home. Her face grew hot. She was ready to run again and leave her friends stuck in this mess. Who would do something like that? What kind of friend was she anyway? The same question flitted over Flynden's face. Sophie rubbed her eyes to avoid looking into his.

"Okay," she said in a small voice. "Let's go to the Garden then."

Flynden sat behind her on Nelwyna's back and scooted toward the rump some more. He said nothing. Once she turned around, but he looked away and off into the woods.

Nelwyna walked along the narrow path between the trees, and her hooves thudded on the leaf-strewn forest floor like the dull ache in Sophie's chest. Sophie breathed deeply, but even the calming peppermint scent didn't do anything to make the ache go away. The wind swayed the crowns above them. A bunny crossed their path, eyeing the tall horse for a second before it hopped past and had gone. A flock of crows swooped through the branches, their loud caw-caws jarring the stillness. A squirrel jumped from branch to branch to the right, almost like it followed them. When they reached the small clearing, Pelifeles came dashing from the trees, now a cat again.

"Hey, why the moping?" he asked. "You should be glad. We tricked those men."

Leave it to Pelifeles to sum up the mood right away.

"What's wrong?" He jumped in front of Nelwyna.

The horse shied. Her front hooves left the ground. Sophie was too slow to grab the mane and Flynden didn't have a chance at all. They both slid over the rump and into the grass.

"You are fortunate I did not trample you, fur ball," Nelwyna snorted. "What were you thinking?"

"What's going on? I want to know," Pelifeles hissed.

"You are not in charge."

"Neither are you."

"Stop it, guys." Sophie picked herself up off the ground and brushed grass off her pants and tunic.

"Sophie wants to go to the portal," Flynden said as he got up and crossed his arms. "She can't wait to go home." He had a big frown on his face.

Leaving us in this mess, Sophie finished for him in her mind.

Pelifeles blinked at Sophie and started grooming himself, saying nothing. He did a thorough cleaning job, licking his right front paw then his left, even though they were already as white as he could make them. When he had finished the paws, he pulled them over his ears a few times before he twisted to do his back and haunches, and finally pulled his tail through his mouth.

They waited for him to finish. She wasn't sure why, but somehow she had the feeling he was going to yell at her. Pelifeles blinked again.

"We can't open the portal alone. You know that, Sophie," he said.

Sophie nodded, shook her head, and shrugged.

"But," she started, "but you and Nelwyna and Flyn, have powerful magic. Can't you do something?"

"We can do something, but something won't be enough." Pelifeles stretched his front legs, shifted his weight forward and stretched his quivering hind legs. Then he sat back. "The Mother Flora is powerful, but even she can't open the portal with her magic alone."

"Why not?"

"Because it was an accident. Mixed magics ripped the portal open, and only a similar accident can do so again. Even so, it might not open the same portal."

"You mean, maybe I can't go home?"

"Maybe."

Sophie opened her mouth and shut it again. Did that mean she might never go back home? She clenched her teeth. She needed to go home and check on Trudy. Master Eigil had to come back, too.

"She's just worried about herself, don't you see?" Flynden said. "She doesn't care about any of this, about us."

"That's not true!" Sophie yelled. "I'm… I don't know."

Flynden turned away. Pelifeles slunk around Sophie's ankles and purred.

"You're scared." His tail wound around her leg. "Let's go back to the Garden and let the Mother Flora say what needs doing."

Sophie nodded and hung her head.

"Come on." Pelifeles padded across the clearing. "The sooner we…" He stopped and stuck his nose in the air.

Sophie smelled it, too. *Sour Apple. Oh no.* The wicked yellow-green light flickered between the trees.

"Run," Nelwyna said and blocked the path. "Run. Now."

"Come on." Flynden spun around and sprinted toward the path leading to the Garden. "Come, Sophie. Nelwyna knows what to do."

"She can't fight him all by herself." Sophie stopped.

"Come." Flynden ran back and tried to pull her away with him. Zap.

"Ouch." Sophie snatched her arm from his grip. "What if he hurts her?"

Sophie ran back to Nelwyna and patted her neck.

"Run, girl." The horse shook her hand off and nickered. "I have ways to protect myself. If you do not go now, he will surely hurt you. Go."

"Come, Sophie." Flynden stood poised and tense. He

swiveled his head between her and the coming yellow-green light like he watched a tennis match.

"Be careful," Sophie said with another glance at the light. She gave Nelwyna another pat and ran with Flynden across the clearing. Pelifeles jumped around them almost like herding them into the woods.

When they had entered the trees, Sophie slowed to take a last peek at Nelwyna. The horse dropped her head and started grazing, looking peaceful. A lone horse in a clearing looked innocent enough. Would Makimus take the bait? The men had seen the horse with them and would have told him. She went cold and shivered. Nelwyna shouldn't get hurt because of her. But what could she do to help?

"Keep going." Pelifeles urged her. "There is nothing you can do. Run."

With a final look over her shoulder, she dashed after Flynden. Pelifeles stayed behind her, making sure she kept running. Somehow, the forest seemed darker than before. Maybe it was getting close to evening. They would get to the Garden late after the Flora had turned and could talk to the Mother Flora right away.

They hadn't run far when Nelwyna's scream ripped through the forest. Flynden stopped dead. Sophie crashed into him. They stood wide-eyed, peeking through the trees toward the clearing. An acidic smell stinging her nose replaced the peppermint smell, almost like the forest was getting angry.

"We must help her." Sophie shivered, hunched her shoulders, and tried to rub the goose bumps off her arms.

Another scream tore through the woods and right through Sophie.

"Get going, Sophie." Pelifeles hissed. His fur stood on

end and started glowing. "Flyn, make her go. I'm going back to help the old nag."

Flynden swallowed and nodded, but he looked like he didn't like Peli's idea one bit. Before he could say anything though, Pelifeles had disappeared down the path.

Flynden and Sophie stared at each other.

"What can we do?" Flynden asked.

"You could protect them with your magic."

"I don't know how. It might not work."

"We could use the Flora blossom." Sophie pulled the sack from her pocket.

"You don't know what it'll do, if it'll do anything at all. I know for sure Makimus will take it from you if he catches us again." Flynden tried to pull her down the path but his fingers sparked and the Flora blossom turned hot beneath the cloth. Sophie stuffed it back into her pocket.

Another scream ripped through the forest followed by a big boom, like a bomb exploding.

"Let's go, Sophie." Flynden started running.

Sophie still didn't move. They couldn't just leave Nelwyna and Pelifeles. What should they do? Boom! Boom! Behind them, the forest lit up white and yellow-green, taking turns. Pelifeles must have gotten to the clearing.

"Sophie, come!" Flynden yelled. "You can't help them. Come on!" He ran back to her and pulled both of her arms to make her go with him.

Zap. Zap. His fingers sparked and stung her arms. The Flora blossom seared her leg.

"You're hurting me. Let go." Sophie tried to twist from his grip, but this time, he held on tight.

"I'll let go if you promise to come with me."

The pain brought tears and blurred his face. The stinging and burning got so bad she wanted to scream, too, like Nelwyna.

In the end, Sophie gasped and nodded.

"I promise. Just let go. Please."

Flynden released her. As she swung around to follow him, another terrible scream pierced her eardrums.

❧ *Chapter 23* ❧

Eigil huddled by the dirt-filled sacks, hugging the Celarim with his good arm, and his injured arm hung limp and throbbing at his side. The trembling prongs of the pitchfork pointed at his chest, giving him no chance to switch arms or try to hide himself with his magic.

"Got you, didn't I?" Spittle sprayed Eigil's face as the caretaker spat out the words, more excited than angry. "I knew it. Knew I wasn' going nuts." His feet shuffled sideways in a nervous dance. "What're you doing here? Speak up." The prongs pierced Eigil's arm.

Eigil jerked back, stung, his legs hit the sacks. The heavy book slammed him backward, but he dared not let go; it was his lifeline. He stopped the fall with his elbows, silently begging the book to aid him, to give him strength to call up his own magic.

"Speak up, I said," the caretaker spat. "Don't have all day."

Eigil remained still. What could he have said in answer to the old man's ranting? Instead, he preserved what little strength he had.

"I'm gonna call the cops now," the caretaker said, his face grim. "You got some answering to do." The man jammed the pitchfork into his left armpit, the prongs still pointing at Eigil, and with his right hand, pulled a palm-size metal object from his coat pocket. With his thumb, he flipped the top part up, punched little buttons on the other part with his left-hand forefinger, then held it to his ear, his eyes squinting at Eigil. A momentary silence hovered within the shed, except for their breathing.

"Hello?" the caretaker's voice boomed into the silence.

Eigil flinched. A tiny voice barked from the object, words Eigil could not understand. What magic was this?

"Yes, I'm the caretaker at Second Street Cemetery, you know, the small one up the hill. I've got somebody here." Again, the tiny voice in the object spoke. "Yes. Yes. Henry Mullen, caretaker." He nodded. "Think he might've had something to do with the girl gone missing." The voice again. Another nod. "Yes. Got him cornered." The tiny voice sounded agitated. The caretaker shook his head. "No. No chance. He's hurt. Can't do much." The voice barked something again. "Yeah, think so. Good idea." The voice again. The caretaker nodded. "Just hurry. Okay?" He flipped the object shut with one finger and slipped it back into his pocket.

"Won't be long now, old man. The cops will straighten you out." He took the fork into both hands and held it over Eigil. With his chin up, he leaned over and looked down on Eigil from half-closed eyelids. "Say something." He flipped the fork around and prodded Eigil's rips with the butt end. "Are you dumb?"

Eigil groaned. Perhaps if the old man believed him too weak and injured to talk, he would stop pestering him. The caretaker must have called someone, perhaps guards. He needed to be gone before they came. Yet, his weakness would not let him move. More than anything, he wanted to close his eyes and sleep. Perhaps he could handle the caretaker, but not the guards. May the light brighten your path and protect you, Master Eigil, he wished for himself and pressed the Celarim closer. As the book's hard edge dug into his bad arm, pain flared and jostled him to his senses. His mind cleared. The Celarim sent soft, pulsing magic bursts into his chest.

"What's the matter with you?" The caretaker leaned over Eigil all the while keeping a firm grip on the fork.

Eigil closed his eyes, not wanting the old man to see his life and strength returning.

The man poked Eigil's good arm with one finger, but jerked back as if stung.

"What's going on here?"

Eigil opened his eyes a bit. With a grim but surprised face, the caretaker examined his finger, which now sported a red burn mark. The Celarim weaved its magic around Eigil, protecting him. He could not be touched. Relief flooded through him. Maybe he had a chance. Maybe he would be strong enough at the right moment to disappear; otherwise, his vows not to harm would be tested.

The caretaker squinted back and forth between his finger and Eigil.

"Gimme that book." The old man reached out. "If it's a book." He hesitated.

Eigil groaned again and moved his head from side to side, groaning louder. The old man backed up.

"You stay put. Cops gonna be here any minute." Fear laced his voice. He stepped back far enough to clear the door. Perhaps he had decided a safer distance was called for.

Fine with me, Eigil thought. When the guards arrived, the caretaker would turn around. It would be his chance, perhaps the only one.

The book's pulses came steady and strong now, pumping magic into him. Would it be enough?

In the distance, a wailing rose and ebbed, coming closer. Eigil gasped. Demons? Had the old man called demons? Were these cops, as he called them, demons and not guards? His courage sank, and suddenly, the Celarim stopped pulsing. Fear pierced his heart. He lifted his head to look at the book. The uneven pages viewed from the top glowed for a moment, then faded. Was the book deserting him, now when he needed its strength the most? He wiggled it a bit, but wanted to shake it and ask what happened, but it did not work that way. The book grew dark and cold, and so did Eigil's innards.

The wailing pitched higher then choked into silence as a horseless carriage entered the burial grounds. Bright flashing lights flickered across the shed. Two doors slammed.

"In here!" the caretaker shouted. "Over here!" Standing a few steps outside the door, he waved both arms.

Eigil reached deep inside himself, probed deeper, prodded, nudged, but his magic did not stir. Instead, a fear and helplessness he had never known filled him from the crown of his head to his cold feet, paralyzing him. By the light, what was he to do?

Another wail rose in the distance, ebbing and rising, also approaching fast.

"He's in here." The caretaker said to someone out of view and pointed inside where Eigil lay. Blue, red, and yellow flashing lights danced through the cold morning.

Eigil watched through slits as two men, one stocky,

the other slim and tall, dressed in identical dark blue coats and leggings entered the shed. Guards. Men. Another wave of relief washed over him. The caretaker squeezed in beside the two men, who looked more curious than dangerous, yet their faces were stern.

"Okay, old man, what's going on here?" The stocky man asked.

Eigil decided to keep his silence and shook his head, groaning, hoping he appeared too weak to respond.

"He seems ill to me, Jim," the slim guard said.

"Right." Jim, who seemed to be the one in charge, leaned forward. "An ambulance will be here shortly, old man. The EMTs will have a look at you." He then asked the caretaker. "You found him?"

"Yes, the guy's been hanging around here." He jabbed his finger at Eigil. "Saw him the first time the girl gone missing."

"I see." Jim glanced at Eigil and back to the caretaker. "Doesn't look like he's capable of abducting anyone. More like he's going to pass out."

"He could've had an accomplice. Never know. Work in pairs."

"I watch those TV shows, too." Jim grinned, but his grin changed soon into a frown and his voice sounded strict. "We appreciate your help, um?"

"Mullen. Henry Mullen," the caretaker barked.

"Thank you, Mr. Mullen, please wait outside. We might've more questions later," the slim guard said and gave Henry Mullen a stern look.

"Fine," the caretaker grumbled and moved outside, but suddenly swung back. "You better watch him." Spittle landed now on the guard's face. "You might get zapped."

"What do you mean?" Jim asked.

"When I tried to take the book from him, I got zapped like touching an electric wire."

Jim and the other guard wrinkled their brows and eyed the Celarim. Then Jim took hold of the book and pulled it from Eigil's arm. Eigil let it happen because he had no strength to prevent it. Now, the Celarim appeared to be only a large book and he only an ordinary man. Fear made him grow colder.

"You must've picked up some static, Mr. Mullen." Jim grinned again. "Please wait outside now."

"Fine." Henry shuffled out.

The other carriage's wailing choked into silence outside the shed. More flashing lights mingled with the first set. Jim walked out.

"Keep an eye on him, Bart," he said over his shoulder. "Make sure he doesn't do anything."

"Right," Bart laughed. "He's gonna jump at me any second now."

When Jim had left, Bart placed the Celarim on the sacks to Eigil's left, opened the cover, frowned at the few pages he turned, and let the cover fall shut again. He seemed not all too concerned about Eigil and stepped to the open door, watching what happened outside.

Eigil reached inside himself again. Deep and deeper he went but searched in vain for a flicker of his powerful magic. What was happening to him? With a groan, he pushed himself onto his left side. When he reached for the Celarim, his right arm came up short. Bart gave him a quick glance and made a step toward him. Eigil fell back.

A man and a woman in different matching garments of gray leggings and white shirts entered the shed, bringing with them a white hard-case bag. The man felt his pulse. The woman took the stump and unwrapped the bloody cloth binding it.

"What happened to you, old man?" Her voice was brisk but friendly.

Eigil looked into her brown and kind eyes and exhaled. They were here to help, not to harm him. For the third time, relief grabbed him. He relaxed a bit and closed his eyes.

"We need to get him to the hospital," the woman said. "He's lost a lot of blood. I'm surprised he's alive."

Eigil opened his eyes once more as she spoke to Jim and Bart. "Get the stretcher, guys. Hurry up."

The two guards hurried from the shed.

"Give me a hand, Allen," she said to the man who had arrived with her. "We need to get him out of here. The stretcher'll never fit."

Together, they lifted him off the sacks. The two guards returned and helped carry him outside. The sun rose above the horizon, shooting an orange blaze across the burial ground. The wind blew sharp and icy on Eigil's cheeks, stinging the inside of his nose. They placed him on a high cot on a metal frame he assumed was the talked-about stretcher, and the woman covered him with a warm blanket.

"You'll be fine." She patted his shoulder, giving him a wide smile. They wheeled him toward the open door of a box-like carriage with red glyphs and a blue cross. No, they could not take him away from here. He would never find his way back.

"No." Eigil kicked off the blanket.

"What?" the woman asked. "What is it?" She bent close, because he had only whispered the word. "Wait a minute," she said to Allen and stopped moving. "He's trying to say something." Again, she bent over him. "What is it, old man?"

"Cannot leave." Eigil breathed the words. "Must stay." If he could delay them, perhaps his magic would awaken soon once more.

"We cannot leave you here. You'll die." Her concerned gaze made her look even prettier. Two locks of her golden-blond hair had come loose and framed her face. For one moment, she reminded him of the young Mother Flora, when he had still called her Marguerite. He tried to reciprocate the woman's smile, but his cold and stiff facial muscles would not obey.

"Must stay." He repeated the words and with his right hand grabbed her arm.

Shock registered on her face, but then she placed her hand over his.

"He doesn't know what he's saying, Maggie. He's probably out of his mind."

"For you, all old people are out of their minds. Wait until you get there." She squared her shoulders and straightened. "You'll see that's not true. I think he's trying to tell us something."

"Like what?" Jim said. He stepped beside her and leaned over.

"Don't know. Something."

"Do you know anything about the missing girl?" Jim grabbed the stretcher, preventing Allen from pulling it to the carriage's open door.

Eigil needed more time. Should he say yes or lie? Which answer would purchase him the time?

"Yes."

"See. See. I knew it." Henry Mullen danced toward the stretcher. "I knew he'd something to do with it."

Now, they all bent over him.

"Come on, old man." Jim said. "Let's have it."

"Must wait," Eigil whispered. "Child will return."

"Oh right." Allen rolled his eyes. "He's stalling. Don't you see?"

"Go get busy on the radio," Maggie said. "Let them know we're coming. Go on, and get the IV ready." She pushed Allen away from the stretcher.

"What do you know, old man?" she asked. "Do you know where the girl is? Is she hurt?"

Eigil wished he knew the answer. Was the girl hurt? Was she still alive? If so, would she find her way back? Would he be here when she did?

"Must wait," Eigil repeated. "Not leave."

Then Allen returned, carrying a transparent tube with liquid and a long needle attached to it.

"What are you doing, Allen?" Maggie sounded alarmed.

"We'll give him a nice shot and he'll sleep until we get to the hospital. No messing around."

"You'll do no such thing." Maggie slapped his arm away with her free hand, sending needle and tube flying.

Good girl. Eigil liked her more with each passing moment. He tightened his grip on her arm, looked from her to Jim, and breathed. "Please. The book."

Both Maggie and Jim straightened and exchanged a concerned look.

"Get the book, Bart," Jim said, wiggling his hand toward the other guard.

Bart trotted into the shed and returned with the Celarim. Maggie took it from him and placed it close to Eigil's feet on the stretcher. Eigil lifted his head and reached for it.

"It'll be right here. I promise," Maggie said and placed her hand on his forehead, pushing him back onto the soft pillow.

"How long can we wait?" Jim asked. His brow furrowed into a vertical line on the bridge of his nose.

Maggie shrugged. "A few minutes, no more. He should've been in the hospital days ago."

"You've got to be kidding, right?" Allen stooped, his voice came muffled from somewhere below the stretcher. "When have we ever asked an injured person what he wants? He'll be dead if we don't get moving."

Jim scanned the forest to the left, then to the right. His eyes caught Maggie's and nodded.

"We'll wait. Five. No more."

Maggie smiled at him and patted Eigil's hand, then faced toward the forest as well.

Eigil reached once more deep inside, searching, prodding, until he found a mere flicker in his heart, surprised to find it there. Perhaps the thought of Marguerite, or the similarities of the two women, had let it flare and let him discover it there. After all these years, he surrendered to the longing, to the love, and to the pain his choice had given him. Now, this love had to save him, so that he could save his love and his land.

Eigil's magic quickened, and he knew he would be able to sit up, grab the Celarim, and disappear. It might take him a few moments to leave the stretcher, but if they could not see him, they would look elsewhere, giving him more time.

He let the magic grow. Already, the sage scent wafted through the air. He took a deep breath, sucked it in, which brought him Maggie's concerned look. He closed his eyes. She did not move toward him. Instead, she removed her hands. She stepped away, and soon, angry whispers issued from nearby. Perhaps she continued to argue with the man called Allen.

Eigil watched Jim through narrow slits. The guard paced at the foot of the stretcher, keeping his face averted from him. His moment arrived. His chance had come.

The magic grew and quivered within his chest. With a sudden burst, he unleashed it into his body and let it cloak him. Moments later, it flung him upright. He reached for the Celarim. His hand closed on its spine as the magic engulfed him, and his arm with the Celarim disappeared. He had a moment long enough to slide his legs off the stretcher, to stand on his feet, alas unsteady, and to start tottering along the path toward the forest.

"He's gone!" Henry Mullen yelled and rushed to the stretcher. "He's gone!"

The others joined him.

"I told you." Allen laughed. "He was pulling your leg, Maggie."

"Shut up," she said.

Eigil grinned.

❧ *Chapter 24* ❦

Sophie and Flynden ran until they reached the forest edge, taking a few seconds here and there to catch their breaths. By the time they made a final dash across the space to the Garden wall, it was dark. The moon hung low above the hills, a round lantern ready to roll left or right. The two Flora, Rose and Lily, stepped from the blue shadows by the gate almost like appearing out of nowhere.

"Come, the Mother Flora is waiting," Rose said.

Flynden hesitated, but Rose waved him on.

"You are welcome once more, Flynden," Rose and Lily chimed together.

Flynden thanked them and ran with Sophie over the hills and into the Garden town, leaving Rose and Lily behind. Like before, Flora stood and stared at them along the narrow paths and ways. Without slowing down, Sophie and Flynden hurried on to the Mother Flora's cottage, heading straight to the back and into the courtyard.

The Mother Flora sat with Gritta, Thistle, and Bramble outside. When Sophie and Flynden ran up to them, they hurried to the gate.

"Sophie!" Bramble waved.

"What has happened?" the Mother Flora said without greeting. "Where are Nelwyna and Pelifeles?"

Gasping, bending over, Sophie and Flynden pointed back from where they had come. Gritta brought cups of water that they gulped down right away.

"There were two men," Sophie said, breathing hard. "Guarding the path in the woods. They saw us after we got the Flora blossom." She pulled the cloth sack from her pocket and offered it to the Mother Flora, who shook the blossom onto her hand. Tiny sparks danced above it like lightening bugs. With a loving gesture, she pressed it to her chest, holding it there, and closed her eyes for a moment.

"Go on," she said.

"Nelwyna saved us and carried us away. Makimus must've been close because we didn't get far when he came after us with his magic."

Flynden nodded. "Nelwyna told us to run." He swallowed hard. "We heard her scream."

"Pelifeles went back to help her and we came here right away." Sophie hugged herself. "I just wish we could've done more."

"You did well, children," the Mother Flora said. "You would not have been able to stand against Makimus. The spirit mates have a better chance by themselves without having to worry about you two. Let us hope the light will protect them."

"But can we not go and check?"

"They will be here before long. You will see." The Flora beckoned Sophie and Flynden to join her in the courtyard.

Gritta went inside and came back with two baskets

filled with fruit and bread and poured more cold water into their shell cups. Sophie was so scared and worried for Nelwyna and Pelifeles, she couldn't eat a thing. Flynden ate nothing either and sat with his hands balled into fists.

Sophie leaned back in her chair. "Does Makimus really hate everyone?"

"Perhaps." The Mother Flora smiled at her. "Most of all, he hates himself."

"Why's that?"

"I think he wanted to be a normal boy and have his mother belong only to him, not go away and live with the Flora." She folded her hands in her lap and rearranged the folds of her gown. "It is the reason he hated Eleta so much, I think, because she wished for a normal life for herself and Flynden, and she stood up for her wish, something his own mother failed to do."

"But it's an honor to be a special boy and to become a councilor of the High Council," Flynden said.

"True. Yet some people would prefer to live normal lives and not have the responsibility of being special. All they want is to earn a living and be with their loved ones. I do understand this. It is the reason why I force no woman to take the seed."

"What happened to his mother?" Sophie asked.

"She disappeared one day, and I never saw or felt her presence again. I assume she passed on into the light."

"And what happened to the sickly child? The one I was supposed to take the place of?" Flynden asked.

The Mother Flora chuckled. "He surprised us all. Vaughn did become a councilor apprentice. With his mother's help, he grew strong and healthy." Her voice trailed off and her face took on a thoughtful look.

"Vaughn?" Flynden's eyes popped. "What will happen to me now?"

"Master Eigil will decide when he returns, Flynden." She smiled at him. "Do not worry. There will be a place for you at Council Hall."

"I'm not sure that's right for me." Flynden shook his head. "I always wanted to be more like Stace not like Kir. Stace always said I wouldn't even make a good servant. And now…"

"You will be fine. We are all here to support and guide you."

"Not Makimus though."

"No." The Mother Flora shook her head. "Not Councilor Makimus."

Flynden frowned but said nothing. The Mother Flora walked into the cottage and winked at him from the door. He grumbled something and unclenched his fists.

The whole time, Thistle stared at Flynden and shifted in his chair, looking like he had to work up the courage to say something to him. "The Mother Flora told me," he said.

"Told you what?" Flynden snapped.

"You're my brother."

"Mine, too." Bramble piped up.

"The creature was your ma, and Gritta's our grandma." Thistle's face lit up when he looked at Gritta. He had a thin blanket tucked around him and still seemed a bit weak, but happy.

Thistle had family now, someone to help him look out for Bramble. Bramble hopped off Gritta's lap and crawled beside him onto his chair. He buried his nose in her hair.

The yellow moon rose over the Garden and made the

shadows bluer and purplish. Its bright light sparkled on the shell pitcher and cups on a small wooden table by the cottage door. Thistle's and Bramble's white-blond hair almost glowed in the moonlight.

Gritta leaned back with a heavy sigh. Bramble slipped from Thistle's lap and wiggled herself into Gritta's arms again. The old woman embraced the little girl while tears trickled from her chin into Bramble's hair. Thistle watched, looking jealous. Gritta wiped her eyes and chin with her apron.

Thistle nibbled on his lips. Sophie could almost see the wheels in his head turning with questions.

"Grandma, why did you leave us and go to the Flora?" He asked, looking straight into the old woman's eyes.

Gritta didn't blink or look away and spilled more tears when she did look down.

"Your grandda grieved himself to death over Eleta. You were still small and Bramble not yet born. Tadd never forgave himself for letting things happen the way they did. He became ill and never recovered. After he died, your da became insufferable. Your ma begged me to stay, and it broke my heart to leave her and you, but I could not remain under one roof with Braen. First, I did not know where to go, but then I thought I might find work in the village as a servant or sew for a living. Eleta, after all, had learned her sewing skills from me. I found a wealthy family who took me in. A short time later, Bramble was born. I heard about it from neighbors and went home, but Braen would not even let me see her."

She sighed.

"I didn't know Da was so mean to you. He was always good to us."

"Yes, he was, and I am grateful to him for that." She

got up and gently tucked the blanket around him. She patted his head and returned to her chair. "A few years later, terrible news reached me. Moirae and Braen had been found dead. You and Bramble had disappeared. One day, I went to the farm to look for you, begging the light to guide me, but I could not find you anywhere. Fear stole into my heart. The neighbor who had found your ma and da had said they saw no sign of struggle or violence. How could Braen and Moirae be dead if this was so? The neighbor agreed to look after the farm until I had things sorted out. Then I sought the Mother Flora and asked her for help, but even she had no answers for me. She thought it might not be safe for me to return to the farm, so she invited me to stay and promised to make inquiries about you and Bramble. I have been living here and caring for the Mother Flora ever since."

Thistle threw off the blanket, scrambled from his chair, and hugged her hard. She pulled him onto her lap.

"I am sorry, child. I know I should have been looking for you and Bramble, but I thought you were dead, too. You did a fine job hiding."

Thistle grinned.

"We both did fine. I looked after Bramble, and Bramble behaved most of the time."

"All the time, Grandma," Bramble said and nodded, making her curls dance around her face. Gritta smiled and laid one hand on Bramble's head.

"I think you were wise to leave, Grandma."

Thistle told Gritta what the Mother Flora had said.

"He killed when he has sworn to serve the light and the people of Nugateris?" Gritta's shoulders slumped, and her face seemed more wrinkled than before, like a shriveled up potato.

Thistle placed one hand against her face. "Master Eigil will come back and put him in his place."

Gritta nodded, but seemed to be deep in thought. After a moment, she said, "I think it is time for you to go to bed." Gritta gave Thistle and Bramble a quick hug and ushered them inside. "Are you two coming?" She asked Sophie and Flynden over her shoulder.

Sophie yawned and barely made it off the chair to go inside. Flynden stumbled after her, looking just as worn out.

Gritta showed them to their rooms and tucked them all in. "Sleep well," she said and walked out.

❧ ❧

Gritta woke them while it was still dark. They went outside where the Mother Flora waited at the fountain dressed in her flowing white gown. The wind sang in the big tree above them. The old woman fidgeted and leaned from one foot to the other, back and forth, like a dance. The Mother Flora hugged her.

"We must talk, Mother Flora. Before you turn," she said.

"You look concerned."

"I am. We must talk." Gritta's brows furrowed. With her wrinkled face and bushy eyebrows, she looked like an old man, and now when she furrowed them, she looked even more so.

"Come then. We will talk inside."

Together, they ushered the children before them into the cottage. Thistle still wobbled a bit, but he took Bramble's hand and went ahead into the kitchen. Inside, Gritta pulled a chair for the Mother Flora and asked Thistle and Bramble to sit on one side of the table.

Sophie and Flynden settled across from the siblings. In the rush of making tea, Gritta dropped a beautiful shell cup. It hit the floor and splintered into a hundred pieces.

"I am sorry, Mother Flora." She brought out a broom but made an even bigger mess by flicking the pieces all over the place.

"Never mind, Gritta," the Mother Flora said, following her movements with raised eyebrows. "We will take care of it after you have spoken your mind." She smiled at the old woman and gestured for her to sit down. "Gritta, it must be important if you rush so to make tea."

"Yes, Mother Flora. Forgive me. I feel compelled to hurry." Gritta folded her hands on the table but did not touch her tea. Instead, she fumbled with bread and fruit baskets for a while.

"Well?"

"It is like this, Mother Flora." Gritta took a deep breath. "After hearing Councilor Makimus' bad deeds, I think we should prepare for the worst. In case he comes here. I admit, I am scared."

"Do you trust me, Gritta?"

The old woman nodded.

"I am certain Councilor Makimus will come to the Garden because now he knows Sophie possesses the Flora blossom. He will want to prevent her from reaching Master Eigil. Yet, I do not know if I can stop him from doing more harm. Therefore, I have given considerable thought to our wellbeing," the Mother Flora said.

"What will you do?"

The Mother Flora smiled her secret smile.

"We will hide beneath the roots of Hen Wyneb, and I

will seal the tree's entrance. Then Councilor Makimus will not know where we are. He might detect the magic, but since magic is all around us, he will not know the difference."

Gritta exhaled and relief smoothed her wrinkled forehead.

"Mother Flora," Thistle asked, "will he really come to the Garden?"

The Mother Flora reached out to him and placed one hand on his.

"I believe so. However, the light favors the prepared. It does no harm to hide for a little while. Do you think?"

Thistle and Bramble shook their heads. Thistle looked like he would've rather gone somewhere far away instead of waiting for Makimus. Bramble seemed to like the idea of the councilor coming. First, she pouted, but then she frowned and squinted.

"We'll catch the man with the big rings," she cried and banged her fists on the table, startling them.

Teacups jumped and rattled. Deep in thought, the Mother Flora regarded Bramble for a while, her silvery eyes intent. It was almost scary the way she looked at her.

Why was the Mother Flora staring at Bramble like that? Was she upset with her? Bramble was only a little girl. The Flora children must have temper tantrums sometimes.

"Thistle, would you prefer to leave the Garden with Bramble and Gritta?" the Mother Flora asked, giving now Thistle the same intense look.

"Em, yes, I would." Thistle said and nodded. "I'm afraid of Councilor Makimus."

"Understandably so."

"I don't want to leave," Bramble cried. "I want to help."

"You will, Bramble." The Mother Flora rose and closed the door to the courtyard. "Come, I would like to talk to you."

"The sun will be rising soon," Gritta said.

"Over the past few hundred years I have acquired a great amount of patience. Every so often, I can let the turning wait for a short while."

"What about the portal?" Sophie asked. "Shouldn't we be thinking about that, too?"

"We will be talking about it as well, child."

Thistle got up, too. "What is it you want to tell Bramble? I want to hear it, too."

"Yes," Gritta pushed her chair back and stood. "I would like to know what you tell Bramble." The worry in her voice made the words sound hoarse.

The Mother Flora answered none of their questions; instead, she studied them for a moment like making up her mind about something and walked from the room.

"Come then," she said over her shoulder, "and I will tell you of my plan."

Gritta took Thistle's and Bramble's hands and followed the Mother Flora down the hallway. Sophie and Flynden exchanged quick glances. Flynden nodded and they hurried after the Mother Flora, too.

They walked through the cottage and out the front door to narrow stairs with rope handrails winding around the giant tree the Mother Flora had called Hen Wyneb. Single file, they climbed after the Mother Flora, who strode ahead, keeping her eyes raised. Round and round, they went. The dizzying trek made Sophie's head spin. She held onto the rough ropes, not daring to let go or look down until they reached the top-most platform overlooking the Garden town.

Out of breath, they reached the platform, a room like a tree house with a roof and big glassless windows. Gritta sank into a chair with a colorful cushion. Benches, woven from reeds, lined the walls around the room. Sheer white curtains dressed the windows and fluttered in the breeze that sounded like a storm up here. Thistle, Bramble, Sophie, and Flynden leaned out and looked down through the branches to the paths and cottages bathed in the soft yellow light of the moon.

"Children, be careful," Gritta warned and straightened in her chair.

Thistle leaned back and pulled Bramble with him because she wouldn't listen and leaned out farther. The little girl mimicked Flynden who hung from his waist over the windowsill.

"Come, join me." The Mother Flora patted the cushions beside her.

Thistle pulled Bramble across the room and sat with her on one side of the Flora while Sophie sat on the other. Flynden chose to sit on a woven rug and leaned against the wall below one window. The breeze ruffled his hair that had turned a light blond after the fight by the wall. Gritta stayed in her chair, still mopping the sweat off forehead and neck with her apron.

"Now listen," the Mother Flora whispered even though nobody could possibly hear her this far up. "Councilor Makimus wants to steal the three special seeds I carry, and with them, grow the legendary seed tree. If he succeeds, the Flora will perish—all of us, not only me."

She held out her right hand where three pea-size bumps showed under the skin of her palm. They all leaned forward and peeked at the outstretched hand.

Bramble hopped off her seat for a closer look. Gritta squinted at the Mother Flora, frowning and looking like Bramble, only older.

The Mother Flora closed her eyes; her brow furrowed. The small stoma-like slit opened over the three bumps. One after the other, three shriveled pea-size seeds popped out and lay on her hand.

"What are you doing, Mother Flora?" Gritta's frown deepened.

"It will be fine." The Mother Flora smiled. "Take these seeds, Thistle and Bramble, and hide them some place where no one would expect." Then she went all serious and intense again. "Councilor Makimus must not find you. When he comes, he will be looking for me. I will make certain it will take him a while before he realizes I no longer possess the seeds. It will take him even longer to figure out who has them, if he finds out at all. Therefore, do not tell me or anyone else where you go."

"But the demons, Mother Flora." Gritta gasped. "If you give up those seeds, you will die, and then they will come."

Would they all die? Sophie understood enough of their talk that panic rose like vomit from her stomach.

"Master Eigil will have returned before they come." The Mother Flora knitted her brows. "He will protect you against the demons and Councilor Makimus with the Celarim and the Flora blossom. I believe we can trust Councilor Druce Lar, perhaps the other councilors as well. It must be this way to save the Flora race."

"Who will be the next Mother Flora? You must choose a successor."

"I will be Mother Flora as long as I can." Again, the Mother Flora looked at Bramble with tender and kind eyes, but her gaze was also determined and a bit scary. Thistle hugged Bramble closer and squinted at the Mother Flora. She regarded him and placed her empty hand against his face.

"I need your help with this, Thistle, yours and Bramble's."

Thistle shook his head, but Bramble nodded. What did the Mother Flora want Thistle and Bramble to do?

"I want to help you, Mother Flora," Bramble said.

"No, Bramble. You're much too little. You don't know what you're saying." Thistle pulled her away from the Mother Flora, but Bramble struggled free and twisted away from him.

With a very grown-up voice, she said, "We must help, Thithle, and stop the man with the big rings or he'll hurt more people."

Thistle shook his head again and looked at Gritta.

"I don't like it either," the old woman said, more to the Mother Flora than to Thistle. "No good will come of it."

"What do I do, Mother Flora?" Bramble sounded unfazed and ready to go ahead with whatever the Mother Flora had in mind.

Again, Thistle tried to pull Bramble away with him toward the stairs, but she tore herself loose and knelt before the Mother Flora, her face open and willing.

"What do you want me to do?" she repeated.

"Bramble, no." Thistle cried but didn't try to pull her away this time.

What was this all about? Sophie tensed until her whole body hurt.

"Bramble," the Mother Flora caressed the girl's hair and held the palm with the three seeds before her face. "I want you to take one of these seeds, and Thistle and

Gritta will help you to keep the other two safe until you are wise enough to know what to do with them."

Bramble closed her eyes, tilted her head back, and opened her mouth. The Mother Flora's hand traveled from Bramble's crown along her face and cupped her chin.

"No!" Thistle yelled. He lunged, knocking Bramble to the floor and the seeds from the Mother Flora's hand. The Mother Flora gasped and reached for the seeds, but Bramble quickly picked them up one by one, and before anyone could stop her, she had popped all three seeds into her mouth. With a heavy sigh, Gritta fainted and slipped to the floor.

"Bramble, no! Don't, please don't!" Thistle slung his arms around Bramble and cried, "Please don't swallow those seeds, Bramble."

Teary eyed, the Mother Flora sat on the bench, looking all scared now.

"Do not swallow those seeds, Bramble. I do not know…" she said but didn't get to finish.

Unafraid, Bramble gulped and swallowed. A big grin split her face.

"You shouldn't have done that!" Thistle yelled.

The Mother Flora closed her eyes and dropped her chin. Her hand found Thistle's shoulder.

"Promise me, Thistle, to look after your sister and protect her, no matter what. I did not want it to happen this way."

Thistle went still and nodded, still holding onto Bramble.

"What will happen to Bramble?" he asked. "Is it going to hurt her?"

The Mother Flora opened her eyes, spilling tears onto her hands in her lap.

"She will be Mother Flora, perhaps more. I do not know."

"It isn't right. Bramble is only little," he said with no tone in his voice. His eyes were dry and flat.

"Nothing will happen until she is grown. With your help, she will be fine."

Gritta came to as white as a sheet. Sophie and Flynden rushed to help her back into the chair. "What have you done, Mother Flora?" she whispered and rose. "What will become of Bramble?"

The Mother Flora shook her head and didn't answer the question.

"You must leave now, Gritta. Take the children and go. Bramble will be the Flora's last hope."

"What will you do?"

"I will take Sophie to the clearing in the forest and open the portal for her. Master Eigil must return and set it all right."

Wow, it looked like Master Eigil would have his hands full when he got back.

"While Councilor Makimus concentrates on Sophie and me, you will slip out of the back door, so to speak." The Mother Flora walked to the stairs. "Let us prepare for your journey." She hunched her shoulders like she carried a heavy weight and started down the stairs.

Gritta looked too shocked and overwhelmed to protest. She scooped Bramble up and kissed the girl's face. Bramble still smiled and snuggled into Gritta's arms, her head on the old woman's shoulder. Hugging her close, Gritta hurried downstairs, but Thistle stood like a stone statue.

"What'll happen to Bramble?" Sophie crossed her arms. Why didn't the boys say anything? "Thistle, are you okay?"

Thistle started sobbing. He shook hard and made no move to follow his grandma and sister downstairs.

"What's going on?" Sophie mouthed to Flynden, but the boy shook his head, his face scrunched up in his usual way.

"Come, Thistle," Sophie said. "It'll be fine. I'm sure." But she wasn't sure about anything at all.

"She…she," Thistle cried and gasped. "She won't be my sister anymore. She'll be the Mother Flora."

Flynden went up to the boy, grabbed his shoulders and put his face close to his.

"It won't be for a long time. Bramble needs to grow up first. You heard the Mother Flora."

"You d…d…don't know that. Bramble i…i…is so little. She d…d…doesn't know what she's d…d…doing. The Mother Flora shouldn't have done it."

Sophie put her arm around Thistle. "Whatever happens, you and Gritta will be there for Bramble and watch out for her. Come, your sister needs your help now more than ever."

Thistle twisted away. "Bramble won't need us. She'll be powerful and strange. Maybe she won't even know us."

"Don't be silly," Sophie said. "She loves you."

Thistle shook his head and cried even harder. When Sophie made a move to hug him, he tore himself away, sidestepped her and clambered downstairs.

"What now?" Sophie asked and threw up her hands.

Flynden raised his shoulders with a heavy sigh and shook his head.

When they got back to the kitchen, Thistle stood with his arms around Bramble by the door. The Mother Flora packed food into a large basket. Nobody said a thing. The sun hadn't come up yet, and the gray morning made the kitchen look gloomy and cold. After a few minutes, Gritta returned, carrying a small pack slung over her shoulder.

"Morning is approaching," the Mother Flora said. "You must leave before the sun rises." She hugged the old woman, but Gritta didn't hug her back, standing straight and stiff, staring ahead over the other woman's shoulder.

"Do not be angry with me, Gritta. In time, you will come to understand."

Gritta pressed her lips into a thin line in a Trudyish way. Now, Sophie understood how much love and care this thin mouth meant.

On her knees, the Mother Flora reached for Bramble. The girl twisted from her brother's arms and went to the Mother Flora. They held each other for quite some time without speaking before the Mother Flora took Bramble's face into her hands.

"May the light always brighten your path, Bramble, Mother-Flora-to-be. May it protect and guide you. May you give it strength and love. Cherish it and give it care." Bramble nodded, her face serious, like she understood.

Sophie understood little and maybe it was better that way. Relief surged through her because it wasn't she who had to shoulder that responsibility, but right away guilt made her face grow warm.

The Mother Flora stood. "You have your orders, Gritta. Do not fail." She said it almost harshly to the old woman.

Gritta cried and gave her a curt nod before the Mother Flora led them outside.

"Bye, Sophie." Bramble slung her arms around Sophie's waist and squeezed. Sophie bent down and let Bramble give her a wet kiss on the cheek.

"Bye, Bramble. Take care." Sophie hugged her back. "Miss you."

"Miss you, too." Bramble moved to Flynden and hugged him around the waist, too. He didn't let the little girl kiss him, but hugged her back. Sophie grinned despite being sad, and hugged Gritta and Thistle.

"Wait here until I call my Flora children and the women," the Mother Flora said to Gritta. "When I start telling them about my plan, take your grandchildren and leave."

Gritta nodded and took her grandchildren's hands, standing ready to go.

Sophie waved once back to Gritta and the siblings and followed the Mother Flora back through the cottage to the colorful stone path. The Mother Flora called to Rose and Lily, asking them to gather the Flora and the women right away. Within minutes, they came, filling up the grassy area and the stone walk in front of her home. The Mother Flora waited until the last stragglers hurried toward her. She seemed to know when everyone was there. A sad smile spread over her face when she cast a quick look over her shoulder toward the cottage. Taking a deep breath, she started talking.

❧ *Chapter 25* ❧

Eigil leaned against the rough bark beneath the evergreen branches. The Celarim stood upright beside him against the trunk—dark, cold, and lifeless. He leaned against the book with one shoulder as regrets and sorrow churned inside of him. He should not have written the instructions for the seed tree, the Mother Flora's secret, onto the pages. Once written, it would be forever part of the book. It could not be undone. At the time, he thought it wise, a precaution, but now his actions seemed foolish. How could he have known Councilor Makimus would turn on the council and use the sacred book for his devious ends? Of course, Eigil had thought of tearing the page out, but it would have been as if ripping a limb from a living being. The magic's wrath would have killed him. At times, he thought he deserved such a fate for his foolishness, but his death would serve no one.

Now all he had done seemed to be for naught and he was slipping away, not into the white cold, but away into the light. The magic's burst, which had saved him from the guards and the caretaker, had ebbed away and left him weaker still.

"Now would be a good time, child," he mumbled and

realized he had spoken aloud, addressing the girl who had not returned. "I must go home, child," he muttered. "My country, my home, and my love depend on it."

Despite the biting cold, the forest air smelled fresh and clean, bringing back good memories of Nugateris. Eigil sucked it in and winced. Even breathing had become painful. He blinked through the boughs across the burial ground. The white cold had iced over the old gate with a thick white coat and its wrought iron wings hung dead and silent on its hinges. Past the gate, the forest stood dark. He should not have closed the portal. Perhaps he would have found a way back without the Flora blossom, or perhaps he was only an old man fooling himself. He huddled within his torn tunic and pulled the soiled cloak tighter around his numb body.

The sun set behind the mountain that kept watch over the town and its small burial ground. If the child did not return, this would be his last sunset, a feeling bone-deep and certain. He had always loved the colors of the ending day, the anticipation of the Flora turning, of seeing Marguerite. There had been the satisfaction of a life lived well.

Eigil tried to stretch his stiff legs but his knees would not straighten. It mattered little now. He knew, soon he would fall asleep and slip away, here in the burial ground, fitting for his old aching bones.

Eigil gazed into the wide yellow, orange, and red band that was stretching across the sky behind the distant mountains as if being pressed into the dark by the indigo sky. With one last flash, the fiery ball dipped behind the mountain. Even if the sun had not warmed him as such, the thought and color had warmed his heart. His head bobbed forward, his chin lowered to his chest. It would not be long now.

A while later, Eigil raised his head and blinked, his eyes crusty with frost. With the darkness, the temperature had dipped lower than ever. He must have dozed off, but not for good. Relief warmed and soothed while his shoulder pained him where it dug into the tree. As if his body had morphed into ice, his limbs refused to obey when he tried to stretch them. Like a frozen claw, his hand clasped the cloak, the stump hung lifeless beside him. The hand no longer shook as he made the effort of pulling the garment tighter but he could not even lift a finger.

The rumbling noise belonging to a horseless carriage had woken him. Its light speared the dark, first up then down as it crested the hill and crawled along the path between the burial sites. Through frozen eyelashes, Eigil watched it stop by the shed. Perhaps Henry Mullen had come back, but this was not the caretaker's carriage. The old man's carriage was big and rusty, with a loading surface in the back, while this small and yellow one had a shiny coat that sparkled within its own lights. The door swung out, expelling first a pair of slim booted legs, before the rest of the woman unfolded from the small carriage. Eigil tried to glimpse more of her, but she wore a wooly hat pulled far down over her ears. She walked around the carriage and stood looking at the shed, her hands jammed into the pockets of a big puffy jacket. As she turned her head, black profile against bright light, he recognized her. Maggie had not given up on him, showing a surprising likeness to Marguerite by coming here alone. Marguerite, caring, always hopeful, had not given up on him either, and would be waiting for his return. He would hold on.

Maggie checked the padlock on the shed's door, rattling it, and slapped it down against the wood. Her golden hair, released from its braid, rippled like sunlight from underneath her hat down her back. It swung gracefully with her moves. She walked once around the small structure and perhaps peeked into the back window to find him within.

"I am over here, Maggie." He whispered and wished his voice were stronger, wished she would hear him, no longer caring if his secret came to light. He must survive. He would explain if he could only catch her attention.

"Maggie." Of course, the rumbling carriage would not permit her to hear his feeble voice.

"Old man, where are you?" she called.

"Here, Maggie, over here." The wind snatched away his whispered words like the soft flakes once more dancing from the sky.

Maggie hesitated for long moments. She pivoted on the spot, this way and that.

"Let me help you!" Maggie called and listened, then hurried around her carriage, turned it off, but left its lanterns burning.

An icy silence settled in the night. Eigil had not even strength to whisper. It seemed as if these short hopeful moments had been only a respite at best from the inevitable.

"Old man?"

His lips made an attempt to form an answer, but his words were thoughts she could not hear. Helpless, he watched her walk one more time around the shed, watched her slap her carriage's roof before she climbed back in and slammed the door. The carriage hummed to life and rolled around the path that started and ended at the hill where it had entered.

He could not let her leave. He must stop her. The faces of Maggie and Marguerite merged in his mind, giving him hope, lending him strength. Once more, the magic flared. He fed his love and hope and joy into it, everything good he possessed, trying to send a light she could see.

The tiny sparks formed on his frozen fingertips, crackling and sputtering like a candle about to die. He waited until the carriage came alongside. He let go. The purple color sparked once and winked out even quicker. Bright lights danced before his eyes instead.

The wheels crunched past; the carriage's hum rumbled once more through the cold night, over the rise, and out of the burial ground. She had not seen it.

A sudden painful tightening in his chest ripped him away from the fading sound of the carriage. He gasped, "Nelwyna." The bond severed and his spirit mate slipped away, too, leaving him ever colder and lonelier.

A heart-shaped face surrounded by white petals and golden hair swam into view. Silvery eyes shining with life, filled with warmth and love, gazed back at him. Marguerite. He reached out to her with his heart and mind. Her features blurred and tore apart as if the cold wind snatched them up too, leaving nothing but darkness.

❧ *Chapter 26* ❧

The Mother Flora's plan sounded crazy, but in this case, it might be a good thing because only a crazy plan might work. She would be going home. If the plan worked, Makimus would come to the Garden first. When he didn't find anyone, he would go to the clearing. Having a powerful and evil man come after you wasn't comforting, but they needed Makimus' magic to open the portal again, the Mother Flora had said.

"Home," Sophie whispered to herself. Even saying the word tasted yummy. Like forever, she hadn't felt at home anywhere, not since before Mom and Dad died in the car crash. If this maniac weren't after her, she could almost feel at home here with Flynden. But no, she had to go home to Trudy and make sure she was okay. She just had to be. Guilt twisted in her stomach. If she got out of here in one piece, she would make up for it all. *Promise.* She would be a better kid. She would listen to Trudy and be nice to her. In her head, she promised everything she could think of, if only she would make it home.

Sophie pulled the rose-scented blanket to her chin, feeling nice and cozy under the warm softness.

The day had dragged along. After the Mother Flora's

short speech, she had stepped close to Hen Wyneb, the giant tree, and placed both hands against the trunk. With closed eyes, she had mumbled to herself for quite some time until the earth beneath her rumbled. The trunk split right where her fingers pressed against the bark. A gasp went through the Flora. A few little ones cried. With cracking, heaving and moaning, the split widened between two thick roots until it measured two arms' lengths wide. A fresh earthy smell rose from a dark hole and silence settled over the scene.

"Come, children." The Mother Flora beckoned the Flora and walked ahead of them down the hole into the tree.

Curious, Sophie and Flynden followed with the helper women. Stone steps led down into the earth. At the bottom, the Mother Flora lighted a vaulted cave with white globes. Sophie, Flynden, and the women waited on the stone steps and watched.

A musty, earthy smell, nothing bad though, rose warm off the soft ground. The Mother Flora strode with encouraging and calming words among her children, assuring them they would be safe here. When dawn came, she turned with them in the cave's warm earth.

Earlier, she had instructed Sophie and Flynden to wait at the mouth of the cave and keep watch. But what could they do if Makimus did show up? The Mother Flora claimed Flynden would protect them all with his magic. Neither Flynden nor Sophie was quite so sure. The look on the women's faces told Sophie they thought along the same line, but they said nothing. They had brought woven mats and blankets, given one to her and Flynden, then had settled and waited with them.

Nothing happened all day, and Sophie thought she

would maybe die of boredom instead of being killed by Makimus. She tossed on the mat and snuggled deeper under the blanket. If she could stay under there, smell the fresh Flora scent, and not have to deal with any of it, she would be content. But Master Eigil counted on her, and so did Trudy. Trudy would be worried sick by now if she hadn't died already.

Frustrated, Sophie flopped onto her back, pulled the blanket higher, changed her mind, and folded her arms on top.

The Mother Flora's plan had a tiny snag. That snag was tricking Makimus into using his magic at the same time with her friends to rip the portal open. Sophie believed he would come because now he knew she had the blossom. How she would do her part, she couldn't even begin to imagine. What if she got killed trying?

Sophie tossed a few more times, crossed her arms behind her head, and stared through the branches into the darkening sky. Nearby, some women knitted blankets of the kind that covered Sophie, and only their needles click-clicked in the silence. Their faces looked grim.

Sophie's eyelids grew heavy and she started to doze off when Flynden got up from his mat and walked down the colored stone path.

"Where are you going?" Sophie called after him and sat.

"I'm going to the main gate. Maybe I can see something."

"You're supposed to watch, remember?"

He kept walking, ignoring her. She wasn't going to disobey the Mother Flora, so she would stay put. A bit miffed, she lay down again and fell asleep despite promising herself not to.

A hand on her shoulder woke Sophie.

"It is time, child. Come," Rose said.

Sophie flung the blanket aside and scrambled to her feet. Still half asleep, she followed Rose down into the cave where the Mother Flora waited.

"Are you rested, child?" she asked.

"I'm fine." Sophie wasn't, but complaining wouldn't help now.

"Where is Flynden?" the Mother Flora asked.

Sophie blushed, like it was her fault. "He was going to the main gate, he said."

The Mother Flora shook her head, but just then, Flynden pushed past the women, running down the stairs, cradling Pelifeles in his arms.

"Mother Flora!" he yelled. "Pelifeles is hurt."

The Mother Flora met him halfway and knelt. "Place him on the ground."

Flynden placed Pelifeles near her knees. The cat's fur was burned to the skin in most places, the skin blistered, and his tail stuck out funny like an L-shape.

"Oh no." Sophie slapped one hand to her mouth. "Did Makimus do that?"

Flynden nodded. "Calleo and Kir found Peli, but they couldn't heal him. They're hiding now with Councilors Druce Lar and Tulio in the forest." Flynden bit his lip and rubbed his eyes, but he couldn't hide how upset he was.

The Mother Flora guided her hands over the small, furry body, moving them back and forth, up and down, for some time. The whole time she worked on Pelifeles, a light flowery scent rose from her skin. Under her hands, the blisters dried and healed, the fur started growing back, and the tail straightened and looked whole again.

"Will he be fine?" Flynden scooted closer.

"He is on the mend now." The Mother Flora smiled.

"I doubt the injuries will have dampened his spirit."

"What about Nelwyna?" Sophie asked. "Where's she?"

Pelifeles' tail twitched, and he opened his eyes.

"Nelwyna is still lying in the clearing," he hissed. "Makimus slashed her with his magic until she went down. I tried to fight him off, protect her, but he let his whole fury out on us. We couldn't win. So, I played dead. When we weren't moving anymore, he left."

Oh no. Sophie held her head with both hands and stared open-mouthed at Pelifeles.

"I crawled to her," Pelifeles whispered, "but she lay still, barely breathing. I decided it would be best to find help and made it to the road not far from Gwern where I found Kir, Calleo, and Councilors Druce Lar and Tulio."

"Will they help Nelwyna?" Sophie asked.

"*We* will." The Mother Flora patted her arm. "Rose!" She called and the Flora hurried over. "Go to the forest by the main gate. Kir, Calleo, and two councilors are hiding there. Tell them to wait for us in the clearing where Master Eigil disappeared and not let anyone see them."

"Yes, Mother." Rose hurried up the stairs and out into the night.

"We are leaving now. Come." The Mother Flora ushered everyone but her Flora children from the cave. Flynden carried a protesting Pelifeles and cuddled him close. At the top of the stairs, the Mother Flora turned to gaze at her children. She stretched her arms wide like she wanted to hug them all.

"May the light always brighten your path." Her voice echoed off the cave walls. "Take care, my children. Be safe."

"Aren't they coming?" Sophie asked. "What'll happen to them?"

The Mother Flora glanced at her children and shook her head. "It is better for them to wait here."

The Flora broke into their strange humming song and raised their arms together, reaching for their mother. The Mother Flora turned away and Sophie stepped outside with her.

"Stand back now," the Mother Flora said to her, Flynden, and the women who waited with them. She then placed one hand on either side of the split in the tree and closed her eyes. With the same cracking, moaning, and heaving, the bark, roots and earth moved until the split closed and the tree stood whole like before.

"Hen Wyneb will protect my children until Nugateris is safe for them once more."

"How will they survive without sunlight?" This wasn't right. She was burying them alive. Sophie shivered and felt nauseated. What else was this woman going to do? But the heartbreaking look in the Mother Flora's eyes made her regret those thoughts.

The Mother Flora told the women to leave and find shelter on the farms and in the towns. She thanked them for their help and service and sent them on their way. Some wanted to hug her, wish her well, but she shook her head.

"Leave now. You are in danger, too."

The thirty or so women rushed away. Soon, only Sophie, Flynden, Pelifeles, and the Mother Flora stood at the roots of the old tree.

❧ ❧

The moon shone in a sky sparkling with stars and cast blue and purple shadows that followed them like phantoms through the grass. A breeze played with Sophie's hair and cooled her hot face from the quick walk. They hiked through the night over the hills and reached the low wall much quicker than she'd thought. For a while, they huddled low behind the stones near the gate and watched the forest. When nothing moved near the trees, Flynden opened the gate. With Pelifeles leading, they hurried across the open space into the forest. The cat didn't look like he'd ever been injured at all. Maybe the Mother Flora could do whatever she did to Pelifeles to Nelwyna, too, and save her, if she got to her in time.

When they entered the trees, the crowns blocked out the moonlight, but neither Pelifeles nor the Mother Flora slowed one bit in the darkness. Pelifeles let his fur glow just enough for them to see the path. The Mother Flora strode after the cat like she thought nothing of this strange hike in the night. Fear and excitement pushed Sophie ahead as they trekked deeper into the forest.

The usual peppermint scent wafted around them, a fragrance now so pungent, it stung in her nose and made her sneeze. The trees knew. The thought flashed through her mind. They knew something important and dangerous would happen in their forest.

Sophie couldn't tell how long they'd walked, almost forever it seemed, when Pelifeles slowed.

"We're almost there," he hissed. His words came out in a whisper. "Nelwyna lies near the trees at the far side of the clearing."

For a moment, they all listened into the dark. An owl hooted somewhere in the branches above them. A breeze stirred the trees and the peppermint smell hung strongly in the air. Up ahead, the moon bathed the clearing in a soft blue light.

The Mother Flora beckoned them forward.

At the clearing's far end, a black bulk lay in the grass, not moving. Sophie's throat tightened. She swallowed hard and clasped her hands to stop them from shaking.

Instead of crossing the clearing straight ahead, the Mother Flora wove a path along the trees until they stood close to Nelwyna. The Mother Flora held up one hand and waited. Sophie listened, but only a breeze stirred the trees. When the Mother Flora dropped her hand, Flynden and Sophie rushed forward and slid to a stop beside Nelwyna's body. Sophie placed her hand on the white tear-shaped blaze and stroked the horse's feverish forehead, down to the nostrils where a bad cut cleft her soft nose. She was still alive. Maybe they weren't too late after all. The rib cage rose and fell ever so little. Nasty gashes criss-crossed the neck, flanks, and rump. Blood oozed from them. The front legs were broken and stuck out in a way they shouldn't.

"Nelwyna," Sophie whispered, choking. "We've come to help. Hang in there. Okay?" She got a weak snort for an answer.

The Mother Flora knelt by Nelwyna and touched the white tear above the eyes, but all too soon, she sat back onto her heels, folding her hands in her lap. Did she make Nelwyna well again? Sophie watched, but the mare didn't move, only her rib cage kept rising a bit.

"We are too late," the Mother Flora said, sad and accepting.

"What do you mean?" Sophie asked and grabbed the Mother Flora's arm. "Can you not heal her like Pelifeles, please?"

The Mother Flora shook her head. "No, Nelwyna's wounds are deep, much deeper than Pelifeles' injuries were."

Sophie rounded on Flynden. "Flynden, can't you do something?"

Flynden shook his head, too.

"Pelifeles?" Couldn't they do anything? "Maybe together?"

Sophie gazed from Pelifeles to Flynden to the Mother Flora. The look on their faces told her more than any words could have.

"But…" Sophie knew as soon as she said the word there was no but. They were too late. Oh no, what would she tell Master Eigil? He would be devastated. Or would he be angry? Guilt twisted in her gut.

"It's all my fault," Sophie whispered.

The Mother Flora took Sophie's hands.

"No, it is not your fault, child. Nelwyna did what she had to do. She would not have wanted it otherwise. She knew how important it is for you to return home and give Master Eigil a chance to do the same."

Sophie hung her head and leaned her forehead against Nelwyna's shoulder. The horse's rib cage rose and sank, rose and sank.

"I'm so sorry, Nelwyna. I didn't want this to happen. I promise. I'll help Master Eigil come home. I will."

Nelwyna's last breath whooshed out of her, and then her rib cage moved no more. Pelifeles touched his nose to hers. A tiny spark jumped between them. He sat back and hung his head. Flynden caressed Nelwyna's forelock and patted her neck.

Sophie stared, pushed the shoulder a few times, and turned to the Mother Flora.

"She is gone," the Mother Flora said. "Come now." She pulled Sophie up with her.

"Are we just going to leave her here?"

The Flora nodded. "There is nothing more we can do. We must hasten."

They couldn't just leave Nelwyna. What would happen to her?

"Come," the Mother Flora said again, her voice stern now, and she strode back to the path. Pelifeles padded along side her, dragging his tail, his ears drooping. Flynden took Sophie's hand and pulled her away across the clearing into the night.

❧   ❧

Sophie and Flynden trekked after the Mother Flora and Pelifeles. The clearing where the portal had been wasn't far, and a short walk took them there.

At the clearing's edge, the Mother Flora stopped. Sophie peeked past the massive trunks. For a moment, they stood in silence, listening to the night sounds. A night bird sang a sad song somewhere in the giant trees. Sophie glanced over her shoulder, but of course, she wouldn't see the black body on the ground from here. She pinched her nose with two fingers and stifled a sob. No, she wouldn't cry. She would be tough and see this through. More than ever, she wanted to stop Makimus. Flynden took her hand again and held it. She squared her shoulders.

Up ahead, the moon bathed the clearing in a soft light. A soft breeze, like breathing, whooshed through the crowns of the trees and through the grass.

"Now what?" Sophie whispered, but the Mother Flora

pressed one finger to her mouth.

How would she know what to do? Was she supposed to go out there and confront Makimus? Well, so far, the man hadn't shown up—yet, and neither had the apprentices nor the councilors.

Sophie let her gaze travel around the clearing, checking into the dark spaces between the trees, but if Kir, Calleo, and the councilors were there, they stayed hidden.

The Mother Flora beckoned her to lean close.

"It is time for you to step into the clearing, child," she said, and gave Sophie's arm an encouraging squeeze. "For our plan to succeed, you must be the only one seen looking for the portal."

"You really think we can fool Makimus?" The butterflies in Sophie's stomach danced one of Trudy's polkas. Sophie shook herself.

"We have to believe we can." The Mother Flora gave her an assuring smile.

Sophie raised herself on tiptoe and twisted to have another look. In the moonlight, the clearing looked peaceful like a fairytale scene. Her eyes flicked to Flynden's.

"We will be here and watch over you," the Mother Flora continued. "No harm will come to you, I promise."

How could the Mother Flora be so sure?

Flynden nodded, his face scrunched up again. He hugged her and Sophie hugged him back. For a long time, they held each other. Her eyes burned, but she swallowed hard and blinked. No point getting all mushy. Maybe this was the last time she'd ever see Flynden. She wasn't a crybaby, and she had a job to do. She gave him another squeeze and let go.

Pelifeles slunk around her ankles. She scooped him up and cuddled him close, sticking her face into his silky fur that had grown back in the short while. Why couldn't the Mother Flora have healed Nelwyna? Sometimes magic seemed to be a good thing, but for some things, even magic wasn't enough.

She let go of the cat and faced the Mother Flora, who took her hands, flipped her left hand palm up and placed it into Sophie's. Amazed, Sophie cupped the hand and watched as the stoma opened like before, and three perfectly round pea-size seeds popped into the hand. The Mother Flora kept her eyes closed, her brows wrinkled as she concentrated. When the three seeds had settled on her palm, the stoma closed, and the Mother Flora opened her eyes again.

Sophie collected the seeds with thumb and index finger and placed them into her hand and stared at them for a moment.

"You must not…" the Mother Flora started.

Sophie brought her hand up and popped the seeds into her mouth.

The Mother Flora gasped. "You must not swallow them," she finished saying, her voice stern again.

"I won't. Always hide gum in my mouth. Nobody ever finds it even when they tell me to open my mouth to check." She grinned. The Mother Flora's mouth remained open for a second before she snapped it shut.

"Don't worry, Mother Flora," Sophie said. "I'll be careful. Honest."

The Flora sighed and shook her head. "I will trust you. These are only regular seeds, but they still might do harm to you if you swallow them. If our attempts fail and Makimus confronts and threatens you, tell him I gave you my three special seeds." She hugged Sophie. "Hand them over, it might save your life."

She then pulled two pouches from her gown's pocket. "Here are more seeds. Take them to Master Eigil. By now, he may have need of them." She sighed and handed a tiny silky pouch to Sophie.

Sophie stuffed the lumpy little pouch into her pocket and held out her hand for the other pouch.

"This one contains the Flora blossom. Do not let it touch your skin."

Sophie nodded. As she slipped the pouch also into her tunic pocket, the blossom's warmth seeped through the fabric and warmed her hip. With her tongue, she moved the three seeds from left to right, like hiding her gum, but unlike the fruity taste of her favorite strawberry gum, these seeds were yucky. Now all she had to do was walk into the clearing and wait for her friends—and Makimus—to open the portal, then run home. Of course, it wouldn't be so easy, and the butterflies in her stomach knew it, too.

"What about you?" she asked the Mother Flora. "What will happen to you?"

"Do not worry about any of us. Go home and send Master Eigil. He must return as fast as he can."

"You sure you'll be fine?"

"Yes, child." The Mother Flora hugged her but then pushed her toward the gap between two trees. "Go on. May the light always brighten your path, child."

Sophie nodded. "Good luck to you, too."

"Be strong, child. We count on you." She reached up and cupped Sophie's face with her hands—lovingly, like a mother. "Tell Master Eigil," the Mother Flora said, her voice fierce. "Tell him."

"Like what?"

"Tell him, I…" The Mother Flora took Sophie's hands. "Tell him to remember me."

"Okay. Will do." Sophie hugged the tiny woman one more time, and with another parting glance at Flynden and Pelifeles, she stepped out into the blue moonlight—to be shot at. She grimaced.

❧ ☙

Sophie wished she hadn't popped the seeds into her mouth. What would she give for some gum right now? In her tunic pocket, the Flora blossom pressed warm and somehow comforting against her side. She walked a few steps ahead and hesitated. The urge to swing around was great, but it might be giving her friends away, so she kept walking.

The ancient trees stood like silent sentinels around the clearing. Moonlight shining blue from between the trees now glowed golden in the clearing's center. The whole scene looked peaceful. The butterflies had changed into a big hard knot sitting heavily in her stomach. She trailed toward the area where she thought the portal had been. She couldn't be sure, but the Mother Flora had said close would be good enough. The sweep of all magics together would cover a wide area, including the spot where the portal had been. What if the portal was gone for good?

Would she be quick enough to flatten herself on the ground when her friends fired their magics? Part of her wished Makimus would show up soon; the other part of her wished she would never see him again—ever. He would be aiming at her, not at the portal. Her knees went weak just thinking about it.

She wandered across the wide-open space, at first aimlessly, but then lifted her arms, fingered and grabbed the air before her as if searching for something invisible. It probably looked stupid, but she was here to trick Makimus. She had to look like she was searching for the portal and doing it all wrong. Maybe he would think she could open it with the blossom. Maybe he would try to get it from her before he did anything else. What could she say to tempt him to fire his magic?

The knot in her stomach tightened, making her feel sick. Her legs wobbled a bit and her kneecaps vibrated up and down in her knees. Her hands stretched out in front shook like some alien things at the ends of her arms. Sophie took a deep breath of the peppermint smell. She had to keep her wits. When the moment came to act, she couldn't be all mushy and wobbly.

Where had the portal been? She whirled on the spot, once around, before going forward again. The Mother Flora had told her she would see nothing floating in the air. Maybe something on the ground would make her remember. How could a patch of grass she'd seen only once look familiar? Despite her doubts, Sophie kept searching. Grass, grass, and more grass. She veered right and left, spun on the spot, once around again. There, hadn't there been a cluster a bit bigger than the others? No. Wishing wouldn't get her anywhere. A few more steps to the right, then left. Grass, nothing but grass.

Then, some buttercups shone deep yellow in the moonlight. She remembered squashing the little flowers when she dived through the portal into the clearing. Excited, she walked around the flowers. She had found the right spot. Shaking hard, her excitement and fear mounted, but she couldn't let it show and took a deep calming breath. She combed her fingers through her hair, once, twice, three times: the sign they had agreed on.

A branch broke in the forest. Sophie flinched and peeked into the dark. She wanted to run, not be the biggest target around, but she had to stay for the plan to work. They wouldn't get a second chance. It had to work the first time.

The minutes crawled by. How long had she been standing on this spot? Wouldn't it look odd to Makimus if she stood here waiting? Maybe she should be doing something. Keeping her eyes on the buttercups, she began a weird dance she'd seen on TV. Arms stretched above her head, she waved her body like seaweed in the ocean, wiggling her butt at the same time, mixing it with the stamping of a Native American dance she'd seen at a festival. If nothing else, the movement helped her to relax.

She started to get into the groove of it when the yellow-green light appeared. The round light bobbed in the darkness like a ping pong ball on the ocean. By the time it reached the clearing's edge, it had grown to basketball size and glowed bright yellow-green. Makimus had come and sour apple stank up the air.

Sophie's knees shimmied up and down, her hands shook at her sides, her stomach turned over. Sophie swallowed. She wanted to hug herself around her waist, but it would look weak. Instead, she stood tall and folded her arms across her chest, holding onto her upper arms. She bit her teeth together and hoped she wouldn't throw up.

The yellow-green light lengthened to the size of a big man and flared brighter before fading away, leaving

Councilor Makimus standing there.

"Well, well, well," he said. "Here you are, child. You departed rather quickly the last time." He strolled to the right, not toward her.

"What d…d…do you want?" She sounded like a sissy. It didn't matter. Being cool wasn't required, only getting the job done.

"Oh, but what could I possibly want from you, child?" Makimus spread his arms widely as if wanting to fold her into his arms.

Eek. Her eyes followed him circling her.

"Well, y…y…you wouldn't be here if you didn't want something, right?"

"All I want, child, is to help." He stopped and took a step toward her. "Is this so difficult to believe?"

Sophie nodded and tightened the hands on her arms, pinching them. The pain somehow helped. "You don't want to help anybody but yourself. Creep," she added, hoping that maybe if she made him angry, he would use his magic. So far, he still smiled. Well, he had taken one bait, why wouldn't he take another. For a moment, she was like a cat playing with a mouse, but then she wondered who was who. She wanted this to be over; she wanted to go home and tensed, clenched her fists and jaw, even her butt.

"Tut, tut. Is this the way to show respect toward your elders?"

"You're not my elder. You're just a big, fat creep." She nodded to underscore her words. What else could she say? Which words would hurt him enough to make him lash out? She would have to find a weak spot. Hopefully, he had one. Insults didn't seem to do it.

"Who'd want some elder like you anyway?"

"Oh, let me think." He scratched his beard and lifted his eyes to the sky. "Apprentices of the High Council, children of Gwern-cadarn-brac, young men and women looking for guidance from a benevolent councilor."

"Who'd listen to you?" Sophie raised her voice. "No mother or father would want their child dealing with you. Your own mother didn't have any use for you."

Makimus went rigid. For a second, he stopped smiling.

She'd found his weak spot and would keep picking on it.

Then he changed tack.

"You sound brave for someone all alone." His smile reappeared, now wider, and more fake.

Sophie couldn't help chancing a glance at the forest.

"Are you counting on your friends?" He started walking again, calm now, hands behind his back. "If you do, I have to inform you, regrettably so, that they are otherwise occupied at present and could not meet you here."

He was lying. Her eyes flicked to the forest where she searched for a sign of Kir, Calleo, and the councilors. They had to be there. This was too important.

"Ah, but you were counting on them." His gaze flicked to the forest.

Did he know about the Mother Flora and Flynden, too? Sophie held her breath.

"I visited the Garden. It seems the Mother Flora took her children somewhere safe. No help will come from her. So, who remains?"

Sophie swallowed. Don't listen. Stick to the plan. Keep taunting him. She had nothing else left to do. Her friends would be there. She had to believe it.

"So, why did your mother give you away?" She raised

her chin, trying to look haughty.

"What do you know of my mother?" He resumed his circling walk. "She was a fine woman. The finest."

"Well if that's so, why did she give you to the Council? Huh?" Sophie leaned forward, staring at him, making her face as fierce as she could. "Your mother probably couldn't stand you. So why would anyone else?"

He stopped and brought up his hands. Yellow-green sparks crackled at the fingertips and stank of sour apple.

"So, where is your beloved mother now? Huh?"

He sucked in his breath. Then his smile was back, more fake than ever, all teeth, and through them he hissed, "I killed her."

Sophie's mouth fell open. He killed his own mother? What chance would she have? Maybe she was just like him because hadn't she killed Trudy?

For an instant, they stood with their eyes locked. Any second now, she could feel it, and he would kill her, too. Sophie swallowed hard and pressed her legs together to keep from peeing herself.

He raised his hands higher. Yellow-green fire flashed. Sophie dropped to the ground and flattened herself. An instant later, the magic hit the air above her with a bang like a shot. She threw her arms over her head but peeked beneath her elbow. Brilliant white light hurtled from the forest where the Mother Flora and Flynden stood, meeting the yellow-green magic above her head. Another bang tore at her eardrums, exploding above her and throwing Makimus across the clearing where he lay still.

Sophie twisted around and looked up. Close to her and a foot off the ground, an uneven ring of sparkles and flames twisted in the air. The portal had reopened.

"Run!" Flynden shouted, striding toward her, his

hands aglow with white light. "Run, Sophie! Now!"

Fear and panic grabbed her and kept her down. She jerked her head from side to side and tried to peek into the dark. Why weren't the councilors coming? Where were Kir and Calleo? The moment to go home had come, but she was too scared to move.

"Run!" Flynden yelled again and placed himself between her and Makimus.

When she still didn't move, the Mother Flora and Pelifeles emerged from the forest.

"Go, child, go!" The Mother Flora called, striding toward her.

Finally, Sophie found movement in her arms and legs, scrambled up and swung around. Makimus heaved himself to his feet, shaking his head like trying to clear it. Fury twisted his round face into an evil, distorted mask. His raised hands flashed yellow-green.

❧ *Chapter 27* ❧

Sophie jumped. Hands and arms first, she dove forward like a swimmer from a diving board. The portal sizzled, flashed, and sucked her in. Her hands broke the fall, her elbows buckled. She crashed face down, her nose and chin scraped through fine sand. Before she even stopped sliding, she was up again and swung around.

Through the shimmering portal, a battle of white and yellow-green magic raged in the clearing. Bangs, booms, and cracks tore the air and rocked the ground, reaching all the way into the portal and vibrating under her feet.

She stepped toward the portal. What could she do to help? The Mother Flora's words rang in her mind. "Any friend in the range of Flynden's magic will always be safe." But could Flynden handle this?

White light flashed, once, twice, like the end of fireworks, bringing daylight to the clearing. With another boom, the light vanished and plunged the clearing into darkness. The councilors and apprentices hadn't come. What would happen to Flynden, Pelifeles, and the Mother Flora now?

Sophie waited a moment like she always did when the fireworks were over, just in case one last rocket whizzed by. She stood still in the dull gray world, while the portal's uneven ring flickered before her. When nothing else happened, she swung around and ran into the gray haze.

After some time, she realized there was no light ahead. She jogged in place and squinted right and left. Was she going the right way? The portal in the cemetery had disappeared right after she'd gone through. Was it closed, too? That's all she needed. How was she supposed to open it by herself? Maybe she'd have to go all the way back and get her friends to open this one for her, too.

She looked back. Far away, the other portal flickered. Was the Mother Flora okay? Flynden and Pelifeles? She could always go back. No, she couldn't. She could do nothing to help them, and her friends couldn't help her now either. She'd have to find her way back, alone. Her friends needed Master Eigil most, and only she could bring him back.

When Dad was still alive, he'd say, "Onward and forward," when something hadn't quite worked out. So, onward and forward. Her tongue tucked the seeds into her cheek before she swallowed to get rid of the taste. With another deep breath, she strode straight ahead.

A few minutes later, white forms slithered toward her. Those creepy ghosts again. Goosebumps rippled up her arms, over her shoulders, and down her back. She picked up her feet and ran harder, but before she got too far, the white ghosts had formed a circle around her, hemming her in. She stopped and turned on the spot.

This time they didn't shriek. Hard-to-make-out forms glided in a circle around her until one, a small figure, formed into someone more solid. Something familiar about it struck her as the ghost picked up its own smaller, closer circle. Sophie's heart skipped.

"Tommy?" She stepped toward the small ghost. "Tommy is that you?"

The ghost floated closer. More features formed into Tommy's; his arms, legs and torso became solid. He wore his pjs with the funny monsters on them. Who would've thought Trudy so thoughtful, dressing Tommy in his favorite pjs for his funeral. The pj-arms stretched toward her and when only a few feet remained between him and her, he stopped.

"Tommy." Sophie knelt to look into his white and dead eyes. She shrank back. Eek. He said nothing, stood and smiled at her, but it was Tommy. Her mouth went dry. Master Eigil had told the truth.

"Tommy." She reached out. "I miss you. I wanted to say good-bye."

"Why didn't you?" Tommy glided forward. His gray misty hands reached for her, icy and unreal. More goose bumps traveled up her arm where the gray hands grazed her skin.

Tommy's mouth opened. "Where were you, Sophie, when I needed you most?"

"But I was always there for you." What was he talking about?

"No, you weren't. Trudy was. You were always off trying to find ways to run away, stealing and lying. You weren't a nice person anymore after Mom and Dad died."

Open-mouthed, Sophie stared at him. "But…"

"You never appreciated what we had. You always messed up."

"I'm sorry, Tommy. I really am." She reached to touch him but her hand swished right through his chest. "I wanted to make things better for us. Find a good home."

"We had a good home. We had Trudy already. All you ever did was make excuses for messing up." Tommy floated backward. "You weren't always a good sister. Maybe if you'd been there, I wouldn't have died."

His words slapped her face. She had told herself the same thing, but Tommy's words hurt. Guilt and pain cut deeply.

"Go home, Sophie. Maybe there's still a chance for you to make it up to Trudy."

"Don't leave." She reached for him when he backed up farther. "I don't know where home is because you're not there anymore."

His palms came up, turning ghostly again, but they stopped her. One hand pointed ahead. His gray mouth formed the words, "Be smart, Sophie. Go home." He floated back farther until his form merged with the other figures. Stunned and shocked, she watched his pointing hand disappear.

Tommy was right. She'd never appreciated any of the good things they'd found after Mom and Dad died. There wasn't anything good left. That's what she thought anyway. She'd always been on the look out for better. Better than what? Now everybody was gone. Tommy. Maybe Trudy, too. Now she had no one, no home, nothing. Emptiness filled her hollow insides, a gray nothingness like the one around her.

The ghosts came roiling in one big, white and gray swirl toward her, shrieking now. Sophie clamped her hands over her ears and jumped to her feet.

"Stop!" she screamed. "Stop! You awful things."

The shrieks and wails tore at her, hurting her all the way down into her chest. When she hugged herself and dropped to her knees, the Flora blossom grew hot in her pocket. She pulled the pouch out. Maybe the blossom would help her find the way and open the portal in the cemetery. With one hand she held her tunic's hem, with the other, she shook the blossom from the pouch and held it high with the cloth. The blossom sparkled. Thin light beams speared the air like a mirror ball. Shrieks and wails stopped right away. Ghosts, mists, and swirls slithered away and left her standing alone in the dull and empty space.

The Flora blossom pulsed. When Sophie raised her hand a bit more, the blossom pulsed quicker. She lifted her hand even higher until a white light flashed ahead and speared the gray, cutting through the gloom. Sophie ran after it until the beam hit a spot in mid-air. The light sizzled and pierced the spot, burning it black.

A tiny flame flickered to life. It licked and ate away at the black mark spreading outward, wider and wider. Within the fire's circle, the black spot thinned and flaked away like burned paper. A ragged-edged portal opened to a snow-covered world.

Sophie stood, open-mouthed, gazing into the forest. *Home.* She dropped the Flora blossom back into the pouch and slipped the pouch into her pocket. With a big breath, too impatient for the portal to open wider, she took aim, her arms forward like before, and dove through it. She landed on her belly in the snow.

"Whew!" Sophie gasped from the cold, slid a few inches, and lay still. After a few seconds, she flopped onto her back. High in the night sky, a full moon greeted her, casting purple shadows over snow, graves, and the peak. Home. She was home. She wanted to holler, but changed her mind. Maybe not such a great idea. She didn't want to be noticed just yet.

Sophie sat. Wow! That was something. So, magic wasn't all bad. Her tongue probed her cheek for the seeds. *Phew*. Good, she hadn't swallowed them.

She tucked her legs under, leaned forward onto her hands, and peeked through the trees to the dark and silent cemetery. No police. No Master Eigil either. She crawled a few feet and used a tree to pull herself up. Burr, was it ever cold. The thin tunic and pants didn't keep her warm in this kind of weather. Now they were wet, too. She shivered and trudged through the deep snow to where tire tracks showed the cemetery drive and hurried toward the shed where she had last seen Master Eigil. He would be hiding in there, but the padlock on the door was iced over. So much for that idea. She high-stepped through the snow around the building to the window in the back, cupped her eyes and peeked into the gloomy shed.

"Master Eigil?" Her knuckles rapped the glass. "Master Eigil, are you in there?" She knocked again and pressed her ear to the cold glass. Nothing.

Back in front, she scanned the rows of graves. Not even an animal scurried through the freezing night.

Maybe Master Eigil hung out over by Tommy's grave, waiting for her there. She frowned when she thought of the ghostly Tommy in the passage. Master Eigil had told the truth. At least that gave her a warm fuzzy feeling. Everything he'd said was true. More shame and guilt nibbled away on her. He did need help, and she'd been so rude to him, hadn't even listened much.

Sophie slid and slipped along the icy path. No footprints surrounded Tommy's grave when she got there. Nobody seemed to have been there for a while. The grave lay tucked away, peaceful and calm, under a thick snowy blanket. A few wilted flowers peeked through the white layer. Sophie folded her hands the way Trudy did when she prayed. Sophie tried to think calm, pious thoughts, but only the word "sorry" came to mind.

A noise somewhere to her right ripped her away from the one pitiful word. Throwing caution aside, she faced the cemetery and yelled, "Master Eigil!"

She waited, listening, and let her voice ebb away. She took a deep breath and gave her voice a bit more force. "Master Eigil? It's me, Sophie. I'm back." Again, she listened. She let her eyes travel along the cemetery's boundary, ticking off the trees along the edge and peered at the black gaps between them. She glanced toward the cemetery's other side where the road came up over the hill. No, he wouldn't be anywhere near there.

"Master Eigil?" she called again. Where was he and why wasn't he answering? She held her breath, listening, and squinted into the dark. Hadn't something moved over there? There was no wind, but between the shed and where she stood, the wide branches of a blue spruce sent an avalanche of snow to the ground.

Sophie dashed toward the tree, slid, fell, got up again, and slid on her knees beneath the sheltering branches. Like a sorry pile of skin and bones, Master Eigil lay crumbled within his cloak.

"Master Eigil?" She took his icy hand. "Are you okay? What happened?"

Frost-crusted eyelashes parted. Darkening blue eyes blinked at her.

"Child, beautiful child," he croaked.

"Come." She pulled on his arm. "The Mother Flora and the others need you." The sudden thought of Nelwyna made her let go of him. "Nelwyna..." she started to say.

"Know," he breathed. "Felt her slip away."

"You must go."

"No." The word wheezed out of him.

"You must," Sophie cried. She spat out the three seeds and placed them onto his chest. "The Mother Flora gave me these to help you, and these, too." She pulled the pouches from her pocket. "See, and I got the Flora blossom."

His fingers tightened around hers. "Late," he mumbled. "Celarim to the Mother Flora."

"No, no. I can't." Sophie picked one seed. "Here." With one hand, she tried to push it between Eigil's lips, grabbed a handful of snow and pressed it against his mouth, too. He didn't move his lips nor swallowed the seed. His fingers slipped through hers, and his hand fell into the snow.

"Master Eigil?" Sophie whispered. "Master Eigil?" She shook his shoulder, but his summer-blue eyes were as dark and blank as the window in the shed.

Sophie bent forward and rested her forehead on his chest, grabbed the cloth, and held on. She squeezed her eyes shut tight and bit her lip. Suddenly, she understood what the Mother Flora had meant by "tell him to remember me." She was dying, too.

Sophie sat up. With two fingers, she closed Master Eigil's eyes the way she had seen it done in a movie. Now, he looked asleep. She took his hand and the stump, and crossed the arms on his chest and over the three seeds. She pulled the hood around his neck and tucked the cloak around his body.

After a while, Sophie sat back on her heels, resting her hands a moment longer over Master Eigil's hand, looking at the old man's peaceful face. She slipped the pouch with the Flora blossom and the tiny silky pouch with the other seeds back into her pocket. With a deep sigh, she rose into a squat and searched for the Celarim. What did it look like? Had he left it in the shed?

She crawled past Master Eigil, and there, against the tree's trunk, half covered with snow, leaned the big book more than twice the size of a coffee-table book. She grabbed the top and pulled it over. And three times as heavy. She lifted it with both arms and hugged it close, feeling warmth radiating from the cover. Right away, the Flora blossom flared in her pocket. She pushed the Celarim away.

In the book's center, a dark hole no bigger than the blossom peered at her like an eye. Did she have to place the blossom into this hole? She pulled out the blossom again, and with the pouch over her hand, exposed the blossom, trying it this way and that. Yes, it was the right size. The hole in the book began to glow at the same time the blossom burned her hand through the pouch. She dropped it. With a hiss, it landed in the snow and melted it away. Fear tickled her stomach. She shouldn't be touching these. With her tunic's sleeve pulled over her hand, she picked the blossom from the snow and slipped it back into the pouch and into her pocket. Better take it back and let the Mother Flora deal with it.

She stood the book on end and held it with one hand, while she leaned forward and gripped Master Eigil's shoulder with her other.

"Bye, Master Eigil," she whispered. "I'm sorry, I failed you, too."

Dragging the book with her, she crawled out from under the branches and stepped back into the snow.

The moon hung low and a pale blue stripe lined the edge of the horizon of the new morning. Sophie slipped along the drive and over to the shed where the snow wasn't so deep from there into the forest.

The Celarim and the Flora blossom had to go back, no arguing about that. She dreaded running through the gray passage again, but there was no one else to do it. She twisted and looked to the arc above the cemetery entrance. It would've been great to just go home if she still had one. She couldn't even bear thinking of what that meant. Sophie squeezed her eyes shut, hoping and wishing.

An old truck rattled up the short road to the cemetery. She stepped behind the shed and peeked around the corner. The cemetery caretaker climbed out. *No, not him.* She couldn't let him see her.

He stomped around his truck to the shed, grumbling and rattled the padlock, checking it.

Sophie frowned and backed away from the shed and behind the nearest tree. The man huffed, making so much noise, he wouldn't hear anything, but she couldn't count on it. He came around the shed. How could she get away without him seeing her? She hugged the big book to her chest, standing still, holding her breath. He would see her footsteps for sure.

The caretaker frowned and pressed one hand to the shed to steady himself. For a while, he peeked into the back window. What was he waiting for?

Cold and fear made her teeth rattle. She tensed, ready to run.

Suddenly, the caretaker swung away from the shed, and with a few quick steps, he had her. As he grabbed her arm, she pulled away. Her tunic sleeve ripped at the shoulder. She twisted away. He reached for her again. In an effort to fight him off, she dropped the book and punched his chest hard with both hands. He staggered but caught himself on a tree beside him, giving her a few seconds to pick up the book again and swing it at him. She caught him on the shoulder and head, and sent him flying into the snow. Losing her balance from the swing, she landed in the snow beside him. The book slid away. She scrambled up and a few steps back, scared the caretaker would grab her again, but he lay there, out cold.

The sky brightened. Cars rumbled by now and again, people driving to work. Headlights pointed up the steep road to the cemetery. Someone else was coming. Sophie lifted the book, pressing it against her chest, and stumbled toward the portal. She didn't stop when she got there and ran right through into the gray passage. She peeked once over her shoulder. A car crested the rise under the arc. The caretaker would be fine. Someone would find him, she told herself.

Sophie ran as fast as she could with the big book toward more trouble at the other end.

❧ *Chapter 28* ❧

The heavy book slowed her down, but she ran until she couldn't run anymore. Sophie stopped and doubled over, panting and gasping for air. The Celarim warmed against her chest and sent the warmth into her body. Her lungs expanded and air rushed in. A moment later, she straightened.

Thoughts tumbled over and over in her head, making it spin, making her want to throw up. What had she done? What kind of person was she anyway? She had hit Trudy with a stone; she had stolen from her best friend's mom; she had lied. Now, she had knocked out the caretaker. Even though she didn't like this nosy and rude man, it wasn't a good reason to hurt him. Mom and Dad had taught her to be honest and kind, and never hurt others, at least not intentionally. And now? Was she just as bad as Makimus?

Sophie fled through the passage like Makimus was after her, keeping her eyes open for Tommy, but he didn't show this time nor did the other ghosts.

The Celarim grew hot in her hands. The Flora blossom flared, burning her side through the cloth. Sophie stumbled to a stop, placed the book on the ground, pulled the tunic sleeves over her hands, and picked it up again. She twisted on the spot but couldn't see the portal. Gray, nothing but gray everywhere, it even filled the hollow space inside her. She wanted to go neither forward nor backward, but drop the book and the blossom for good, and turn into a ghost, too.

Sophie almost opened her hands to let the book slip to the ground, when one face after the other appeared in her head: Master Eigil's, Flynden's, the Mother Flora's, and Trudy's. No, she would see this through and would start by being honest with herself. Even though she was tired and scared, whatever was going to happen from here on, she wouldn't mess up again.

With her resolve came an energy burst, and her feet moved almost by themselves. She leaned into the jog, head down, like working against a strong wind. The portal had to be somewhere ahead. What if she couldn't go back home after? No, forward first.

She held onto the book like grabbing a lifesaver. The edges dug into her upper thighs and arms with every step. On and on she went but still no portal showed. She slowed and shifted the Celarim into her left arm. Too weak to hold the heavy book with one arm, she let it slip into the fine sand. Her fingers fumbled for the pouch with the Flora blossom, pulled it from the pocket and held it high. Like a beacon, the blossom's light pierced through the cloth and the grayness. She pocketed the blossom and lifted the book with a groan. Luckily this wasn't a tome written in stone otherwise she'd be in real trouble. She hugged the book to her chest and veered to where the beam had pointed. The book pulsed in her hands, up her arms and into her body, scary and exhilarating at the same time. The blossom answered with its own pulse in her pocket.

Sophie tugged the tome along, then tried the Flora blossom again, stretching her arm over her head, holding it high. The light pointed ahead this time.

There, the portal shimmered not far away, its sparkling, burning edges glowing like ambers. She jogged closer and stopped just out of reach.

On the other side, black and burned tree trunks ringed the clearing. Bushes still burned. The fire had scorched the grass. Did Flynden and the Mother Flora flee? Would Makimus strike as soon as she came out?

The portal burned large enough for her to jump through, but when she stepped toward it, it sizzled and hissed worse than before. Even if it burned her, she had to get through no matter what. She took a deep breath, backed up, and tightened her grip on the Celarim. The book grew hotter and singed her tunic. A stink like burned fingernails stung her nose. She sneezed.

Now or never.

For a second, she jogged in place, then pushed ahead, gathered speed, and jumped.

Bang! With the crack of thunder, the portal flashed and exploded. She wanted to cover her ears but the explosion threw her forward into the grass, and she held onto the book instead. Sophie twisted in mid-fall and crashed on her back, her breath knocked from her, the Celarim like a shield still in her arms. Her head smacked back, hit the ground, and she almost passed out. She fought to stay alert when the yellow-green magic hit the Celarim and bounced off the book cover. At the same time, the magics' white, yellow, lavender, and purple-blue flashes whizzed everywhere. The battle wasn't over after all. They had waited for Master Eigil, but now, they got only her instead.

Bathed in sweat, Sophie stayed on the ground and kept hugging the book. The Flora blossom grew even hotter in her pocket. She wanted to pull it out but didn't dare drop the book.

Another yellow-green strike missed her and exploded into the ground, spraying grass and dirt at her. Smoke roiled above the spot where she lay. Sophie screamed.

"Help! Someone help!"

Another yellow-green volley answered her scream and hit the ground right beside her.

She balanced the book on her chest and groped for the pouch with the Flora blossom. Too scared to care, she pulled the blossom from the pouch with her bare hand, but rather than getting hotter and burning her palm, it did nothing.

Two yellow-green strikes hit close to her head, singeing her hair, the sour apple stink worse than before. She made herself as small as she could behind the Celarim, but the book wasn't *that* big. Something else would have to happen soon, or she would be dead.

Makimus stepped from the trees draped in his magic. It flickered around the edges of his body, protecting him from the other magics flying at him from all sides now. As he walked toward her, he threw one volley after another, hammering and burning the ground between him and her. Soon, he would have her.

Like they had heard her silent wishing, Druce Lar and Tulio and with them Kir and Calleo, strode from the forest toward her as well, hitting the ground with their magics in front of Makimus. But he kept walking, not looking scared at all or like he even saw the others.

A few yards to go, Makimus swept both his arms to his sides and wind-milled them around. His magic lifted councilors and apprentices off their feet and threw them toward the forest where they lay still.

"Stop!" The Mother Flora's voice rang out. She rushed from the trees, Flynden and Pelifeles right behind her.

"No!" Sophie croaked from her dry throat.

Unafraid of Makimus, the Mother Flora strode forward. The big man halted and regarded her. Behind the magic's shield, his face twisted into a hateful mask.

Sophie tried to stand, but Makimus' magic exploded before her, throwing her back down. Dazed she lay still, holding on to the Celarim and the Flora blossom.

"Makimus! Stop!" The Mother Flora shouted. "I forbid you to continue this madness. Let the child be."

"Hold your tongue," Makimus sneered. "Today is a new beginning. A land free of the Flora's reign. It is time for you to meet the light, Mother Flora."

Makimus stretched his hands forward, shot yellow-green lightning bolts at her, and blasted the tiny woman off her feet, lifting her high to the first tree branches and holding her up like flying a kite. His laughter rang through the clearing. Screaming like mad, Flynden dashed across the small space and smashed into him, but his white magic only flickered and winked out. He couldn't make it work. Pelifeles jumped past Flynden onto Makimus' chest and clawed his face. With a glowing yellow-green swipe of his hand, the big man tossed Flynden and Pelifeles aside like rag dolls. He withdrew the magic from his other hand and released the Mother Flora's body, letting it crash to the ground into a crumpled, lifeless heap.

Silence settled over the clearing. Only Makimus stood now, and laughing like a crazy man, he dropped his magic shield and approached the Mother Flora's body.

He took her small right hand into his large one. From his tunic's folds, he pulled a thin dagger and with a swift slash, cut the Mother Flora's palm. For a moment, Makimus stared at the hand before he slapped it away, disgusted.

The seeds, he was looking for the seeds the Mother Flora had given to Bramble.

"I have them," Sophie called. "Here, I have those seeds. She gave them to me."

Makimus looked up. "Give the seeds, the blossom and the book to me, child, and no harm will come to you."

"I can't get up. I think my leg is broken," she lied.

Makimus strode toward her. What should she do when he reached her? She had left the three seeds on Master Eigil's chest, but she still had the tiny pouch with the other seeds. Maybe Makimus would realize too late that they weren't the ones he was looking for and would be too distracted to do anything more to her.

Sophie placed the Flora blossom beside her in the grass and gathered the pouch with the seeds in her fist.

Makimus stepped over Flynden and Pelifeles who had dropped in his path. She had to stop him now. He was close enough. Sophie threw the pouch.

Makimus stared at the pouch in the grass. Surprise and humbleness washed his face clean of malice, and for a second, he looked like Santa Clause, but only for a second. He stooped to pick up the pouch, gently, almost reverently, like a delicate butterfly.

Desperate for something to do, Sophie did the one thing she could think of and inserted the Flora blossom into the dark hole of the Celarim cover. It settled with a soft click. Instantly, the book cooled in her hands, vibrating. She trembled with fear of having done something terrible. Raised on one knee, she held the book before her, facing Makimus. White magic burst from the blossom, hammered into him and threw her backward, but she hung on.

Like the yellow-green magic that had tossed the Mother Flora into the air, the white magic flung Makimus up, twisted and tumbled him above the clearing. It spun into a twister and swept Makimus higher and higher toward the sky that was now turning lighter with a new day. The magic glared and brightened until it was blinding white and sucked Makimus in.

With a loud whoosh, whoosh, the magic rushed once around the clearing and returned to the Celarim where the Flora blossom drew it in. It flared once more and winked out. Sophie staggered and dropped the book. Exhausted, she sank into the grass beside it.

The hurricane-like winds died down to a breeze and blew away the smoke and the sour apple stink. At the edge of the clearing, Camshron stood in the shadows between two trees, watching. He took one last look at her before he swung around and disappeared into the woods.

Flynden tried to get up on hands and knees, shaking his head. Pelifeles struggled to his paws, his fur singed again like the Mother Flora hadn't fixed it earlier.

Dawn rose over the clearing in the ancient forest. Like a fresh breath, the wind blew peppermint scent through the trees at Sophie and cooled the sweat on her face. The trees seemed alive and maybe they'd helped defeat Makimus. She wanted to hug them all. For a second, she smiled, but when she looked toward the Mother Flora, lying twisted where she had fallen, her smile faded away. The Mother Flora's arms and legs stuck out in odd angles the way they shouldn't. Green blood dripped from her cut hand and her mouth.

Sophie pushed herself up onto wobbly legs. All her bones hurt. She stumbled over to the Mother Flora's body. Even in death, she looked serene. The dirt on her face couldn't hide her delicate and beautiful features. The once-white petals around her face had wilted to yellow and brown already, like autumn leaves. Sophie straightened the Mother Flora's arms and legs and managed to make her look like she was resting. Then she sat back onto her heels and hugged herself, shivering. She gasped when the Mother Flora's body turned brown and wrinkled like an old shriveled up potato. Her face grew old and older. The whole body shrank in the white gown until only shreds of brown withered-leaf-like stuff remained and even that turned to dust.

Sophie still stared open-mouthed when Pelifeles pushed under her arm. She picked him up and cuddled him close.

Groaning, Tulio and Druce Lar stirred, helping each other up. Young and nimble, Kir and Calleo jumped to their feet first, helping the struggling councilors. Flynden remained in the clearing's center, staring up to the spot in the pale blue morning sky where Makimus had vanished.

Druce Lar approached Sophie and knelt beside her. Kir, Calleo and Tulio bent down onto one knee and watched the dust of the Mother Flora's body seep into the ground. With hanging heads, councilors and apprentices folded their hands like praying monks.

In the clearing's center, Flynden stood with hanging head and shaking shoulders.

"By the light, child, you saved us all," said Druce Lar,

his face grave.

Sophie shook her head. "Not the Mother Flora though," she sniffed.

"No, not the Mother Flora." Blinking a few times, he scratched his beard and cleared his throat. "You saved the Celarim and the Flora blossom for us and defeated Makimus."

"What good is that now?"

Druce Lar sighed and nodded like he agreed. "Perhaps, the good of it will reveal itself after a while." He placed one hand on her shoulder. "Tell me child, what has become of High Councilor Eigil?"

Sophie looked down. "I...I was too late," she whispered. "The Mother Flora gave me seeds to make him better, but he was too weak to eat them. He told me to take the Celarim back to the Mother Flora."

"You did well," Druce Lar said. "We will miss the High Councilor, but more so the friend."

"Maybe I could've done more..." Sophie wiped her nose on her sleeve.

"You did fine, child," Tulio said. "You and Flynden showed more wisdom and courage than your elders. We should make you Council Members." He winked at her.

Sophie gave him a lopsided grin and walked over to where Flynden wavered with hanging head. Pelifeles slunk alongside and brushed against her legs, like giving her support.

"Flyn, are you okay?" She stopped a few feet away.

Flynden nodded, then nodded again, looking at her. His hair had turned white, and his face pale without freckles, but a fire burned in his eyes that hadn't been there before. The spunky happy boy had left for good.

"Will you tell the councilors about Bramble and the

Mother Flora's seeds?" Sophie asked.

"What for?" Flynden spread his hands wide, all sad and helpless.

"Nugateris needs a new Mother Flora, Flyn," Pelifeles said and pushed against Flynden's leg. "We'll be in big trouble if we don't have a new Mother Flora to keep us safe from those." He pointed up with his nose. "Look."

Dark clouds roiled in the sky over the forest. A breeze quickened into strong gusts. The trees bent, agitated again.

"Is there a storm coming?" Sophie asked.

"That's no ordinary storm. Demons more like it. The Mother Flora's magic held them at bay." Druce Lar joined them. "Without her magic, the demons will overrun the Isle of Nugateris once more." He placed one hand on Sophie's shoulder. "We must leave."

"Will you come with us?" Flynden asked Sophie.

Sophie took a deep breath. She wanted to stay, but she had other things that needed fixing. She shook her head.

"I'd like to, but I need to find out if my foster mother is okay."

Flynden said nothing, his face sadder. "Will you come back though?"

"Son, the portal should not remain open," Druce Lar said. "It was a mistake and will always be a risk." To Sophie he said, "If you want to go home, child, you should do so now. We need to seek shelter from the demons until we are prepared to fight them."

For a moment, Sophie looked from Flynden to her other friends.

"I want to go home."

"Then go, child," Druce Lar said. "Go with our gratitude, and may the light always brighten your path."

Sophie hugged the tall councilors and apprentices around their waists, then crushed Flynden into a bear hug. She picked up Pelifeles and rubbed her face into his soft fur. He said nothing but purred like a little motor in her arms.

Above the clearing, dark gray and black clouds filled with shrieks much like those in the gray passage. Like fog and mist, the gray mass sank into the clearing. Together, the trees whipped back and forth, branches slapping at the clouds. An acidic smell replaced the peppermint.

Pelifeles wiggled from her arms and jumped ahead. With Flynden and Calleo's help, half carrying her, Sophie pushed against the wind and fought her way to the portal.

"Go!" Flynden yelled and pushed her away.

Sophie hugged him one more time before she swung around. The portal hissed and sizzled, but she had jumped already through it and swiveled on the spot. Druce Lar waved his hand with his lemon-yellow magic, and for a moment, she watched Flynden and Pelifeles running toward the trees, Tulio picking up the Celarim and hurrying with Kir and Calleo across the clearing; then a bright yellow flash cut off her view.

๛ *Chapter 29* ๑

Sophie stared into the swirling gray and reached out. To do what? Knock and say she changed her mind and wanted to go with them after all? No, she couldn't reach her friends anymore. With a grimace, she pulled her hand back. She had to check on Trudy and face whatever punishment waited.

Sophie slogged through the gloom. No ghosts came to bother or greet or shriek at her. In her loneliness, she would've welcomed even them. She needed to find her way back now with no Flora blossom and no friends to help her. After a short walk, her worries disappeared because the cemetery portal flickered not far ahead.

Would the police be waiting or the irate caretaker?

Sophie halted and hesitated but shook her head. No, no more running away. With squared shoulders, she walked toward the portal and peeked out into the snowy forest. The sun glistened on the snow and ice, but no one waited for her. She took a step back and lunged through the portal into the cold mountain air. The morning sun rose over the cemetery. Sophie drew her hands into the tunic's sleeves. *Brrr. Freezing.*

A loud whoosh and crackle startled her. For a few

seconds, she watched the portal's edges sizzle and burn, shrinking smaller and smaller, until it closed with a final hiss behind her. It shimmered a moment longer before only crisp cold air filled the space between the trees.

Sophie sat back onto her heels and let out a heavy sigh. Snow melted under her legs and the water seeped into her leggings. She had to get up and get moving.

By the shed, the snow lay flat and trampled where the caretaker had fallen. Someone must've found him and taken care of him, or he hadn't been hurt at all. She would find out later. Now, she had something more important to do.

Sophie trudged through the snow along the cemetery's edge, ducked beneath the branches of the pine tree, and gasped. Master Eigil's body had turned to dust in the short while she'd been gone and had seeped into the ground like the Mother Flora's dust, leaving his crumpled tunic and cloak. Maybe it was right this way. The tree would shelter him forever and she would say hello with every visit to Tommy's and Mom and Dad's graves. Maybe somewhere, Master Eigil and the Mother Flora were together again. Wishful thinking, but she liked the thought.

The three seeds still lay on the tunic where Master Eigil's chest had been. Sophie knelt, picked them up, shook out tunic and cloak, and scraped snow over the dust. She rolled the seeds into the fabric, and tucked the bundle under her arm. With one sleeve, she wiped her nose and crawled away from the old man's resting place. Time to go home.

With a parting glance, she slipped and slid along the path and beneath the cemetery's arc. On the small rise before the road dipped down, she turned around to look back. Silent and peaceful, the cemetery lay behind her, fitting for those sleeping there. She pulled her mouth into a lopsided frown, shivered, and hurried downhill.

At the bottom, a row of cars lined up at the McDonald's pick-up window. She hurried past, keeping her head down. If she kept to the side streets, she would make it home, hopefully without anyone noticing her. If only for a little while, she didn't feel like answering questions.

☙ ☙

She turned the corner into Walnut Street, her street. Without looking left or right, hoping none of the neighbors would spot her, she hurried to number fourteen. At the house, she snuck around back and headed for the garden shed. She would hide the bundle with the seeds in there and decide later what to do with it. She pulled the shed door open. It creaked. Oh no. She forgot it always did that. She took an old plastic bucket with a lid and stuffed the clothes and seeds into it, then hid the bucket behind an assortment of flowerpots. She pushed the door closed with another squeak, when a stifled scream made her jump.

"Um Himmels Willen, kind! Where haff you been?" Trudy yelled with a heavier-than-normal accent. Sophie grinned despite her foster mother's anger. Feeling so relieved seeing her alive, she didn't care one bit about what was coming. Trudy hurried from the deck, down the stairs and across the yard. A white bandage covered most of her head, but otherwise she looked fine.

"This is no laughing matter," she hollered, grabbing Sophie's shoulders, shaking her. "Answer me. Where haff you been?"

What should she say? She hadn't thought of this at all, and she'd promised not to lie anymore, but telling the truth now might be worse.

"Um, I stayed with friends."

"What friends?" Sophie got another shake. "Look at you. Where are your clothes? Your mom's jacket?"

Sophie hung her head. Her eyes burned.

"I helped friends in trouble and lost the jacket."

Trudy held her at arm's length and scowled.

"Inside. Now." She pushed Sophie ahead of her, up the steps to the deck and through the backdoor into the kitchen. "Bathroom. Shower." She pointed. "When you're done, we talk." When Sophie didn't move, she yelled. "Now!"

Trudy had never been so angry before. She'd always been nice and tried to be patient and understanding, but even Trudy seemed to have her limits.

Sophie tiptoed across the hall into the bathroom, trying to make as little noise as possible. Not aggravating Trudy more would be best right now.

Despite the rough welcome, Sophie more than ever enjoyed the smell of ironed laundry and the clean fresh smell hanging around the house. She breathed it in like perfume while she wiggled from her dirty and ripped clothes. When they lay in a pile on the bathroom floor, she looked at them and squatted down to touch them. All the faces left behind swam before her face. She missed her friends already, but she would never see them again. It would be better to forget about it, but she never would. Had they found shelter from the demons? Would they find Bramble and keep her safe?

"Sophie, are you taking a shower?" Trudy hollered

through the bathroom door.

"Yes, I am." She turned on the faucets and let the water run.

For a few minutes, she stood under the hot water until her cold, stiff body felt more like her own again. She toweled herself off and walked with the towel wrapped around her into her bedroom.

How often had she complained about it being too small? She had complained about the curtains with the horseshoes on them that Trudy had sewn for her. She went to her beautifully carved dresser and traced the back of the porcelain horse with one finger. Trudy had given her the figure last Christmas. She twirled on the spot, taking it all in. There lay Trudy's parenting magazine minus the adoption agency ad. For a moment, she stared at it and the pink pack of gum that lay beside it. She snatched both off her desk, and with a "Wheee!" tossed them across the room where they landed on the bed, slipped over the edge and out of sight.

"Sophie?" Trudy called.

"Be right there." A big lump in her throat made her swallow. She bit her lip and stifled a sob. Quickly, she dressed in jeans and a t-shirt, not bothering with socks.

The smell of roasted chicken and home fries greeted her in the kitchen. Trudy had made her favorite food. This wouldn't be so bad.

"Sit," Trudy snapped.

Or maybe it would.

Trudy pointed to a chair at the table and took the one opposite.

"Now, where haff you been, kind? I was worried sick."

"With friends, Trudy, honest."

"You were gone for over a week. No word. No note.

Nothing."

"Sorry." Sophie kept her hands folded on the table and her eyes on her hands.

"Sorry isn't enough," Trudy threw up her hands. "Dianne and her parents, most of our neighbors have been looking for you. I hung up flyers with your picture at stores and the post office. The police have been searching for you, and all you have to say is sorry?"

"But I am," Sophie squeaked. "I don't know what else to say."

"What about those friends? Who are they and where do they live?"

Sophie groped for some plausible-sounding answer, but couldn't come up with anything. If she told the truth, Trudy would be even angrier. She would never believe it and think Sophie made fun of her. So what could she say?

Sophie pushed her chair back and dashed around the table. She fell to her knees beside Trudy's chair and took Trudy's hands in hers.

"I'm sorry, Trudy," she started. "I really am." She wiped her face sideways on her t-shirt sleeve. Tears she'd tried so hard to hold in now fell steadily. "Sorry for all the trouble and hurt I've caused you. Not just now, but before when Tommy was still alive. I know I've been a brat and made your life really miserable. You were always nice to me and Tommy and took good care of us and I never appreciated any of it." Sophie started sobbing. "B...b...but I did, I do, I mean. I just never let you know." She took her t-shirt's hem and blew her nose. "You're the nicest person I've ever met besides Mom and Dad."

"Flattery will get you nowhere." Trudy pulled a clean handkerchief from her apron pocket and held it under

Sophie's nose. "Here, kind, don't use your t-shirt."

Sophie took the hankie and breathed in the fresh ironing scent again. Why had she always balked at Trudy's fussing before? How nice Trudy's caring felt.

"I was helping my friends. They were in trouble," Sophie said. "I couldn't get word to you."

"Are they fine now?" Trudy wrinkled her brows. She still didn't look convinced.

"I don't know," Sophie cried.

Trudy pulled her up and onto her lap. The last time she'd sat on Mom's lap was the day she died. Mom had pushed the chair back after dinner and pulled her onto her lap just like Trudy did now. No one had ever cuddled her since then. She hadn't let anyone.

"Ssh, Ssh, kind. Don't cry." The arms held her, warm and comforting.

"I'm sorry, Trudy." Sophie pushed her face into Trudy's shoulder. Her fists dug deep into her sweater. "Sorry I hurt you."

Trudy said nothing for a long time and rested her face against Sophie's hair. The plop-plop of Trudy's tears on her forehead and her quivering chest made it pretty clear how Trudy felt about all this.

The timer at the stove went off.

Sophie raised her head and tried to wiggle out of Trudy's arms.

"I'm not done holding you yet," Trudy sniffled and clutched her closer.

Sophie leaned back into her. "The chicken will burn," she said.

"Never mind the chicken."

Sophie gently fingered the bandage on Trudy's head. "Does it hurt?"

"My heart hurts more," Trudy said.

"I thought you were dead." Sophie started crying all over again. "I thought I killed you."

Trudy took the hankie from her and wiped Sophie's face, keeping her own tear-streaked face stern, gentle, and concerned all at the same time.

"I'm not so easy to kill, kind. I'm happy to have you back, but you will have to make up for what you did. There are consequences."

Sophie nodded. *Anything.* She would do anything to make it right again.

Trudy grinned. "Now, let me get up or the chicken will burn."

Sophie took a shaky breath and hopped to the floor. When Trudy pushed Sophie toward her chair, her fingers lingered a moment longer.

"I'm okay, Trudy, really."

"Yes, but I'm not." She gently squeezed Sophie's shoulder. "I need to hold on to you for a bit longer." She placed her head against Sophie's, placed a kiss on her cheek and let go. Up came her hand with the handkerchief. She blew her nose like a trumpet while she walked over to the stove. There, she slipped on the red-and-white potholders and pulled the pan from the oven.

Sophie jumped up, grabbed plates and utensils from the cupboard and set the table. Trudy stared, surprised. Sophie gave her a lopsided grin. She'd never set the table for Trudy before, not once.

"A little music?" Trudy switched on the small CD player on the counter and Taylor Swift crooned from the speakers. Now, it was Sophie's turn to stare. Trudy tapped her foot and whistled off-key along with Sophie's favorite song she'd always disliked before. Sophie pointed to the CD player.

Trudy grinned. "That song gave me comfort when you were missing." She filled the plates on the table with drumsticks, lots of home fries, and green beans. "Eat, kind, while it's hot." Trudy poured milk for Sophie and juice for herself.

Sophie sang along with Taylor while she waited for Trudy to sit down. Even her favorite food had never smelled so yummy. Trudy sat, a big smile lit her face, her eyes still shiny. Sophie pulled her mouth into a grin, a mix of frown and smile. Trudy pointed with her fork to the plates, and they both dug in.

❧ *Acknowledgments* ❧

This book would not have been possible without all the wonderful people who helped and supported me. A warm thank you and cheers to:

Kristen for editing, critiquing, and sharing her publishing know-how with me;

Vee for listening, her critique and edits, thoughtful comments, and her continued support;

Don, Lorin, Brenda, Jason, and Roman for their helpful suggestions;

Jordan, who edited an earlier version of the story, making this a better one;

Amanda for her excellent copyediting and proofreading magic;

Christine for her beautiful cover design;

Bob for help with the tricky interior layout;

Deb for her knowledge of creating a good painting and sharing it with me;

My family for cheering me on;

And Kayla for her patience, love, and companionship throughout everything.

❧ *About the Author* ❧

Photo: David Erwin

Gabriele loves writing and reading. In addition to children's books, she writes poetry that rhymes and songs that are funny, and plays them on her guitar or her piano, and sometimes on her accordion, which nobody likes but her. She has recorded two CDs of her own songs. When she isn't writing, she's often seen painting pictures of animals and flowers, or anything that strikes her fancy.

Dogs, cats, and horses have always been a big part of her life, and her love for them carries over into her stories. Her pets, past and present, will make regular appearances, like her quirky cat Peppy, who became the Pelifeles character in *Sophie and the Magic Flower*. She enjoys growing plants and gardening, which also play a big part in the story. Her favorite summer activity is hiking with her dog Kayla, a Labrador retriever mix, in the Colorado mountains and taking photos of the beautiful scenery.

Sophie and the Magic Flower is her first published novel.

gabrieleewerts.com

56041103R00231

Made in the USA
San Bernardino, CA
09 November 2017